LOVE'S UNDYING FLAME

Gaby could feel the heat of the horse at her back and the heat of the man in front of her. She felt overpowered by Rayne's tall, lean body, mesmerized by the blue-black lights of his eyes, the line of his bottom lip, the dark head silhouetted against the sunlight as it dipped down toward her.

Their lips met and clung and Gaby wasn't aware that she'd gone up on tiptoe to meet him. She forgot time and place and stood on the hot prairie clinging to the raw-boned strength of him. Her body remembered what her mind and heart had tried so hard to forget. It remembered and responded. She felt the flare of passion, hot and pulsating, igniting deep within her. Yes, this was what she'd yearned for these past weeks. She was a passionate woman and she needed to be loved as only Rayne could love her. . . .

Creole Angel

Peggy Hanchar

AN ONYX BOOK

NEW AMERICAN LIBRARY

Onyx is a trademark of New American Library.

SIGNET, SIGNET CLASSIC, MENTOR, ONYX, PLUME, MERIDIAN
and NAL BOOKS are published by NAL PENGUIN INC.,
1633 Broadway, New York, New York 10019

First Printing, December, 1987

1 2 3 4 5 6 7 8 9

PRINTED IN THE UNITED STATES OF AMERICA

For Steve, my sweet husband,
for all the becauses.

1

"Someday, Gaby, I'm going to sail away on one of these ships," Alcee Branche said. His thin face was wistful as he gazed at the shipping vessels lining the New Orleans wharf.

The girl walking beside him nodded her head in understanding. Her silvery laughter danced on the muggy air. She was dressed in the drab homespun clothes of a domestic, but her bright beauty and flashing smile drew speculative glances of more than one man as they moved along the docks. She seemed not to notice.

"How can you sail away on a ship when your mother won't even let you come to the docks alone?" she asked. Her dark eyes sparkled with teasing lights. Alcee didn't take offense at her laughter or her question. Gabrielle Reynaud had been his friend for most of their childhood. He loved her and trusted her.

"I'll find a way," he muttered now, his angry scowl more for his overly protective mother than for Gaby.

"I'm sure you will, Alcee," Gaby replied kindly. She was sorry she'd poked fun at him. "Perhaps someday I'll be rich enough to own one of these boats and we'll sail on it together."

"How will you get rich?" Alcee scoffed. He was a tall, slim boy of fourteen, towering over the slender girl who was four years his senior. The pallor of his face hinted at his failing health. Like others whose lungs couldn't stand the moist air of the Louisiana coast, he would probably

7

not reach manhood. A surge of pity made Gaby grasp his hand.

"You're probably right," she declared. "You'll have to do all those things for me." Glancing about, Gaby pointed to the tall smokestacks of one of the palatial steamships. "Alcee, it's the *Delta Rose*. Let's go look at her closer." Hand in hand they hurried toward the stately ship.

"Get outta here, nah," a dockhand called as they raced across the wooden wharves. Bales of cotton and tobacco were stacked high on the side. Barrels of spices, crates of silks, and other goods were being unloaded from one of the squat steamships. Gaby and Alcee slowed as they passed stacks of cowhides and horns shipped from Texas. They were on their way to the eastern markets. Barrels of tallow and pickled beef vied for space with boxes of china and crates of furniture from the northern cities.

Now that the war was over, the river trade was picking up again, although there were some who believed it would never reach the magnitude it had once enjoyed. Still, the wharves were a busy and exciting place to be. Gaby and Alcee hurried on.

New Orleans had been an occupied city from early on in the War Between the States. The city was still under martial law, and her streets and buildings were filled with the blue uniforms of the Yankee soldiers and by carpet-baggers looking to make their fortune.

"Isn't she beautiful?" Alcee breathed, looking at the *Delta Rose*. The huge showboat looked like a palace floating on the muddy Mississippi waters. Above her pristine paint, her smokestacks rose in the air as if to announce to one and all that she was still the queen of the river.

"Someday I'm going to France on the *Delta Rose*," Gaby mused, her eyes wistful, her smile dreamy. Looking at her, Alcee felt a stab of jealousy. Gaby probably would go to France. She nearly always did what she said.

"You'll never go anywhere," he scoffed, suddenly angry with her and with himself and the illness that held him captive. "You'll just stay there at your old Cour des Anges with all the other prostitutes. One day you'll probably die there, the way your mother did."

"I won't, you horrid boy," Gaby cried, stung by his cruel words.

"Yes, you will," Alcee taunted. "Mama says you will." Gaby's hand flashed through the air, striking his pale cheek; then she whirled and ran along the dock away from him.

"Gaby," he called after her. "I'm sorry, truly I am. Don't leave me behind, Gaby." He ran after her.

Gaby paid him no mind until she heard him beside her, gasping as he tried to keep up. He shouldn't exert himself like that, she thought, but anger kept her slender legs churning as she strode across the wharf.

"Gaby, please don't run away," he called plaintively. He stood in the middle of the wharf, his thin chest heaving, his pale cheeks flushed. As always, Gaby's anger melted in a surge of concern for him. Her steps slowed, although she did not go back to him. She would bend only so far, she thought, and waited as his footsteps drew closer.

"Don't be mad at me, Gaby," he mumbled.

"You deserve it," she cried, and turned to face him. Tears stood out on her rounded cheeks and her eyes glittered with the remnants of anger.

"I shan't die like my mother," she declared. "Perhaps I will become an angel in Madeleine's court, but I won't stay there forever. Someday a rich and handsome gentlemen will come. He'll fall in love with me and want to marry me and take me away to his plantation. I'll have wonderful parties and all the clothes and jewels and food I'll ever want."

"And slaves to take care of you, and the war never really happened," the boy said cynically.

"Be careful, Alcee, or I'll box your ears again," Gaby warned.

"It won't change things back," he answered implacably.

"I know." Sighing, Gaby swung around and began to walk along the wharf again, adroitly dodging the barrels and crates, skipping around the black men who lolled on cotton bales. The war had brought them their freedom, but no one had shown them what to do with it. The war had changed everyone's life, and not always for the bet-

ter. At least it hadn't here in the South, which struggled
to survive in the aftermath of its financial collapse.

A commotion at the end of the wharf drew Alcee's
attention. "The cattle boats got in past the sandbars," he
cried. "The tide must be up. Let's go look at them." He
urged Gaby along. Relenting from her earlier anger, she
hurried with him toward the sound of bawling cows and
swearing men. "Morgan Steamship Company" was painted
on the side of the boat, which carried two decks of cattle
pens.

"They must have come from Texas," Alcee said, greatly
excited. "I'm going there someday."

"Whatever for?" Gaby asked.

"To explore. To fight the Mexicans and the Indians."

"They aren't fighting the Mexicans anymore. They made
peace long ago before Texas became a state."

"Well, they may need to fight them again," Alcee said.
"Besides, they still have the Indians. I'll help capture the
savages and discover where they've hidden their gold. I'll
be rich."

"Those men don't look very rich to me," Gaby observed.

Crestfallen, Alcee lapsed into silence. Girls didn't understand about adventure and exploring new territories,
he thought.

"Let's go up there so we can see," he cried, and began
to climb up on the bales of cotton stacked high along the
wharf. Gaby followed him, hitching her skirts around her
knees. From their perch they were able to look down on
the flat-bottomed boats where rangy men with weather-
beaten faces whistled and called to the wild-eyed, milling
cattle.

The men flailed at them with coiled lariats until the
frightened cows, tossing their wickedly long horns and
rolling their eyes, moved toward the gangplank.

"Dusty, don't bunch them too close or they'll gore
each other," someone shouted, and Gaby's wide-eyed
gaze picked out a tall, lean man perched on the top deck,
one long leg slung over the railing. Silhouetted against
the sky, he was a commanding figure with his broad
shoulders and tapering waist and hips. Heavy of bone and
sparse of flesh, he exuded an aura of strength and stam-
ina. A wide-brimmed, high-crowned hat hid his hair and

shadowed his eyes, but she could see the bold, chiseled lines of his nose and jaws and the wide, uncompromising slash of a mouth. In spite of his rough attire, there was no doubt he was the man in charge.

"Look, Gaby," Alcee said, pointing to a makeshift sling which hauled cattle up from the lower decks. Gaby tore her gaze away from the tall Texan and watched the beehive of activity below her. How different these men were from the indolent Creoles who had learned to move languorously in the moist, hot air. By contrast these men moved quickly, their actions sparse and efficient. When they weren't moving, their long-limbed bodies settled back into a slouch and it seemed they might never move again.

Gaby's gaze went back to the man on the top deck. He seemed to be everywhere at once and to see everything. Under his shouted directions the cattle were brought under control.

Descending the stairs, the man climbed onto a sturdy horse and nodded his head at the man he'd called Dusty. Suddenly the gate was lifted and the cows surged forward, down the gangplank and onto the wharf, the sound of their hooves like thunder on the wooden planking.

Gaby drew in her breath as the cattle swept by below her. Seen up close, their long horns were evil-looking and dangerous. The span from tip to tip was wide enough for Gaby to stand upright between them.

Freed at last from their swaying prison, the bawling cattle ran wildly, looking for a way to escape. They bumped into kegs, overturning them, the contents spilling over the wharf, to be trampled underfoot by the cows that followed. Some ran into buildings and stopped short, stunned by the impact. The stacked bales where Gaby and Alcee lay rocked as the cows brushed past. Gaby screamed as they shifted and wobbled beneath her.

"Gaby," Alcee called, and scrambled backward to safety. There was no time for her to move. The bale that held her swayed, then tipped forward, pitching Gaby downward toward the milling cows. Frantically she gripped the hemp binding thus breaking her fall. She landed near one of the cotton bales and huddled back against it.

The cows surged around her, their hooves sending up waves of choking dust. The heat and smell of their bodies was overpowering. Terrified, Gaby clung to the bale, her eyes fearful as the cows veered closer, narrowly missing her with their sharp horns.

"Alcee," she screamed.

"Hang on, Gaby, I'll get you," Alcee called, and held out a hand, but Gaby was too far down to reach him and he was too frightened himself to get closer.

"What the hell," someone shouted, and suddenly the cattle were prodded away from her. She was shielded by the sweating, heaving sides of a horse. Lean, hard hands reached down to lift her off her feet. Strong arms wrapped around her, holding her about the waist as if she were a rag doll. She was half-perched on a muscular thigh, and the hard wall of a chest and shoulder supported her comfortingly from behind. Gaby turned her head to see her rescuer, and her gaze collided with the startling blue eyes of the Texan she'd watched on the boat.

He paid her scant attention as he expertly guided his horse through the cattle, managing to head off a steer that seemed intent on going his own way. The man took her some distance from the stampeding longhorns and unceremoniously dumped her on a bale. With a cry, Gaby fell in a heap, her skirts tangling around her legs, her dark hair flying out of its pins.

"Stay away from those cows. They're dangerous," the man commanded, glaring down at her. Angrily Gaby sat up and glared back. He needn't have treated her in such an undignified fashion, even if she had gotten in his way. She turned her furious blushing face to his, her dark eyes snapping with anger, and once again their gazes clashed.

Rayne stared down at the girl. He'd mollycoddled nearly three hundred head of cattle over on the boat from Galveston. The trip itself had taken only two days, but they'd sat outside the sandbar at the mouth of the river waiting for the tide to come in so they could dock. Now his cows were frightened and he was tired and irritable. He'd meant to ride away, but the girl's beauty caught him. The feel of her small warm body was still with him, the smell of her hair still in his nostrils. He stared down into her dark eyes, feeling his body respond to her beauty, then shook his head and glanced away, back along the wharf at his bawling cows. He'd been out on the range without a woman too long, if a mere child could arouse him.

"Stay out of the way," he snapped, and without a backward glance, turned his horse toward his men. The memory of the girl went with him, the small pointed chin, the dark flashing eyes, bright and alive, the creamy complexion that seemed to invite a man's touch, the full trembling lips, and the dark hair tumbling about her shoulders. Involuntarily his eyes had lowered, searching her chest for soft mounds, proof of her womanhood. The baggy dress had given him no clue.

She was a child, he told himself. One day she would be a beautiful woman, one who would break men's hearts. He felt a moment of regret that he wouldn't be there to see her then. One woman was much like another, he told himself, and prodded his horse with a booted foot. He had Lorna waiting for him back in Texas. He had no time to think of a child now.

With his coiled rope, Rayne Elliott slapped at a lagging steer. He'd gotten his herd here with less mishap than he'd expected. His decision to ship his cattle to New Orleans rather than drive them to markets in the North had been a good one, in spite of the high cost of the cattle boat. His profit might be less, but it was quicker. He'd be back at the ranch in time to gather up another herd and drive it to Kansas in the fall. For now he needed some quick money to put the ranch back on its feet.

Rayne's thoughts drifted back to the Rocking E Ranch. He'd been shocked when he'd returned from the war and had seen the neglect. Without cowhands and the incentive to keep the ranch going, his father had let it fall into neglect and near-ruin. Some of the buildings were on the verge of falling down, corral fences broken apart, the cattle gone and wandering southward. It was the way of most of the ranches after the war.

"Ho, Rayne, everything all right?" Dusty Simmons, his foreman, rode up to meet him. He glanced back down the dock toward the girl and boy.

"Some younkers got in the way," Rayne said, and dismissed all thoughts of the girl from his head.

"What d'you say, after you get rid of these here cows,

we go down to one of them fancy places and get us some good liquor and bad wimmin?" Dusty asked.

"Sounds good to me," Rayne agreed. He hadn't made any commitment to Lorna yet and it had been a long time out on the range. He kicked his mustang into a trot, suddenly eager to be off the docks and rid of his herd.

Gaby lay where she was, watching the two men gallop across the wharf with the last of their herd. They were headed toward the cattle pens. She felt stunned, as if her breath had been knocked from her. She could still feel the hot brush of the Texan's glance across her face and body. Boldly he'd looked down on her, assessing her, and then he'd dismissed her as if she were nothing. He'd no doubt forgotten her by now, but Gaby couldn't forget his warm blue gaze or the feel of his hard body against hers. Sensations she'd never felt before clamored alive and insistent deep inside her. She felt frightened by them.

"Gaby, are you all right?" Alcee asked, coming to the edge of the bale.

"I'm all right," she snapped. Sitting up, she made an attempt to refasten her hair.

"Good thing for you that Texan came along when he did. I was afraid one of those cows would gore you with his horns."

"You were certainly no help," Gaby said shortly. She pulled her skirts free and pushed herself over the edge of the bale and landed lightly on her feet on the wharf.

"Hey, wait for me," Alcee cried, but she walked away, heading back in the direction they'd come.

"Where are you going?" Alcee hurried to catch up.

"Home," Gaby snapped. "I'm tired of these stupid, childish adventures of yours."

"You promised you'd come with me so I could see the wharf."

"You've seen the wharf and the steamboats and the cattle boats. Now I'm going home."

"Don't go yet," Alcee called, but Gaby kept walking and he was forced to follow. For once she didn't slow her pace to make it easier for him.

"Are you angry because I didn't come down and help you?" he demanded. "It wouldn't have done you any good for me to be gored too," he said reasonably.

"It doesn't matter," Gaby said.

"Then why are you angry?"

"I'm not angry," Gaby shouted and people in the street turned to look at them. "I'm not angry with you," she repeated in a lower tone. She had no intention of telling him that she was angry with herself and with the arrogant Texan with the hard body and the bold eyes. Silently they hurried through the brick-paved streets of the French Quarter and down the narrow alley to the Cour des Anges.

"Well, good-bye, Gaby. Thanks for going with me," Alcee said, but she made no answer, just swung open the wide cast-iron gate and walked through the shadowed passage to the courtyard beyond.

What was wrong with Gaby? Alcee wondered. She was so moody lately. He shrugged and turned back to his own house, his thoughts on the sights of the wharves. Someday, he told himself, he'd go down to the wharf by himself and he really would sail away on one of those ships. Someday he'd show Gaby.

"Gaby, is that you, *ma chérie?*" Madeleine Porcher called from the gallery that overlooked the courtyard.

"*Oui*, Maddie, it is I," Gaby said, and paused at the fountain to dip her handkerchief in the cool water and bathe her flushed face. She had hurried too much and now she was hot and sweaty. She sank down on one of the cast-iron benches in the shade of a willow tree and rested. She was tempted to take off her shoes and stockings and dangle her feet in the fountain as well, but decided against it, since Madeleine was nearby. It would only bring about another lecture on decorum for young women.

Gaby glanced around the courtyard. It was quiet and lazy in the afternoon heat. Soon the gardens would be filled with men, young and old, each come to spend the evening with the woman of his choice. Lanterns would be lit in the gardens and the doors from the drawing rooms and all along the gallery would be thrown open invitingly. Servants would move about discreetly, offering trays of drinks and other light refreshments.

The women of Cour des Anges, garbed in the latest gowns from New York or Paris, would chat pleasantly about affairs in New Orleans. As glances grew bolder, more provocative, and desires mounted, the couples would move quietly up the stairs and along the gallery to the bedrooms, where the doors were closed and locked. Privacy was demanded and assured for Madeleine's customers, for they were often the richest men of New Orleans.

Madeleine carefully screened her patrons and assured them they would receive something rare and special in her house. Now that the octoroon balls no longer existed, the Cour des Anges and other establishments like it had flourished. Likewise Madeleine demanded that her girls behave like ladies at all times except in the bedrooms. Gaby wasn't one of Madeleine's angels, but her mother had been, and she assumed that one day she would be too.

"Where have you been, *chérie?*" Madeleine asked. She'd come down from the gallery and seated herself beside Gaby on the bench.

"I walked Alcee to the wharf. His mother forbids him to go by himself."

"So you take him there against her wishes," Madeleine scolded.

"I didn't take him, I accompanied him," Gaby insisted. "Soon he will be a man, and his mother treats him as a child."

"That is true," Maddie said, "but now, *chérie,* I worry about you. I have told you not to go to the wharf. It is much too dangerous. There are men there who would hurt you."

"They think I am a child," Gaby said in disgust, remembering the lean, brown Texan who had rescued her. He had obviously thought so.

"There are some men who would not care if you *were* a child," Madeleine reprimanded.

"I had Alcee with me."

"Alcee! Pah!" Madeleine scoffed. "He is not protection. It is time you started to behave like a woman. You must begin to think of your future and what you wish to do with it. When your mother died, she asked me to care for you until you were old enough to take care of yourself. The time has arrived, *chérie.* I cannot leave you to run through the streets all your life."

Gaby looked at the beautiful red-haired woman seated beside her. Once Madeleine Porcher had been a famous beauty, as had Gabrielle's mother, but now time was etching its passage on her lovely face.

"You have been very kind to me since my mother's death," Gaby said contritely. "I'm grateful."

"I do not wish you to be grateful, *ma petite,*" Maddie said in dismay. "This I owed your mother. She was a sister to me. I made a promise that I would care for you and protect you from the unkindnesses life offers. This I have done. Now you are an adult and you must begin to make decisions for yourself."

"There is nothing to decide," Gaby said, shrugging. "Someday I will become an angel here."

"Are you sure, Gaby?" Maddie asked.

Gaby shrugged again. "*Mais oui,* Madeleine," she said with rounded eyes.

"Gaby, that someday is here," Madeleine said softly, and watched the dark lashes fly upward as the girl turned startled eyes to her. "All of us here at the Court of Angels must do our share," Maddie continued. "Although the war has ended, food is still scarce and very expensive. Everything goes to the Union soldiers and to the carpetbaggers with the jingle of real coins in their pockets. I fear if we are not to go hungry as we did during the war, we must work very hard, each of us."

"Oh, Maddie," Gaby exclaimed, mortified that she hadn't realized the true condition of things here at the Court. She had taken Madeleine's care for granted. "I want to pay for my keep," she declared. "I'll go out and find a job today."

Madeleine smiled at the girl's youthful naiveté. "*Chérie,* what job will you find? What will you do? You have no skills."

"I can . . ." Gaby hesitated, her mind racing. "I can become a maid in one of the mansions along the river." She seized on the idea, picturing herself in a maid's uniform, gallantly scrubbing a floor to earn money for food for Maddie and the others. Gaby smiled bravely. It would not be so bad, she consoled herself.

"That is not for you, *chérie.* Soon the master of the house or his son would notice your beauty and would come creeping up the back stairs in the night. You would have no choice but to submit or lose your position. And when you are with child, he will deny everything and force you to leave as if the shame is all yours." Madeleine's eyes flashed with anger and outrage as she spoke.

"It doesn't always happen that way," Gaby said.

"More often than you might imagine, Gabrielle. Many of my girls began that way." Madeleine's eyes grew sympathetic as she looked at the young girl, remembering her mother when she first came, pregnant and frightened, to the Court of Angels. Elysse had been different from the other girls Madeleine had helped. She'd insisted on keeping her baby. Madeleine had never regretted her decision to take both the mother and the child under her wing. Now, looking at the beautiful dark-eyed girl, Madeleine sighed. She must do her best for Gaby.

"You are no longer a child, Gaby." She spoke sternly. "You are well past the age when most women have known the caress of a lover's touch."

"But I have no lover," Gaby cried, resisting the leaving behind of childhood for the burden of being an adult.

"Then we must find you one," Madeleine said, smiling. She understood all too well Gaby's reluctance, but she'd already given the girl more years than she herself had had. She could do no more.

"I . . . I don't think I'm ready yet," Gaby protested.

"It is time, *chérie*. I cannot protect you longer. Already my girls ask why you are given privileges they do not enjoy, why you run about the streets like a wild pony, undisciplined and untamed."

"I'm sorry, Maddie," Gaby said contritely. "I know I displease you."

"You do not displease me, *chérie*. The things you do displease me. You go to the docks, where no woman should go. You wear the clothes of a servant." Madeleine reached out a hand as if to touch Gaby's sleeve, and drew back. Her expression hardened. "In my kindness, I have neglected you, Gabrielle, and now I must do better by you."

"It's all right, I don't mind," Gaby said quickly and with some foreboding.

"Your mother would mind, Gaby. She didn't want you

brought up in the streets. She asked me to wait until you were old enough to make your decision about becoming an angel. You are eighteen now and it is time for you to decide what you want to do with your life."

Gaby's head bowed as she thought of everything the beautiful Madeleine had said. The Court had been a haven for her mother and now for her. One ringed, elegant hand came out to gently lift her chin. Madeleine studied the young face. Oh, to have such youth and beauty again, she thought. She could do great things with such assets. But her time had come and gone. Now she must teach Gaby. Together they would find a bright future for Gaby. It was what Elysse would have wanted.

"It is not such a bad way of life, *chérie*," Madeleine began gently. "You are very beautiful, Gabrielle. We will find you a rich benefactor, one who appreciates your beauty and fire, one who will take care of you and give you beautiful things. We will find someone who will give you a beautiful house all your own, and you will be happy and secure there. But this cannot happen if you run about the streets and if that which men value so highly is taken from you carelessly. You must preserve your value until the giving of this special gift you have can be exchanged for something of equal value. It is the only thing we women have to bargain with. We must bargain wisely."

"I understand, Madeleine," Gaby said softly. She'd not lived in the Court of Angels all her life without understanding clearly what was expected of the women who resided there.

"There are few men of such wealth left since the war," Madeleine went on. "One of them is coming here to-night, and we must be ready."

"Tonight?" Gaby asked, appalled. She'd known this time would come, but she couldn't believe it was upon her so quickly.

"Tonight, Gabrielle. We must prepare you. We have wasted much time." Madeleine waited for some response from Gaby, and after a long pause the girl nodded her acceptance.

"Ruby?" Madeleine called to the large black woman who served them well, seeing that the Court ran smoothly even if Madame Madeleine Porcher herself should become busy with a favored patron.

"Yas, Miz Madeleine." Ruby waddled out into the courtyard. Her round face pulled into a scowl. She took her duties seriously. She could have moved on after Lincoln's proclamation, going to Texas or one of the other promised lands offered to the freed slaves, but she liked New Orleans and her position at Cour des Anges. She had no need to be paid for her services. She'd been handling the household accounts ever since she'd come here as a young woman more than fifteen years before. Her enormous bulk had ended any chance of her becoming one of Madeleine's angels, but she'd proven herself invaluable with her quick intelligence and steadfast loyalty.

"You want sumpin'?" Ruby asked now in the patois of the New Orleans blacks.

"Ruby, we must make this little street urchin into a beautiful woman by tonight," Madeleine instructed.

The large black eyes fixed on Gaby. "Impossible!" Ruby snapped. "Her nose too little, her eyes too big, and she ain't got no meat on them bones. Ain't no man goin' wan' her. They think she a boy!"

"That's what we have to work on," Madeleine said with a wink at Gabrielle. "When we are finished with her, we want every man to think she's the most beautiful woman he's ever seen. We want him to burn with desire for her."

"Lawd, we can do dat. We had lotsa practice." Ruby chuckled. "Come on in here, girl." Ruby motioned toward the bathhouse. "First we got to get yo' a bath. Yo' smell like the stockyards." Gaby cast a last pleading look at Madeleine, who imperiously motioned her to follow Ruby.

Two hours later, Gaby sat in her bedroom, one dainty foot resting on a cushion, her clean hair falling down her back in shiny black waves. She was surrounded by the other women of the Court of Angels. Some were younger than she and some were older, nearing the end of their careers. All cheerfully offered her advice on how to behave with a gentleman.

Under Ruby's watchful eye, Salome, a young black maid, worked on her hair while another carefully painted her nails. Gaby was exhausted. Her body had been soaked and massaged, pounded and laced and perfumed until she could hardly move a muscle. She wanted only to tumble into her bed and sleep forever, but even that comfort was denied her.

Her own small bed had been taken from the room, and a new one with a wide downy mattress and large, deep pillows had replaced it. The new bed had been made up with snowy white sheets and lace-edged pillowcases. Fresh netting had been hung about the bed to keep out the insects. New sheer lace curtains fluttered at the windows between rich velvet draperies of burgundy. Woven carpets had been laid and now her room had obtained an opulence it hadn't shown before. Even the large mirror sitting in the corner had been added.

"Some men have peculiar fantasies," Marie said when Gaby asked about the mirror.

"Madeleine says no fantasy is peculiar," Clarisse replied. "She says some people are just less ashamed of their bodies and their needs." Gaby looked at the mirror again and glanced away, suddenly feeling hollow in the pit of her stomach.

"Don't look so frightened," Clarisse giggled. "It's not so bad, and you'll receive presents and bonbons."

"We can tell who gets the bonbons," Marie said dryly. She was a thin, sharp-tongued girl who thought the fluffy blond weak-willed and foolish. Clarisse made a moue of disapproval at her.

"You have to forget yourself and have fun," she observed with a knowing wink at Gaby.

"Keep your head at all times," Marie advised. "Remain a little bit aloof. Keep them guessing. It keeps them coming back."

"I never pretend," Clarisse cut in. "I never have to."

"It takes imagination to be able to pretend," Marie said archly.

"I just relax and let whatever happens, happen," Clarisse said. "We all have a good time. Do you know who Madeleine has arranged for you tonight?"

"Monsieur Barbieri," Gaby said faintly.

"Oh." Clarisse stopped smiling and her friendly, candid gaze moved about the room. "He's so old and his breath smells and he—"

"Clarisse," Marie said, her dark eyes taking in the stricken look on Gaby's face. "He is not so bad," she said kindly. "He will finish very quickly and then he sleeps."

"He may finish quickly with you," Clarisse said, arching an eyebrow, "but he never does with me."

"Perhaps not. It is understandable that it takes longer when he feels no passion, *chérie*," Marie said with mock sympathy. "Monsieur Barbieri told me himself he has an aversion to fat thighs."

"What?" Clarisse shrieked.

"Ladies, ladies," Madeleine said, entering the room. "No more of that." Instantly the two girls fell into sulky silence.

"How does she look, Ruby?" Madeleine asked, turning to study Gaby.

"She need more at the top, Miz Maddie," Ruby said, "and there ain't nuttin we kin do 'bout dat."

"Let me see." Gaby was made to stand in the center of the room while the lace negligee was lifted from her slim shoulders and the two women perused her figure, skimpily attired in the lace underwear.

"She's perfect," Madeleine proclaimed, nodding her approval over the exquisitely shaped figure with its small, well-shaped breasts. "We don't have to be overblown for a man to appreciate our charms, Ruby."

"Yas'm," Ruby said, but it was clear she didn't agree. Most men liked a woman with a little flesh on her. Wasn't that what her man told her? Ruby wriggled her ample hips in unconscious response to her own memories.

"I think we'll put her in the white satin gown with the pink trim," Madeleine said, studying the girl's pale face. "Yes tonight it should be the white. After all, she is a virgin, *n'est-ce pas?*"

"Maddie . . ." Gaby swallowed and looked at her benefactress with large, eloquent eyes. "What will Monsieur Barbieri expect of me? Clarisse says—"

"Clarisse talks too much," Madeleine said, turning to frown at the blond girl. Clarisse bit her lips and looked away. "You are not to worry, Gaby. We have trained you well," Madeleine reassured her ward. "Barbieri is a gentleman."

"But . . . but how am I to kiss a man if his breath smells?" Gaby wailed. "I . . . I have never kissed a man before. Do they all have bad breath?"

Madeleine's bustling steps halted and she turned to look at Gaby. Her quick eyes flashed to the faces of the other girls and back to Gaby, who stood in misery and uncertainty.

How difficult this first time was for a woman, Madeleine thought sadly. Men placed such importance upon it and yet it was only when the initiation was behind a woman that she was truly able to find pleasure herself and thus learn to please a man. Madeleine remembered her first lover. How young, how bold he'd been.

Gaby should have such a man.

"It will not be so bad," Madeleine reassured Gaby, and herself as well. Quickly she turned away from the bright sparkle of tears in the girl's dark eyes.

"Hurry, ladies," Madeleine cried, clapping her hands. "It is time to dress for our guests," The room broke into a flurry of activity as the women gathered up their things and hurried back to their own rooms to prepare for the evening. Gaby remained where she was in the center of the room as if frozen.

"Here, Miz Gaby, we slip dis on," Salome said, holding out snowy white petticoats. Mutely Gaby stood while the maid helped her dress. When she was ready, Gaby looked in the mirror. In spite of her finery, she looked like a fragile, broken flower, her eyes so tragic that even Ruby went away shaking her head.

Madeleine, gowned now in a beautiful magenta satin which set off her auburn hair, stopped by Gaby's room again. A black beauty mark had been penciled on one cheekbone and her extravagant red hair was piled high on her head. Madeleine looked at Gaby and caught her breath. She looked so young and untouched. Her mother would have been proud of her.

"You are beautiful, *chérie*," Madeleine said softly.

"Oh, Maddie, please don't make me do this tonight, not tonight," Gaby cried, suddenly frightened.

"It must be tonight. Monsieur Barbieri has already

been notified. It does no good to wait, Gaby. It is time you got on with your life. You are no longer a child. Now, dry your tears and smile. It will not be so bad. Tomorrow you will laugh at tonight's tears."

Gaby blinked back her tears but she could not summon a smile. Descending the stairs to the courtyard, Madeleine carried with her an image of Gaby's sad face.

The breezes were warm and fragrant with the scent of magnolias. The stars were bright in the black velvet of the night sky. It was a time for romance, Madeleine thought. She pushed away the guilt Gaby's tears had aroused in her. She had protected the girl long enough. She had done her best. Even now she was striving to give Gaby to someone who would be captivated by her young, untried charms, someone rich enough to take care of her in a grand style.

In her youth, Gaby had known only death and hunger and the streets of New Orleans. Monsieur Barbieri could give her so much more than a young lover might. Love was not so important after all. In a few years, Gaby would see that and thank Madeleine for her decisions this night.

"Miz Maddie . . ." Zack, the black man who'd guarded the Court for many years, stepped out of the shadows. "There's two gentlemen at the gate. One says yo' might 'member him. His name's Dusty."

"Dusty Simmons?" Maddie asked in surprise. She remembered the Texas cowboy only too well. He'd come to New Orleans early in the war before the city's capture and occupation by the northern troops. He'd stayed a week, and in that week, Madeleine had forgotten for a time that she was a businesswoman.

"Dusty, you came back," she cried, and threw herself into his arms. He laughed and hugged her tightly, his arms strong and sure around her. No man had ever held her that way since Dusty had left. Oh, the years had been long, Madeleine thought, and hugged him back.

"I told you I'd be back someday," Dusty said, drawing back to look at her. "You look good, Maddie, real good." Madeleine knew he lied. The years told on her as well as they did him. His hair was graying now and his shoulders sloped a little, but his body was still as hard and lean as when he was younger.

"It's good to see you, Dusty," she said in a voice that had gone strangely husky. Dusty drew her into his arms again, his mouth settling on hers on a long, satisfying kiss.

Madeleine had been vaguely aware of a tall figure waiting in the shadows. Now she heard the sound of a throat clearing, and with a laugh Dusty released her and stepped back.

"Maddie, I want you to meet a friend of mine, Rayne Elliott. He used to be my commanding officer in the army and now he's my boss on the Rocking E Ranch."

"How do you do?" Madeleine said graciously, extending her hand to the tall, lean cowboy.

"Ma'am, it's a pleasure to meet you," Rayne Elliott said. Dusty had been right. The woman was a stunner. She had class and the kind of good looks that would endure the ravages of age.

"Listen, Maddie, girl, Rayne and me are in New Orleans for a few days. We just brought over some cows and we're fixin' to enjoy the sights before we head back to Texas. We been out on the range for quite a spell and ain't had nothin' to keep us company but them mean-tempered, ugly steers. We got us a mighty big cravin'. Have you got someone real special for Rayne here?" He didn't ask for someone for himself. They both knew Madeleine would spend the night with him.

Maddie looked at the long-legged man who was Dusty's friend, noting the breadth of shoulders, the slim tapering hips, and the strong, clean-shaven jaw. He and Dusty were of the same cloth, she thought. Beneath the black hair sweeping back from a widow's peak, compelling blue eyes stared back at her unwaveringly. Madeleine caught her breath. In the arms of such a man as this, a woman would know she was every inch a woman. Madeleine remembered Gaby waiting tearfully in her room for an old man to claim her virginity. First she deserved a night with a man like Rayne Elliott.

Madeleine made up her mind. Gaby would have her night of passion and love. Later would come the nights of loneliness and disillusionment, the nights of pretending and compromise. Never mind that she would no longer be a virgin. Maddie had fooled many an astute patron with a little fish bladder filled with blood, and thus a young girl could be a virgin time and time again.

She would give Barbieri to Clarisse. She would give Gaby one last gift in memory of her mother. Madeleine turned back to Dusty and smiled.

"I have just the girl for him," she said gaily. "She is a very special girl, my tall, handsome Texan. a treasure such as most men only dream about, and she is a virgin."

Madeleine's laughter filled the fragrant, warm air.

2

Gaby stood at the window looking down on the brick-paved alley. It had started to rain and the streets looked slick and shiny in the pools of light cast by the gas streetlamps. Here in the side street, all was quiet. The bright lights and gaiety of New Orleans' frenzied nightlife took place on some other street.

Gaby felt alone, isolated from other people by the coming event. Like any other girl, she'd dreamed of a handsome prince who would come someday and sweep her off her feet. Instead, fate had allotted her doddering, half-witted old Barbieri. Behind her the door opened and there was the sound of a boot on the wooden floor. It was time, Gaby thought. She must put away her romantic dreams and be practical. She must welcome Barbieri and make him believe she'd been eagerly awaiting him.

Drawing a trembling breath, Gaby parted her lips in a seductive, inviting smile as she'd been shown by Clarisse, and turned to face her first customer.

She was beautiful, more beautiful than Rayne had expected. He'd only half-listened to the madam below, believing her words were exaggerations. He hadn't minded. He'd wanted to be enticed and seduced. It was all part of the allure of a place like this. Cour des Anges was a whorehouse, but it was a lot fancier than any he'd been in so far. The girls were presented in a little more discreet fashion, but the outcome was the same.

He'd bought the services of a whore for the evening, and since he'd paid more than usual, he'd expected her

to be beautiful. She'd surpassed his expectations. He
stood silently taking in her fragile, sultry beauty, and for
some reason he thought of the little hoyden he'd rescued
on the wharf that afternoon. Was every Creole blessed
with the same dark-eyed innocence, the same smoldering
passion in every glance? Her smile was knowing, experienced, and in spite of the madam's assurances of her
virginal state, Rayne guessed she'd entertained men often here in this room.

"Bonsoir, monsieur," she said. Her voice was soft and
melodious, with just the hint of Creole accent. She smiled
again and the curls that were pinned behind her ear
danced with the movement of her head.

"I am Gabrielle," she said, and extended her hand.

Gripping his hat in his hand, Rayne moved forward
into the light. He heard her quick intake of breath and
saw the consternation on her face, but he was too preoccupied by his own responses. He felt awkward and out of
place in the elegance of the room and in the presence of
the dainty creature before him. She stood with her hand
still outstretched. Rayne took it and bent to place a kiss
on the tips of her fingers.

His blue eyes met hers and Gaby drew in her breath as
she recognized the cowboy on the wharf.

This was not Barbieri.

He bent again and this time planted a kiss in the warm
palm of her hand. A tingling sensation began at the touch
of his lips against her skin. Gaby trembled, trying to
regain control of her senses.

"I'm Rayne Elliott," the Texan said, straightening so
his eyes once again met hers. Gabrielle had to tilt her
head back to look at him. In the soft lamplight she
studied his face. It was like no other face she'd ever
seen.

His strong features seemed chiseled from stone. There
were deep lines along his lean cheeks and at the corners
of his mouth and eyes, as if he often squinted against the
sun. His forehead was tanned to a line where his hatband
had rested, and above that line, his dark hair, thick and
vibrant, swept backward from a peak. His deep-set eyes
seemed to look right through her, and she felt herself
flush.

"Go away," she wanted to cry to him, but her tongue wouldn't speak. She simply stared up at him. Rayne returned her gaze.

She was younger than he'd thought when he first entered the room, and more beautiful. His hungry gaze fell on her full mouth and he flipped his hat on the bed and swept her into his arms. His eager mouth descended to hers and he tasted the sweetness, felt the softness of her against his own body. He'd meant it to be a mild kiss, simply to break the ice, but he felt his control slipping.

"Please, *monsieur*," Gaby cried. "There has been a mistake. I am to be with Monsieur Barbieri."

Rayne drew back to look into her eyes. "Didn't you say your name is Gabrielle?" he asked. "The lady downstairs told me the third door for Gabrielle."

"Madeleine sent you to me?" Gabrielle gasped. Relief flooded through her that she would not have to be with old Barbieri that night; then relief fled as she realized she hadn't been given a reprieve at all. This tall man with the weather-beaten face and penetrating gaze was to spend the night with her instead. Fear washed through her. It was one thing to dream of a handsome man when you were never likely to see him again, but when he stood in the middle of your bedroom with an expectant air about him, it was another matter indeed.

"I see," she said, moving away from him and toward the chest that held bottles of liquor. "Would you like some whiskey or champagne?" she asked, stalling for time.

"Whiskey!" His gaze never left her, taking in the slim, straight back, the sway of her hips beneath the petticoats. She was short and her figure small and petite. There was about her an air of dainty womanliness. The scent of her perfume drew him across the room toward her, so when she turned with the tumbler of whiskey he was right behind her. She gasped and the whiskey sloshed over the edge of the glass and onto her pale fingers.

Rayne took the glass and drank the contents in one swallow, his eyes never leaving hers. Then he lifted her fingers to his lips and gently kissed away the whiskey that had spilled on them. The hot rasp of his tongue on her hand made her shiver and jerk away.

Rayne looked at her in surprise. Wasn't she here to please him? Why was she so skittish, especially when he was trying to please her as well? He seldom took his pleasure from a woman without giving something in return.

Quickly Gaby turned away from him, moving with an unaccustomed rustle of satin skirts to look out the window again.

"Have I offended you?" Rayne asked, and Gaby turned back to face him, a tremulous smile on her lips.

"Oh, no," she said, her gaze not quite meeting his. Unconsciously she made her smile wider. Rayne crossed the room to stand before her, his lean hands gripping her arms.

"You are very beautiful," he said huskily. He lowered his mouth to hers and once again Gaby felt as if she were drowning in emotions she couldn't control or understand.

"Please, *monsieur*," she cried when he released her mouth. His lips grazed a path along her jaw to the warm softness of her throat. Her small hands pushed at his arms and shoulders.

"Please wait," she cried again.

"Why?" he whispered against her skin.

"Would you . . . like some more whiskey?" Gaby said desperately, trying to evade the hot, moist rasp of his tongue on her sensitive skin. Her nerve endings tingled with his invasion of her senses. He didn't answer. His mouth covered hers once more, his tongue probing against her soft lips, forcing them open. Gabrielle moaned and didn't know it. If she hadn't been gripped so tightly in his arms, she was sure she would have fallen down. Her head was reeling. He released her mouth long enough for her to try again.

"Are you hungry, *monsieur?* Would you like some food?" Clarisse had told her she must offer these things.

"Yes, I'm hungry," Rayne Elliott muttered low in his throat, "and no, I don't want any food." He swept her up in his arms, her ruffled skirt trailing over his arms as he carried her to the bed. He seemed not to notice that he'd crushed his hat. Suddenly all the fears Gaby had experienced during the afternoon came back to her. His hard, masculine body was alien-feeling beside hers on the bed, and she was overwhelmed by the insistency of his passion.

He lay half across her, the weight of his lean body arousing further confusing emotions within her. She pushed against his shoulder, struggling to free herself from him.

"Please, *monsieur*, there has been a mistake," she gasped against his lips, but he wasn't listening. He'd spent too many weeks out in the chaparral, and now beneath him was a woman more beautiful than any he'd dared dream about. She was his for the night. There was no need to waste more time talking. His hands moved to the buttons and fasteners of her bodice.

Suddenly it occurred to Gaby that she was overpowered by the man who held her. She had no choice in what was about to happen to her, and the realization left her shaken and frightened. Tears she'd tried to hold back filled her eyes. She lay silent, shamed and resigned to what she was about to become.

She made no more protests as he quickly unfastened her clothes and removed each garment carefully, as if removing the petals of a lovely flower, trying to reach the very heart of her. But she would never reveal her heart, Gaby thought bitterly. She would never give that part of herself.

She lay nude before the gaze of the strange, handsome man and felt her vulnerability. His brilliant blue eyes darkened with passion as he looked at her and she shut her eyes so she wouldn't see his expression. With them open she was too aware of the violation of her body that was about to occur.

Lightly he touched her, his finger barely grazing the little red starlike birthmark on one breast. Then the touch was gone. The weight of his body left her. Was he displeased? Had he disliked the mark on her breast? Had he thought her flawed? She opened her eyes. He was taking pity on her after all, she thought, but he had only risen to strip off his clothes. His shirt was flung to the floor and Gabrielle quickly shut her eyes again, the image of his bare chest already etched in her mind.

She felt the weight of him as he settled above her again. She was surprised that his skin was so smooth. Weren't men great hairy beasts? She caught her breath as she felt his hot breath fan her cheek, felt the scrape of his chin against the delicate skin of her shoulder. His head burrowed in the sensitive hollow of her throat and a tide rose within her.

She trembled as his hands moved gently across her skin and settled at her breasts, lightly touching the sensitive, virginal nipples. Emotions warred within her. She wanted to respond to the touch of this man she'd met only a few hours before, while her heart and mind fought against his possession of her body and spirit.

Tears stung her eyes and coursed down her cheeks to the pillow beneath her, and her body trembled with repressed sobs. Rayne drew back and gazed down at her, puzzled at the tears on her cheeks.

"Have I hurt you?" he asked softly, and with her lips clamped tightly shut lest she emit a sound, she shook her head that he hadn't.

"Why are you crying?" Gently he smoothed the dark strands of hair from her flushed cheeks. Her slight body trembled but no answer came. Puzzled, Rayne looked at her. She was young, younger than he'd thought, now that her hair was tumbling about her shoulders and the finery was gone from her.

"Don't you feel well?" he asked, uncertain of how to handle this problem. He'd never had a woman cry when he was making love to her. Had he lost his touch out in the bush? Was he rushing her, doing something wrong? He lay watching her, torn between wanting to fling himself out of the room in anger and demand another girl and wanting to be here with her no matter what the problem or how long it took to solve.

Gaby opened her eyes and looked at him, and he recoiled, staring at her incredulously.

"You're the girl on the dock," he said in amazement. Gaby stared at him in surprise. Now he recognized her, she thought. How like a man. "Aren't you?" he demanded, and Gaby was surprised to see he was angry.

"*Oui!*" she said quickly.

"But you're only a child," Rayne exclaimed, standing up and reaching for his pants. Damn, as in need as he was, he wouldn't take a child, no matter how experienced she was.

"I am eighteen, *monsieur*," Gaby said indignantly. She sat up and gripped the sheet to her breasts. Rayne paused and looked at her. She looked like an angel sitting there.

"You don't look eighteen," he said doubtfully.

"Nevertheless, I am. My birthday was in March."

"I don't understand then," Rayne said, fastening his pants about his trim, hard waist. "Why are you crying?"

"I am sorry, *monsieur*." Gaby lowered her gaze to her tightly clenched hands. "It is the first time I will be with a man. I am a little frightened and a little sad."

"You're a virgin?" Rayne demanded in disbelief. True, the madam downstairs had said she was a virgin, but he hadn't believed it. It was a claim made by all madams about their wares.

"Look, this isn't necessary. I don't care if you've been with other men or not. I don't expect a virgin. I've been alone for months and I just want a—"

"A woman, *monsieur?* A whore?" Gaby flared. "Well" —she shrugged and smiled sadly—"that is what I am."

"But you're . . . a virgin," Rayne said as if she were scarred with some horrible mark.

"*Oui*," Gaby said more calmly than she felt. "But all women start out as virgins, Monsieur Elliott. It is not something so unusual. It is only you men who set such great store by a woman's virginity at the same time you take it so carelessly. Is it any wonder we cheat a little bit?" Her eyes were dark and snapping with anger as she looked at him. Suddenly Rayne felt guilty as hell, and then the guilt turned to anger.

"Look, sweetheart, I didn't come down here for a Sunday-school lesson," he said, pulling on his boots, "and I have no particular desire for a virgin. I like a woman with a little experience behind her." He stamped his boot on and reached for his shirt.

Suddenly it occurred to Gaby that if he left, she would be stuck with Barbieri again, and the thought appalled her more than the thought of mating with this man.

"*Monsieur* . . ." she began as he buttoned up his shirt.

"Look, don't call me '*monsieur*.' My name is Rayne."

"Rayne," she repeated obediently. "You are not leaving?"

"You bet I am," he said, reaching for his coat.

"Please, Rayne. Please don't go. I beg you," she cried, getting off the bed and hurrying to him. She laid a hand on his chest and looked up at him with wide, appealing eyes.

"Look, I don't take virgins," he said, backing away. "I just came here wanting a woman to spend the night with."

"And you have her," Gaby said, deliberately making her voice seductive. "Am I not attractive enough for you, *monsieur?*"

"You know you are, you little devil," he said, his voice tight, his blue eyes boring into hers, "but I didn't come here to break in an untried filly." Gaby stared back at him in bewilderment until the full import of his words came to her.

"I was lying," she cried. "We are told to behave like frightened virgins, so the men will like us better. Please don't leave. If you do, I will be shamed by the others." She could see him wavering. "I am a woman of much experience in these things," she pressed. Still he wavered.

"If you leave, Madam will beat me and I will not be allowed to eat all day long," she said, making her voice piteous. Rayne looked at her in surprise and a sudden rush of anger. Was she telling the truth? Suddenly he wanted to strike the redheaded woman who had gone off with Dusty. No wonder the girl was so little and skinny.

"Have you ever gone hungry?" he asked harshly.

"*Oui, monsieur,* many times I have been hungry," Gaby said. She didn't tell him it was due to the early years of the war and not to Madeleine's punishment.

He stood looking down at her indecisively, and Gaby began to unbutton his shirt slowly. When it was open, she pushed it over his shoulders and arms. She'd never touched a man in such an intimate way before. Her fingers lingered on the curves and slopes of his muscular chest and back. Once again her fingers traced across the whipcord leanness of his ribs and fluttered of their own volition across his flat midsection to his waistband.

At her touch, a light flared in Rayne's blue eyes. He gripped her arms and pulled her against his bare chest. The sheet she'd clutched to her fell to the floor and she felt her bared breasts against his warm skin. The emotions she'd struggled with earlier were there again, but this time she didn't fight them. His head dipped and his mouth was on hers, hot and demanding. Her body conformed to his familiarly now.

She could feel a growing bulge press against her lower stomach and was surprised at the throbbing response that rose somewhere deep within her and spread downward into her thighs. Her mouth opened in surrender beneath his probing tongue and her senses were invaded as never before. Unbidden, her arms came up to wrap around his neck, and she stood on tiptoe, straining against him.

Rayne scooped her up and placed her on the bed. This time she kept her eyes open. She saw the flare of passion that darkened his eyes, saw the thrusting manhood of him, and her own senses were inflamed by him. Instinctively she followed his lead, opening herself to him, and gently, expertly, he led her to a peak of passion and desire that was new to her. Her fright was behind her and now there was a pulsing anticipation.

When he entered her, she cried out briefly against the pain and he paused in disbelief and would have withdrawn, but she clasped her arms around him and welcomed him. He'd been too long without a woman; she'd aroused him too well. He stopped fighting and moved against her gently until he saw the pinched look of pain give way to pleasure, then he rode her through the night sky to a land beyond all others where they both found a new wonder and ecstasy.

"You were virginal," he murmured against her temples later when they lay resting.

"Now I'm a woman of experience," she said, and snuggled against him. How could she have been so frightened of something so wonderful? She closed her eyes and slept.

She wasn't used to the feel of a man in her bed and she woke several times during the night. Each time, he caressed her, teaching her new ways to pleasure. Finally, near dawn, she fell into an exhausted sleep, satiated beyond a point she'd ever thought possible earlier in the evening. She was unaware that her dark-haired lover lay wakeful and confused beside her. He'd never known such a night of satisfaction with a woman. Woman, hell—

despite what she said, she was little more than a child. Yet that child had given more generously than any woman he'd ever known.

He pulled her small body against his, marveling at its soft perfection. To think he'd found something like her here in a New Orleans whorehouse. He felt confused and angry and wasn't sure what he was angry about.

When the dawn cast mauve shadows across the room, he rose and pulled on his clothes. The girl slept on. He stood over the bed staring down at her. Even after their night together, she still looked like an angel, he thought, a very tired angel. His eyes lost their bemused look and grew serious. He turned away and quietly left the room.

It was nearly noon before Gaby opened her eyes. Ruby was at the door with a tray of hot coffee. Gaby sat up and looked around. She was in her own room, but this wasn't her narrow bed. Then everything came back to her. Quickly she looked around the room for signs of Rayne, but he was gone. She drew in her breath and held it a moment against the sudden rush of disappointment.

"Miz Madeleine, she say yo' prob'ly ready fo' some coffee and some talkin'," Ruby said. "She say she be right heah."

"Thank you, Ruby." Gaby settled back against her propped-up pillows. The sunlight spilled through her curtains but the day seemed bleak and gray to her. She lay thinking of the night before, of the feelings Rayne Elliott had aroused in her, and she blushed.

She'd given herself freely and now he was gone. Was this to be the way of life from now on? Was she expected to give everything in the velvety darkness of the night and be left barren and bereft in the searing light of day? A light knock at the door interrupted her unhappy reverie. Madeleine entered and looked at her brightly.

"*Bonjour, chérie,*" she said, studying Gaby's downcast face in dismay. "You did not have a good night?" Gaby made no answer.

"With such a man as that I thought it would be a night to remember." Madeleine laughed gaily. Her reunion with Dusty had been all she'd anticipated when she'd first seen him at the front gate.

"Do not sulk, my pet." Madeleine seated herself beside

the bed and poured a cup of coffee for herself. Her dark
gaze darted over Gaby's face. Could it be, she wondered,
that a man of Rayne's possibilities had left the girl unsatis-
fied and disillusioned of love after all.

Once more the shrewd Frenchwoman studied the silent
girl's face. No, there were the signs of a night well spent in
the purplish shadows under her weary eyes, the mouth
swollen from the kisses it had received and given. Even
shifting in bed, Gaby gave away the events of the night by
the slight wince she made. Then what troubled the girl?
Sudden understanding swept over Madeleine and she smiled.

"Congratulations, *chérie,*" she said, sipping at the hot,
bittersweet brew. Her eyes were merry over the rim of
the cup. "I think you have made a conquest."

"What do you mean?" Gaby asked, raising her eyes
hopefully.

"The tall, handsome cowboy came to waken me at an
ungodly hour this morning to tell me that I must not give
you to any other man. While he is here in New Orleans
he wishes to have you himself."

Gaby's spirits rose and her face lit up. "Oh, Maddie,
do you think he liked me?" she asked, her dark eyes
shining.

"*Oui,* so it seems," Madeleine said. "But that is not all
with which a woman must concern herself. 'Did he like
me?' Pah! Did you like him, Gaby? Do you want to
spend all your time with him?"

"Yes, oh yes," Gaby cried, sitting straight up in bed,
her face eager and anxious at the same time. Madeleine
looked at the lovely young girl and remembered Gaby's
mother when she was that age, tender and innocent and
unafraid of life. There had been that same rosy glow on
Elysse's face during the time she'd spent with Gaby's
father.

"*Chérie,* do not be so eager. Do not give too much of
yourself or you will be hurt. In a very short while this
good-looking cowboy will go back to Texas, back to his
cows, and back to a woman who will bear all his hardships and his children and die before her time. These
things you do not want. Be careful you are not hurt by
caring too much for him. It is easy to mistake passion for
love."

"I didn't say I love him," Gaby cried defensively. "I only wish to spend time with him. I have known him only a few hours. How can I love someone I don't know well?"

"Love is not practical or logical, *ma petite*. Be on guard." Madeleine rose and with a swish of her skirts turned to leave. "Gaby," she said, her brows drawn together in a puzzled frown, "why did this cowboy of yours tell me I must not beat you again and I must give you food to eat? I do not keep food from you and I never beat you."

Gaby flushed guiltily.

"Ah, I understand. It was a game," Madeleine said. "Some men like to play these fantasies. How clever of you to see that for such a strong man, he would want a woman who is in need of his protection."

"I didn't mean—"

"Of course you didn't, *chérie*," Madeleine said. "You have done well, Gaby. If we are careful, you can have a most illustrious career. You are beautiful enough and clever enough. Now, rest. Your Texan will return in the afternoon with a carriage, and you are to show him New Orleans."

Gaby was apprehensive about meeting Rayne again. How must she appear to him? Should she feel shy for all that had occurred between them through the night, or should she be gay and uninhibited? Should she pretend a worldliness, a sophistication other courtesans showed? She wasn't sure what would please Rayne and she wanted to please him.

She dressed carefully for her afternoon ride, choosing to wear one of the new dresses Madeleine had ordered from New York. The black-and-white dress with its nipped waist and flaring skirt and trim of dull cherry piping at the scalloped hem and sleeves made her feel smart and fashionable. Gaby was glad the steel-and-bone hoops had gone out of style. She liked the swish of petticoats about her ankles.

She also liked the light in Rayne's eyes when he first saw her. His gaze raked over her face and figure, then came back to the soft mouth.

"You look pretty as a red heifer in a flower bush," he

teased her, deliberately drawling the words. His eyes sparkled with laughter. Although the words were unfamiliar to Gaby, their meaning was all too clear. The laughter in his eyes died and his gaze captured hers.

Gaby walked into his arms, raising her mouth for his kiss. Why had she worried this morning about their meeting? It all seemed so natural to be here in his arms. Gaby pressed against him, her body responded to the desire he ignited in her. Rayne drew back and looked down at her with a lazy grin.

"How quickly the angel becomes the temptress," he said huskily, and was delighted by the rosy blush that stained her cheeks.

Rayne lifted her effortlessly into the waiting carriage, marveling at her lightness and the tiny span of her waist. Her perfume filled his head with a seductive message. He stood watching her settle herself on the seat. He'd never known a woman could be so beautiful and dainty. She was hardly any bigger than a minute, yet in the night she'd been all the woman a man could ever want. That tiny, perfect body had hummed beneath his touch and she'd borne his weight easily.

"Is something wrong, Rayne?" Gaby looked down at him where he stood as if awestruck.

"Not a thing," he said, knocking his hat against his thigh impatiently and clamping it on his head before climbing up on the seat beside her. What was the matter with him anyway? He was acting like he had some ailment. Cupid's cramp, the boys back in the bunkhouse would have said. Rayne scowled and picked up the reins. Gaby stirred on the seat beside him, letting her shoulder brush against his, just to let him know she was there and to feel his strength. Rayne felt her softness even through his coat sleeve, and all the irritation went out of him.

The carriage rolled through the streets of New Orleans. Gaby had never seen the city from this angle. She'd always walked. She took Rayne down the Vieux Carré, through the French Quarter, down Canal Street, through the parks, and out along the river road, where the great mansions and plantations of the rich had been built before the war. Now huge cotton plantations were falling into disrepair. There were no slaves to work the cotton fields and help maintain the plantation houses.

"It looks as hard hit as Texas," Rayne observed, and slapped the reins against the horses' backs. They found a grassy place along the riverbank and pulled off.

"What is Texas like?" Gaby asked when they were settled on a grassy knoll looking over the river.

"It's big, bigger than you can ever imagine," he said. "Texas is like a woman. She's got two sides to her. Both sides are beautiful, both are dangerous to man." He smiled down at her teasingly. "But once you've seen her, you can't forget her." Gaby was sure he wasn't talking about Texas anymore.

"It's a tough life out there, Gaby. Someone like you wouldn't survive."

"I'm stronger than I look," she answered quietly.

"You're a little heifer that's barely away from her mother," he teased her again. "Where is your family, Gaby? How did you end up in a place like the Cour des Anges?"

"I am an orphan," Gabrielle began with a sad little shrug. Quietly she told him of her life with Madeleine, of the fever that had taken her mother's life, of the hungry, lean years during the war, made harder because Madeleine wouldn't allow the hated Union soldiers into her establishment. She made him laugh when she told him of how the women of New Orleans emptied their chamber pots on the heads of the soldiers until General Spoons Butler, so nicknamed because of his love for his hostess's silver, issued his infamous Woman Order whereby any woman who showed her contempt for the Union Army would be treated like the lowest woman of the street. Thereafter the ladies of New Orleans had quietly demonstrated their outrage by pasting Butler's picture in the bottom of their chamber pots. Rayne laughed at the thought of the unpopular general getting his comeuppance.

"The women of New Orleans sound as spunky as the women of Texas," he said.

"What are the women of Texas like?" Gaby asked, thinking of what Madeleine had said about them.

"They're hardworking, stubborn women, not afraid of anything, some of them. Others can't take it. They break and run away. Those that stay grow old before their time, worn out by the dust and dirt, half-crazed by the lonesomeness and the constant threat of Indians and wild animals, half-starved during the lean years. It's a pretty rough life."

"Why do people live there if Texas is such an inhospitable land?" Gaby asked.

"You'd have to see it," Rayne answered. "You'd have to ride up into the mountains and watch the sun rising in the morning." He stopped speaking, a half-smile on his lips. "I wish I could show it to you," he said regretfully.

"You love this Texas of yours?" Gaby mused softly. The thought made him seem more aloof from her. There was a part of him she could never share.

"I was born on the ranch," Rayne was saying. His arms were draped around his bent knees and he stared into the rushing water of the river. "My father brought my mother there when she was just a bride. She lasted for a year, until I was born, then she left."

"You must have missed her very much," Gaby said, recalling her feelings of loneliness since her mother's death.

"Not as much as Pa," Rayne answered with a tightening of his lips. "It just about destroyed him." He paused, wondering why he was even talking about these painful old events. He'd never spoken of them before to anyone. Something about Gaby and her gentle ways seemed to draw the pain away.

"I got to meet her once," he said softly. "One day she came riding up to the ranch house. I was about sixteen then. She'd had old man Lewes from town drive her out in his buckboard. I remember how she looked with her hair dyed sort of an orangy red and her face all painted up. At first she looked young, not like the other women I'd seen. Then she got down out of the buckboard and walked up to the porch where Pa was standing." Rayne tossed away the blade of grass he'd been chewing and turned to face Gaby.

"She looked old and haggard, kind of used-up. You could see how pale she was under all that powder and paint. Her eyes looked tired and"—he paused, groping for the right word—"frightened."

"Did she stay with you then?" Gaby asked.

"She wanted to." Rayne's voice changed. It grew bitter as he talked. "She was sick and dying and needed a place to stay. She thought Pa would take her in, but he just stood there and looked down at her. All those years he'd waited for her to come back to him, and now she had. He never said a kind word to her, never said hello, how have you been. He just stared at her, savoring his moment of triumph before her ordered to leave."

"Oh, Rayne," Gaby said softly. "Why, when he'd waited all those years?"

"That's what I asked him," Rayne said. "but he couldn't answer me straight. He just yelled that she was nothing but a painted cat."

"What is that?" Gaby asked.

"A calico queen." From the puzzled expression on Gaby's face he could tell she still didn't understand. "A woman who hired herself out," he explained, acutely aware of Gaby's occupation.

"What did you do?" Gaby asked, to ease the sudden tension between them.

"I saddled up and rode out after her. It took me a couple of days to find her again. I caught up with her in Waco in a saloon. We talked." Rayne paused again. His mind raced back to that scene, the saloon dark and dingy from the smoke of oil lamps, the stench of stale whiskey and unwashed bodies, his own as well, for he'd ridden hard, afraid he'd lose her.

"Why did you leave?" he had demanded. She'd looked at him a long moment and he'd thought she wasn't going to answer.

"It was the wind," she'd said finally. "It was the loneliest sound I'd ever heard, sweeping across the plains the way it did. I used to hear sounds in it, you know, people laughing, piano-playing. I got so I couldn't stand it anymore. I wasn't meant to be a rancher's wife."

"Come back to the ranch. I'll make him let you stay."

She nodded her head slowly, setting the garish orange-red ringlets to shaking slightly. "It's too late, too late," she'd mumbled, reaching inside the satin bodice for a handkerchief and pressing it against her lips while she coughed. When she took it away, he'd caught a glimpse of red, whether from the paint on her lips or something else, he hadn't been sure. She'd raised her head then and smiled, a practiced smile, hinting at secret delights. It had shut her away from him. It had been the veil she'd hidden behind for too many years, and she'd turned it on him.

"Besides," she'd said, "I've always been able to take care of myself. I just got a little tired and lazy back there. I thought I'd drop by the ranch and take it easy for a while. I don't blame Cole for being mad at me. He's got a right to feel that way."

"Come back and rest then, until you're feeling better. You can leave when you want," Rayne had urged, but again she'd nodded her head.

"The wind's still out there," she'd said softly.

The images flitted through Rayne's mind, but he said nothing of them to Gaby. "The next morning she was gone again," he said quietly. "I looked for her for a while, riding from town to town, getting into trouble myself. Finally I got into a fight and killed a man up in Wyoming. I decided it was time to go home and help Pa with the ranch. When I got back to Texas, men were signing up for the war. I joined too."

"Did your father ever ask about your mother?" Gaby inquired.

"No," Rayne answered flatly. "We never talked about her." Gaby remained silent. How sad for all of them. "You know something," Rayne said, shaking his head as if even now he still couldn't believe it. "I never knew her name."

Gaby was shocked at the bitter cruelty of Cole Elliott. "I'm so sorry," she said softly. Rayne glanced at her, the line of his mouth thin and tight, his eyes hard. She could feel him pull away from her. He'd let her glimpse something of himself, but she mustn't feel pity for him.

"After the war I went back to the ranch," he said, speaking crisply. "I didn't realize how much I'd missed it."

Gaby saw the enthusiasm in his eyes as he spoke. Her heart fell at the thought that he would soon leave New Orleans and return to his ranch, while she would be left here with old Barbieri to enliven her days and nights.

The thought took away all the joy she'd felt at their outing and she stared out over the river, a pensive frown on her face.

"Why so sad?" Rayne asked, reaching out to take her hand. "You'll get lines and look old before your time."

"I can't afford to do that," Gaby said with forced lightness. "Then no man will want me."

Her answer made his lips tighten. The thought of another man touching her brought a rage to his heart. "We'd better get back," he said, and got to his feet.

Suddenly he wanted to take her back to the Cour des Anges and forget he'd ever met her; then she put her hand on his sleeve and smiled up at him and his anger melted. He would enjoy her while he was here. When he stepped on the boat and headed back to Texas, he'd put her out of his mind.

That night Rayne took Gaby to dinner at Antoine's, one of New Orleans' most elegant restaurants, where Gaby ignored the food on her plate and openly gazed at the beautiful women and their escorts. New Orleans was recovering from its shame as an occupied city. Its air of gaiety and frivolity was returning. Gaby felt a surge of pride for the gallant Creole city.

In the days that followed, Gaby delighted in discovering New Orleans with Rayne. She regaled him with tales of its history. She took him to Jackson Square to view the buildings the flamboyant Baroness Pontalb had erected in memory of her father. She told him of the scandalous duel between the baroness and her aging father-in-law, wherein he had lost a piece of his ear, and of the haunted house where the evil Madame Lalaurie had tortured her slaves. She took him to the dueling oaks where for generations hot-blooded Creole men had settled their differences with pistols and swords.

"We settle our arguments with guns in Texas," Rayne said, "but we don't get this fancy about it."

In the evening they went to the theater or to a concert or to one of the bawdy nightspots, but always they ended up back at the Cour des Anges in the big double bed. Each night Rayne taught her new ways to make love, and she was an eager pupil. His low, satisfied chuckle told her of his pleasure in her.

One night, satiated and tired from their lovemaking, she lay beside Rayne listening to his even breathing and wondered what she would do if he were to go back to Texas without her. She began to hope he would ask her to marry him and take her away. It didn't matter about the hardships of living in Texas. If a woman loved a man enough, she could overcome anything, and she loved Rayne fiercely. She'd loved him since their first night together, but how did he feel about her? Impatiently she waited, hoping he would tell her. But Rayne made no declaration, and she was suddenly afraid to ask.

One night Rayne planned to take her to the opera. Gaby wanted it to be a very special night, for she sensed their time together was drawing to an end. She dressed with even more care than usual, choosing a soft pink taffeta ball gown and piling her midnight hair high on her head with clusters of curls just brushing the top of her shoulders.

Rayne's breath caught when he first saw her. The lamplight cast a soft glow around her head. Her dark eyes were wide and luminous with a special softness just for him.

The sparkle in Rayne's blue eyes caused shivers of happiness to run through Gaby. The night seemed made of a special magic all its own.

"Take care, *chérie,*" Madeleine whispered when Gaby paused in the drawing room to bid her good-bye. "Such happiness is always followed by pain."

"It doesn't have to be," Gaby answered. "Rayne will ask me to marry him and take me back to Texas with him."

"You are fooling yourself, Gaby," Madeleine warned. "Such men do not marry women like us." Gaby looked at her friend in surprise. This was a different Madeleine from the one she was used to seeing. There was a sadness about her eyes and mouth. Regret was etched in her face. Was Maddie speaking of Rayne and Gaby or was her caution for herself? Soon Dusty would return to Texas as well.

A cold chill of apprehension threatened Gaby's mood.

The opera hall was even more elegant than Gaby had imagined, with its paintings and ornate moldings, the plush seats and brilliant chandeliers. Rayne had rented a box for them and Gaby reveled in the sheer elegance of it. She sat forward and looked around with unabashed curiosity. The ladies' gowns were bright splashes of color against the more somber hues of the men's formal attire. Even with the ruin brought on them by the war, the bon-vivant Creoles maintained their style the best they could.

Suddenly Gaby became aware of someone looking back at her as intently and audaciously as she herself had stared. She turned her head and encountered the gaze of a slim dark-haired man seated in one of the other boxes. He was flamboyantly dressed, his clothes achieving a certain style and flair few others had. There was almost an effeminate air to him.

Gaby flushed and looked away, aware that he was still staring at her, but her eyes were drawn once more to him. He seemed to glitter with a special beauty that at once repelled and fascinated her. Rayne stirred, his hard leg brushing against hers.

"Is that man bothering you?" he demanded, glaring at the fancily dressed Creole.

"No," Gaby said, glancing away. There was something evil about the man, she decided. He was too beautiful, too sure of himself. She watched the way the other women's eyes were drawn to him.

Rayne got to his feet, his eyes turning to meet the Creole's in an unspoken warning. Suddenly the man threw back his head and laughed, then made a mocking bow to Rayne. Turning to the man beside him, he gestured toward the box. It was obvious they were discussing Gaby and Rayne. The two men laughed, the sound drifting on the perfumed air.

Gaby felt Rayne stiffen beside her and turned to put a reassuring hand on his arm. Rayne looked into her dark eyes, and pushed aside his annoyance. Tonight was to be special for Gaby. He didn't want to ruin it with a fight. Besides, he could hardly blame the two men for staring.

She was a beauty. He dropped a light kiss on her soft lips and squeezed her hand reassuringly and Gaby felt the tension drop away from her.

The opera was wonderful. Gaby lost herself in the soaring notes and pageantry of a more romantic time than she'd ever known. She could feel Rayne shift restlessly beside her and guessed he was more used to a night under the Texas stars listening to the coyotes than he was to opera.

During intermission they wandered down to the lobby. Rayne went to get her a glass of champagne. Bright-eyed Gaby looked around at the magnificent opulence of the opera house and the people who seemed to take the richness of their surroundings for granted. She sensed the presence of the man at her elbow even before he spoke.

"Mademoiselle," the handsome Creole said in a smooth voice that seemed to glide over her. He was even more mesmerizing close up. Every feature was perfect, possessing a prettiness that Gaby found hard to reconcile on a man.

Suddenly she wished Rayne were back and felt apprehension at the thought of what he would do if he were there.

"Allow me to present myself," the man said, "I am Antoine de St. Amant, known to my friends as Toto." He bowed deeply, while Gaby looked at him in amazement. Who had not heard of the famous Toto? His name was spoken with admiration and awe in the streets of New Orleans. He was a fencing master and was rumored to have killed more than a hundred men, all of them in duels. How could a man of such an awesome reputation look so harmless?

"May I inquire the name of this beautiful and delectable creature who stands before me?" he asked.

"You may not, sir." Rayne's voice was cold and hard as he stepped forward. Although he hadn't touched her, Gaby could feel the strength of his body behind her and was comforted by it. Something about the way Monsieur de St. Amant looked at her alarmed Gaby.

"Is it the custom of the Creole gentlemen to accost a lady?" Rayne demanded.

"A lady?" de St. Amant repeated, his smiling gaze

sweeping over her face and shoulders. "No, it is not. I did not think I was speaking to a lady." Gaby's face flushed with mortification at the implied insult.

Swiftly Rayne stepped forward, but before he could take hold of the man, the Creole had taken Gaby's hand and raised it to his lips.

"I thought I was speaking to an angel," he said with mock reverence, his voice sly with innuendo. Bowing, he placed a moist kiss on the back of her hand. Gaby heard Rayne's growl of rage deep in his chest, and the answering light in de St. Amant's eyes frightened her.

"Rayne, no please," she cried, putting a gloved hand against his chest. "No harm was meant."

"*Ah, monsieur, la belle ange* is correct. No harm was meant. I am sorry, *mademoiselle*, if I have offended."

"I am not offended, *monsieur*," Gaby said quietly. keeping her eyes downcast. She was aware of other people turning to regard them with some curiosity.

"This time I will forget your insult to the lady," Rayne said, "but don't come around her again."

"You are her . . . protector, sir?" de St. Amant asked. Gaby held her breath waiting for his answer.

"I am," Rayne replied evenly, his hard gaze still holding that of the Creole.

"Then I bow to your wishes," de St. Amant said. The man turned on his heel and walked away, but Gaby wasn't watching him now. Her glowing gaze was turned to Rayne. He'd said he was her protector. Did he understand what that meant? He was taking responsibility for her welfare. He wouldn't leave her now.

Rayne glanced down at her shining face. "Come on," he said, "let's get out of here." Taking her arm, he led her out of the hall and down the street to the carriage. Once inside he pulled her into his arms possessively.

"Gaby," he whispered, his breath warm against her temple, "I can't bear to have another man look at you, much less touch you." Gaby's heart swelled with love. Rayne didn't want another man to have her. He wanted her just for himself. He loved her too.

"Let's go back to the Court of Angels," he whispered urgently.

Impatiently they endured the ride back to the Cour des

Anges. In her room at last they went into each other's arms eagerly. Tenderly they loved one another, trembling in the intensity of their feelings. Later they lay in each other's arms and slept, their limbs entwined, their bodies embracing even in sleep.

3

He would never leave her now. She was sure of it. Gaby stretched luxuriously and settled back against the pillows. Her mouth still tingled with Rayne's kisses. Reluctantly he'd gone to tend to some business, then he would be back and they would spend the whole day together, perhaps drive out into the country for a picnic.

Gaby stretched again, too happy to lie still any longer. She would go to Texas with Rayne, she thought. She'd help him run his ranch and make it bigger and more prosperous than he'd ever dreamed. In her happy preoccupation, Gaby gave little notice to Madeleine's pinched face and red eyes. She hurried through breakfast and bathed and donned a summer gown of small shepherd's checks and dots with a high white collar and a straw bonnet to match. Her eyes sparkled with anticipation. Impatiently she awaited Rayne's return.

When Zack sent a girl up to tell her that she had a caller, Gaby fairly flew along the gallery and down the stairs toward the courtyard, her wide crinolined skirts flowing out behind her on the steps. A dark-haired man stood with his back to her. Gaby paused on the stairs, her eyes wide in surprise and sudden misgiving.

Her caller was none other than Antoine de St. Amant. He smiled when he heard her startled exclamation, his dark eyes gleaming at the sight of her.

"*Mademoiselle,*" he said, crossing the courtyard to stand below her. "I have found you at last." He took her hand and placed a kiss upon it.

"*Monsieur,*" Gaby said, trying to draw her hand back, but he held it fast.

"You are even more beautiful than I remembered you," he murmured. "Last night I thought I was seeing an angel, and now today"—he swept one hand around to take in the courtyard—"I see I am right. You are one of Madame Porcher's famous angels. I think that is my good fortune."

"*Monsieur,* you are mistaken," Gaby said faintly. The thought had occurred to her that Rayne might return any moment, and what would he think if he saw de St. Amant there?

"But there is no mistake, *belle ange.* You are here, I have found you. I am here, Mademoiselle Gabrielle Reynaud"—he bowed formally—"to invite you to join me for dinner and the theater tonight."

"I am sorry, Monsieur de St. Amant, I cannot," Gaby said, feeling light-headed with her anxiety. She wished him away from the Court of Angels.

"Please, call me Toto, as all my friends do."

"Monsieur Toto," Gaby repeated, "I am otherwise engaged tonight."

"Ahh, that is too bad," Toto said. "But this is not just a social engagement I wish, *mademoiselle.*" His dark eyes bored into hers. "I wish your services for the night." His insolent gaze raked over her boldly, pausing at her small breasts and nipped waist. His eyes were hard and hungry when they met hers again. Gaby felt her legs quiver beneath her. Suddenly she felt frightened of this dandified man with the reputation of a killer.

"I am sorry, sir, I've already told you that I'm spoken for the entire evening," she replied evenly. She longed to snatch her hand from his, but was afraid of offending him.

He saw the fear in her eyes and was untroubled by it. Many times when charm had not netted what he wanted, he had used his reputation to bring the recalcitrant into line. He wasn't squeamish of doing that now. Still holding her gaze with his own, he let his thumb slide across the back of her hand in a suggestive circular motion. He could tell by the expression on her face that she knew what he wanted. Toto de St. Amant smiled. Part of the pleasure was the chase and capture, especially of such a quarry as this.

"I think you should change your plans, my little angel," he said lightly, "and join me tonight."

"I cannot," Gaby said stubbornly.

"Why not, *ma chérie*? Is it because of this peasant you were with last night? Do not be afraid of him."

"I'm not afraid of him," Gaby said, then rushed on, hoping the Creole would have pity. "We are in love."

"Ah, love. It is a very tender emotion," Toto said contemplatively, a smile on his lips. "Many people will do anything in the name of love. They will even risk their own lives to save the life of the one they love." His dark eyes turned back to hers. "I do not ask you to risk your life, *chérie*, only to spend the evening with me." The implied threat was all too clear. Gaby stared at him, seeing the evil in the man, and she was sickened by it. Still, fear mounted in her for Rayne. He was a stranger to their land and their customs. He was unskilled in the ways of the duel. He'd have little chance against Toto, a master fencer.

"Please, *monsieur,* I beg of you," she began, her voice low and vibrant with urgency. "Do not demand of me what I cannot give you."

"Cannot or will not?" Toto said, and now his hand gripped her cruelly. "I am used to having what I want, *mademoiselle,*" he said, and the face was twisted and ugly with anger. Wildly Gaby looked around the courtyard, but there was no one near to help her. She could hear the peal of the bell at the gate. Rayne was near. Hope flitted across her face, then died as she looked at the Creole's evil face. Rayne must not see them here together.

"Yes, all right. I will spend the evening with you," she whispered, and felt his hand release hers. "Now, please go quickly. I beg of you."

"You are very wise, *mademoiselle,*" de St. Amant said. "I will look forward to our evening together." He bowed mockingly.

"Go now," Gaby cried. "Please go!"

The smile left de St. Amant's face. He wasn't used to being dismissed in such a manner. Who did this girl think

she was? She was nothing more than a common whore.
Never mind, tonight he would teach her some manners
and it would be a pleasure he would anticipate the rest of
the day.

"Until tonight, *mademoiselle*," he said lightly, and turning with a flourish, he walked toward the gate. Gaby
stayed where she was on the stairs. Her legs gave way
beneath her and she sat down, her hands gripping the
railing with knuckles gone white, her head resting on her
hands.

What was she to do? she wondered frantically. She
couldn't tell Rayne. She couldn't put him in such danger,
yet the thought of spending the night with de St. Amant
was unbearable. All the happiness she'd felt earlier seemed
forever gone. Rayne found her like that, crouched over the
stair railing, her face pale, her eyes dark and tragic.

"Gaby," he cried, taking one of her cold hands in his.
"What is it?"

"Nothing. It is nothing," she said lightly, forcing herself
to smile up at him. "I came down the stairs too fast and I
became dizzy. I have not been resting well lately and I
have only you to blame for that." Her gamine face was lit
with her smile. The worried look left Rayne's face and he
urged her to her feet and down the stairs.

"Are you sorry?" he asked, smiling because he already
knew the answer. It was there in the shine of her eyes and
the way she looked at him.

"Ruby's packed a basket. We're going on a picnic," she
said with forced gaiety, and fled to the kitchen, where she
tried to calm herself. She couldn't play out this charade,
and yet what would happen if she told Rayne about de St.
Amant? She was too frightened of the consequences.

They took the old river road, driving far inland beyond
the swamps and palmettos to a place where a little creek
ran past a high hillock and weeping willows trailed their
branches in the Mississippi. It was an idyllic spot. Rayne
spread a blanket on the ground and Gaby seated herself.
Leisurely they ate and drank the wine, and when they were
finished, they sat watching the river flow past.

"Do you have rivers in Texas?" Gaby asked pensively.

"Yep," Rayne said. He was lying back, his hands tucked
beneath his head, a blade of grass between his teeth. "We

have a lot of rivers. There's the Rio Grande that separates us from Mexico, and there are the Colorado, the Pecos, the San Antonio, and the Red rivers. There's a place known as the Seven Hundred Springs, and the South Llano River, the Brazos, the Guadalupe, the—"

"Stop, stop," Gaby cried, laughing.

"Of course, none of them are as big as this river, but some of them are just as mean-tempered."

"Texas must be a very big place to have as many rivers and cattle and plains and mountains as you claim it does."

"It is a big country," Rayne said, "a country where a man can be alone if he wants, and breathe air that hasn't already been breathed."

"Someday I'd like to see this Texas of yours," Gaby said softly. It would never happen now.

"Maybe you will," Rayne said, and glanced away. Part of him wanted to ask her to go back with him and part of him was scared of taking her to Texas. She wasn't a woman suited to that kind of life.

"You wouldn't like it much," he said. "There are no stores or theaters or fancy restaurants, no operas like you're used to here. You wouldn't have any reason to dress up in the fancy gowns you like to wear." His mention of the opera reminded Gaby of Toto. She turned a desperate face to Rayne.

"Make love to me," she whispered.

Rayne looked at her in surprise. "Now?" he asked, looking around. They were alone, sealed off from the rest of the world by the drooping branches of the weeping willow.

"Now," Gaby said. "I need you, Rayne." She moved into his arms, her mouth sweet as it met his. Rayne kissed her slowly, savoring the taste and feel of her, marveling at the perfection of her small body. Gaby's eyes were wide and tragic as she watched the emotions flitting across his face. Slowly his hands moved over her soft skin, weaving their magic spell. Gaby closed her eyes and gave herself over to the fiery beauty of the moment.

Afterward they lay gazing up at the cloudless sky. Rayne looked at Gaby with puzzled eyes. She'd been as passionate and responsive as she'd always been, perhaps more so, yet he sensed she'd held something of herself back this time. The thought bothered him. She lay now facing away from him, and as he pulled her against him. he saw that she'd been crying.

"What is it, Gaby, my sweet?" he said, gently cradling her against him. Mutely she shook her head and he felt her body quiver as she held in her tears.

"Tell me what's wrong," he urged, and still she shook her head in denial. Finally, when she had her silent sobs under control, she raised her tearstained face to his.

Once she went to Toto, Rayne would never touch her again. She had no choices. She must give up her love in order to keep him alive.

"Rayne," she whispered, "take me home now. Our time together is at an end."

"What are you saying, Gaby?" he asked in amazement, his eyes searching her tearstained face.

"I don't wish to see you again," she said, forcing herself to meet his gaze. He stared at her, trying to comprehend how she could love him so completely one moment and dismiss him the next.

"I don't understand," he said.

"There is nothing to understand." Gaby shrugged with feigned indifference and began to struggle into her clothes. "We have had our interlude and now it is finished."

Rayne gripped her shoulders. "It doesn't have to end now or ever if we don't want it to." His words tore at her heart. How she'd longed to hear him say them, but now it was too late.

"I want it to," she answered stoically. Taking a deep breath, she pushed herself out of his arms and whirled to face him. "You have been very patient with me, Rayne. You have taught me much, but now I must go on to someone else." She saw the understanding of what she was saying grow in his eyes and saw the look of love turn to anger and then contempt.

"Is this what you really want?" he asked insistently, "or is Madeleine forcing you into it."

"She has nothing to do with this," Gaby said. "I am what I am, Rayne. I can't change that. I must go on to someone else. It is the way of the things at the Court of Angels."

"Gaby," Rayne said pleadingly, moving toward her,

but she turned away from him and stood on the riverbank, staring with unseeing eyes into the muddy waters.

"You have no more money to spend on me," she said implacably. "You've spent all you can afford. The rest is for your ranch. It is time I find another man with a pocketful of money. Please take me back now."

Rayne stared at her a moment as if testing what she'd said, but she kept her face closed and hard so he wouldn't see the pain she was feeling. Silently she moved to the carriage.

"Dusty told me it would come to this," he said bitterly, "that you were like Madeleine and too used to the fancy life you lead here to give it up for a poor ranch in Texas. I wouldn't believe him. I believed you when you whispered you loved me."

"It was love talk," Gaby cried, leaning against the carriage. "We are taught to say it." She swallowed back the tears. "Please take me back now. I have an engagement for the evening."

She didn't see the spasm of pain that crossed his face at her words. His hands clenched into fists and he stalked across the clearing to swing her onto the seat. Without gathering up their picnic basket, he climbed onto the seat, and taking up the whip, flicked the horses into a run.

Gaby held on to the side of the bouncing carriage, trying to hold back the tears until she'd reached the privacy of her room. At the gate of the courtyard, Rayne handed her down, then without a word leapt back onto the seat. He didn't look back as the carriage careened down the street and around the corner.

Madeleine took one look at Gaby's face and wrapped her arms around her. She'd dealt with her own unhappiness the past few days and now she must share her strength and wisdom with this young girl. Had she been wrong to send Rayne Elliott to Gaby's room that first night? Silently she patted the girl's heaving shoulders. She hoped not.

"*Chérie*, do not cry so," Madeleine soothed. "Tomorrow you will laugh at these tears."

"I'll never laugh again," Gaby sobbed tragically. She raised her face to look at Madeleine, and the older woman was stunned by the grief she saw there. "You don't know what happened this morning," Gaby mourned.

"My God, tell me, Gaby," Madeleine exclaimed, shocked by the pain in the girl's eyes.

"Last night at the opera, Toto de St. Amant saw me. He tried to talk to me, but Rayne intervened. Today de St. Amant came to see me while Rayne was gone. He wanted me to join him for the evening. At first I refused, but he . . . he threatened Rayne's life." She swallowed back her tears. "Tonight Toto de St. Amant is coming for me," she cried.

"Gaby, no," Madeleine whispered in disbelief. "You cannot go to this man. He is dangerous and evil. He enjoys hurting people too much. I will not allow him here in my house."

"You must." Gaby raised her ravished face to look at Madeleine beseechingly. "If you don't, he'll kill Rayne, and I couldn't bear that."

"So you go to this evil man to save Rayne's life?"

"Gladly," Gaby cried fervently.

"Rayne shouldn't ask this of you."

"He doesn't know. Don't try to talk me out of this, Madeleine. I must do it," Gaby declared, springing up in nervousness. Resolutely she wiped the tears from her cheeks. "It won't be so bad. I will endure it because, as you say, we women must. Soon Rayne will be gone and safe from Toto's vengeance. Don't worry about me." Gaby's voice broke. She gave Madeleine a sad, brave smile. "Tomorrow I'll laugh at my tears."

Without another word she left the drawing room, sweeping up the stairs to her own room, where she ordered a bath, then flung herself on her bed and wept uncontrollably.

Madeleine remained in the drawing room uncertain of what to do; then, as memory of the rumors she'd heard of de St. Amant and his cruelty came to her, she was galvanized into action.

"Ruby, get Zack, quickly. He must go on an errand for me," she called. She had to save Gaby. She prayed she wasn't too late.

Dusk had fallen, lanterns had been lit in the courtyard. Gaby stood just inside the drawing-room doors watching the dark-haired man.

"Since it is our first evening together, *mademoiselle,*"

de St. Amant said, strolling about the room, touching first one thing and then another, as if assessing its value and finding it wanting, "I have decided we will not attend the theater after all. I think we must become better acquainted." He turned to smile at the pale girl.

"As you wish," Gaby said faintly. She stood with her eyes downcast. She'd worn the plainest of gowns and no makeup, with her hair caught up in a tight knot at the back of her head, all in a vain attempt to make herself less attractive to the Creole. She was unaware that her fresh, unadorned beauty was even more appealing to him.

He was inflamed by her air of innocence, even though he knew he would not be the first. He preferred young virgins, willing or unwilling. Still, there was that untouched look to this Creole girl that excited him. She averted her eyes and he saw her tremble. A pulse began to beat somewhere in his head.

"If you will lead the way, *mademoiselle*," he said thickly, gesturing toward the stairs. Gaby looked at him blankly. It was to happen so quickly, she thought in dismay. There would be no chance to dissuade him.

Resolutely she turned and led the way along the terrace to the loggia. She was acutely aware that he followed behind, his hungry eyes following the sway of her hips as she mounted the stairs. Madeleine was nowhere in sight.

Meekly she led de St. Amant down the gallery to her bedroom and opened the door. He motioned her to enter ahead of him, and she did so. No sooner was the door closed behind them than the Creole leapt on her, his hands entwining in her black hair in a painful grip, his mouth descending on hers in a punishing kiss. Gaby was surprised at the swiftness of his attack and his seeming need to hurt her, but she remained passive under his touch.

"So, my little angel, you do not resist me, but neither do you give me what I want."

"I do not know what you want, *monsieur*," Gaby replied with outward calm. Her eyelids were lowered, so she didn't see the blow coming. She felt it in an explosion of pain against the side of her temple. She stumbled backward. Dazedly she looked at the Creole. He leaned over her, his smile frightening.

"I want you to plead with me," he half-whispered. "Beg me!" He slapped her again and Gaby fell backward against the bed. She caught herself against the post and turned fearful eyes toward him. This couldn't be happening. Through a haze of pain she saw de St. Amant approach her again. Something glittered in his hand. It was a small silver knife, its handle encrusted with gems, its point sharp and menacing. In terror Gaby looked from the knife to his face.

"We have a long night," he said softly. "I will teach you very carefully, my little angel. You will learn well what is expected of you." The knife cut each button holding the bodice of her gown in place.

Terrified, Gaby backed away from him, gripping the carved posts of the bed. There was a mad light in de St. Amant's eyes as he stalked her. Suddenly he lunged at her, his hands ripping at her bodice until it hung nearly to her waist. His dark gaze rested on the small breasts and he reached out to touch the tiny red birthmark. He smiled, glancing up at her with approval. He liked the mark. It made her seem more exotic.

Gaby whimpered as he brought the knife closer; then with a scream she lunged past him and ran toward the door. He was there ahead of her, holding the door closed with his shoulder while he brought the knife up to her throat.

"Do not scream, Gaby," he said in that soft, sinister voice. "Once a girl screamed and I had to quiet her. If she hadn't screamed she would be alive today." Gaby gasped and held her breath to still the whimperings. Her eyes were wide with fear as they studied his face. What would he do to her?

"If she had only been patient I would have taught her to love the fine edge of the knife against her skin," de St. Amant said, still speaking of the girl he'd murdered. "She would have found the blade brings pleasure as well as pain. I will teach you to find the ecstasy of my knife, my dark angel."

"You're mad," Gaby whispered.

"Don't say that until you've tasted the passion my

knife and I can bring you," he snarled, and with a sudden
jerk of his hand she was swung across the room and onto
the bed.

"Please don't," Gaby cried.

"Ah, you are learning very quickly," de St. Amant
said. "Didn't I tell you you'd learn? Plead with me."
Once again he stalked her, while Gaby scrambled backward across the bed, the same bed in which she'd known
such delight with Rayne. Terror gave her the strength to
draw a breath and scream again. Now de St. Amant
charged toward her, his knife held high as if to stab at
her. Gaby threw herself to one side and heard the rip of
her dress as the knife arced downward. She screamed
again and suddenly she heard feet pounding on the gallery outside. Hope flared within her.

"Help me, help me," she cried. The door crashed
inward and Rayne was there. In one quick glance he took
in the scene, saw her torn and cut dress, saw the graze of
blood on her milk-white shoulder, and his hands were
reaching for de St. Amant. Madeleine and Dusty were
right behind him.

"What is the meaning of this?" de St. Amant sputtered
in Rayne's grip. "Madam, when I pay for the services of
one of your whores, I expect privacy."

Rayne's fist ended anything else he might have said.
The Creole fell to the floor and lay rubbing his jaw.
Madeleine crossed the room to put a protective arm
around Gaby, who stood shivering uncontrollably, the
scraps of her ruined gown clutched to her naked breasts.

"You are not welcome in my house, Monsieur de St.
Amant," Madeleine said to the man on the floor.

The Creole looked at the ring of people above him and
slowly got to his feet. He took great care to brush at his
clothes and straighten them. When he was satisfied all
was perfect, he looked at Rayne, his eyes furious.

"You have struck me, sir. In New Orleans that is a
challenge and must be met on the field of honor."

"You mean a duel?" Rayne asked.

"No," Gaby cried, taking a step forward. The two men
ignored her.

"Yes, *monsieur*." The Creole's lip curled in contempt at
this rough Texan who didn't know the first conventions of

dueling. "And since it is you who have issued the challenge, I am to be given the choice of weapons. I choose swords."

"No, Rayne, no," Gaby cried, running to clutch his arm. "He's a teacher of the sword. He's killed hundreds of men."

Rayne looked at her with hooded eyes and saw the bruise marks of de St. Amant's hands upon her pale flesh. His lips tightened in anger.

"So be it," he said quietly.

"Jesus, Rayne, listen to what the girl says," Dusty intervened. "You don't know a damn thing about fightin' with a sword." Rayne said nothing, his eyes boring into de St. Amant's.

"I know how to kill a man," he said. For a moment the Creole's gaze flickered, his confidence shaken; then he reminded himself that no man had beaten him yet, and his bravado returned.

"We will meet at the dueling oaks at daybreak," de St. Amant said. The four of them were left staring at each other, the sound of the Creole's footsteps fading down the stairs. His challenge meant sure death for the Texan. Gaby leaned against Rayne's chest and sobbed uncontrollably. The very thing she'd tried so hard to prevent had happened after all. Rayne stood cold and unresponsive to her weeping.

"We must do something," Madeleine said.

"He's gonna kill you, Rayne," Dusty said.

"You must leave," Gaby urged tearfully. "Get on the ship, get away while you can."

"I don't run away from fights," he said, gazing down at her coldly.

"Perhaps we could teach you to use the sword," Madeleine said, thinking out loud.

"There's not enough time," Dusty answered. The two of them kept talking, discussing possibilities. Rayne remained silent, his body tense.

The blue of his eyes was nearly black in the shadowy lamplight, but Gaby knew it was more than that. She could read the cold rage in their depths. He didn't understand why she'd gone from him to de St. Amant.

"We've got to do something to unbalance the Creole,"

Dusty was saying. "If he's so danged good with swords, he's gonna be too sure of himself, maybe get a little careless. We've got to give him something to even the odds, make him worry a little."

"Since de St. Amant chose the weapons, Rayne gets to choose the place the duel is fought," Madeleine said thoughtfully.

"You mean the duel don't have to be fought down by the oaks?" Dusty asked.

"No, some men have even fought in a cemetery and fallen into the grave that was dug for them. Duels can be fought wherever and however you wish, as long as they follow the rules."

Something clicked inside Gaby's head and she turned to look at the two of them.

"He can fight on horseback, if he wishes," she said.

"On horseback?" Dusty exclaimed. "That'd do it, Rayne. Ain't nobody better'n you on a horse."

Rayne turned to look at the three of them, his gaze coming to rest at last on Gaby's face. "Okay, Dusty," he said wearily. "Tell de St. Amant we fight on horses. Get word to him tonight. Maybe it'll keep him awake."

"Ruby, send Zack," Madeleine cried, and hurried out of the room. Dusty followed her. In silence Rayne looked at Gaby, then turned toward the door.

"Rayne, wait, let me explain," Gaby cried.

"You said everything this afternoon by the river," he said, and stalked down the gallery toward the stairs. Gaby ran after him, clutching her torn dress to her. Rayne was already halfway down the stairs. She'd never catch him. "Rayne," she cried leaning over the railing. "Please, don't go." Tears filled her eyes.

He paused in the courtyard below. "What is it you want, Gaby?" he said. "Do you want me to come back up and share the bed you would have shared with de St. Amant?" When she could make no answer, he left, closing the gate quietly behind him.

The morning air was soft and moist. The mist clung with insidious fingers, waiting for the sun's warmth. Sounds were magnified in the quietness. The creak of a saddle, the rattle of carriage wheels over cobblestones spoke of early risers abroad in the streets.

Madeleine and Gabrielle huddled in the morning chill as their driver whipped the horses through the streets. Gaby sat quiet and withdrawn, only her eyes showing agitation, the dark circles evidence of her lack of sleep. The driver guided the carriage onto the road leading out of town, and at last they came to a wide field where several people had already gathered. Word had spread of the duel on horseback, and the morbid curiosity seekers had come to watch.

Rayne and Dusty rode into the clearing on their horses. Dusty tipped his hat to Madeleine, but Rayne looked straight ahead. Gaby wanted to call to him, but was afraid she might distract him as he prepared for the duel.

The crowd of onlookers cheered, and suddenly Antoine de St. Amant rode into the clearing on a beautiful white horse. Affectionately the crowd called to him. As usual he looked elegant and unruffled, an easy smile on his face. Gaby shuddered. She knew only too well the sort of man who hid behind that friendly smile.

The rules were read to the two men, who galloped off to opposite ends of the field. Both men stripped naked to the waist. The Creole preened a bit as he showed his sleek, muscular physique, but there were some betting men who put their money on the tall Texan with the whipcord muscles. The rest were too cautious to go against de St. Amant's reputation.

The two men sat their quivering mounts, each watching the judge's hand, which held a red handkerchief aloft. The air was tense as people held their breaths. The judge's hand dipped downward and both men spurred their horses forward.

The Creole seemed not to be disturbed at all by this way of dueling. As his horse drew near Rayne's he drew his sword high, ready to strike his opponent. The blades flashed and cracked together as Rayne managed to ward off the first attack. Perhaps he could hold off the mighty Toto until the crowd was satisfied and demanded the duel be called off, Gaby thought hopefully.

Again the two men rode toward each other. The Creole raised his sword again and aimed a blow at Rayne's head.

Once again Rayne knocked the blade aside. Now the two men circled each other, guiding their mounts with their knees as they slashed out with their swords. Steel clanged against steel. Gaby could hear the labored breathing of the horses as they wheeled and circled. Suddenly the fencing master lunged, his sword aimed at Rayne's head in a blow that would have severed it from his shoulders if Rayne hadn't slipped out of the saddle, clinging to the side of the horse.

"No," Gaby cried out, standing up in the carriage.

"Don't worry, little lady, that's a Comanche trick," Dusty said, and sure enough, Rayne swerved his horse to the right and was once again in his saddle. Angry now, de St. Amant lunged at him again, his movements awkward as his mount danced about trying to maneuver into the position his rider needed.

The Creole's blade flashed downward but this time Rayne's hand shot out and gripped de St. Amant's sword arm while his own blade flashed through the air. Rayne drove the blade deep into de St. Amant's chest and the fencing master fell to the ground, a look of astonishment etched on his face.

Rayne dismounted and stood over the dying man. The crowd looked on in silent dismay. Toto de St. Amant, one of the greatest fencing masters in New Orlean's history, looked up at the Texan.

"*Coup de maître!*" he whispered, and died. The crowd cheered. A master stroke, the dying master himself had said of the Texan's victory. The master had died as honorably as he'd lived. Few knew of the cruelty of the man. Within a few hours his name would become even more legendary, and none would dare raise a voice to tell of his true nature.

Gaby bounded out of the carriage and ran toward Rayne, joyfully crying his name. He had won. He hadn't been killed. How foolish of her to have worried. She ran to throw her arms around him and hold his dear, strong body against hers. He was alive and she thanked God for it. She could feel Rayne's strong hands gripping her arms. The comfort and reassurance they gave quickly ended as she felt herself pushed away from him. Startled, she looked up into his accusing face. His eyes were cold as they flicked over her face.

"I hope you're satisfied, *mademoiselle*," he said. "Because of you, I killed a man." He let go of her so abruptly she stumbled backward. He blamed her for this, she thought blankly.

"Toto was an evil man who deserved to die," she cried.

"I had no wish to be his executioner," Rayne said. He held her gaze for a moment more, then turned and mounted his horse. "Come on, Dusty," he said wearily. "Let's get out of here." The two men galloped across the field and down the road toward town without a backward look.

Gaby stood as if frozen, while all around her men hurried to tend to the dead man's last needs. A wagon was brought out on the field and the body laid in back; then the wagon rumbled away.

"Come, *chérie*, we must go." Madeleine led her back to the carriage.

"He hates me," Gaby sobbed as the horses moved down the road. "He blames me for everything."

"Shhh, *chérie*," Madeleine said. "When he is gone, you'll forget about him."

"I can never forget him," Gaby wailed; then, as the import of Madeleine's words reached her, she raised a tear streaked face. "When are they leaving?" she whispered.

"As soon as the tide is in so the boat can clear the sandbars at the mouth of the river," Madeleine replied. And none too soon, she thought. As long as Rayne Elliott was in New Orleans, Gaby would be heartsick over him. It was clear the girl was in love with him. Madeleine wasn't surprised when Gaby gripped her hand.

"Maddie, you must help me," the girl beseeched her. "I must go with Rayne on that ship."

"*Chérie, c'est impossible!*" Madeleine exclaimed.

"No, don't say that. If he sails without me, I'll lose him forever." Gaby turned to the driver. "Go to the wharf," she instructed. "Hurry, hurry." The urgency in her voice impelled the man to take up his whip and brandish it over the backs of the galloping horses.

"My poor Gaby," Madeleine said, but the girl wasn't listening. She was leaning from the carriage to see how far they had to go. The wind whipped against her tear-dampened cheeks and pulled the pins from her hair, but she didn't notice. All uncertainty was behind her. She was going to Texas with the man she loved.

4

"Am I doing the right thing, Dusty?" Gaby asked. He'd helped smuggle her aboard and had hidden her in his cabin until the steamship had cleared the mouth of the river and was sailing into the blue-green waters of the Gulf. Now Gaby looked at him, all the fear and uncertainty she felt clear on her face. "What if Rayne doesn't want me?" she whispered.

"I think you're just what's needed along about now. Come on, he's up at the front of the boat."

Rayne stood at the railing. He'd changed his clothes from the suits he'd worn when he called on Gaby. Now he wore the rough twill pants and vest she'd first seen him in on the docks. The broad-brimmed hat was pulled low over his eyes. Once again he seemed strange and enigmatic, of a different land and breed of men. She couldn't lose him.

She turned back to Dusty, and the light in her dark eyes was joyous. If he were younger, Dusty thought, he'd do everything in his power to win her for himself.

It was obvious that girl was in love with Rayne. She fairly glowed with it.

"Thank you, Dusty."

"My pleasure," he said, taking the small hand. He could feel the fine, delicate bones beneath the smooth skin. "If that fellow over there don't treat you right, you just come on back to me."

Gaby smiled at his jest, then stood on tiptoe to plant a light kiss on one cheek. "Rayne is very lucky to have you as a friend," she said softly, then was gone, moving lightly along the deck toward the tall figure.

Dusty stood and watched her go. "Rayne doesn't know just how lucky he is," he muttered. When he saw Rayne swing around, Dusty walked back along the deck and his thoughts turned to Madeleine. Maybe they'd been wrong, he thought. Maybe they could have made it work. They should have been willing to give it a try like Gaby.

"Rayne?" She said his name softly and still he heard her. He whirled, his face showing his astonishment.

"Gaby, what are you doing here?" he asked, his startled gaze flickering over her as if she were an apparition standing before him. His knuckles were white as he gripped the railing.

"I came to tell you I love you," Gaby said simply. What else could she say? Nothing else should be as important as that between them. "I couldn't bear the thought of never seeing you again. I know you're angry with me because of Toto, but I swear . . ." Tears gathered in her eyes and she had to pause and swallow against the lump in her throat.

Rayne swept her into his arms, his lean cheek pressed against her temple. "Gaby," he whispered over and over. "I was so afraid I'd lost you because of my own cussedness. I was going back for you on the very next boat to New Orleans."

Gaby's heart lifted at his words. Still, she wanted to make everything clear between them. "I want to explain about Toto."

"There's nothing to explain. You were right. He was an evil man and deserved to die."

"I only went with him because he threatened to kill you if I didn't."

"He threatened me?"

Gaby nodded. "He said he would call you out. No one had ever beaten him before, Rayne. I was so afraid he would kill you." She cradled his lean jaws in her slender hands and gazed earnestly into his eyes. "I couldn't have lived with myself. I had to do something."

"You did it for me," Rayne mused. He'd never had a woman defend him before. The fact that Gaby had tried to do so was touchingly funny.

"I would do it all over again," Gaby vowed, "if I had to, even knowing what a sadistic, evil man Toto was. I love you, Rayne."

He crushed her small body to his, rocking her while he looked at the sky and sea. She'd been willing to give her life for him. She'd come on board the ship bound for a strange land, even when she wasn't sure he'd have her. There was so much courage and determination in her small, dainty body. He set her back on her feet.

"Gaby, about going to Texas . . ." he began hesitantly.

"Don't you want me?"

"You know I do," he answered fervently, "but are you sure, Gaby?"

"I belong with you, Rayne," she replied without hesitation.

"It's not too late if you want to change your mind."

"Yes, it is," she said with a mischievous grin. "The boat can't turn back now."

"There are boats that go from Texas to New Orleans."

"But I won't be on any of them." The grin was gone. Her eyes were serious and direct as they met his.

"It'll be a rougher way of living than you're used to, Gaby," he said. "There are no women close by to talk with, no operas or theaters or restaurants."

"Will you be there?"

"Some of the time." She was surprised by his answer. "Sometimes I'll be out on the range for days, or gone for months on a cattle drive. You'll be alone with just a hand or two to keep you company."

"Then I'll be there when you come back," Gaby said softly.

"You'll be lonely."

"I'll manage."

"How, Gaby?" Rayne's finger traced across her cheek. She was so young and untried. She had no idea what she was taking on. She looked at life through the idealistic eyes of love.

"I'll think of you every minute," she said, and wrapped her arms around his trim waist. "Let's not talk about it anymore." She rested her head against his chest. She could feel the warmth of his skin through the shirt he wore. Her fingers slid enticingly down the length of buttons and paused at the waistband of his trousers.

"How long before we get to Texas?" she asked.

"A long time," Rayne replied huskily, and caught her to him. Their kiss was long, full of promise and passion.

"The cabin is this way," Gaby said breathlessly, and Rayne wasn't sure if he could wait until the door was closed behind them.

To many passengers the crossing was uneventful. To Rayne and Gaby it was blissful. It took two days to cross the Gulf and they spent most of the time in their cabin. They delighted in the touch of each other, finding reassurance that they'd not lost their love. The hot midday sun beat down on the staterooms, heating them to a fever pitch, then cooled into late-afternoon shadows. When they lay exhausted and momentarily satiated by their lovemaking, they rose and dressed and walked along the deck, watching the rose-hued setting of the sun over the Gulf waters before returning to the pleasant solitude of their cabin.

On the morning of the third day, a dark smudge of land appeared on the horizon and Rayne pointed it out to Gaby. She stood within the circle of his arms, secure and happy as she caught her first glimpse of her new homeland. Would it be hospitable to her? She hoped so. As long as Rayne remained in Texas, so would she.

Dusty came to join them as the boat drew closer to shore. "It's nice to be back home," he said, and Rayne glanced at him sharply. The trip to New Orleans hadn't left his friend happy. Rayne suspected it had something to do with Madeleine Porcher. Unconsciously Rayne's arm tightened around Gaby.

The wharves of Galveston were much like those of New Orleans, teeming with the same noise and confusion. The same rough-looking dock gangs hauled barrels and crates. The same indolent blacks, suddenly freed and unsure of a place to go, lolled about. Bales of cotton sat around the docks waiting to be loaded on boats bound for the northern factories. Gaby looked at Rayne in surprise.

"We grow cotton here too," he said. "There are some big plantations in the eastern portions of Texas."

"Listening to you, I thought Texas just had cattle and deserts and Indians," Gaby teased.

"The rich black bottomlands along the coastal plains support a style of living every bit as sumptuous as that enjoyed by the Louisiana planters," Rayne explained.

The squat boat maneuvered with surprising ease into the bay and up to the docks. Hands leapt ashore to secure the thick ropes that held the boat captive.

"There's Little Finger," Dusty said, and pointed to a slight old man wearing a beat-up hat and the bushiest whiskers she'd ever seen. Nearsightedly he peered at the people standing at the rails, and when he spied them, he waved.

"Yo, Rayne, Dusty," he called.

"How're things going, Little Finger?" Rayne called as he took Gaby's arm and led the way along the railing toward the gangplank. On the dock below, the fiesty old man kept pace with them.

"Jest fine," he called up. "The boys had a little trouble one night, but they got it straightened out. Slade and Billy spent the night in jail."

"Where are they now?" Rayne asked as they stepped onto the wharf.

"Havin' theirselves a last drink afore we pull out. They'll be here directly."

"They'd better be," Rayne said, and Gaby perceived he must be an exacting boss. "Dusty, take care of the horses and the supplies. Get them loaded on the wagon when the men get back. I want to leave at sunrise."

"Sure thing, Rayne," Dusty said.

"Make sure the men are here on time in the morning," Rayne continued, "even if you have to go looking for them tonight."

"I'll take care of it," Dusty assured him. "In fact, I'll go looking for them right now. I could use a drink myself."

"If there's any trouble, you can find Gaby and me up at the hotel."

"What have you got there?" Little Finger inquired, realizing for the first time that Gaby was with Rayne and Dusty.

"Gaby, this is Little Finger, the best cook west of the Mississippi."

"And, Little Finger, this is a real, genuine woman. You ain't too old to recognize one anymore, are you?" Dusty teased. A hoot of laughter sounded from along the dock.

"Like as not he wouldn't remember what to do with one if he recognized her," a voice said, and everyone turned to look at the man standing nearby. He was about Rayne's age, Gaby saw, and nearly as tall, but there his resemblance to the rangy, hard-muscled rancher ended. This man's body had a softness about it that suggested he didn't spend as many hours in the saddle as Rayne and his men.

His hat was shoved back to reveal sleek blond hair, and his eyes, pale gray, were challenging as he met Rayne's gaze. He was dressed in a shirt and vest like the other men, but his were edged with silver trim and coins. His boots were new and still shiny, and silver spurs were attached to the backs of them. They made a tinkling sound when he moved, and he moved around a lot, as if he couldn't stand still for long.

Gaby felt a shiver of apprehension run through her and instinctively she stepped closer to Rayne as if to protect him from this man and the unspoken threat emanating from him.

"Hello, Rayne," the man said.

"Thad," Rayne's voice was clipped.

"I hear you took some cattle to New Orleans."

"That's right," Rayne said evenly, and Gaby could sense the tautness in him.

"Well, you ain't brought them back, so you must have sold them."

"It appears that way."

"Hope you got a good price for them."

"Good enough," Rayne said tersely.

"It'd be a shame to go to all that trouble and not get a good price," Thad replied with mock concern. His glance slid to Gaby. "But then, New Orleans does have its compensations, don't it?" Gaby could feel Rayne's arm quiver and suddenly she understood that the man wanted to bait Rayne into a fight.

"My name is Gabrielle Reynaud," she said, stepping forward and holding out her hand. The man looked at her in surprise and then relaxed, his grin aimed at her now. He took off hat off and nodded his head courteously, but his gaze was too bold.

"I'm right glad to meet you, ma'am," he said. "I'm Thadeus Martin. You'll be a welcome addition to Texas."

"Thank you," Gaby said.

"I didn't know Rayne had such an eye for the pretty women." Thad's tone was sly and his eyes slanted back at Rayne, gauging his reaction. Once again Gaby felt Rayne's hand at her elbow and this time it was biting, causing her to wince.

"Dusty, see to the supplies and get them loaded on the wagon," Rayne repeated his orders to the foreman, who had remained nearby, his jacket pulled back and away from his gun.

"Don't worry, Rayne. The boys and me'll see everything's all right," Dusty said without looking at his boss. His eyes were steady on the man who had lingered in the background. He looked mean and he also kept his hand close to his gun. Gaby felt alarm race through her.

"You brought back supplies from New Orleans, Rayne?" Thad asked. "You figuring on staying on out at the ranch?"

"It's my home. Where else would I go?" Rayne snapped.

"Oh, I don't know. Since your father's laid up and can't reach much anymore, I kinda figured you'd be looking to sell."

"Not me, Martin, you'll have to look for some other land," Rayne said, and turning his back on the man, guided Gaby along the dock toward the streets.

"Well, think about it, Rayne," Martin called. "I could give you a real good offer on those acres." Rayne kept walking, without looking back or replying. His long legs covered the distance swiftly, and Gaby was forced to trot along beside him to keep up.

"Rayne," she called breathlessly, and he stopped and looked down at her. "Did I do something to make you angry with me?"

"I'm not riled with you, Gaby, but you've got to stop trying to protect me. If there had been any gunplay back there, you would have been caught in the middle. I couldn't have returned Martin's fire for fear of hitting you. Stay out of the way, Gaby. I've never used a woman's skirts to protect myself before and I'm not starting now."

"I'm sorry," she whispered. "There was just something about him that frightened me. He reminded me of Toto."

"He's not that bad. He's always been a little wild. I thought the war would take some of that out of him, but it didn't. Don't worry about him anymore. I can handle him."

Gaby said nothing more. She couldn't hurt Rayne's pride any further expressing her doubts. She'd seen the flare of hatred in Thad Martin's eyes. He wanted Rayne dead.

"Why does he hate you so much?" she asked. Rayne paused to look at her, a smile crinkling the corners of his eyes.

"You don't miss much, do you?" he asked.

"Not when it concerns you," she replied with an impudent grin. "Tell me about Thad Martin."

"Not much to tell," Rayne replied, and turned back toward the street. Small houses and shops crowded along each side, but Gaby paid them little mind, too intent on Rayne's words. "We were boys growing up together on the prairies. Our fathers started their ranches at about the same time. At first we were close as brothers, but as we grew older, Thad turned wild. He was always trying to prove himself. It bothered him if he thought someone could ride a horse faster or shoot straighter." He didn't say it, but Gaby knew Thad hadn't been able to best Rayne at those things. Still, it wasn't enough reason to kill a man as Thad wanted to kill Rayne.

"I hadn't seen Thad for a lot of years; then he was assigned to my division in the war. I caught him dealing in contraband. There was going to be a court-martial. Then the charges were dropped and Thad was assigned to a different unit." Rayne's words were terse. He didn't elaborate on anything, only stating the bare facts as they'd occurred. Gaby guessed at how he must have felt to discover his boyhood friend's illegal activity.

"Let's forget Thad Martin and see the sights," Rayne said, taking Gaby's elbow.

At daybreak Rayne woke Gaby and she hurried into

her clothes. Excitement mounted in her. She was actually in Texas and they were beginning their journey to Rayne's ranch. They were to take a river raft up the Brazos to a landing several miles inland. From there they would take their wagons and horses and travel overland into the heart of the Texas prairie.

The wagons and horses had already been loaded when Rayne and Gaby got to the river landing. Several men stood around or lounged on barrels and any makeshift seating they could find. Some of them glanced up when Rayne and Gaby approached.

"Boys, this is Gabrielle Reynaud," Rayne introduced her. "She'll be going back to the Rocking E Ranch with us." Some of the men eyed her speculatively. Gaby kept her chin high. Rayne hadn't explained to them that she was going to be his wife, she thought with a flash of irritation.

"Gaby, you've met Little Finger. This is Bailey, Ramon, Turner, Slade, and Billy."

"Pleased to meet you, ma'am." Billy stepped forward and touched the rim of his hat respectfully. The other men stood and did the same. Gaby was touched by their politeness. From their rough appearance she'd expected them to be an unmannerly lot. She smiled back at them, not sure which name applied to which man. It didn't seem to matter anyway. After the first polite greeting the men slumped into their former positions, their hats pulled low over their eyes. They weren't being unfriendly, Gaby realized. It was obvious some of them suffered from hangovers. There was a cut lip or two and the young man named Billy sported a black eye. He grinned back at Gaby.

The lines were cast off from shore and the riverboat headed upstream. Eagerly Gaby watched the town disappear behind them, catching a final glimpse of stately town houses and hardwood trees sculpted to exotic shapes by the salt-laden winds from the ocean. Gaby was surprised by the greenery. The river ran past cotton plantations much like those in Louisiana, with shabby great houses and abandoned fields of rich black loam.

All day they traveled by river, and although the lush tropical greenery had become more sparse, still there were no deserts, just rich, flat alluvial plains stretching away on either side. It was dark by the time they reached the landing. The men maneuvered the clumsy rough carts off the flat-bottomed boat.

"Where is the hotel?" Gaby asked, looking around. She heard one of the men stifle a laugh.

"There ain't any hotels out here," Rayne said. "We passed the last way station some miles back."

"But where will we sleep?" she asked.

"Right out under the stars," Rayne replied. "You won't be afraid, will you?"

"Of course not," Gaby answered, and looked around. Darkness was rapidly falling. "I've never slept outdoors before. It will be . . . interesting."

Rayne suppressed a smile. She seemed so tiny and dainty to him, and yet she was trying hard to be brave. He took special pains to stay near her as they began to set up camp.

Two campfires were built, one against a log overlooking the river and the other some distance away near the wagons. Rayne used canvas to set up a lean-to near the river. It would afford Gaby some privacy and give added warmth against the cool night. Dusty and the other men spread their bedrolls under the supply wagons.

Gaby watched the efficient movements of the men as they worked. The smell of coffee and frying meat came to her and she realized how hungry she was. She cast a look at Rayne. His horse had been hobbled near the lean-to and his saddle flung on the ground near the log. As she watched, he lowered his lean frame to this makeshift seat and leaned back against his saddle. He seemed perfectly at ease.

"Come here, Gaby," he said, holding out a hand to her. She went to him, nestling down on his lap, and he pulled a blanket from his bedroll and wrapped it around her.

"The nights can get chilly here, even if the days are hot," he said, and wrapped his arms around her protectively. Gaby snuggled against him, no longer worried about what was beyond the light of their campfire. The moonlight cast a silvery glow on the river water and lit the flat open land.

"It's much bigger than I'd expected," Gaby said in a small voice.

"It is a big country. If you don't tame it, it'll be the death of you."

Suddenly Gaby felt frightened again. She'd thought of Rayne as fearless and indestructible, but even he seemed to hold the wildness and beauty of this land in awe.

"If you make the land work for you, it's a good life here," he said softly. "Life won't be easy this next year or two, Gaby, but I'm going to make it pay. There's money in cattle, and cattle is about the best thing we can grow here in Texas. Someday I'm going to be one of the biggest ranchers in this state. Stick with me, Gaby, as long as you can."

"I'll stay with you forever, Rayne," she answered simply, and he hugged her close.

She meant it now, he had no doubt, but later, when boredom and fatigue set in, she'd get her fill of it and she'd leave. Too many women did, women who'd been born here. Gaby would too. He couldn't expect her to stay when even some of the women who'd been raised here in Texas had trouble with the isolation and poverty and the constant fear of Indian or outlaw attacks. He'd keep her here as long as he could; then he'd let her go. For now she was beside him and he'd savor each moment with her.

Little Finger brought them plates of beans, sourdough bread, and beefsteaks, thick and burned nearly black on the outside, pink and juicy inside. They had a taste like no other beef Gaby had eaten before, but she ate a good portion before laying aside her plate and cradling her tin cup of hot coffee in her hands. Thoughtfully she stared into the fire.

"Tell me about life on the ranch," she asked Rayne, and when he started to speak, admonished him, "Don't tell me the bad parts—you've been doing that from the beginning. Tell me about the good times, the times that brought you back to the ranch after all those years away."

Rayne cast her a quick, surprised look. His shrewd Gaby! He should have known she'd look beyond his words and see the reason for them, but now she was asking for more, and happily he shared his life as a boy growing up on the ranch.

From the other campsite came the sound of a guitar and someone singing softly as if not to shatter the tranquil peace of the night. Rayne told Gaby of his first horse and of his first roundup. He told her of wild mustang ponies that roamed the prairies, and of the longhorns, and of how important a good horse was to a cowman.

Even after they'd undressed and rolled themselves together in blankets beneath the lean-to, Rayne talked on, telling about branding and old legends he'd grown up with. Gaby lay with her head pillowed on his shoulder, drowsily watching the dying embers of the fire. In the distance there was the howling of an animal, but Rayne seemed not to notice, so Gaby didn't worry about it. At the other campfire, the singer put aside his guitar and all grew still.

"Then there's the Wilson boys, who hunt down the longhorns in their bare feet, or so I've heard tell, although I find it hard to believe any fool'd go into the chaparral without his boots on." Rayne chuckled and glanced down at Gaby. Her eyelashes lay along the curve of her cheeks and she was fast asleep. She looked like a little girl, not more than nine or ten, but he knew better.

He'd do everything he could to keep her here, he vowed. He'd try to make life as easy for her as he could, and maybe if she knew how much he loved her, maybe she wouldn't leave.

5

They rose early the next morning when the sun was just staining the eastern sky, and loading up their supplies, set out cross country at an angle from the Brazos River. Sometimes it appeared they'd left the river behind them for good, and then it wove back around to meet them. The land was changing even more now. They were leaving behind the rich fertile fields and traveling through prairies, their tall grasses already turning brown under the hot summer sun.

That evening they camped in the open again. Gaby walked out over the vast prairieland, glad of the chance to stretch after the bumping, lurching ride she'd had all day. Rayne had padded her seat, but after a few miles, even that hadn't helped. Gaby could see Little Finger, the cook, gathering firewood.

"I'll help you," she called, and before he could object, began gathering up the round black disks.

"Why are you called Little Finger," she asked him as she bent to her task. "Is it your real name?"

Little Finger glared at her. Didn't she know it wasn't polite to ask too much about a man's name? He looked at her innocent face and realized she didn't. She had a lot to learn about Texas ways. Still, he liked her. She was a pretty little thing.

"Folks started calling me that when I first came here," he said. "I got captured by a bunch of Comanche and they cut off one of my fingers afore I got rescued." He held up his right hand and Gaby could see his little finger was missing.

"You must have been very frightened," she said faintly.

"Some," he said. "It ain't so bad, though. Coulda been worse, much worse. It kinda reminds me that them Injuns ain't ever to be trusted."

"Are there many Indians here in Texas?"

"Some," Little Finger answered. At the look on her face he went on. "The Comanche stay mostly over in they own territory in the Cross Timbers west of here."

"Do they attack people and scalp them?" Gaby asked.

"Not so much anymore. They've been quieted down in the past years. They still come out and steal cattle when they're hungry, but not enough to make a fuss over. If someone gets killed, more likely it's by some of the young bucks who are still avenging their ancestors."

"Oh," Gaby said, finding little comfort in Little Finger's words, although he'd meant well. "This is very strange wood," she said when one piece crumbled beneath her fingers.

"Yes, ma'am." Little Finger chuckled. "You might say that. But if it weren't for squawwood, many a man out on the prairie would have to eat his meat raw."

"How does it come to be here like this?" Gaby asked innocently. "Does it grow like this?"

Little Finger looked at her quizzically. "Well, you might say that," he began reluctantly. "You see, ma'am, this here comes from the buffalo, when he . . ." Little Finger gestured wildly with his hands. How did you explain such things to an eastern woman? he wondered. He wasn't about to. "Yes, ma'am," he said lamely. "It just kinda grows there."

When they had enough fuel for the supper fires, they headed back toward camp.

"You'd best not wander around out here on your own, ma'am," Little Finger said. "Ain't much telling what kinda snakes you might find."

"Snakes?" Gaby said, and hurried to keep up with the fiesty old man with the whiskers and the missing finger. "What kind of snakes?"

"Oh, we got us rattlers here, real mean they are. They get taller than a man, so when they spring at you, you cain't hardly get out of their way. By the rivers, they's cottonmouths you have to watch out for, and then there's the little coral snake and the—"

"Never mind," Gaby said, and trudged so closely behind him, she almost trod on his heels. Little Finger repressed a smile. Just like a tenderfoot. They always hated snakes.

Gaby watched closely as Little Finger built a fire. One day she might have to do this herself and she wanted to be ready. Little Finger set up metal holders and laid a rod across them. From the rod he hung a coffeepot so it swung from a hook just above the flames.

She offered her help so often that Little Finger soon tired of trying to walk around her and asked her to fetch water from the stream running nearby. Happily, Gaby went about her assigned tasks.

She was learning to be a frontier woman. She'd make Rayne proud of her. He'd never be sorry she'd come to Texas with him. Carefully she watched Little Finger mix up the sourdough bread and set it to baking in the Dutch oven, with coals piled high on its iron lid. It looked simple enough. She was sure she could do that much. Her confidence grew.

Rayne and Gaby ate supper with the rest of the crew and afterward sat around listening as the men swapped tales about roundups and trail drives. Gaby didn't understand a lot of what they were talking about, but she listened attentively.

Their talk turned naturally to the war years, for nearly all of them had been involved one way or another. Some, like Rayne and Dusty, had fought for the South, while others stayed behind and protected Texas and its borders from Indians, outlaws, and troublesome bands of Mexicans.

"Whooee, I remember things was bad back in sixty-three," Little Finger said, "what with the drought'n all. Then them northers hit us. They say Galveston Bay even froze over that year. Wal, them winds and that snow sweeping down into Texas just pushed them cows southward, thousands of 'em." He paused and took a chew of tobacco.

"Me an' ole D. W. Sanders, a feller with jest one eye, we took a herd o' cattle and started out to Mexico to git some supplies for some of the wimmin. We had us mebbe three hundred head of cows. We couldn't git no good help, all the men bein' away at war and all, so we jest used us some younguns, some of 'em not hardly outta they dities.

"Wal, sir, one night something spooked them cows and we couldn't hold 'em; we couldn't even turn them dadblamed critters, so we jest run 'em. Run 'em all night, we did, and come mornin' we ain't lost nary a one of those beeves. I'd say we done right well for a coupla ole men with a brood a younguns." He punctuated the end of his story with a spurt of tobacco juice aimed into the fire. It hit a hot stone and sizzled.

"Did you ever git them cows to Mexico?" Slade Harner asked. His eyes glittered with derisive laughter as he looked to the other men to join in his ridicule of the old man. Gaby felt a wave a irritation toward the younger cowboy. She'd come to like the crusty old cook.

"Dadburn right, we got 'em to Mexico," Little Finger snapped. "Got a good deal for 'em too. Ask Billy there. He was one of the younguns we tuck with us." He nodded toward the young cowboy with the black eye. When he saw all eyes turned to him, he shyly ducked his head and looked at the ground.

"What'd you get with yo'r money, Little Finger?" another cowboy called, and it was obvious they didn't believe him.

"Ask Billy," Little Finger said indignantly. "He'll tell you right enough." Billy looked around the circle of men and saw they were waiting for him to speak.

"Well, we . . . uh . . . we got us some real knives and forks, the metal ones." He raised his head to see if the men were as impressed by that as he had been. They weren't.

"Bet the ladies were grateful," someone said.

"They ware," Little Finger snapped, greatly offended now. "During the war we didn't have a lotta that kind of thing around here. We had to eat off'n those wooden ones or with our fingers. The wimmen said they felt lak they was civilized again onc't they had forks. They was real hard-up."

"In more ways than one, from what I hear," another

cowboy said suggestively, and someone kicked his leg and nodded toward Gaby.

"Go on, Billy, what else?" someone prodded.

"Uh, we got some bridle bits and some flour and salt and some coffee," Billy said.

"The real stuff, mind you." Little Finger couldn't stand his abstinence from the conversation any longer. "None of that bellywash we was drinking."

Some of the other men laughed. "Back in Georgia," one man drawled, "we was down to parched peas and corn ground together."

"We tried jest about everything," Little Finger said. "Okra, chicory, even acorns. A couple of times I figure they even tried bilin' their boots."

Everyone laughed at the old man's remarks, then sat silently reflecting on the war years. They had been hard, both at home and on the battlefield. The future didn't look much better, except that they were back on Texas soil doing what they did best, punching cows. They lolled back by the campfire and reflected on the first cattle drive since returning home. They were broke already, but they had a job and soon there would be another trail drive and money to spend on the calico queens and whiskey. They sighed in pleasant contentment. Ramon took out his guitar and began picking a tune. His voice was rich and full as he sang the words of a ballad: "Last night as I lay on the prairie, and looked at the stars in the sky . . ." The song was plaintive and seemed to reflect the mood the men had fallen into.

Then Ramon burst into a rousing tune that soon had them tapping their toes and clapping in time to the music.

Slade Harner rose and walked to where Gaby sat on a log. "Ma'am?" he said, and the music died around them while every face turned toward Gaby. Every man there knew she was Rayne's woman, and they knew the unspoken code of chivalry Texans held toward another man's lady. Slade Harner was stretching the code.

It seemed to Gaby as if all activity was suspended while everyone waited for her reaction.

"Would you care to dance a jig with me, ma'am?" Slade asked again when she made no response. "That is, if Mr. Elliott don't mind."

"The choice is the lady's," Rayne said offhandedly. Gaby hesitated a moment more. Something about Slade made her feel uneasy. Several times she'd noticed him boldly watching her. Nevertheless he worked for Rayne and she had no wish to offend him. Reluctantly she held out her hand and felt Slade pull her to her feet.

A cheer went up from the other men, and the music and foot-stamping began anew. Slade swung her around the hard-packed ground so fast her feet barely touched. Before they'd made a complete circle another cowhand was there, insisting on his turn to dance with the pretty woman from New Orleans. Gaby danced with all, save Ramon.

She was wondering how to end it when Rayne stepped forward, taking her hand and enclosing her in his arms. The music slowed to a waltz measure and everything else faded from Gaby. Other men formed couples and began to dance around the circle, but for Gaby there was only Rayne and the feel of his strong arms around her. His long, lean body led them in a rhythm that was theirs alone.

The men fell silent as they watched the couple glide around the campfire. It would be a while before they were back in town and had their own women again.

Slade Harner stood back in the shadows watching Gaby and Rayne and his eyes glittered. She was some woman, all right, some woman for a whore. He knew New Orleans and he knew the district where she'd said she'd lived. He'd even heard of the Court of Angels. Slade changed his stance to ease the sudden tingle in his groin. Be patient, he advised himself.

The dance ended and Rayne turned toward his own campsite.

"Good night, boys," he said, touching his hat with one finger, one arm still holding Gaby close to his side.

Ramon's music played on, quiet and reflective now. It followed Gaby and Rayne across the short stretch of prairie ground to their canvas shelter, where they undressed and hurried under the warm covers. The night had turned chilly.

They snuggled together, letting their shared body heat and growing desire warm them. Looking up at the patch of night sky, visible beyond the edge of the canvas, it seemed to Gaby that the stars were bigger and brighter, closer to them somehow. Then Rayne moved and his shoulders cut off the vision of moonlight and stars and she forgot everything except the passion between them.

It was hard to leave the warmth and comfort of the makeshift bed the next morning, but Rayne prodded her out. The smell of coffee and the promise of the warmth of the campfire prompted her to hurry into her clothes. Rayne filled a basin of water from the barrel in the wagon and she quickly washed her face and hands, shuddering at the coldness of it. Another day had begun, she thought, and sat down to eat some of Little Finger's flapjacks. She was already getting used to the strong bitter brew they called six-shooter coffee.

"Ain't no good unless you kin float a six-shooter in it," Little Finger had told her. She was coming to like the colorful way the Texans talked.

The day warmed quickly, and by midday Gaby was nearly faint from the heat. The white-hot sun seemed to sear everything under its merciless light. The heat rose from the hard-baked prairie floor, trapping man and beast alike. There was no place to go to escape it save onward, so they moved toward the shimmering horizon.

Little Finger gave Gaby a wide-brimmed hat to shield her from the sun's glare and she was grateful, but it did little to alleviate her discomfort. What she wanted was some shade, certainly more than was afforded by the canvas slung over the metal frame of the chuck wagon, and she wanted a bath and one of those tall, cool drinks that Ruby used to make back at the Court of Angels.

Still the men pushed on. They must be hot too. They had not even the shade of the canvas to shield them, and they weren't complaining. She gritted her teeth and remained silent.

At noon they stopped for a meal and Gaby hurried out onto the flat brown prairie to gather up rounds of squawwood for Little Finger's fire. Despite the heat she was determined to do her share.

Rayne's horse cantered out to where she worked. "What are you doing, Gaby?" he asked, his eye concerned as he glanced down at her.

"Why, I'm gathering wood for Little Finger's fire."

"Do you know what you're gathering?" Rayne asked.

"Yes, Little Finger told me. It's squawwood," Gaby answered in surprise, and caught a hastily concealed look of amusement on Rayne's face.

"It's not wood Gaby," he said gently. "It's buffalo droppings."

Gaby looked at him blankly and then with growing horror as she realized what he was saying. Quickly she dropped her armload of chips and brushed at her gown and hands. Now Rayne's mirth was unchecked.

"Oh . . ." Gaby sputtered. "I was just trying to help, trying to do my share," she declared, near tears.

Rayne's laughter ended abruptly and he swung down from his horse. "Don't try so hard, Gaby," he said, taking her into his arms. "It will work out."

"I just don't want you to be sorry I'm here," she said, her eyes bright and anxious.

"I'll never be sorry," Rayne answered, and lowered his head to place a kiss on her lips. He held her in the circle of his arms and wondered that she didn't know how grateful he was that she had come to Texas.

Gaby leaned against his tall, rawboned body, reveling in the feel of it against hers.

"Gaby," he said, and she heard the ache in his voice. It echoed her own need. Heedless of who might see them, she raised her mouth to his once more. With a gentle, lingering touch, Rayne set her away from him.

"We'd better get back to the wagon and have a bite to eat," he said reluctantly. "We still have long way to go before we reach the Rocking E Ranch."

"Will we get there today?" Gaby asked eagerly as she fell into step beside him.

"I plan to," Rayne said, casting a measuring look at the sky and terrain, as if just from those he could determine exactly how many miles they must go.

They made a quick meal of it and were on their way in little time. Everyone was eager to get back to the Rocking E.

"If we want to get to the ranch before nightfall, why aren't we going faster?" Gaby said impatiently.

"Too hard on the animals in this heat," Little Finger

said. "Best to set a pace and hold to it like we're doing. We'll get there. The other way, we might not." He spat a stream of tobacco juice over the wagon wheel.

Gaby grew drowsy from the heat, her head nodding, her lids drooping. Apologetically she smiled at Little Finger.

"This climate takes some gittin' used to," he said, "and that's a fact."

"How long have you been out here?" she asked. Perhaps if they talked, she could stay awake.

"Wal, let me see if I can recollect," the old man said, scratching his jaw beneath the whiskers. "I come here with Cole Elliott and we both wasn't much bigger'n shavetails. Cocky we war. Thought we could lick the world. Dadburn did, at times. Leastwise we helped whup the Mexicans. Yessiree, that was a time in a young man's life. That was back in thirty-eight, but Cole and me, we come out earlier'n that. Things got bad back east. Warn't much of a future there for neither one o' us, so one day Cole and me we jest lit out. Didn't wait for our folks to give us they blessin', 'cause we knowed it wouldn't be a-comin'." Little Finger paused and scratched at his chin again.

"Ole Davy Crockett, he come out here along with Jim Bowie and the others. Met him onc't, that was afore the Alamo, mind you. Cole and me, we was goin' to the Alamo, but Cole got hisself into a gunfight. He got shot up pretty bad and I kinda figured I couldn't leave him. I stayed back and waited for him to heal up, only by then the Alamo warn't no more. Them was sad days for Texas, I can tell you."

Gaby listened to the old man talk and she pictured a much younger man, still fiesty, with one finger missing and maybe the beginnings of a beard, as he and his buddy roamed the west.

"Cole was barely on his feet when he taken off and offered our services against them murdering Mexies. We whupped 'em good with ole Sam Houston leadin' us. Couldn't nobody whup a Texan after that. Still can't. We jest got hooked up with those Secessionists who couldn't hold they own against them Unionists. It was a sorry day for the South, all right, but even sorrier for Texas. Now we're under military government, but we'll git our own

back." Little Finger's voice droned on and on and soon
Gaby began to doze again.

A man shouted. Gaby opened her eyes and looked
around. The man was pointing toward something on the
prairie up ahead. Little Finger stopped talking and headed
his team in that direction. Rayne had already reined his
horse around and was galloping toward the brown humps.
They looked innocent enough, Gaby thought, and yet
sensed a tenseness in Little Finger and the other men as
they drew closer. Large black birds wheeled and circled
above the area.

"Vultures," Little Finger grunted, and pulled the wagon
to a halt some distance from the other men. A smell of
rot and decay was carried on the wind. Gaby peered
ahead. The carcasses of dead cows lay to one side. Two
of them had been skinned and the hooves and horns
removed. Their hides lay in bundles nearby. Even as she
sat watching, two of the cowhands got off their ponies
and went to examine the skins. Gaby caught a glimpse of
boots protruding from one of the hides.

"Whooee, this one's a goner, sure," Slade Harner
called.

"What are they talking about?" Gaby cried. "Surely
there aren't men in those hides."

"The Spanish call it the Death of the Skins," Little
Finger said. "They wrap the skins, fresh off a cow, around
a man. In this sun the skins draw up and harden like iron
around him. It's a slow, painful way to die."

"No more," Gaby cried, and leaned over the wheel to
retch into the yellow prairie soil. "Did the Mexicans do
this?" she asked weakly.

"No, ma'am," Little Finger replied. "I don't figure
they did. Jes' someone who learned from 'em."

"This poor devil's had it too," Rayne said, checking
the second bundle.

"Who is it, Rayne?" Little Finger called.

"Cook Avery and his oldest boy," Rayne answered.

"Reckon who done it?" Little Finger asked bitterly.

"That's the Bar M mark on the hide he's wrapped in."
Slade pointed to a mark on the skin.

"Thad Martin and his men for sure," Little Finger said.
"But how come they done this to Cook and his son."

"He got caught taking some of the Bar M cows," Rayne said angrily. "We all know some of the little outfits are stealing back cows they think are theirs."

"Seems like he'da taken more men than jest his son if'n he was going up against Thad Martin and his men," Little Finger said.

"You can't use what you haven't got," Rayne said. His face was grim, his eyes dark with anger. "Avery didn't have men, just his kids." He stood up and looked around. He could see Gaby's pale face, the dark eyes as bleak and grim as he felt. Rayne cursed under his breath. He should have anticipated something like this when he saw the vultures and had Little Finger go on without stopping. It was too late now.

Rayne looked at the sky, bleached by the hot sun. It was already midafternoon and they had a way to go to get to the ranch before nightfall, but he couldn't leave Avery and his son out here.

"Some of you men get them up on the back of the supply wagon. We'll take them back to the Avery ranch."

Gaby sat huddled on the wagon seat. What kind of country was this, she wondered, that men died so cruelly?

They snaked across the prairie until they came to a small huddle of buildings looking forlorn and forgotten against the dun-colored prairie. As their horses drew near, a tired-looking woman came out of the sod shack and stood watching them approach. A small child clung to her skirts. Two other faces peered from the door of the shack. A boy, hardly more than ten or twelve years old, paused near the corral fence.

"Mrs. Avery . . ." Rayne brought his horse to a stop before her.

"Mr. Elliott," she said, and stepped forward, wiping her large rough hands on her apron. "Cook ain't here right now. He's off. You folks look hot and tired. Git down and set a spell. I'll have my boy draw you some fresh water."

"I'm afraid we can't stay, Mrs. Avery," Rayne said, getting down from his horse. "We want to make the ranch before nightfall. We brought your husband and your boy with us."

"You got my man with you?"

Silently Rayne looked at the woman and the grim message was evident in his face. "Yes, ma'am," he said finally. "We've got them on the back of the wagon."

"No," Margaret Avery said in a small tight voice, and walked to the back of the supply wagon. Gaby expected to hear her cry out and lament her dead husband and son, but she stood quiet and still, too defeated by the harsh life here on the Texas plain to accept this final blow. Slowly she raised her head and looked at Rayne. "Why?" she asked. "How come they done this to him?" He was a good man, and Sonny was jest a boy." Her voice broke.

"They got caught rustling cattle."

"Cook warn't no rustler," she flared. "You knowed Cook Avery, Mr. Elliott. He warn't no thief and I won't have you comin' in here and callin' him so in front of his younguns."

"I'm sorry," Rayne said, and went to stand near her. Something about her fierce loyalty for her husband and children touched him. "He was found with Bar M cattle," he explained. "You know what folks are going to say about that."

"He warn't stealing cattle. He was jest tryin' to get back what was ours. Thad Martin's men've been taking our cattle all spring."

"Can you prove it?" Rayne asked.

Miserably the woman shook her head. "We cain't prove it, but everybody around here knows who's takin' the cows from us little ranchers. He's been doing everythin' he can to drive out the little ranchers so he can take over their land."

"Did you talk to him about the problems?"

"Cook tried. Him and Sonny went over to the Martin ranch, figuring to talk to the old man. Cook didn't accuse no one. He jest said he thought they got some of our cows by mistake, but they beat him up for accusin' 'em of stealin'. They beat him up real bad. It took him weeks to git over it, and all that time he kept talkin' how he was goin' ta git his cows back."

"Maybe someone else took his cows," Rayne said.

"Who else?" she flared. "Ever since Thad Martin come back from the war, he's been after us. Whatever his men see, they jest take, and we ain't strong enough to fight back. The old man don't do nothin' to stop him. Thad Martin means to take over this territory. You watch out, Rayne, your land'll be next. It'll be your cattle he'll be takin', then he'll find some excuse to kill you too." Her words and the memory of Thad's goading back at the dock made Gaby shudder with sudden fear for Rayne.

The woman's tirade ended and she stared at Rayne as suddenly it hit her that her husband and son were dead, wrapped in skins that couldn't be removed from their bodies even for burial. Cook Avery had lost his fight and she couldn't carry on alone. She would no longer be engaged in this battle against the weather and droughts and evil men who wanted what wasn't theirs to take.

Margaret Avery stepped back toward her sod home and her children came to cluster about her in a shared sorrow. She raised her head and looked at the fresh-faced young woman seated on the wagon beside Little Finger. Rayne Elliott had brought himself back a woman. She sat with eyes full of sympathy. Well, let her keep her pity for herself, Margaret thought. She would need it. Ahead of her were more hardships and sorrows than a body had a right to.

"I'm much obliged to you for bringing my man home," she said, pulling her tattered dignity about her. It was more heartrending to Gaby than tears would have been.

"I'm sorry it wasn't better news," Rayne said. "I'll leave a couple of my men here to help you bury your dead. In a couple of days I can send over someone to help you out with your work until you make other arrangements."

"Ain't no need to do that," Margaret Avery said. "Me and the kids, we're goin' into town and live. I'll git me a job cleaning houses or doing wash until I can git enough money together to go back to Tennessee. Tell your daddy if he wants to buy our land he kin have it for what he kin pay."

"We can't pay you much, Mrs. Avery," Rayne said. "You might want to try selling it to someone else."

"Who'd want it but you and Thad Martin—and I ain't selling it to him. I won't give my land to the man who

murdered my husband and my boy. Think on it some. I'll
take whatever you can pay me."

"I'll let you know," Rayne said, and touching his hat
brim, led the men and wagons out of the yard and headed
west. The sun was already sinking low.

They moved out over the prairie, feeling dwarfed by
the wide sky and vast expanse of flat land. Gaby thought
of Margaret Avery and her children and the dirt shack
that sheltered them. What would the Elliott ranch be
like? she wondered with some misgivings. Could she live
as stoically as Margaret Avery had, bearing her husband's children, enduring the hardships, and accepting
his death as that woman had done? It wouldn't be like
that for Rayne and her. She was sure of it. Yet doubts
tugged at her as they continued their journey.

The sun was nearly gone by the time they came to the
Rocking E Ranch. Its light, reflecting in the western sky
in a final flamboyant show of color, cast purple shadows
over the hills and hollows. The ranch house sat nestled
into the hillside and the last rays of sunlight cast a golden
glow over its stone-and-adobe walls. A wide low porch
ran around the front and side of the building.

Near the ranch house were several sheds and barns
built in the same squat manner as the ranch house. They
seemed to hug the ground and become one with their
surroundings. Beyond the outbuildings were the corrals,
made of roughly hewn rails.

"There it is, Gaby." Rayne glanced at her, his eyes
eager, and Gaby sensed how much he wanted her to love
his house.

"It's beautiful," she said, and meant it. The house sat
on the prairie soil, solid and substantial, as if it had been
built to last forever. Now it would be her home and the
home of the children she would give Rayne.

They swept down the hill toward the ranch house. Men
working around the barn and corrals halted what they
were doing and raised their hats in greeting. The cowhands let out whoops and shrill calls as they galloped into
the yard amid a cloud of dust. Little Finger drew the
wagon up near the porch and set the brake.

A tall, stoop-shouldered man came out of the house
onto the low porch. He was an older version of Rayne

Elliott. His leanness had turned to gauntness, but the remnant of past strength still clung to him.

"We made it, Pa," Rayne said, sitting easily in his saddle. "We got a good price for our cows and we brought back the supplies we needed, with a little left over."

Cole Elliott made no reply. His gaze moved around the group of new arrivals and turned glacial when he saw Gaby still perched on the wagon.

"What's that woman doing here?" he bellowed, and the yard grew quiet as the men stopped talking and looked at him. It seemed to Gaby as if they quailed beneath the old man's fierce gaze.

Rayne ignored his father's question. Leisurely he swung a long leg over his mount and slid to the ground. The smile had left his face and his blue eyes were flat-looking. "We had a safe trip," he answered evenly. "We didn't lose any cows or men." The old man missed the anger, coiled and held in check.

"Who's that woman out there?" he demanded again. "Where'd she come from?"

Rayne mounted the steps to the porch and faced the unyielding man, his face as cold and set as his father's. "That woman is Gabrielle Reynaud," he answered evenly. "She's from New Orleans."

"You brought back a New Orleans whore?" the man spat out and Gaby cringed at the contempt in his voice. "Get her off my land."

"She stays," Rayne answered, and his voice was too quiet, his face too calm. They'd been heading for a showdown for months, and he wasn't about to back down in front of the men and Gaby. To the watching ranch hands there was little question of who'd win this argument. They'd ridden with Rayne Elliott and they knew he could be as hard as iron about some things.

"I won't have a whore on this ranch. I did once and—" His words were cut off by Rayne's fist at his chest, balling the front of his shirt in an iron grip. Rayne shoved his father back against the side of the house.

"Don't ever call her a whore again. Her name's Gaby and she's here to stay as long as she wants."

"That won't be for very long," Cole raged. "Her kind

don't last long. They feel the call to move on to some other place, some other man."

"I'll face that when it happens," Rayne said.

"It will happen," Cole retorted. "It's just a matter of time. She's a whore." The fist tightened on the material and Cole felt it cut into his neck. He looked at the fury of his son's face and felt a tremor of fear, fear of losing what little bit of this hard-faced man he could still cling to, but then, Cole Elliott didn't cling to any man, not even his own son.

"This is my ranch—" he began.

"You gave it to me, it's mine now," Rayne said. "I've worked it since I was a kid. I watched you drink away the profits. You gave up during the war. Well, you gave it to me, and what I say goes. I say she stays. If you can't live with that, then leave."

"I might have known you'd turn on me," Cole snarled. "You're her son, all right." Rayne clenched his fists tighter. The accusation rang in his ears. He'd heard it often enough in his lifetime. Gaby was sitting white-faced, watching them. He'd wanted her homecoming to be better than this. Taking a deep breath, he let go of Cole's shirt and stepped back, his gaze hard and condemning as he looked at his father.

"Every day I live," he grated, "you make me happier to know the truth of that." He whirled on his heel. Stay with me, Gaby, he thought as he walked to her.

Cole watched his son's stiff back. He'd pushed him too far this time. It was the war. It changed men. He'd seen it back in '38 in the war with the Mexicans. That was when he'd given up his wild, free ways and brought Lily out here to start ranching. Even now her name conjured up a vision of red hair, smiling lips, and pale rounded breasts. He'd won her in a barroom brawl and persuaded her to come to the ranch with him. She'd been a tall, leggy woman, nearly as tall as him, not like this woman Rayne had brought home. She looked little more than a child.

Rayne handed her down and she stood in the yard looking around with big dark eyes. They seemed to take in everything, corrals, bunkhouse, and barn; then those great dark eyes turned to Cole. They seemed to plead with him for something he didn't have in him to give. He looked away first.

Rayne took her arm, his grip reassuring on her elbow, and accompanied her up the porch steps.

"Mr. Elliot . . ." she began, and her voice was womanly soft to his ears. "I'm glad to meet Rayne's father at last." She held out a small hand to him.

In silence he looked out over his ranch, and she might as well not have been there.

Gaby lowered her hand and turned away. Perhaps with time he'd come to accept her.

Rayne's arm, strong and comforting, helped take away the sting of his father's rejection. They entered the house and Gaby looked around her new home. It was rough and dingy. There was no hint of a woman's touch from the hooks driven into the walls where hats, gunbelts, and spare clothes hung, to the cowhide chairs and mounds of gear resting in every corner. The table and chairs were homemade and rough hewn, albeit worn smooth in spots from use.

"It's rough," Rayne said, looking around the room with new eyes. Remembering the satins and cut-glass chandeliers of New Orleans, he was even more worried about Gaby's reaction. She was too quiet.

"It just needs some fixing up," she said finally. She was with Rayne. Nothing else mattered. She turned her luminous smile on him once more and he felt some of his anxiety slip away.

"Welcome to the Rocking E Ranch," he said, and took her in his arms. His mouth was firm and warm on hers. He cradled her against his chest.

"Stay with me, Gaby," he whispered. "You won't be sorry you came, I promise." Unknowingly he echoed the words his father had uttered to his mother so many years before. Standing out on the porch, Cole Elliott heard them and cursed under his breath. Straightening his shoulders, he headed for the barn. He knew where there was a bottle of whiskey hidden out there.

"Rayne, about your father. I can't stay here if he doesn't want me."

"It's not you, Gaby. It's all women he has a grudge against."

"Still, if he doesn't want me—"

"Maybe you can change his mind about things," Rayne said. "You're good at getting men to change their thinking." He grinned wickedly and Gaby forgot his father as Rayne swept her up in his arms and carried her down the hall to their bedroom.

"Welcome home, Gaby," he said as he gently laid her on the bed. Suddenly she felt at home, and in that moment she began to love the ranch too. She felt a rare contentment seep through her and she raised her arms and drew Rayne's head down to her breast.

6

When Gaby awoke the next morning Rayne was gone. Sleepily she lay looking around. Where were the canvas coverings and the clang of pots and irons at the cook fire? No hard ground bruised her body. She felt warm and pampered. She stretched and lay remembering Rayne's gentleness and passion the night before. She'd sensed a joy in their lovemaking. They were home and together.

Home, Gaby thought, looking around the bedroom. Shabby though it might be, it was nice to think she had a home all her own. Seized by a sudden restlessness, she leapt from the bed and donned the gown she'd worn from New Orleans.

The sun was already high, pouring its heat and light down on the scorched earth with malevolent glee. Gaby shaded her eyes against its glare and looked around. She had no idea where to look for Rayne. The corrals and barnyard were deserted. She gazed at the long, low building that made up the ranch. Perhaps he was in one of them.

Stepping into the glare of sunlight, she felt the clamminess begin across her brow and back. What would it be at midday? she wondered, and was relieved they weren't still traveling across the prairie. How could Rayne and his men stand it?

There was no one in the barn. At the farther end of the corrals she could see someone repairing a fence, but it wasn't Rayne. There was a low, narrow building with a

mean porch clinging to its side. Gaby mounted the steps
and looked around.

"Hello," she called, but no one answered. Cautiously
she opened the door and poked her head inside. Rows of
beds stood along each side of the room and clothes hung
from pegs driven into the rough walls. Someone had
decorated the spaces in between with calendars and pictures, tacked up without benefit of frames. Her cheeks
turned red as she glimpsed the subjects of some of the
pictures. Nude women of voluptuous proportions hung
side by side with ornate scrolls of Bible verses.

"Hello." A male voice sounded from one of the beds,
causing Gaby to start and turn.

"I . . . I didn't realize anyone was in here," she said,
her eyes darting to the figure on the bed.

Slade Harner crossed one leg over the other and lolled
back against the pillows. His brown hair was tumbled
over his forehead and his chest was bare.

"I was looking for Rayne," Gaby stammered.

"He's out gathering strays. He'll be gone all day,"
Slade said softly, and his voice seemed to hold some
special message of intimacy.

"Why didn't you go with him?" she asked uneasily.

"I'm sick," he replied, and grinned as if at some private joke.

"Where are all the others?" Gaby asked, looking around.
Surely she hadn't been left alone here on the ranch with
this man.

Slade swung his legs off the bed and came to stand
near her, too near for Gaby's comfort. She could smell
the sweat on his body and took a step backward.

A half-smile curved his lips. "You don't need to worry,"
he said, bringing a hand up. Lightly he touched the
smooth curve of her cheek. "If you're needin' someone,
I'm right here."

Gaby drew away from him so quickly she bumped into
the door and heard it click shut. Slade stepped forward
and she was pinned there against the door. To open it
again, she must move closer to his half-naked body. She
cowered where she was, a cry of denial springing to her
lips.

The sound of hoofbeats in the ranch yard made Slade

raise his head like an animal sniffing the air for danger. Hastily he moved to one side. The doorknob gave under Gaby's trembling fingers and then she was out in the searing air again, the heat only intensifying her flushed state. Beads of moisture formed on her forehead and upper lip and her cheeks were stained red.

She paused on the porch of the bunkhouse, grasping one of the posts as if for support as the tall figure swung down from the horse and turned in her direction. Her heart sank when she saw it wasn't Rayne. Cole Elliott looked at her with cold eyes.

"What are you doing there in the bunkhouse?" he demanded. Before she could utter a word, a soft, sly voice spoke up.

"She's just lookin' for her man," Slade said. He'd followed her out onto the porch. He hadn't bothered to put on a shirt, and from his bootless feet to his tousled hair, it was all too obvious he had been in bed. Gaby turned back to Cole and read the condemnation in his eyes. She wanted to cry out against those unfair assumptions, but to do so would only make her appear more guilty.

"I was looking for Rayne," she said instead. "Where is he?"

"He's out there workin'," Cole said coldly. "You oughtn't to be down here. Decent women don't go into bunkhouses." He gave her no time to defend herself. His eyes focused on Slade, steel blue and piercing. "You look fit enough to be on a horse," he snapped. "Saddle up and meet us out on the south range." Cole climbed back into his saddle and galloped back the way he'd come.

"He sure looks mad about something," Slade said with a cunning look on his face. "I reckon he's got a burr under his saddle." He grinned at Gaby and turned back inside the bunkhouse. Gaby picked up her skirts, ran back to the house, and slammed the door behind her. She wouldn't venture outside again without Rayne, she vowed.

Muffled hoofbeats sounded hard and fast. Slade had left the ranch as well. She was all alone here.

She fought against the panic she felt. What she needed

was a good cup of coffee and then to get busy with
something. Ruby always said a little hard work took care
of the blues.

Gaby walked through her new home, taking stock.
Besides the front parlor, one end of which served as a
dining area, there was another bedroom besides Rayne's
and hers. Gaby guessed it belonged to Cole. A third
room might once have been intended for a bedroom but
had been turned into a storage room and held all manner
of cast-off furniture, worn saddles and broken bridles,
kegs and barrels and trunks. Everything was covered
with a layer of gray-yellow prairie dust. A stairway led
upward to a small loft with two tiny rooms, and at the
back of the house was a lean-to kitchen and another
small room meant to store food. Every dish, every pan,
even the top of the wood-burning stove was covered with
so much dust that it was clear the kitchen hadn't been
used in years. Obviously Rayne and Cole had been taking their meals with Little Finger and the other men
down in the bunkhouse.

Gaby rolled up her sleeves and set to work. She would
learn to do many things and she would make their home
beautiful. Her spirits rose as she envisioned the transfor-
mation she would bring about and Rayne's surprise when
he saw what she was capable of doing.

She found an old flour sack and tied it around her
gown. Taking a roughly made broom of reeds and prairie
grass, she swept the cobwebs from the corners and ceil-
ings. She hauled saddles and gear out of the parlor onto
the porch, dragging things across the floor when they
were too heavy to be toted.

The house grew warmer as the sun rode higher. Patches
of sweat discolored the bodice of her gown. She worked
on with dogged determination.

Rayne returned at midmorning and found her sitting
on the floor in a puddle of dirty water, the overturned
bucket beside her, cobwebs in her hair, and her dirt-
smudged cheeks wet with tears. Brightly she smiled at
him, ducking her head to scrub at the tears and dirt with
one hand while she continued to cradle the other in her
lap.

"Gaby, what are you doing?" Rayne cried, crossing

the room to kneel beside her. She glanced up at him, wide eyes filled with pain and discouragement, and child-like, held up her hand. A splinter of wood protruded from her palm, ugly and painful-looking. "Let me get that out," he said, and gently took her hand in his. With infinite care he removed the splinter and smeared an ugly, evil-smelling salve over it. He bound the hand with a clean white rag.

"Leave that on so you don't get an infection," he said, and studied her somber face. She hadn't said a word while he worked on her hand, and now she sat with her eyes downcast.

"What's wrong, Gaby?" he asked so gently that she raised her head to look at him, tears starting afresh from her brimming eyes.

"You left me here alone without anyone around except that man in the bunkhouse. Then Cole came and made him leave and I was all alone and . . . and . . ." She stopped talking and wiped at her tears.

"You weren't alone," Rayne said. "Little Finger was in the cookhouse."

"Little Finger?" Gaby said, pulling back. A glossy strand of hair clung to her damp cheek. Gently Rayne pushed it back. "I would never have left you alone," he said softly, his tone warm and reassuring.

"I didn't know," Gaby said contritely, looking down at her bandaged hand.

"Pa should have told you." Rayne looked around at the half-scrubbed floor and the puddle of water. "What are you doing here?" he asked quietly.

"I . . . I was trying to mop the floor and I overturned the pail and . . ." she hiccupped. "I want it to look nice for you when you got back."

Rayne couldn't have loved her more at that moment. All his past fears seemed laughable now. This was his Gaby, trying vainly to be brave and grown-up enough not to cry.

"It looks very nice," he said, pulling her into his arms and patting her back. "The things you've done really make a difference." He looked around the room. Where the devil had she put his spare saddle? he wondered, but wisely kept silent.

"No, no, it doesn't," Gaby sobbed, wallowing in the luxury of having his strong arms around her. "I tried so hard, but I . . . I'm not very good at this. I never kept . . . kept house before. Ruby and the servants did it." She didn't see Rayne's lips tighten but she felt a stiffening of his body. He had warned her it wouldn't be easy, and now here she was the very first day, whining like a spoiled child. She had to show him she had more backbone than this. Gently she pushed away from him, her chin raised stubbornly as she met his gaze. "I'll have it looking better by tonight," she vowed.

"Gaby . . ." Rayne began reluctantly. He didn't want her to do this kind of work. It wasn't what he expected of her. He looked around at the dingy, neglected room. He couldn't blame her from trying. He'd spent little time indoors since his return to the ranch. His days were spent in the saddle and often his nights were spent out under the stars. "Dry yourself off and change clothes."

"I haven't got anything else to change into," Gaby said, looking down at the wet and dirty skirt of her gown. The flour sack had done little to protect her.

"Hold on," he said, and walked back to the storage room. Gaby could see him rummaging through things, and soon he returned with a blue silk gown. "See what you can do to make it fit," he said, handing it to her. "At least it will be clean and dry."

Gaby carried the dress back to the bedroom and changed. Once the gown had been a fine garment, but its lace had yellowed. The neckline was cut low but the skirt flared around her prettily before ending in a tangle on the floor. It's original wearer had been much taller than Gaby, and much rounder.

"Gaby?" Rayne called to her from the parlor, and gathering the voluminous skirts up in her arms, Gaby hurried out. His face broke into a grin when he saw her, and he gathered her up in his arms. "Gaby, where are you?" he cried in mock horror, his hands roaming over her freely as he pretended to look for her in the folds of the dress. He found her ribs and tickled her until she collapsed against him with laughter.

"Do you think it's too big for me?" she asked, pretending to seriously consider the gown. Laughter sparkled in her dark eyes as she thought of how she must look. Rayne studied her lively face. There was so much he must learn about this elfin creature.

"The gown's not too big, the trouble is with the body inside. You need to grow some."

"This belonged to your mother," she said softly.

"Yes, it did." Seeing Gaby in his mother's dress, remembering her tears earlier, Rayne felt the laughter squeeze out of him. He was reminded of his father's harsh words. His mother had run away from the loneliness and hard work of the ranch. Gaby would too someday, but not now, not yet. She was here now, and if there had been tears, there had also been laughter between them. It would be all right. Somehow he had to make it right.

Rayne swept the small figure up in his arms, raising her high before settling her against him. He buried his face in the warm, fragrant softness of her breasts, nearly crushing the breath from her. "Gaby, don't ever leave me," he whispered harshly.

Her slender arms came up to enfold him, cradling his head against her. "I'll never leave you, Rayne," she answered. Her lips left soft, petallike kisses on his brow and cheeks, then found their way to his mouth. She felt his mouth grow firm and demanding beneath hers. His kiss was long and deep, leaving her breathless. She lay in his arms, her feet dangling above the dirty plank floor. Forgotten were her bright plans. Her thoughts were only of Rayne. Her fingers threaded through his dark locks as she gave herself up to the desire that swept over her.

Their kiss ended and once again Rayne's head rested against her breasts; his hot breath seared her skin. He could feel her pulse, wild and erratic, shaking her slender body.

"Gaby, I love you so," he cried, feeling joyous. He swung her around the room, her dangling feet flying out from him. She clung to his broad shoulders, her body arching against his as she threw her head back and laughed gaily. Whooping, Rayne spun around until both of them were breathless and giddy, and when he came to a stop, their glances met and clung, the question and answer of their need clear in their eyes. Before Rayne could carry her off to the bedroom, a shadow darkened the sunlit patch of the open doorway.

"What's going on here?" Cole Elliott's voice, hard and angry, whipped through the air, shattering the spell they'd created. Turning to face his father, Rayne placed Gaby back on her feet. The dress slithered back into place, falling in pools of bright satin. Cole Elliott gave a start when he saw what she wore.

"Where'd you get that dress," he demanded belligerently. "You had no right to snoop around in things that aren't yours."

"I gave it to her," Rayne said quietly. His eyes were steely as they met his father's. "Her own clothes were wet and she had nothing to wear."

"I guess it don't make any difference to me," Cole said, "It was one yo'r ma left behind when she went. Your woman might as well have it. A whore's dress for a—"

With balled fists Rayne stepped forward. Cole bit off the rest of his words, but they hung in the air between them. The words hurt. Gaby bit her lips to still their trembling.

"Be careful what you say, old man," Rayne said. For a moment the two men squared off as if they might exchange blows.

Cole backed down first. "I'm taking some of the boys down in that stand of mesquite south of here to round up strays," he mumbled, and clamping his hat on his head, stalked out. Rayne turned back to Gaby, but the light of passion had died between them.

"I'll send Sam into town to get you a couple more dresses and to find some Mexican women to clean up the place a little," he said, turning his hat in his hand. "I know it's pretty run-down."

"It's not so bad, Rayne, really it's not," she cried. "It just needs some cleaning up. I'll wash the walls and the floor and . . . and . . . It just needs a little . . ." She looked around, her words trailing off. It needed a great deal. They could both see that.

"I'll have Little Finger mix up some whitewash and leave Billy behind to paint the walls for you tomorrow.

I'm sorry there's no wallpaper and nothing pretty for you."

"It's pretty enough," Gaby cried, her heart aching. Rayne loved his home. She didn't want him to think she didn't love it too.

Rayne looked at her glowing eyes, at the love shining there, and for a moment a smile lit his bleak expression. "It will be pretty, Gaby. Just as soon as I can make it that way. Give me a little time."

"We have all the time we need. We have the rest of our lives," she cried, but Rayne had already swung around and stalked from the room. She watched him cross the porch and in one powerful, fluid motion mount his horse. With a finger he touched the brim of his hat in a final farewell and rode away.

Standing alone in the doorway, Gaby had never felt more lonely. She was not alone on the ranch, she reassured herself. There was Little Finger crossing to the well, and a couple of cowhands further out in the corrals, breaking in wild mustangs, yet she felt alone.

Sam returned just before dusk. He'd ridden hard. He pulled the wagon to a stop before the porch and tossed a package down to Rayne.

"I ran into Miss Lorna at the store," Sam said. "She helped me pick out the dresses. She was real surprised you were back. Wants you to come by and see her."

Rayne said nothing. Casting a quick glance at Gaby, he handed her the package of dresses. Perched on the back of the wagon were two Mexican women. One was plump with a kindly-looking face and gray streaks in her dark hair; the other was young and slim, with lively brown eyes.

"I am Jacinta," the older woman said as she got down from the wagon, "and this is my daughter, Maria. You need help with your house, eh?"

"I'm Gaby. We certainly do need you," Gaby said. She liked the looks of the two women. There was an air of quiet capability about Jacinta and a sparkle of good-natured humor in both their eyes. Maria started to haul some of the supplies from the wagon into the house.

Jacinta looked around, her face carefully guarded as she observed the sad state of the ranch house.

"We will fix it up in no time," she said cheerfully.

"That's what I thought," Gaby said. "It's harder than I'd expected."

"Now there will be three of us. The work will go quick." Jacinta went to look at the sleeping arrangements. "We will sleep in here for tonight," she announced, indicating the second bedroom. "Tomorrow we will move to the loft, is best, *si?*" Gaby had no chance to reply before the woman had sailed off to something else. In no time their belongings had been carried to the bedroom and Jacinta was bustling around the rest of the house, shaking her head and making little tsking sounds under her breath. Her eyes fairly gleamed with eagerness. It was obvious she was needed here, and she already liked the looks of the girl who was to be her mistress. She also liked the tall, lean cowboy who hovered over Gaby protectively. Whenever he looked at the girl, his face softened. It was obvious he was much in love with her in spite of her odd dress.

Jacinta even liked the old man who was the father. She would make all these people comfortable, and perhaps it would ease the tension she felt between them.

At a loss for what to do now and not sure she would have the energy for it anyway, Gaby trailed back to her bedroom looking for Rayne. He was nowhere in the house and she surmised he'd gone to the barn. The package of new dresses lay on the bed. If she hurried she could be dressed and waiting when he returned. She'd like him to see her in something other than the ragtag outfit she'd worn all day.

Eagerly she opened the packet of gowns, wondering who Lorna was. Rayne had seemed uncomfortable when Sam had relayed her message. Had he and Lorna been friends or lovers? The answer was all too clear when she stripped away the brown paper. Inside were three of the dowdiest dresses she'd ever seen. There was not even a row of lace or a ruffle to relieve their severity, and they were all of the same dark, serviceable color. Well, she wouldn't have to worry about their getting soiled, Gaby thought with a wry smile. A knock sounded and Maria entered.

"Here is your water, señorita," she said shyly. "May I hang up your new clothes for you?" she asked, and at Gaby's nod, moved forward to shake out the wrinkles and hang the dresses on the pegs. Her face remained pleasant and unrevealing.

Such ugly gowns, she thought. A beautiful woman such as her mistress should not wear such clothes. Maria sighed. The Texas women had no eye for color. They all seemed to wear these somber clothes. She shrugged and left the room.

Gaby sponged her tired body, feeling better just to remove some of the grime she'd acquired in one day's work. Things didn't seem so bleak to her as they had an hour before. Even the somber dresses couldn't mar her mood. At least they were clean, and they fitted, snuggling up against her tiny waist and flaring over her hips. The bodice was almost too tight across her small breasts, and the high neckline chafed, so she left the top buttons undone, exposing the shadowy hollow between her breasts. Gaby brushed her hair until it gleamed and piled it on top of her head, then sighed as she looked in the mirror. How she longed for something pretty to wear for Rayne.

They ate by candlelight. Rayne was too caught up in the sparkle of Gaby's smile and the light shining in her eyes to notice her dowdy dress. He'd thought of her all afternoon, remembering the hot, quick passion between them. He longed to throw aside the concealing garment and gaze at the pale, soft body he'd come to know as well as his own.

"They might as well be eating cornmeal mush and beans," Jacinta grumbled good-naturedly. It was just as well they were too preoccupied with each other to notice the meal. It had not been her best. There had not been enough time. Tomorrow would be better, much better, and like Gaby earlier that day, Jacinta looked around the room with a keen eye while she plotted what was needed to turn Señor Elliott's ranch into a thing of beauty and comfort.

In the days that followed, Gaby saw the ranch change before her very eyes. Although she worked hard herself to bring about those changes, she had to admit it was Jacinta and Maria who made the difference.

True to his word, Rayne had Little Finger mix a thin white paint and Billy Fuller came to brush it on the mud-plaster walls. Freed of their dinginess, the rooms took on spacious proportions. The women were so pleased with the results in the parlor that they enlisted Billy to do all the rooms, and Rayne, pleased to see Gaby happy and occupied, forgot that he needed every man to gather strays and allowed Billy to stay and help in spite of much grumbling from Cole.

Often when Billy was there working, Maria contrived to be in the same room, her dark eyes watching him shyly from beneath lowered lids. Whenever Billy spoke to Maria, Gaby observed, his face turned red. As the work progressed, he seemed less able to talk freely when Maria was in the room. Gaby hid a smile and looked at Jacinta. The older woman was all too aware of the attraction that was developing between the two young people, and she was carefully guarding her daughter.

With Jacinta's help, Gaby went through the spare storage room, and was surprised to discover a nearly new sofa and matching upholstered chair. Pulling and tugging together, the three women hauled the old wooden furniture outdoors on the porch and placed their new finds strategically before the fireplace. Jacinta rubbed oil into the leather upholstery until the pieces shone like new. Kerosene lamps, their glass shades polished until they gleamed, were placed around the room. A woven rug appeared on the pale wooden floor, the planks gleaming now from repeated scourings.

The pegs driven deep into the parlor walls, which had once held an assortment of clothes and odds and ends, now held a pair of rifles and hats on one side. On the wall at the other end of the room they hung a beautiful Mexican *colcha*.

"It is just the thing," Jacinta said, looking at the covering. "My mother made it many years ago. I remember her working on this when I was but a child."

"It's beautiful, Jacinta," Gaby said. It was the finest piece of handiwork she had ever seen.

"It took her nearly twenty years to complete," Jacinta said. "It is a rare skill brought from Spain."

"Are you sure you want to hang it here?"

"*Sí*. This is my home now too," Jacinta replied. The two women stood admiring the beautiful hanging. Bright prairie flowers and grasses blazed against a creamy white background. It brightened the room considerably.

Slowly the rooms changed, reflecting a different kind of beauty than Gaby had at first envisioned. There were no crystal chandeliers, no gilt-edged furniture, no fine rugs. The rooms and the furnishings seemed to reflect the new land and its people. Everything must serve a purpose. There was no room for the elegant little étagères filled with useless painted china so popular back in New Orleans.

When Rayne returned home each night, he seemed not to notice the changing ranch house. His eyes were only for Gaby. After they'd kissed until they were breathless, Gaby would take his hand and lead him about, pointing out every little addition or improvement. Dutifully he would declare his approval and sweep her back into his arms.

Cole Elliott often expressed his disapproval, muttering and lamenting under his breath, threatening to move to the bunkhouse. His attitude might have undermined Gaby's enthusiasm for work on the house if not for Jacinta.

"Pay him no mind, señorita," Jacinta said. "Some men like to complain. It is part of their nature. He has not moved out yet. When he does will be soon enough to worry." Soon even Gaby began to understand the old man better and to be amused at his constant grumbling. Somehow it made Cole seem less formidable.

Gaby was learning how to live in the hot climate as well. She made it a habit now to rise early, although never as early as Rayne, and to take a nap during the hottest part of the day. She'd learned the importance of opening the shutters to the cool morning and evening air and closing them against the hot glare of the sun. The low adobe-and-stone house stayed surprisingly cool.

Gaby learned to forgo the petticoats and corsets that were so much a part of a lady's dress. Although Maddie had sent her trunk with a variety of gowns and slippers,

Gaby seldom wore them around the ranch. They were unsuitable to her life now. Instead she wore a light cotton blouse and a colorful calico skirt like Maria and her mother wore. Gaby's long dark hair was often twisted into one fat braid and pinned on top of her head during the day, but at night Gaby always dressed, taking time with her appearance, for she loved the look in Rayne's eyes when he saw her thus.

Included in the trunk was a beautiful little music box inlaid with pearl and jade, a gift from old Barbieri thanking her for a most unforgettable evening. The box by rights belonged to Clarisse, Maddie wrote, but she was sending it on to Gaby, knowing she would find a special delight in something so lovely.

Gaby thought of returning the music box, but made the mistake of setting it on the mantel and listening to its gay little tune. It brought back a reminder of home and the people she loved. She was grateful Maddie had sent it.

She seldom saw Rayne during the days now. The men were ranging farther from the ranch house, gathering mavericks for Rayne's herd. He rose before dawn and never returned until well after dark. Gaby was grateful for the presence of the two Mexican women. The days would have been unbearable without them, just as the nights would have been unbearable without Rayne.

Rayne seemed to feel that way too. Little Finger had pulled the chuck wagon out onto the prairie and cooked meals for the men there. At night most of the men just slept out under the stars, too tired to make the ride back to the ranch. Somehow Rayne always forced himself over the miles to get back to Gaby.

Every morning before dawn, he tore himself from Gaby's arms and slung his weary body back into the saddle for the long ride back to camp before his men were stirring. He knew the men looked at each other with knowing winks and joked about his long rides, and he swore he would stay in camp that night, but as the sun fell in the western sky and the purple shadows crept across the land, he turned his mount toward the ranch. Gaby was there. She might not be there tomorrow.

Gaby hated seeing the fatigue and creases of worry on

Rayne's face when he returned late in the evening. Sometimes he seemed too tired even to eat. Tenderly she coddled him, turning back his bed and kneeling to pull off his dust-covered boots. Lovingly she bathed his face and body with warm scented water.

"You'll have my men laughing at me when I ride by," Rayne would protest lightly, but Gaby would only give him a smoldering, enticing smile and let the warm cloth dip lower, washing away the grime and sometimes the fatigue, so that his manhood stirred beneath her fingers and he would clasp her to him. One night they lay drowsing in the aftermath of their lovemaking and Gaby watched Rayne's face, seeing the harsh lines return to his mouth and cheeks.

"What is bothering you, Rayne? Why do you worry so?" she asked softly, running her hands lightly over his bare chest and shoulders in a soft, comforting caress.

"Nothing," he said, catching her hand and carrying it to his lips for light kisses.

"Perhaps I can help you," she insisted.

Rayne turned to look at her earnest face and smiled; then his face turned serious again. "I won't be able to come home nights like I have been," he said. "I'm going to have to stay with my men out at the camp."

"No, Rayne," Gaby protested.

"We have rustlers taking our cows, Gaby. They're slipping in at night and taking what we've worked hard all day to round up. It's taking us twice as long to gather up a herd."

"Can't Dusty and your men stop them?" Gaby asked.

"So far they haven't been able to. The rustlers seem to know just when to come in and help themselves. My men are riding double duty now. I can't ask them to do that while I ride home to be with you. It wouldn't be fair."

"But your father stays there overnight," Gaby protested halfheartedly.

"Pa's getting old now. He can't handle it. It's my responsibility, Gaby," Rayne explained gently, and she saw his concern for her.

"I understand," she said. "You must do it. I'll miss you so much, though." She threw herself into his arms.

Rayne pulled her slight body close to him. It would be
hell for him too. And coupled with the torment of missing her would be his ever-present fear that she'd grow
tired of waiting and would leave him.

"Gaby," he whispered against her throat, and once
again she felt his passion rise, as if for both of them it
could blot out the inevitability of their separation.

So the long days and nights apart began. Occasionally
Rayne returned to the ranch for a night, but more often
than not he was out on the prairie somewhere. Some
nights when the moon was high and full, casting its glow
over the grassy knolls until they were etched in silver and
the shadows of the hollows looked like soft velvet, Gaby
longed to ride across the wild prairie to find Rayne and
be with him, if only for a few hours. But she couldn't ride
a horse.

One afternoon as a haze seemed to lie over the land,
Gaby lay in a hammock on the front porch, her freshly
washed hair trailing over the edge. She lay dreaming of
Rayne, wondering when he'd be back, when she heard
the sound of hoofbeats. The horse and rider turned
toward the barn.

Rayne had returned for something! Afraid she'd miss
him, Gaby hurried across the yard.

She'd just reached the barnyard when Slade Harner
emerged from the dark interior. He grinned when he
caught a glimpse of Gaby, a hot light flaring behind his
pale eyes. Hungrily his gaze slid over her, taking in the
flowing black curls tumbling nearly to her waist. The thin
white blouse clung to her warm body, and one side of the
wide neckline had fallen from a pale, soft shoulder.

Gaby paused when she saw Slade, and a gust of wind
caused the full Mexican skirt to pull tight against her,
outlining her slim hips and tapering legs.

If not for the paleness of her skin, she might have been
mistaken for a Mexican, but the proud lines of her face
and the blue-black of her hair proclaimed her Creole
ancestry. Hot-blooded Creoles, Slade thought, remembering the tales of the other soldiers around the campfire, and he longed to touch her.

Gaby saw the intent in his eyes and backed up. "Where's
Rayne?" she asked.

"He's back at the camp. He sent me back here to get this branding iron." It wasn't exactly the truth. He'd grown bored with chasing down half-wild cows, and tired of the stench of burning hair and hides as they were branded. He'd managed to lose one of the branding irons and on his own had decided to return to the ranch on the pretext of getting another.

"I see," Gaby said, disappointed that Rayne hadn't come himself. She caught the sight of the metal iron he held. "What is it used for?" she asked.

Slade smiled. At least she wasn't running away from him. Who knew where it might lead from here, with a woman like her? He thought of the warm darkness of the barn just a few steps away and of the half-filled hayloft.

"Well, you see, ma'am," he began, "we use these here irons to put the Rocking E Ranch brand on every cow we find that ain't already marked. When we get enough of 'em branded, we'll drive 'em to market and they won't nobody be able to steal our cows."

"Rayne says rustlers are taking the cows already," Gaby cut in.

"Well, there might be some men who take a few head," Slade said. "It ain't that many. Besides, the cows don't belong to nobody until they been branded. Onc't they're branded, the rustlers have to change the brands in order to keep claim to the cattle."

"How can they do that, if the brand is already put on the cows?" Gaby asked.

"Like this," Slade said. "Come here and let me show you." He put the iron to the ground and pressed down, leaving an imprint of the brand in the dust. Purposefully he'd made it closer to the barn, so she was forced to move nearer to see it.

"It seems impossible to change a brand," Gaby murmured, studying the mark on the ground.

"It's easy to do," Slade declared, forgetting himself as he picked up a stick and began to make other drawings in the dirt, always moving closer to the barn. "For example, if they find cattle that have an S brand, they just make it into a figure eight or they add a bar or a box or a circle, anything to make it different."

"You mean like this?" Gaby asked, and picking up a twig, completed the curved line below the E of the Elliott brand until a full circle had been made. So absorbed in her drawing was she that she didn't see the jerk of Slade's head or the narrowing of his eyes. He'd revealed too much, he thought, or had he? Did she already know something? Had Rayne said something? Was Rayne suspicious of him?

Maybe this would be a good time to clear out, but first he'd have a taste of the delights this New Orleans woman had to offer.

Hoofbeats sounded. Slade whirled around, his hand moving toward the gun on his hip. He half-expected to see Rayne riding up to accuse him. He relaxed a little when he saw the old man. Crotchety bastard that he was, Slade felt no concern over him.

"What are you doing down here at the ranch, Slade?" Cole demanded.

"I'm just leaving, boss," Slade said placatingly. "We lost an iron and I came back to get some extras." He held up the branding iron.

"We had extras at the chuck wagon," Cole snapped.

"Well, now, I never gave that a thought," Slade said, and this time he let insolence creep into his smile. There was nothing the old man could do anyhow. Everyone knew it was Rayne who ran things now. Offhandedly Slade kicked at the ground, letting the dust fall over the drawings he'd made.

"Get on back out there," Cole snapped. "We need every hand we got to gather them cows."

"Yes, sir," Slade, and making a mocking salute, ambled away toward his horse.

Cole turned back to Gaby to give her the tongue-lashing she deserved. No decent woman would stand out in the yard half-dressed, talking to one of the ranch hands.

Gaby, anticipating Cole's reactions, had already turned her back and was striding back toward the house.

"Jezebel," Cole spat. He'd kept his voice loud enough for her to hear, but she made no answer. She climbed the steps and went into the ranch house without a backward glance. Cole glanced back at the ground where they'd stood and caught sight of the scratchings in the dirt.

Part of an E and the circle around it were still visible. Thoughtfully Cole studied the drawing, then rode out over the prairie toward camp.

7

"No, no, you cannot do this," Jacinta protested. "You will hurt yourself and Señor Elliott will blame me."

"No, he won't. I'll tell him it was my idea," Gaby said, and continued toward the barn. Jacinta and Maria followed.

"Ha," Jacinta cried, throwing up her hands. "Such stubbornness in a woman is not pretty."

"I have no wish to be merely pretty," Gaby said crisply. "I want to learn to ride horseback."

"Wait until Señor Rayne comes back. He will teach you," Jacinta implored.

"Billy has agreed to do it," Gaby replied. "Besides, I want to surprise Rayne."

"He will be more than surprised when you are dead or injured."

"Nothing will happen," Gaby reassured her housekeeper, but Jacinta's words were chipping away at her own courage. They reached the corral, where Billy waited with two saddled horses. Apprehensively Gaby peered through the railing. They were two of the meanest-looking horses she'd ever seen. The horses stared back at her, their eyes rolling, their nostrils flaring as they stamped the ground to disperse the prairie flies that landed on their flanks.

"I've given you Gray Lady," Billy said, indicating a mare. "She's about the gentlest horse we've got."

"She's awfully big," Gaby said weakly.

"Would you rather wait until Mr. Elliott is here to help

you?" Billy asked hopefully. His question merely stiffened Gaby's resolve.

"No, I'm going to learn now," she said, and crawled through the fence. She'd donned a pair of Billy's old pants and her own walking boots for this attempt. Even Billy's pants had proven too big for her and she'd tied them up at the waist with a rawhide sash. They bagged at the seat. She knew she looked funny. Maria had barely been able to suppress a giggle, but it didn't matter. No one but the three of them would see her anyway, and she was determined to learn to ride a horse. One day she could go riding across the prairie with Rayne.

"Put your left foot in this stirrup and pull yourself up into the saddle," Billy said, and then, eyeing her short figure, looked around the corral. "We'll have to find a mounting block for you to stand on," he said over his shoulder as he headed toward the barn. But Gaby hadn't heard his last comment. She placed her foot in the stirrup as he'd instructed and as she'd seen Rayne and his men do hundreds of times. It was higher up than she'd expected and she couldn't get enough leverage to pull herself the rest of the way up into the saddle. The horse shied at the uneven weight on her saddle. Awkwardly Gaby tried to hop closer to the horse, but again the horse moved and she was dragged across the corral, her foot still stuck in the stirrup. Frantically she clung to the edge of the saddle, as the horse became increasingly nervous and began to prance around the corral.

"Billy, help her," Maria cried, and Billy ran back from the barn, his astonishment growing as he saw Gaby clinging to the saddle of the prancing horse. Even as Billy watched, Gray Lady broke into a gallop around the corral, brushing dangerously close to the railing in an attempt to brush away her clinging burden.

"Hang on, Miss Gaby," Billy called, and ran toward the horse. If Gaby lost her grip, she might fall back and be dragged behind the horse. So intent were they all that they didn't hear the dull thud of a horse approaching.

Gaby's arms felt as if they were being pulled from their sockets. She couldn't hold on much longer. She could feel her hands slipping, and wildly she flailed out, her grasping fingers scrabbling at the saddle. An involuntary scream escaped her.

"Don't scream," Billy cried. "You'll spook the horse more." It was too late. The mare reared up on her hind legs and Gaby was thrown free, rolling over and over on the hard ground while the frightened horse galloped away to the other end of the corral.

Gaby rolled to a stop and lay stunned for a moment. Jacinta and Maria hurried into the corral and bent over her anxiously.

"Señorita Gaby," Jacinta cried, and when Gaby didn't answer, clasped her hands together. "Santa Maria, she is dead." Gaby opened one eye and looked at the poor woman.

"No, I'm not, Jacinta," she said wearily. She sat up and winced as pain shot through her hips.

"Gracias a Dios," Jacinta babbled, rolling her eyes and crossing herself. "I thought you were dead. Señor Rayne will never forgive me if you are dead." Jacinta helped Gaby to her feet.

"I'm sorry, Miss Gaby," Billy said, looking at her anxiously.

"That's all right, Billy. It wasn't your fault." Gaby swiped at her clothes. She was smeared with dirt and her hair had tumbled down from its braid and lay untidily around her shoulders. "I'll try again tomorrow."

"Are you Gaby?" a voice asked, and everyone swung around to find a woman with a much-bemused look on her face sitting astride a horse. She looked so at ease there, Gaby couldn't help feeling envious. She was dressed in pants much as Gaby was, except that hers fit, showing off her long, lean limbs and rounded hips. She wore a jacket over her shirt and a wide-brimmed hat to ward off the sun.

"Yes, I'm Gaby."

"I'm Lorna Blake," the woman said. "I'm a friend of Rayne's."

Had she emphasized her relationship to Rayne?

Raising her chin, Gaby stepped forward and smiled graciously. "I am Gabrielle Reynaud," she said, giving her full name. She had a need for a little extra dignity right now, she thought wryly.

"You're the person who needed the dresses," Lorna said.

"Yes, I am," she said lightly, "and I haven't thanked you for your kindness. My own clothes hadn't arrived yet and I was in need of something to tide me over. How clever of you to guess my size so closely. They fit very well."

"What are you doing here?" Lorna demanded bluntly, and Gaby pretended not to understand the reason for her question.

"I was learning to ride a horse," she answered, and saw Lorna's lips tighten in annoyance.

"Before you can learn to ride a horse, you have to get on it. I don't think you made it," she said smugly.

"You sit a horse so well," Gaby said. "Did you have trouble learning to ride?"

"None," Lorna answered. "My father put me on a horse when I was three and I've been riding ever since." The woman was impervious in her superiority. She smiled at Gaby as if to a child.

"You said you are a friend of Rayne's," Gaby said, feeling less and less friendly herself.

"Yes, friends," Lorna answered, and once again the word implied more. Gaby bit the inside of her lip to hide the anger.

Jacinta and Maria stirred beside her. "Señorita Gaby, I will go to the house and prepare a little something to eat and drink," Jacinta offered. Although she didn't like the woman, certain rules of hospitality on the plains must be observed.

"Thank you, Jacinta," Gaby said, and turned back to Lorna. "You will join me for tea or cocoa?"

"Tea or cocoa?" Lorna repeated derisively. "Oh yes. Sam told me you were from New Orleans." Obviously it was a place without any redeeming qualities in Lorna's estimation.

"Yes." Gaby nodded and tried again to be friendly. "Have you always lived here in Texas?"

"All my life." Lorna climbed down from the horse and tied the reins to the railing before turning to face Gaby. "Like Rayne, I'm a Texan fully born and raised. We are a sturdy stock." The pride was evident in her voice.

"How lovely," Gaby said, and the Texas girl missed the irony in her voice. They followed Jacinta and Maria up to the house; Gaby matched her stride to Lorna's longer-legged one. She was growing used to half-running to keep up with these Texans. Proudly she led Lorna into the parlor. The other woman couldn't keep the surprise from her face when she saw the changes that had been wrought.

"You've done a lot of work here," she acknowledged. "You look like you're settling in for a long stay."

"A very long stay," Gaby affirmed. "Please make yourself at home while I wash off some of this dirt." She hurried away toward her room.

Once there, Gaby tore off the baggy pants and the now-dirty shirtwaist. Quickly she washed the dirt from her face and arms, then took out one of the gowns Maddie had sent her from New Orleans. It was a deep mulberry color with a small black print, and was one of Gaby's favorites. It made her look more grown-up and elegant. Quickly she pulled her hair back into a loose knot on top of her head and pinched some color into her cheeks. It was the best she could do on such short notice. Good manners dictated that she not take longer.

She returned to the parlor, her head high, her cheeks flushed from her haste. Lorna stood before the mantel, the tinkling notes of the music box filling the air. She whirled, looking guilty when Gaby entered, and promptly closed the lid, although it was obvious she'd been enjoying the little box.

"It's very pretty, isn't it?" Gaby said. "It was a gift to me."

"A gift?" Lorna repeated, and it was plain she wondered if the gift had come from Rayne. Gaby didn't enlighten her. "It's a frivolous toy for out here on the prairie. The dust will get inside the works and clog it."

"Perhaps," Gaby replied, "but then, maybe it's sturdier than it looks."

Lorna glanced at Gaby. The Creole girl was quicker on her feet than Lorna had expected. The message had been given and made clear. Gaby might look like a hothouse flower, but she was determined to stay and survive here on the Texas plains.

"You know, a little whitewash doesn't do the whole job," Lorna said, and her voice was challenging. "Much more than that is needed."

Gaby studied her words. "That's true," she admitted, "but it's a beginning. The rest will follow in its proper time."

"That's what I'm counting on," Lorna replied.

Jacinta brought the tray of refreshments and Gaby poured coffee for Lorna and cocoa for herself.

"Is Rayne around?" Lorna asked, as one would inquire of a servant the whereabouts of his master. Fire flared behind Gaby's eyes, but she kept her voice polite and held out a small plate of Mexican cakes Jacinta had baked the day before.

"No. He's out at the camp. They've been gathering up strays for a fall roundup."

"I'm on my way out there now," Lorna said. "I thought Rayne and I could ride out together."

"You're going out to the roundup camp?" Gaby asked.

"Yes, I've ridden out there several times." Lorna smiled. Gaby struggled to keep her dismay from showing. "I suppose you haven't seen Rayne for several days now."

"No, I haven't," Gaby replied stiffly.

"He's well, a little tired perhaps. He isn't resting well at night, what with the cattle rustlers and"—she paused significantly, casting a glance from under her lashes—"other things."

"I see," Gaby said, and hoped her voice was even. Inside, she was seething with anger.

"They'll soon have enough cows for a good-sized herd. What with our herd and Rayne's, we should have more than three thousand head to drive to market."

"Will your cattle be going with Rayne's?" Gaby asked.

"Yes, Rayne and I talked it over and decided it was wisest. We'll have more protection that way."

"Will you be going on the trail drive too?" Gaby asked tightly. Her rage mounted. While she had sat home docilely waiting for Rayne to have time for her, this woman had ridden out to see him several times and now she was planning to go on a trail drive with him.

"We've talked about my going with him," Lorna said smugly, leaving the impression that she and Rayne had talked extensively about many things. When she'd let the pause stretch unbearably long she smiled at Gaby. "I always follow Rayne's advice about these things."

"Whatever did you do during the war?" Gaby asked, deliberately keeping her eyes wide and innocent.

Lorna's gaze flicked up to Gaby's face, then back to her cup. "I waited for him," she said simply, and once again raised her head to meet Gaby's gaze. All the hostility she felt for this Creole usurper was there in her eyes. Gaby had taken her man, but Lorna wasn't giving up without a fight.

There was about the Texas woman a sense of independence and freedom that was new to Gaby. She felt sure she would have liked Lorna if there had not been Rayne between them. She felt saddened by the thought. She'd begun to understand that there were few women in the area and most of them lived far apart. Maybe in time, when Lorna saw that Gaby was here to stay and had given up on Rayne and chosen some other man, maybe then they could be friends. With that thought in mind, Gaby rose and held out her hand.

"I'm glad to have met you, Lorna," she said. The tone of her voice was friendly and warm, taking Lorna by surprise. Lorna looked at the hand, then took it for a brief handshake. The Creole girl's hand was soft and small like a child's, Lorna noted, and yet the grip was firm and sure. Troubled, Lorna turned to the door.

"Rayne tells me you have no people back in New Orleans. You're an orphan," Lorna said.

"That might be said of me," Gaby said faintly. How could Rayne have discussed her with his old mistress? Gaby felt betrayed.

"How did you survive? Were you in an orphanage?"

"No, a friend of my mother's took care of me after she died." Then: "Look," Gaby cried, grateful for a distraction, "someone's coming."

A plume of dust rose on the horizon, then grew bigger. Obviously it was several riders approaching the ranch house. With bated breath Gaby waited as the men rode into the ranch yard. They were covered with dust and bearded with several days' growth, but the figure in the saddle of a big roan was too familiar to Gaby now for her not to recognize him instantly.

"Rayne," she cried, and fairly flew off the porch. He dismounted and caught her up in his arms, crushing her to him. His kiss was hungry and long, wakening smoldering fires in her. Happily Gaby planted little kisses all over his face, mindless of the stubby beard that scratched her soft skin.

The creak of leather as his men dismounted and led their weary mounts to the barn reminded them they were not alone. Gaby drew back, her face flushed, her eyes dancing with soft lights that delighted Rayne.

Lorna saw the looks on their faces and her heart turned cold with fear. She'd seen the love in Rayne's eyes when he'd spoken of Gaby, but she'd thought it an infatuation he would soon outgrow. Now she began to doubt, but pushed that doubt aside. She wouldn't give him up that easily. She'd known Rayne as a child, they'd grown up together, Thad, Rayne, and her. When he'd come back briefly to see his father before going off to fight for the South, Lorna had decided then to wait. Someday she intended to marry Rayne Elliott. Their two ranches together would make one of the biggest spreads in Texas.

They were Texans, Rayne and she. They belonged together. He'd soon grow tired of this pale, helpless bit of fluff. Anchoring a smile on her face, she started down the steps as if she already owned the ranch and its land.

Rayne raised his head and looked at her. "Hello, Lorna," he said in surprise.

"Hello, Rayne," she said easily. "I came to meet your little"—she paused—"friend. We've been getting acquainted."

"That's nice of you. I've worried about Gaby out here without anyone to talk to except Maria and Jacinta. I haven't had much chance to introduce her to people yet."

"I haven't needed anyone else," Gaby replied, gazing up at him. His arm tightened about her and his eyes glinted with a special message for her.

"That can be remedied after the fall roundups," Lorna replied, keeping the smile on her face, although her jaws were beginning to ache. "There will be dances in Fowler."

"Good, I'll take Gaby to some of them," Rayne said, smiling down at Gaby, delighted at the prospect of showing her off. Remembering his manners, he looked back at Lorna. "Can you stay and have dinner with us?"

"Dad's waiting for me. Perhaps another time."

"Thank you for coming, Lorna," Gaby said. She felt less threatened by the tall, brusque woman now that Rayne stood at her side, holding her.

Lorna untied her horse and mounted with ease. One day soon, I'll do that too, Gaby thought, and waved farewell. Rayne's arm slid around her waist and upward to lightly brush her breast, and suddenly Gaby felt breathless as she turned to smile up at him. Hand in hand they walked back to the ranch house.

Lorna cantered out of the ranch yard and down past the corrals. Slade Harner was leaning against the rail fence smoking a cigarette.

" 'Afternoon, Miss Lorna," he drawled, his hazel eyes bright and hard as he ran his gaze up and down her body. Lorna bit back a scathing retort and contrived to be friendly.

"Slade," she answered in greeting, then reined in her horse as she remembered something she'd heard the cowboy say once. "You've been to New Orleans. What do you know about Gabrielle Reynaud?"

Slade turned a sly smile on her. "What happened, Miss Lorna?" he asked, leisurely drawing on his cigarette. "Somebody take your man?"

"Don't be impertinent, you polecat," Lorna snapped. She sat considering the cowhand with a long, hard look that made him squirm a bit. Lorna hadn't lived on a ranch all her life without learning how to handle the men that drifted in and out.

"I've heard some talk about cattle rustling up north of here," she said crisply, "and who they suspect did it."

Slade's eyes darkened as he met her gaze. "I don't know what you're talking about," he asserted.

"Don't you?" Lorna asked. "Folks around here are getting kind of anxious about the cows they're losing. If I were to drop a word or two, what do you suppose they'd do if I mentioned your name?"

"You bitch," Slade snarled. His mouth looked vicious,

his eyes deadly. "She came from the Court of Angels," he said reluctantly. "It's a fancy house of prostitution back in New Orleans."

Lorna's eyes widened in surprise and delight. So Rayne's little mistress had grown up in a whorehouse. The Creole girl wasn't as innocent as she appeared. Lorna couldn't imagine Rayne bringing a prostitute back to his ranch. No wonder Cole Elliott hated her so much.

Now she smiled and eased back in the saddle. She was torn between feeling anger with Rayne for leaving her flat for a mere whore and elation that the girl could be easily routed.

Lorna studied Slade Harner. He'd been surprisingly malleable when she'd mentioned the rustlers. It had been a shot in the dark. As long as he stayed away from Bar B cattle, she wouldn't say anything just yet. She might have need of Slade Harner's services again.

She leaned forward and smiled down at Slade. "Have you told anyone else about this?" she asked, and he shook his head. "Why not?" she demanded, and read the answer in his eyes. Somehow he would blackmail his way into Gaby's bed. Lorna smiled again. "Good luck," she said, and wheeled her horse to leave, then thought of something else.

"Your secret is safe with me," she said. "I can't even remember the name of the man they mentioned." She galloped away. Slade Harner stood watching her and the way her trim buttocks fit the saddle. She was a dangerous woman. She knew more about him than he wanted anyone to know, and she wouldn't hesitate to use it when it best suited her purposes. Next time she might want something from him that he couldn't deliver. Slade Harner's eyes narrowed. He might have to get rid of her, he thought, tossing away his cigarette butt.

The night was long and satisfying. Gaby's body hummed from Rayne's touch, her skin grew tender from the brush of his lips and the chin that was at first prickly and unshaven and later smooth and brown beneath her fingers. They loved one another, and rested only to waken and touch again. Their need seemed insatiable. And when the first rays of light began to brighten the eastern horizon, they lay at last exhausted and fulfilled, wrapped in each other's arms.

"Want to go into Fowler with me?" he asked over a plateful of eggs and beefsteak.

"You mean now, today?" Gaby asked. Her face brightened at the prospect and he realized he hadn't taken her anywhere since bringing her to the ranch.

"Now, today. I have to go to the deeds office and handle things on the Avery property. After the fall drive, I'll have the money to pay for the land."

"I'd love to go," Gaby cried, and hurried away to her room to dress. She chose one of the New Orleans gowns and took special care with her coiffure, then perched a tiny elaborate bonnet on top of it all. It felt wonderful to dress up again.

Fowler wasn't much of a town, if one compared it to New Orleans or even to Galveston, but to Gaby it was fine. With bright, curious eyes she stared at the wooden frame buildings and the people moving about the dusty streets and plank walks. She was too busy looking to notice the glances she received, but Rayne's head was high with pride.

Rayne pulled the wagon to a stop in front of the general store. "I thought you might like to look around in here while I go on down to the deeds office," he said.

He took Gaby inside the store and introduced her to the proprietor, a slim man with graying hair and wire-rimmed spectacles. Even as Rayne was introducing Caleb Greene, the shopkeeper's alert gaze moved from one corner of his store to the other, checking his customers' needs and keeping an eye on his merchandise.

Gaby browsed. She was amazed at the variety of goods the store had to offer. There were barrels of nails and foodstuffs and tables piled high with cloth and ribbons. In the corners stood plows and on the wall hung rifles and handguns. At one end of the store were shelves of boots and hats and stacks of heavy canvas trousers. Leather chaps hung beside calico gowns. Jars of coffee beans, spices, and peppermint candy sticks sat on the wooden counter.

"Good mornin', Mrs. Ames," Caleb said to a woman in a calico bonnet. She carried a basket.

"Caleb, I brought you some eggs this morning," she said.

"I can use 'em." He began to count out the eggs, and taking out a ledger, wrote down the amount.

"Caleb, I'm needin' some extra things this morning," the woman said. "I'm wonderin' what you can give me on this brooch." The woman held out a piece of jewelry. "It belonged to my mother. She give it to me when I was first married, but now my man and me need the money."

Caleb took the brooch and studied it, and finally offered her a price.

"Seems like it should have been worth more than that," the woman said, "but I reckon I'll take it." Gaby listened as the two completed the deal, marveling at the way of commerce here in the western town.

"Did you find anything you want?" Rayne asked, and Gaby swung around to greet him. He'd taken less time than she'd expected.

"No, I haven't," she answered, "but I enjoyed looking."

"Are you hungry?"

Gaby nodded, suddenly realizing she was. It must be well past noon and they'd risen and eaten an early breakfast before starting for town.

"The hotel has a dining room. We'll go there," Rayne said, and together they left the store.

"Well, if it ain't Rayne and his little woman," a voice said, and Thad Martin stepped up on the walk. Gaby hadn't seen him since that first day on the dock in Galveston, but she couldn't forget his face. This was the man who had wrapped Cook Avery and his son in raw hides and left them to die.

"Martin," Rayne said, and Gaby sensed him shifting his weight forward so she was partially blocked from Thad's view.

"How is the lovely Miss Reynaud?" Thad asked, tipping his hat in a mocking greeting.

"I'm fine, thank you, Mr. Martin," Gaby replied stiffly.

"I understand you've been out talking to Cook Avery's widow." Thad turned his attention back to Rayne.

"That's right. Somebody killed her husband and the poor woman needs some help."

"Well, that's right neighborly of you to pitch in like

that, Rayne," Thad said with a grin. "Could it be you're buttering up the widow to buy her land."

"Mrs. Avery's already offered her land to me. I'm buying it," Rayne stated bluntly.

The grin on Thad's face faded. "I wouldn't bother, if I was you, Rayne. You ain't going to need any more land."

"Don't threaten me, Thad," Rayne snapped. "I'm not one of your sniveling gunmen or one of the small helpless ranchers you've been harassing. Pa and me have been ranching in this territory all my life and we aren't going to stop doing it because someone like you tells us."

"That's a real uncooperative attitude, Rayne," Thad said, balancing his weight on the balls of his feet. The spurs on his boots jingled restlessly. "My men and me'll have to do something to change it."

"You and your men don't scare me, Martin. Stay out of my way." For a moment Thad tensed as if about to draw, and Gaby felt the same tenseness in Rayne. This time she knew better than to get in the way. She drew back toward the general store. The moment passed. Someone shouted. Passersby glanced at the two men, then paused to watch, but Thad glanced around as if looking for someone, then backed down. He flashed his teeth in a smile that never quite reached his eyes, and held out his hands palms up.

"Now, now, Rayne. No need to go getting all riled, when we can work things out in a neighborly fashion."

"There's nothing to work out, Martin. Stay away from me and stay off my land." Turning, Rayne caught Gaby's elbow and hurried down the street. Gaby couldn't resist trying to look back, fearful of what Thad Martin might do.

"Don't look back," Rayne admonished.

"But he might shoot you in the back," Gaby cried.

"Not while there are witnesses," Rayne said, and kept walking toward the hotel.

8

"Gaby, you can't go." Rayne's voice was adamant. He threw back the covers and reached for his pants.

"Why not?" she insisted.

"It's no place for a woman," he answered gruffly, pulling on his boots. He stamped his foot against the floor to settle the boot on more comfortably and looked at the small figure on the bed. His heart sank as he noted the determined slant of her chin. In the few months they'd been together he'd come to know that look and understand what it meant. When Gaby made up her mind, she wasn't easily dissuaded.

"Lorna Blake goes out to the camp," Gaby said. Her voice was accusing as she glared at Rayne. He glanced away. Sometimes Gaby saw more than he wanted her to. He cursed under his breath. Lorna wasn't making this any easier, either, by showing up at the roundup camp and coming here to tell Gaby about it.

"Lorna's not like other women," he mumbled in a vain attempt to explain. Even as he said the words he realized they were a mistake.

"Oh?" Gaby's fists were planted on her hips, her eyes challenging as they met his.

Rayne sighed. "She's not a woman like you," he said, and knew he'd made matters worse. Rising from the side of the bed, he reached for her, trying to woo her out of her mood. "Lorna's not the sweet . . . and dainty . . . and"—he dropped light kisses on her face and lips with each compliment—" and helpless . . . and—" Sharp elbows thrust against his chest, driving a wedge between them. Rayne stood back and looked down at the small body quivering with indignation. The sweet mouth worked angrily.

"I am not helpless, Rayne Elliott," Gaby sputtered. "I am not a dainty little Creole doll to be kept in the house while you go off to do your man's work. I can do anything any other woman can do. Once I've learned to do something, I can do it better than most people." She knew she sounded boastful, but her pride was hurt.

"Gaby, you can't even ride a horse," Rayne said, trying not to show his amusement. He loved her defiance and independence, but he hadn't the time for it this morning.

"How do you know I can't ride?" she demanded.

"You told me so, remember?" His eyes sparkled with laughter; then the light died away as he thought of something else. "Besides, I saw Lorna in town yesterday and she told me what she saw when she rode out here the other day. I don't want you to try riding again. You'll break your neck."

"Don't coddle me so much," Gaby flared. "I won't break, Rayne."

"I don't want to take that chance. I love you, Gaby. I want to know that you'll be here waiting for me when I ride in at night." The words of love that normally would have warmed her, only added fire to her anger.

"That's all you ever want from me," she cried, venting the frustrations that had been building for weeks. "I can do more than just sit here and wait for you to spare a few minutes out of your day for me. I want to be a part of your life outside of this room." She waved an arm around their bedroom. "I want to know what it is you're doing out there all these weeks. I want to know the dangers and weariness. I want to share it with you, Rayne."

"Gaby . . ." He came back to gather her up in his arms. "Don't you know I think of you a thousand times a day. I can hardly keep my mind on my work sometimes. I warned you that life out here would be different from anything you're used to. I know you get lonely, but you have Maria and Jacinta. You'll have to make that do. I can't share the ranch work with you. Trust me when I say it's not fitting for a woman to be out on the range. It's

too dangerous. The sun would burn your beautiful skin."
His hand glided up her arm.

"I have a parasol," Gaby said, refusing to respond to
his kiss. Rayne sighed and let her go.

"Those little bits of lace and silk aren't going to protect
you from the prairie sun. You remember what it was like
when we traveled here. That was spring. It's much worse
now that it's summer. Take my advice and stay here at
the ranch. If you get too bored, Billy can take you and
the other women into town." He turned away and this
time there was finality in his voice. "Billy will be instructed that he is not to saddle a horse for you."

"Rayne!" Gaby cried in outrage, and looking back at
her angry face, he relented a bit.

"Wait until I have some time after roundup," he said,
"and I'll teach you to ride, but I forbid you to try it again
now." He went out, closing the door behind him. Gaby
stood where she was, her dark eyes stormy, her brows
pulled down in defiance. He forbade her. How dare he?
For weeks she'd been docile and accommodating to his
every whim; now he thought her obedient! Well, Rayne
Elliott was about to learn a new side to Gabrielle Reynaud.
Purposefully she turned toward the table that held the
pitcher of water and began preparing for the day.

"I don't think Mr. Elliott's going to like this," Billy
said later as Gaby stood in the middle of the corral,
impatiently tapping her foot in the dust.

"He told you not to saddle a riding horse for me,
didn't he?"

"Yes, ma'am," Billy said. "But—"

"He said nothing of hitching up a wagon for me, did
he?" Gaby's dark eyes pinned him down without mercy.

"No, ma'am," Billy said, feeling defeated already.

"Then hitch up the wagon, Billy," Gaby ordered. "We're
going out to the roundup."

"Yes, ma'am," he said, and hurried off to do as she'd
bidden. He hated to contemplate Rayne Elliott's face
when he came driving up with Miss Gaby.

It took them longer to reach the roundup site than
Gaby had thought it would. They jostled and bumped
across the prairie beneath a burning sun. She'd left behind a disapproving Jacinta, but Maria sat on the back of

the wagon. With a bone-rattling jar the wheels rolled over yet another ridge.

With one hand Gaby grasped the seat so she wouldn't be thrown from the wagon. With the other she tried to shield herself from the glaring sun with the lace-and-silk parasol. It was nearly midday and the sun was at its peak. A sheen of perspiration rested permanently on her upper lip. She'd long ago given up wiping it away. Her face itched with a coating of sweat and dust and she could feel the trickle of moisture roll down her scalp toward one ear. Her determination was flagging and for a moment she thought of the shaded ranch house and the cool drinks Jacinta brought to her throughout the day. She couldn't back down now.

"There they are," Billy cried, and relief and dread mingled in his voice. Gaby stiffened her spine and sat up straighter, risking her hold on the edge of the seat to dab at her face with a handkerchief.

In a flurry of hoofbeats and a cloud of dust, Rayne was upon them. "Gaby, what the hell are you doing out here?" he demanded. "I thought I told you to stay at the ranch." His eyes snapped with irritation and his mouth was a thin, hard line. Gaby looked at his angry face, feeling less certain, and then she caught the movement of another rider coming toward them.

"Looks like you forgot to tell Lorna Blake to stay home," she said sweetly.

Rayne glanced over his shoulder at the approaching rider and shrugged. "The Bar B ranch is branding here too," he explained with a casualness that seemed feigned. "Clarence Blake is going with me on the drive."

"Howdy," Lorna called, bringing her horse to a stop near Rayne's.

"Hello," Gaby answered. The two women eyed each other. Lorna grinned when she took in the beribboned hat and dainty parasol Gaby carried. Lorna wore a high-crowned, wide-brimmed hat much like the men's and she sat her horse confidently. Once again she was dressed in pants and a shirt and seemed to belong there. In her pale dress Gaby felt frivolous and out of place, and irrationally grew angry at Rayne for that.

"I see you've given up trying to learn to ride a horse." Lorna said, looking at the clumsy wagon.

"Only temporarily," Gaby answered, her gaze locked with Rayne's. He glanced away from the anger he saw in her eyes.

"Billy," he ordered, "I want you to turn this wagon around and take Miss Gaby back to the ranch."

"Yes, sir," Billy said, and picked up the reins.

"But we've just arrived," Gaby protested.

"And you're just leaving," Rayne said adamantly.

"I came to see what a roundup is all about." Gaby insisted.

"There's nothing here to see," Rayne said. "You'll just get in the way." His words ignited Gaby's anger.

"I'm sorry you consider me so much trouble," she said evenly.

"I didn't mean it that way."

"Let her stay, Rayne," Lorna said. "I'll keep an eye on her for you." Rayne looked at the woman who'd been his friend nearly all his life. For a brief time before the war, they'd been more, but that was behind them now and nearly forgotten. Rayne had no room in his life for any other woman than Gaby. Now he considered Lorna's offer. It would be one way of ensuring Gaby's safety while he returned to his men.

"You can stay as long as you remain with Lorna," he said finally. Gaby sensed she had little choice.

"How kind of you to offer to escort me around," she said, smiling charmingly and twirling her parasol. If she were being forced into the role of a helpless doll, she would play it to the hilt, she decided. "Rayne worries about me far too much. He's so protective."

She turned back to the dark-haired man, letting a smile cover the simmering resentment he'd aroused. "Rayne, honey, don't let me keep you. Lorna will take good care of me."

Gaby watched him ride away. He looked tired and worried. The powerful shoulders drooped with fatigue, and still he pushed himself. Were the rustlers still harassing the herds? she wondered. Was there danger to Rayne? Concern for him twisted within her chest and softened her beautiful face.

"It was a surprise to see you here," Lorna was saying.

"I love surprises," Gaby responded, meeting the challenge in Lorna's gaze with one of her own. Lorna sat her horse, studying Gaby. Had she been wrong to dismiss this interloper so quickly? Behind that innocent smile, was there a flash of iron will? Perhaps the battle would be more interesting than she'd thought.

"Have you been to a roundup before?" she asked.

"No, I haven't," Gaby replied, glancing around the valley and noting the noise and movement generated by the men and cattle.

"Then you're in for a few surprises yourself," Lorna nudged her horse with a booted heel. Billy slapped the reins against the horses' backs and the clumsy wagon followed Lorna down the incline right into the melee. Wide-eyed, Gaby watched as men expertly cut a bull out of the milling herd. A grass rope was swung in wide lazy circles, then dropped expertly over the bull horns. Another cowboy rode up behind the steer and cast his rope, snaring the animal's hind legs. Seemingly without any command from the rider, the sturdy pony came to a halt, his hooves digging into the soft prairie soil. The ropes tightened and the bull seemed to be pulled in both directions. He toppled to the ground.

"Oh, he's hurt!" Gaby cried. Lorna merely looked amused. While the bull lay struggling against his ropes, two men rushed forward. One man leaned his weight on the struggling front legs while another man pressed an iron against the hindquarters.

"What are they doing to him?" Gaby asked.

"They're branding him," Lorna said, surprised that Gaby didn't know even that much. "Let's go take a closer look."

"I'm not sure we should," Gaby said weakly, looking round for Rayne.

"Nonsense. Don't be a greener," Lorna said derisively. "It isn't dangerous." Before Gaby could protest further, Lorna rode away. Warily Gaby motioned Billy to follow. The wagon rattled across the bumpy prairie and closer to the branding fires. A stench of smoke, sweat, and singed hair permeated the air. Gaby felt her stomach roil and quickly clasped a lacy handkerchief to her nose. Down here, nearer the herd and the fire, the sun seemed to burn hotter.

Dust rose in the air, kicked up by the working men and their horses and by the frightened cattle. Gaby gasped in the dust-laden air. There was a confusion of sound, smells, and sights. Cowhands yipped and called to the cows they were herding. A staccato of pounding hoofbeats ended abruptly in the frightened bawl of a calf as it was roped and yanked on its side.

Logs flanked either side of the firepit, and iron rods leaned against them, their ends resting in the hot coals so the letters and symbols glowed red.

"The iron has to be hot enough to burn through the hair into the hide and leave a scab that peels away clean, without blurring the brand," Lorna explained.

"You mean they put these hot irons on the cows?" Gaby asked.

"Of course," Lorna replied. "The object is to burn in the brand so it can't be easily changed."

"It's so cruel," Gaby said.

"Not really," Lorna replied impatiently. "The cows can't feel anything." The frantic bawl of a young calf as the iron was set against his hide made Gaby doubt Lorna's words. Quickly she averted her eyes.

A commotion near the herd drew her attention. Silently she watched as Slade Harner cut a cow out of a herd. With frightened rolling eyes, the cow darted away from the cowhand's rope, then turned back to the herd. A high-pitched bawl sounded on the air and the cow's head swung back toward her calf. On spindly legs the little one tried to follow his mother's erratic path. With a whistle and a cry, Slade maneuvered the cow around. Distracted by the cry of her calf, the cow made only a halfhearted attempt to elude the rope that slid over her horns.

Keeping his rope slack, Slade flipped it over the cow's flanks and spurred his horse away so the rope pulled taut, forcing the cow's head to the side. The rope bit into the hind legs and with a sickening crunch the cow went down. Her eyes rolled wildly as if seeking help from someone, while she bellowed in pain, struggled, then went still. The calf ran to stand beside his mother's still body, crying for the comfort and reassurance he'd know, but the cow made no move.

"Slade," Rayne called, galloping up. He got off his horse and went to examine the cow. "You broke her neck," he said, and Gaby could hear the anger in his voice.

"It happens," Slade said nonchalantly, recoiling his rope.

"I told you not to rope alone," Rayne said, standing up.

"I work alone," Slade answered.

"Not when you work for me," Rayne bit out. "You work the way I tell you or not at all." He glared up at the cowhand, the message in his eyes as clear as the words he'd spoken. Slade held the gaze for a moment, then glanced away.

"You're the boss," he finally muttered. Rayne stalked back to his horse and mounted.

"Put that calf with one of the other mothers and see if she'll nurse. Drag that carcass away from the rest of the herd and tell Little Finger to come down and butcher her."

"Yes, boss," Slade said without hiding the insolence in his tone. The two men glared at each other and again Slade turned away first. Rayne rode off to watch as another bull was separated from the herd and roped, this time by two men. A flanker ran to wrestle it down while another man brought one of the red-hot irons from the fire. He placed the iron against the bull's flanks and the stench of singed hair and burning hide rose in the hot air.

Another man moved forward, a sharp knife glinting in his hands. Expertly he cut a wedge of the bull's ear away. Horrified, Gaby watched the plug of skin and flesh fall away in his hands, the white fatty gristle of it turning pink from the oozing blood. Nonchalantly the man tossed the plug at a bucket that was already overflowing with similar pieces.

Shakily Gaby stood up in the wagon, her gloved hand pressed against her lips as she sought to contain the bile that rose in her throat. Her eyes were enormous in her pale face as she looked from the bucket to the man with the knife. He seemed little concerned as he moved quickly, and with a few quick cuts, castrated the bull. Once again the steer bawled out his rage and pain, and Gaby, with-

CREOLE ANGEL

out uttering a sound, sank to the bottom of the wagon in a dead faint.

Gaby was back on the hill, the sky blue and innocent above her. Rayne knelt beside her where she stretched out in the back of the wagon. His dampened bandanna was pressed to her forehead. Maria stood nearby, her eyes wide with concern, Gaby's parasol clutched in her hand.

"Gaby," Rayne said urgently as her eyelids fluttered and at last remained open. She looked at him blankly; then memory flooded back over her. Even now she could hear the yip and call of the cowhands as they went about their business.

"Are you all right?" Rayne asked anxiously.

"She's fine," Lorna's voice drawled. "She just fainted, Rayne. You know these greenhorns can't take the heat out here. She shouldn't have come out when she wasn't used to it."

"I'm all right," Gaby reassured Rayne as if from a long distance.

Reassured, he turned to Billy. "Why didn't you stay up here on the hill?" he demanded. "What possessed you to drive that wagon down there?"

"I'm sorry, Mr. Elliott," Billy said contritely. "I guess I just didn't think."

"Maybe this'll help you think the next time," Rayne said, and balling up his fist, slugged him. Billy went down hard, the force of the blow sending him sliding backward in the dirt. Rayne sprang forward, and gripping the boy's shirt front, prepared to hit him again.

"Rayne, stop," Gaby cried, clinging to the side of the wagon. "It wasn't his fault." Rayne hesitated, his fist drawn back.

"That's right, Rayne," Lorna said quickly. "Gaby insisted on seeing everything up close. Poor Billy couldn't say no to the boss's . . ." She paused as if not sure of what to call Gaby, but Rayne was no longer listening. Instead he bent over the young man on the ground. Billy's face was white and scared, his freckles standing out in bright relief. Rayne's grip still bunched Billy's shirt as he pulled the cowboy toward him.

"Listen to me, boy, and listen well," he growled. "I told you to look after Gaby and not let anything happen to her, and that's exactly what I mean. Fail me one more time and you'll be sorry you ever set foot on the Rocking E Ranch. Understand?"

Billy gulped and shook his head. "Yes, sir."

"Now, you climb back up there on that wagon and I want you to drive it back to the ranch real slow and careful-like so Miss Gaby doesn't feel one bump or jar. Have you got that?"

"I'll try," Billy gulped.

"Don't try. Do it," Rayne roared.

"Yes, sir," Billy said, and scurried to climb up on the wagon.

"Rayne—" Gaby began.

"I'm not in the mood to hear any more of your arguing, Gaby," Rayne said. "I can't worry about you out here and keep my men working. Every hand's needed right now. Go on back to the ranch and stay there. I'll come back tonight." Numbly Gaby stared into the unrelenting blue eyes and shook her head.

"All right," she said dully.

"Get going, Billy," Rayne called, and the wagon lurched forward and then settled into a smooth run, as if Billy were willing away every rock and crevice that might jar the wagon bed. Silently Gaby watched as Rayne turned back to his horse, and taking the reins from Lorna, mounted. Side by side they rode back down the hill toward the roundup.

Unheeded, the tears rolled down Gaby's cheeks. How defiant and proud she'd been when she'd started out this morning, and now she was returning in disgrace and humiliation. Seized by another bout of nausea, she lay down in the back of the wagon and looked at the vast blue sky with tearful, unseeing eyes.

9

"It's done," Rayne said over supper. He drained his cup and set it down with a bang to emphasize his words. His eyes were gleaming with triumph. "We've gathered up nearly two thousand head. They'll all be branded by the end of the week. We leave Saturday for the North." He was bristling with anticipation.

"That's wonderful, Rayne," Gaby said, trying not to think of the weeks of separation that lay ahead of them. "How long will it take for the drive?" She looked at her other guests.

"It depends on many factors, little lady," Clarence Blake said. His eyes were the same penetrating blue as his daughter's, but there the resemblance ended. He was a big, bearish man with an untidy mustache and a large belly that sagged over his belt. He had an unending supply of funny stories that had lured even Cole back to the ranch house. Dusty had also joined them. All through dinner, the men had talked of little else but the impending cattle drive.

"There are a mightly lot of things can happen to slow a man gettin' his beeves to market—stampedes, rustlers, Injuns . . ." His voice trailed off.

"Davenport drove his herd up north earlier in the summer and he said they're crying for beef in the East."

"The real problem is gettin' 'em through Kansas," Dusty said. "They're puttin' out posses to hold back Texas cattle. They say our cows bring in the Texas fever."

"I hear some ranchers are turning their cows east across

Arkansas and then heading north," Rayne said. "The Kansas people don't have the right to keep us from the markets."

"What about Slim Fremont's cows?" Cole asked. "Didn't he say he drove them north and bypassed Kansas?"

"Yes," Rayne said, "but it runs the meat off the cows. They bring less when you get them to market."

"I say we take 'em straight on through Kansas," Blake said. "They can't hold us back if we take enough men and guns."

"I'll go along with that," Cole said. There was a glint in his eyes and Gaby was startled by the animation on his face. Obviously he'd begun to take an interest in the ranch again.

"We don't want gunplay," Rayne reminded them. "They've got the law on their side. If we got into a shooting match with the vigilantes, we could end up dead or at the very least in jail."

"Is it dangerous for you to drive your herd to Kansas?" Gaby asked fearfully.

"Could be," Clarence Blake said. "Some's been outright murdered for their herds."

"Then why do it?" Gaby cried, her eyes wide with worry. She glanced at Rayne and caught him surreptitiously signaling the other men to squelch their talk of danger. The men got quiet, looking at each other uncomfortably.

"We do it for the money," Cole Elliott spoke up, "so Rayne can buy you all the little gewgaws he thinks you need to keep you here."

Gaby glanced at Rayne's face. It was flushed and angry as he glared at his father.

"I have all I need, Rayne," she said. "I have you. I don't want anything else. Don't go if it's dangerous."

Rayne reached across the table and took her hand. "It's not that dangerous, Gaby," he reassured her.

"Why don't you take them to New Orleans again?" Gaby pressed. "It would be safer." Cole Elliott snorted derisively.

"It isn't practical," Rayne explained patiently. "We've got too many cows. It would cost too much to ship them."

"Instead we're driving 'em to Sedalia," Cole said scathingly. "Risking our lives to get rich quick. You've got Rayne in a might big hurry to be a wealthy rancher."

Rayne's eyebrows pulled down in a scowl. "And what do you propose we do, old man?" he demanded. "Sit here and starve to death through the winter?"

"We've got enough money from the spring roundup," Cole snapped.

"Barely enough," Rayne said, "if we eat beef and beans all winter."

"Ain't nothin' wrong with that," Cole said. "I've lived through many a winter on that."

"Not me, Pa," Rayne said, and his voice was tense. "I mean to make this ranch grow, and I'm not alone in trying. Men all over Texas are trying to rebuild their ranches and get on with their lives. Cows are what we have to do that with, and we aren't going to let some vigilante groups in Kansas stop us. We can't be scared out of making a good life for ourselves and our families."

"A good life?" Cole roared. "Life is good here in Texas, no matter what."

"But it could be better, Pa."

"Dang fools are losing their lives along the trails to Sedalia," Cole retorted. "What good will all that gold do 'em when they're growin' cold with a bullet in 'em?"

"If you're afraid, stay behind," Rayne snapped.

His words gave Cole pause. Out of pride he'd refused to accompany his son to New Orleans. He wasn't about to make that mistake a second time.

"You need every hand you can get to trail that herd," he mumbled. "Besides, if I don't go, no tellin' what you'll drag back with you this time." He cast a baleful glance at Gaby, his meaning clear to all who sat at the table. Gaby's cheeks stained pink at the insult. Rayne rose menacingly, his fists clenched. Clarence Blake sought to ease the situation by jumping into the heavy silence with a story. The other men listened and soon the tension eased somewhat. Quietly Gaby listened to the talk. It seemed the men thought of nothing but their cows. The smoke grew thick in the room, the level of whiskey in the bottles sank lower, and still they sat on talking.

"Simon Fisher went down in the spring. Drove his

herd right through Indian Territory, made it through a sandstorm, and finally got 'em to Baxter Springs, but them cows was in such bad shape, he couldn't sell a one of 'em. Some feller came out and offered him less than he woulda got if he'da stayed in Texas with 'em. Well, old Simon, he just took them cows out on the prairie and let 'em go. Said he'd rather see a boil on a whore's . . . 'Scuse me, ma'am," Clarence said, and clamped his mouth shut. His face had grown redder from the whiskey he'd consumed.

She was cramping their style, Gaby realized, and rose from her chair, nodding graciously. "If you'll excuse me, gentlemen?" she said, and with a final look at Rayne, went to her bedroom.

She lay listening to the rumble of voices from the parlor, willing the men to leave so she could be with Rayne. They had precious little time together and she was jealous of every moment spent with someone else.

She wanted to have some time to talk to him. She'd been patient enough. It was time they set a wedding date. The long months of separation would be more bearable if she could spend them planning her wedding.

It was past midnight when the house grew quiet and Rayne finally came to their bedroom. She felt the bed sag as he sat on its edge and shucked his clothes.

"Gaby," he whispered gently. She could feel the heat from his body and rolled toward it, her arms going up to encircle his neck.

"Rayne," she whispered, and her voice was a husky caress on his skin. He gathered her into his arms and lowered his mouth to hers in a hungry kiss. "Rayne, I want to talk."

"My sweet Gaby," he whispered against her mouth. "We are talking. Can't you hear my words?" He lowered his head and nibbled gently at the tight pink bud of a nipple. Gaby gasped in air, winding her fingers through his dark locks, pulling his head more tightly against her. All thought of talk was gone. Her mind no longer worked. Only her senses were alive. Her body opened to him like a flower.

Rayne's mouth moved to the other breast with tantalizing, nibbling kisses. He breathed in the fragrance of her, flowery and womanly. It was an aphrodisiac to him, spurring his desire to a hotter flame.

Gaby surrendered to her passion, letting it carry her higher, and when she feared she might never return to earth, Rayne moved across her, seeking her warmth. She felt him plunge against her and willingly followed him, thrust for thrust, until they scaled the final barrier and hurdled forward into a world of swirling silver-speckled fulfillment.

And then Rayne was gone. He rose in the cold darkness of predawn, and when she would have risen with him, he pressed her back against the warm hollow that had held their entwined bodies through the night.

"Don't get up, love," he whispered. "It's too early."

"I can't let you ride off like this," she protested. "I'll have Jacinta make some coffee and flapjacks for you."

"I can get something at the chuck wagon," Rayne said. "I'd rather think of you here in bed, all warm and soft, waiting for me." His hand slid up and down her smooth bare arm in a lingering caress. "You are so beautiful, Gaby. I haven't told you lately how much I love you."

"I know. You show me in so many different ways," she murmured. "You tell me with your eyes and the way you touch me. Oh, Rayne . . ." She sprang up and threw herself into his arms. "I'm going to miss you so much. How can I bear it here without you?" She lay back against the pillows, pulling him down with her. Rayne raised himself on an elbow to look into her eyes. The lamplight cast a glow around her face.

"You won't leave while I'm gone, will you, Gaby?" he asked softly. She saw the uncertainty in his eyes and was surprised by it. Didn't he know yet how much she loved him?

"No," she answered tenderly, "I'll be right here watching and waiting for you," she pledged. His kiss was hard and urgent, seeking reassurance that the words she spoke were true. He found it in the clinging arms and the yielding softness of her lips that sought yet another kiss and another.

"I have to go," he said breathlessly. "Good-bye, Gaby." He gazed into her eyes for a long minute and then he rose and left. It was only later that she realized she had no chance to talk to him about any of the things that bothered her.

Rayne had said he would be gone about two months. It was early September now. She wouldn't see him again until November. She would never be able to endure the lonely months. She huddled in bed and wept until long after the sun had brightened the patch of light at her window. She thought of the night they'd spent together and was comforted by it. Rayne had shown his love in every way, and he'd reassured her that Lorna was not going on the drive.

For the first week after Rayne left, Gaby moped around the ranch, at a loss as to what to do with herself. If she'd missed Rayne when he was out on the prairie rounding up strays, she missed him doubly now.

"Oh, Jacinta," she said one day, her voice brimming with lonesomeness and self-pity, "I don't think I can last until Rayne gets back."

"Of course you will," Jacinta said in her no-nonsense fashion. "Other women do it."

"How do they manage it?" Gaby asked listlessly.

"You must find something to occupy yourself until Señor Rayne's return," Jacinta said.

"You're right," Gaby cried, leaping to her feet. Her face lit up as she looked around the rooms. There was still much to be done at the ranch. She'd spend the time while Rayne was gone making their home more beautiful. First she had to have some money. Her gaze swung back to the little inlaid music box. She would sell it or trade it for goods at Caleb Greene's store. Laughing with delighted anticipation, she wound the box and opened its lid to hear the tinkling music.

"Jacinta, send Maria to fetch Billy. I want him to hitch up the wagon. We're going to buy some curtains and dishes and rugs and . . . oh, whatever else we can think of that we need," she cried excitedly. She whirled around the room in time to the music and came to a stop before the mantel. Pursing her lips, she stood thinking, a twinkle of mischief growing in her eyes. There was one other thing she intended to do as well. By the time Rayne Elliott returned from his cattle drive, she was going to be able to ride a horse.

Imbued now with an energy she hadn't felt in days, Gaby insisted on traveling to Fowler that very morning. Grumbling and disapproving though Jacinta pretended to be on the surface, she and Maria were eager to go to town as well. They set out with a festive air, and in her enthusiasm for her own plans, Gaby failed to notice the dejected look on Billy's face.

Once they'd reached Fowler, Billy parked the supply wagon in front of the general store and ambled away toward the saloon for some solace.

He wasn't given to drinking, but he needed something to make him feel more like a man instead of a nursemaid for a passel of women. Standing before the swinging doors of the saloon, he took a deep breath and stepped inside. The place was only half-filled. A few men stood at the bar talking and gulping down their drinks, while others sat at tables playing cards.

A fat bartender stood behind a great wooden bar mixing drinks and washing glasses by dragging them through a bucket of muddy-looking water.

"Did you want something, boy?" a voice growled, and Billy looked at the men sitting at one of the tables. Thad Martin and his men sat playing cards, a half-filled bottle and glasses before them.

Billy wiped his palms across the thigh of his trousers and took a step backwards. "No, sir," he said, swallowing nervously. "I was just looking for someone, a friend. Guess he ain't here."

"Can't be yo'r boss you're lookin' for," Thad said. "I heard he's taking a bunch of cows up north."

"That's right," Billy said.

"How come you didn't go with him?" Thad asked. "You look like a pretty good hand to me." Billy's shoulders lifted a little at his words.

"He . . . uh . . . needed someone to stay and keep an eye on things," he said.

"That's right," Thad said, winking at his men. "Rayne's got that classy little lady out there now, ain't he?"

"Miss . . . Miss Gaby," Billy said, suddenly feeling uneasy. "She's doing some shopping down at the general store."

"Well, boys, I think Rayne made a right smart choice

when he left Billy to guard his ranch and his woman, don't you?" The other men at the table nodded their heads and voiced their agreement, then turned their slyly smiling faces back to Billy.

"What's your name, boy?"

"Billy, sir,"

"Come on over here, Billy, and have a drink with us," Thad invited. "Yessir, anytime a fellow gets a break, he ought to wet his whistle. Makes that long dry trip back to the ranch a little easier to bear." He poured a glass of whiskey for Billy. "Pull up a chair for him there, boys," he instructed, and a chair was pulled forward.

"Drink up there, young fella," Martin said, and grinned. Billy'd never had much to drink in his young life; now he realized he was facing a test. Taking a breath, he picked up the glass and tossed the whiskey to the back of his throat the way he'd seen some of the other men do. The fiery liquid burned a path down his throat and set his eyes to watering. He coughed. His insides felt on fire. He bent over, trying to control the coughing spasm that hit him. He could hear quickly smothered guffaws of laughter from the other men around the table.

"That man knows how to drink his whiskey," Martin said. "Boys, pour him another drink, my compliments." With a wink Martin rose from his chair and slipped away. Someone else sat down in the empty chair and Billy never noticed his host had left. The coughing had stopped and the burning sensation had eased a little. Resolutely Billy picked up the second glass of whiskey and raised it to his lips.

Gaby carried her parcel into the general store and laid it on the counter.

"What can I do for you, Miss Reynaud?" Caleb Greene asked, and Gaby gave him a dazzling smile, encouraged that he'd remembered her name.

"It's a question of what I can do for you, Mr. Greene. I have this beautiful musical jewelry box. I'd like to sell it or exchange it for some goods from your store." She unwrapped the box and waited while he examined it.

"It's beautiful, all right," Caleb said, "but I don't have

much need for such a doodad." He peered at it more
closely. "Are the gems real?"

"Yes, sir," Gaby said. "Emeralds and rubies, and this
is pearl and jade inlay—"

"It's mighty fancy, but what's it good for?" Caleb
asked.

"It's a music box." Gaby wound the key and the tinkling waltz melody came tumbling out.

"Uh-huh. Where'd you get a box like this?"

"It's from New Orleans," Gaby answered. "It was a
gift to me."

"Somebody held you in high regard or had lots of
money he didn't know what to do with," Caleb observed.
He'd dealt for too long in practical commodities to be
moved by a fancy useless piece like the jeweled music
box.

"I think it was a little of both," Gaby said lightly.

"I'm sorry, Miss Reynaud," Caleb said, "I'm not in the
market for something so grand as this box."

"Oh," Gaby said. Disappointment made her voice flat.
She hadn't considered that Caleb might not want her
music box. All the way to town she'd planned the things
she'd buy.

"If you're needing some supplies, I can let you have
some until Rayne gets back. I hear he and Blake have
driven a herd of cows north."

"Yes, he has," Gaby answered.

"Well, you just pick out what you need and I'll set it
against Rayne's name. He can come in and settle up with
me when he gets back."

"No, I don't want to do that," Gaby said. "It isn't
really supplies I need, so much as . . . other things. I
wanted to buy them myself as a surprise for Rayne when
he comes home." Slowly she rewrapped the box.

A bootstep sounded on the wooden floor as a large
man stepped forward. "I'd like to take a look at the
music box, if it's for sale," he said.

"Certainly, Mr. Spencer." Caleb Greene turned to
Gaby. Once again she unwrapped the box. The man took
the box and turned away as if to find a better light in
which to examine it. Carefully he studied the workman-
ship and lifted the lid to hear its melody.

"It's too beautiful to sell," he said without turning to look at her. Gaby studied his broad back and rounded shoulders. He was a big man with gray streaking the dull gold of his hair. His suit looked of a good fabric and cut, and the trousers and jacket were matched, unlike the odd assortments most Texans wore.

"Why do you want to sell it?" the man asked. His voice was kind and Gaby felt no unease with him.

"There are so many things needed at the ranch. Rayne works hard to make it nice for me. I . . . I wanted to buy some of the things needed and surprise him when he comes back."

"And you don't mind parting with the little box?"

"Not really," Gaby said, and was unaware of the note of longing in her voice. The box was a link with the only home she'd known in New Orleans.

"Would you sell the box to me?" the man asked, closing the lid and setting it back on the counter. She could see his profile now. Like his voice, it seemed gentle and yet conveyed an aura of strength and kindness. Still he hadn't turned, and she couldn't see him completely.

"If you wish," Gaby said, watching him intently. There was something oddly touching about the way he kept his face averted from her.

"How much do you want for it?"

"I . . . I don't know." Gaby hadn't put a value on the box and had no idea of its worth. She'd thought only of the things she wished to buy. The man hesitated and offered her a price, more than Gaby had thought to get. Quickly she agreed and he pulled out a thick wallet and laid cash on the counter. It was more money than Gaby had ever possessed before.

"Thank you, Mr. Spencer," she cried. "Now I can buy the things I'd planned for the ranch."

Aaron Spencer turned to look at the young woman, noting the happy anticipation in the bright eyes. She'd mentioned surprising Rayne. Aaron wondered what it would be like to have a beautiful woman waiting so eagerly for his return.

Gaby glanced back at him and her excited chatter halted as her eyes took in his scarred face. Aaron steeled himself for the revulsion in her eyes. He'd seen it often enough, he'd come to expect it from all women, especially one as beautiful as this. He waited now for her reaction.

Gaby continued to regard him with her level gaze, and after she'd looked at the puckering scars that pulled one side of his face, she looked directly into his eyes and found the beauty of the inner man. Aaron was shaken by the clear, direct gaze. She made him want to weep and laugh at the same time.

"You are very kind, Mr. Spencer," she said softly. "I'm glad my beautiful little box will be going to a man like you, someone who will appreciate its fineness."

"I will think of you, madame, each time I listen to the melody," he said, bowing slightly.

"Are you from Fowler, Mr. Spencer?" Gaby asked.

"I have a ranch north of here."

"Then perhaps we'll meet again," Gaby said, and held out her hand.

"I'll look forward to it." He took her small gloved hand in his and held it for a moment, his gray eyes studying the beautiful animated face.

"It was nice to meet you, Mr. Spencer," she said politely.

"The pleasure was all mine, Miss Reynaud," he answered, and bowed again. He picked up the little box and made his way out into the bright sunlight of the street. Before he left the store Gaby was already making her selections and he could hear her light, happy voice as she inquired about the storekeeper's best tobacco. For the first time in years, Aaron Spencer cursed the accident that had crippled and scarred him.

Gaby lost track of time. Happily she picked out calicoes, bits of lace for trimming curtains, dishes, woven rugs made out of rags, candlesticks, and any other items she felt would add beauty and a touch of homey comfort to the ranch.

"What are you doing in town?" a voice demanded, and Gaby turned to find Lorna Blake regarding her suspiciously.

A flush of anger stained Gaby's cheeks at the woman's attitude. "I had some shopping to do," she said evenly.

"So I see," Lorna replied, raising an eyebrow as she

viewed the pile of goods on the counter. "Rayne won't be pleased that you're running up a bill here."

"I'm paying for these things with my own money," Gaby replied. "They're intended as a surprise for Rayne when he returns."

"That's right, you like surprises." Lorna grinned, and the memory of the day at the roundup flashed through both their minds.

Gaby swallowed her ire and changed the subject. "I want the ranch house to be beautiful for our wedding," she said, and was gratified to see the grin leave Lorna's face.

"Surely you don't believe Rayne intends to marry you," the Texas woman said incredulously.

"Of course, that's why I came to Texas," Gaby answered.

Lorna laughed. "You don't know Rayne very well, if that's what you're planning. He isn't that easy to get to the altar." The old knowing grin was back in place. Gaby was infuriated by her words and attitude.

"You haven't succeeded in your attempts, have you, Lorna?" Gaby let her voice assume the amused tone that Lorna's had. "In fact, you don't seem to have had much success in any of your plans with Rayne."

"Not yet," the other woman answered tightly. "But I will." Her self-assurance was maddening.

"I thought you were going on the trail drive with your father," Gaby said with feigned politeness. "What happened?"

A frown puckered Lorna's brows. "Rayne decided it was best I stay behind. He was afraid the trip might get to be too dangerous. He's so protective," she said, parodying Gaby's words.

Gaby smiled at the woman. "Rayne is like that," she answered easily. "I've seen him show the same concern over a muley." She let her gaze flick over Lorna with the clear message that Lorna was of little more concern to Rayne than a hornless cow that must depend on the cowhands for protection. Billy had explained that muleys were not greatly liked by the cowboys.

Lorna's face flushed with displeasure at Gaby's words. She glanced at the items on the counter. "Don't spend all your money on foolishness," she remarked. "You'll need some to get back to New Orleans." Turning on her heel, she stalked out of the store.

Gaby's pleasure in her shopping had soured now. She chose one or two more items and had Caleb package them. Stepping out on the boardwalk, she looked for Billy and the wagon. Both were gone. Had he taken it to the stable? she wondered, looking up and down the street.

"Miss Reynaud?" A man stepped forward.

"Yes," Gaby answered.

"Your man, Billy Fuller, had an accident, ma'am. He took the wagon back to the stables and asked that I escort you there." The man was dirty and unshaven and yet he held his hat in his hand deferentially. There was a glint in his eyes of some unknown source of sly humor that made her feel uneasy. Still, if Billy had sent him, the man must be all right. Billy might need her. Nodding her acquiescence, she followed the man along the boardwalk and down a side alley toward the stableyard. Sure enough, her wagon was parked in front, the horses chewing contentedly on a pile of straw. Billy was nowhere in sight. Gaby felt her alarm growing.

"Right this way, ma'am," her guide said, and indicated the dark interior of the stables. "He's back there in one of the stalls."

Why hadn't they taken him down the street to the doctor's office, Gaby wondered, unless his injury was too severe for him to be moved. She hurried to the back of the dark stable, picturing Billy wounded and bleeding. Up ahead, one of the shadows shifted.

"Billy?" she called, and stopped. The alarm she felt now was for herself. She could make out the outline of a man lurking in the shadows. "Billy," she called again. "If you're there, answer me." Only silence greeted her words. Alarm, strong and insistent, clamored a warning, but before she could turn and run, she was shoved from behind, pushed ruthlessly toward the back stall. She would have fallen if the man in the shadows hadn't stepped forward and caught her in his arms. In the shadowy light his face was obscured by his hat brim pulled low over his eyes.

"Well, now, look who I found," he said softly, and

Gaby thought she recognized the voice. Panic made her heart beat wildly, and her breath grew tight in her chest.

"Let go of me," she cried, struggling blindly in the man's arms.

"Relax, little lady," he said. "I'm not going to hurt you. We're just going to have a little fun together. You like to have fun, don't you?" Gaby wrenched herself away from him, and as he moved to catch her again the light fell over his face.

"Thad Martin," she cried out, and the man stepped closer, a lazy smile on his face. The intent in his eyes was unmistakable.

"Hello, Miss Gaby," he said, and in spite of his polite words, his voice was soft and sensuous-sounding.

"What is the meaning of this?" Gaby cried in fury, refusing to back down from him, although his steady advance toward her was unnerving.

"I thought the meaning was clear," he answered, and grinned again, his face looking feral and evil in the half-light. "I'm not expecting you to do anything you haven't done already, Miss Gaby," he said, and laughed. He was close enough to her now to reach out a hand and touch her cheek.

"I'm not interested," Gaby said flatly, and turned toward the stable door and the bright patch of sunlight beyond. Her arm was grasped from behind as Thad spun her around, putting himself between her and freedom.

"Rayne's going to be gone for a long time," he said suggestively. "You're going to get mighty lonesome out there on the ranch without him."

"I'll never get that lonesome," Gaby responded coldly. "Now, let go of me." Thad held her arm for a minute longer, as if considering whether to let her go or not. Gaby's heart set up a wild hammering. She tried to keep her fear from showing as she met his gaze. "Let go of me now, or I'll scream so loudly the whole town will be down here," she threatened.

"I don't think you will," Thad said, and the look on his face turned mean. Suddenly, from behind, a gloved hand clamped over her mouth. An arm clasped her, pinning her arms to her side. Gaby struggled against the bonds, lashing out with her feet.

Thad let her struggle, laughing at her attempts to free herself. "Whooee, Jed," he said. "She's some wildcat, ain't she?" He waited until she had tired herself and stood limp and unresisting in Jed's grip; then he stepped forward.

"I have a message for Rayne," Thad said with clenched teeth. "You tell Rayne he has something I want, and what I want, I take, starting with you." His hand shot out, and Gaby steeled herself for a blow. Instead he gripped the bodice of her gown and ripped downward, tearing buttons and lace apart as he bared her breasts in their lacy camisole. Gaby sucked in her breath, a scream building within her.

"Don't make a sound," Thad warned her, "or you'll be real sorry." His voice and look were so deadly she remained silent, although he ripped at her bodice yet again, this time tearing apart the dainty undergarments, leaving her breasts bared to his gaze. Gaby stood silent, her eyes downcast in fear and misery, her arms twisted cruelly behind her by Jed.

"Whooee," Thad said. "Look at these pretty things. Rayne sure knows how to pick the best. They even have a little red star on 'em." He put out a finger and jabbed her birthmark.

"Please don't," Gaby pleaded softly. "If you have any decency in you at all, please don't."

Martin only laughed. "Let her go, Jed," he ordered. "She's mine first and then you can have her." The man released her, giving her a little shove toward Martin.

"Please don't," she implored, her hand going up to pull together the torn edges of her bodice.

"Come on over here," Martin said, grabbing her hand and shoving her toward the back stall. Gaby fell against a thick post and sank to her knees on a pile of hay, the breath knocked from her. Fearfully she looked up as Thad Martin moved toward her, his hands already busy loosening his belt buckle.

"Let her go," a voice cut through the gloom. Startled, Thad whirled, his hand reaching for his gun. "Don't touch that gun or you're a dead man," Billy said, and the metallic sound of a hammer being drawn back made Thad's hand pause in midair.

"I thought you said he was out," he snarled at Jed.

"I thought he was. He was sleeping it off in the back of the wagon."

"Billy," Gaby cried, and ran toward the young man outlined in the door of the stable. As she swept past him, Thad reached out and grabbed her arm, pulling her back against him.

"Not so fast there, little lady," he said, and using her as a shield, took out his own gun and put the barrel against her head. "Now then, boy. You just put that gun down and go on back out there and climb up on that wagon. Pretend like you ain't seen nothing. You just sleep it off until we get done with the lady in here, and we'll send her on out there to you."

"Billy, do as he says," Gaby cried. "He'll kill you."

"You hear that, Billy. She's telling you to do it. She wants to be in here with us, don't you sugar?" Martin raked his stubbled cheek against hers in a parody of an embrace.

"I said let her go," Billy said, keeping his gun leveled at the man, although they both knew he couldn't shoot with Gaby between them.

"Now, Billy," Martin said, "I like you, boy, but you're being awfully dumb. You and I know you can't shoot without hitting the woman, while it don't pay me no never-mind which way I shoot. I could get you first and then her. Now, I think what we've got here is what they call a Mexican standoff."

"I don't think so," Jacinta said from the gloom behind them. "I am Mexican and I don't think so." Startled, the men glanced over their shoulders. "I have a rifle pointed right at your back, Mr. Martin, and I have a real nervous finger." Gaby could feel Thad stiffen.

"Drop the gun, Mr. Martin," Jacinta said. Slowly he dropped the gun in the dirt of the stable floor. "Tell your man to drop his too," Jacinta ordered. "My finger is getting very tired."

"Drop it," Thad ordered, and Jed let his gun slide to the floor as well.

"Now, let go of Miss Gaby and step back," Billy said.

"Real slow," Jacinta called, and the men moved away

from Gaby. Quickly she ran to the front of the stables, taking care to keep out of Billy's line of fire.

"Now, walk on out of here," Billy demanded, "and stay in the middle of the street where I can see you."

Martin stayed where he was, as if debating scooping up his gun and challenging the young man.

"You will have to hurry, mister," Jacinta said from the gloom at the back of the stable. "My finger is getting real tired now."

"Come on," Thad said to his man, and the two of them stalked out of the barn. As they brushed past, Gaby saw the cold hatred in Thad's eyes and knew she and Billy had made a deadly enemy.

Billy kept the gun trained on the two men until they'd reached the main street and disappeared inside the tavern; then the gun drooped in his nerveless fingers. His face looked sickly green. Silently he leaned over and emptied his stomach of the whiskey Thad's men had given him. When it seemed he hadn't a thing left in his stomach, he raised his head and stared with bleary eyes at the two women.

"I'm real sorry, Miss Gaby," he said. "I guess I didn't do a good job protecting you."

"You did a wonderful job," Gaby said gratefully, "and so did you." She turned and hugged Jacinta. She'd never been so happy to see two people in her life.

"Ohh, I was so frightened," Jacinta said.

"How did you know?" Gaby asked.

"Maria and me come to look for you and then we look for the wagon. We find it here, with Billy inside under some canvas. We hear sounds in the stable and we look and bad men are there with you. Billy gave me the rifle and told me to go to the back. He sent Maria for the sheriff, pronto."

"Is something going on here?" a voice interrupted, and they turned to find Maria accompanied by a large man with a drooping mustache. He wore a black topcoat and a gun and holster low on his hip.

"Sheriff Garner," Billy said, and his voice broke with relief as he greeted the older man.

"This girl said there was some trouble back here."

"There was," Gaby said. "Thad Martin and his man

Jed tried to force themselves on me back there in the stable."

"Are you saying they attacked you, ma'am?" the sheriff asked.

"That's just what I'm saying," Gaby replied. "What are you going to do about it, Sheriff?" All four of them looked at him expectantly.

Tom Garner cursed under his breath. Thad Martin was a mean one and he hated the thought of tangling with him. To avoid answering them, he walked into the stable. At the back two guns lay in the dirt. One was the silver-handled pistol he'd seen Thad Martin carry. Sighing, he rose and walked back out to the small knot of people. Where the devil was Abe? he wondered. He was supposed to be here taking care of the stables. No doubt he was down at the saloon wheedling free drinks. The sheriff turned to the Mexican girl who'd fetched him.

"Run back up to my office and tell my deputy I said to get Thad Martin and Jed Lager and bring 'em down here." Maria hurried away. "Now, start at the beginning and tell me how come you went back in the stable with Thad and his man."

"I didn't go in there with Thad and his man. I was tricked." Gaby began detailing precisely and accurately all that had transpired, calling attention to the torn bodice of her gown, which she still clasped to her. Billy and Jacinta had just finished telling their story when the deputy appeared with Thad Martin and several of his men in tow.

"Sheriff," Thad said, sauntering up to the group, "the deputy tells me you want to see me."

"That's right, Thad. Miss Reynaud here accuses you of attacking her in the stable."

Thad looked at Gaby, his eyes cold and unreadable as they flicked over her. "The lady is mistaken," he said. "I've been at the saloon all afternoon playing cards with my men here. They'll testify to that." He indicated the men who'd accompanied him.

"That's right, Sheriff," the men said corroborating Thad's claim.

"They're lying," Gaby snapped.

"Now, Sheriff, you might inform Miss Reynaud and

her party that men don't take kindly to being called liars down here in Texas."

"Did you come to the stables any time today, Thad?"

Thad paused as if thinking about the question. "Not that I can recollect," he answered.

"Can you recollect if any of your men were down here?" the sheriff asked sarcastically.

Thad looked at his men. "Did anyone come down here this afternoon?" he asked with a grin. Some of the men shook their heads.

"A couple of us brought the kid down here and dumped him in his wagon when he passed out," one man said. "We thought that was better than leaving him where he was."

The sheriff remained silent while Thad and his men played out their little charade of innocence. Finally he interrupted. "You mind telling me how your pistols ended up in there on the stable floor?" he asked wearily.

"We lost those pistols this morning in a poker game," Thad said smoothly. "Ain't that right, boys?" His men nodded in agreement.

"Who'd you lose 'em to?" Sheriff Garner asked.

"Never knew his name," Thad responded. "It was some fella I'd never seen before. He come into the saloon for a drink. We played a few games and he rode on out again." Thad glanced at Gaby. "Leastwise, we thought he did."

"Sheriff, this man is lying. I saw him with my own eyes," Gaby cried.

"It's mighty dark in the back of that stable, Sheriff. This lady and me've only met once before and that was months ago when she first came in on the ship in Galveston. I expect she's met several men since then." His voice was snide with innuendo, although he kept his expression innocently bland. "It seems to me she's got me mixed up with someone else."

"But I called out your name," Gaby cried, "and you didn't deny it was you."

"That was a right smart fella, whoever he was," Thad said, shaking his head admiringly. "He answered you, ma'am, because you were blaming someone else for what he was doing." Thad grinned as if pleased he'd unraveled the mystery. The sheriff looked uncertain.

"If you're done with me, Sheriff, me and the boys would like to get back out to the ranch."

"All right, Martin," the sheriff said. "You're free to go."

"No," Gaby cried in outrage.

"Much obliged to you for recovering our guns for us, Sheriff," Martin said. "When I lost mine to that card sharp, I thought I'd seen the last of it for sure." He paused and looked at Gaby, his gaze lingering thoughtfully on her bodice, which she still clenched together with one hand. "I'm right sorry for what happened to you, Miss Reynaud. When you tell Rayne about it, be sure and tell him Thad Martin sends his regrets that things turned out the way they did." He sauntered back down the street toward the saloon and his men followed, exchanging triumphant, conspiratorial grins.

"You let him go after what he tried to do to me," Gaby raged at the sheriff. Her eyes were dark with anger and frustration. What good was a sheriff if he couldn't bring a culprit to justice?

The sheriff read the condemnation in her eyes and shook his head. "You're right, Miss Reynaud. I *am* afraid of Thad Martin and his kind. Any fool with half a grain of sense would be."

"But he attacked me," Gaby cried.

"You ain't got no way to prove it was Thad that did it," the sheriff said. "Who've you got to back up your complaint? A boy that's falling-down drunk and a Mexican woman." At his words, Jacinta drew herself up indignantly. "Thad would have a dozen men swearing they saw him sitting in the bar playing poker the whole time you say this happened."

"Does he just go unpunished?" Gaby asked incredulously.

"I'm afraid so," the sheriff said, and as if to placate her and his own conscience, offered some advice. "Nothing happened to you today. You were lucky. Now, just go on back out to the ranch and forget about it. That'd be best for everyone. You don't want folks talking about this all over Fowler. It could get nasty for you." His advice had turned to a warning, and she could see in his eyes that he halfway blamed her for the trouble.

Drawing herself up to her full height, Gaby looked into the sheriff's eyes. "I want to thank you for your help and protection," she said scathingly. "It makes a woman feel safer just knowing there's a man like you on the job." She turned to the wagon and motioned to Billy and the women to follow.

Despite a throbbing head that made him feel as if he were walking sideways, Billy climbed up on the wagon seat and picked up the reins.

Sighing, Sheriff Garner turned back to his office.

Billy wheeled the wagon to the back of the general store and Caleb Greene came out to help load the supplies Gaby had bought. All pleasure over her purchases was gone now. Silently she watched until the loading was completed, keeping her shawl around her shoulders to hide her torn bodice; then the wagon headed out of town for the ranch. They hadn't gone far when Billy drew to a stop and slumped in his seat.

"Billy," Gaby cried, and quickly he righted himself, but his face was ashen.

"Excuse me, Miss Gaby," he cried, and fell off the wagon.

Jacinta and Gaby clambered out. Together they got the inert body back onto the wagon, where Billy stretched out, his head pillowed in Maria's lap. Jacinta's mouth tightened at the look of tender concern on her daughter's face. She climbed up on the wagon seat beside Gaby and reached for the reins. Expertly she slapped the leather across the horses' rumps and the wagon started for the ranch.

"This was a sorry day," Jacinta mourned, "a sorry day." She shook her head from side to side. "Señor Elliott will be very angry when he hears of all that has happened. He will go after Thad Martin and make him sorry he tried to attack you."

"Or get killed trying," Gaby said, remembering Martin's words.

"What is this?" Jacinta said. "Señor Elliott is a good man with a gun. He will kill Martin."

"I'm not so sure of that," Gaby said. "You heard what

the sheriff said. Thad is wily and sly. He strikes without a warning and he's not particular about shooting a man in the back.''

"He is a bad man."

"Yes, he is,'' Gaby said. "He's trying to provoke Rayne into a fight so he can kill him. He didn't want me today. I was the way to get to Rayne.''

"But he was tearing away your clothes when we stopped him," Jacinta said.

"Oh yes, he would have forced himself on me," Gaby said, "but that wasn't his real goal. We won't tell Rayne what happened, Jacinta.''

"It is not wise to keep this from him," Jacinta advised.

"It's not wise to play into Thad's hands either," Gaby said with conviction, and looking at her set face, Jacinta made no more argument. Slapping the reins, she urged the horses homeward. She remembered the look in Martin's eyes, and she wanted the stout walls of the ranch house around her this night.

10

The weeks that followed were surprisingly quiet and the apprehension they'd all felt in the days after the incident in town faded. Billy spent his mornings on the ranch chores and practicing his roping, and in the afternoons he saddled a horse for Gaby and helped her mount for her riding lesson. She was determined to ride well by the time Rayne returned. The ranch horses were lively and unpredictable, and just when she'd begun to think she was good enough to leave the safety of the corral, her pony would buck and whirl, depositing her on the ground with painful finality. More than once Gaby would end the lesson early to limp back to the ranch house and soak her aching muscles in a tub of hot water.

The house had begun once again to change as the three women worked on it. The changes were subtle, adding touches of hominess and beauty to the previous comfort and utilitarian neatness. Hand-painted china found its way onto the wooden plank shelves of the rough china cupboard and earthenware pottery held dried bouquets of wild flowers preserved by the hot prairie air. The woven rag rugs lay on the polished floor and fire logs were neatly stacked on the hearth waiting to be used on the cool evenings that occurred with more and more frequency now.

As they sat and sewed one evening, glancing up now and then to watch the flickering blaze in the stone fireplace, Gaby told Jacinta of the squawwood she'd helped gather before she'd learned the truth of what it was.

Jacinta laughed and Maria giggled. Even Gaby ended up laughing at the memory.

Jacinta went on to tell Indian stories she'd heard. Gaby listened, totally absorbed. So intent were the three women on the Indian tales that when the door flew back with a bang against the wall, they all jumped and looked around with wide eyes. At the same time, the dull thud of bullets burying themselves in the thick adobe walls sounded. Maria screamed. Billy stumbled through the door and pressed himself against the wall on the one side.

"Put out the light," he ordered hoarsely, "and get down low." Maria hurried to extinguish the lamps and all three women lay on the floor, their faces terror-stricken.

A call came from the darkness beyond the door, a bloodcurdling scream that hung on the still night air.

"Is it Indians?" Gaby cried, thinking of the stories Jacinta had just told of the fierce, vengeful Comanche.

"I don't think so," Billy said.

Another shot thudded into the thick walls and a chimney from one of the kerosene lamps shattered into a thousand pieces, the glass scattering over the floor. Billy took a quick double step across the opening and slammed the door shut. Laughter, high-pitched and cackling, rang through the air; then all was silent. The occupants in the ranch house held their breath, straining to hear any warning sound from beyond the door. It seemed to Gaby they stayed that way for hours. Her muscles were cramped from being held so stiffly.

"Have they gone?" she half-whispered finally.

"I don't know," Billy said softly. He sounded young and scared. Maria cried softly, her face buried against her mother's shoulder. They waited. Just as Gaby had bunched her legs beneath her to rise, she heard a flurry of hoofbeats in the night and the hooting calls of men.

They charged the house and for a moment, from the thunder of their hooves, Gaby thought they meant to ride right into the house itself, but at the last minute they swerved to one side and clods of dirt and stones were thrown against the door. For several minutes it continued, while terror built within. Maria made no attempt now to smother her sobs, and Gaby herself felt like screaming. Who was out there? she wondered.

Finally the bombardment of the house ended and the last hoofbeat faded away. Still they waited, straining to hear. Only the sound of the night wind soughing through the prairie grass and whistling around the corners of the building broke the stillness. Heartbeats slowed and breathing returned to normal. Cramped muscles relaxed as the people in the room tentatively stood up and looked around.

"I think they've gone," Billy said. Lamps were lit and they stood looking at each other as if taking stock of themselves and the room. Except for the broken glass everything seemed just as it had been. Cautiously Billy opened the door a crack and peered outside.

"Billy, be careful," Maria cried, and crossed the room to stand near him. Slowly he inched the door open until all in the room were able to see out onto the porch. Clumps of dirt and offal had been thrown against the door, and in a bloody heap on the doorstep were the entrails of a cow.

"Ahh," Gaby cried out, and Maria hid her face in her mother's shoulder. Billy knelt in the doorway. A crimson path trailed downward, marking the path the bloody mass had taken when flung against the door.

"I'll clean this up, Miss Gaby," Billy said.

"Don't go out there," Gaby cried, and the boy hesitated, part of him wanting to close the door on the evidence of terror and vandalism, while he acknowledged that no one could clean it up but him. He'd seen cows gutted plenty of times, but this was no sight for the women, especially for Miss Gaby.

Billy stepped out on the porch and closed the door behind him, closing away the light and its illusion of safety. The darkness closed around him, menacing in its very silence. Were the night riders still out there, just waiting for him to venture beyond the porch? Were they preparing even now to ride down on them again?

The door behind him was jerked open and Billy spun around, smiling sheepishly at his nervousness. Gaby stood in the light, her eyes dark as they met his.

"Leave the door open, Billy," she said, "so you can get inside quickly if they come back." He nodded his head in agreement, his hazel eyes flashing his gratitude. He didn't feel quite as alone and helpless now. With his boot and a stick he found near the end of the porch, he began to scrape away the worst of the foulness on the porch.

"Jacinta, Maria," Gaby ordered, "get some water. We'll wash the blood off the door before it leaves a stain."

"Sí, senorita," Jacinta said, grateful for something to do. "Maria, get a rag," she ordered, and both women hurried back to the lean-to kitchen.

They cleaned up the mess as best they could in the wavering lamplight, and once again closed the heavy wooden door against the night and all its threats.

"Billy, I want you to sleep in here," Gaby said, and the young man nodded. She brought him a pillow and blankets and he rolled into them before the fire, his gun on the floor beside him.

They spent an uneasy night, and with the pale light of dawn went again to look at the evidence of the night's terror.

Their fears seemed blown out of proportion as they looked around. Jacinta brought a broom and swept the porch clean and Billy got a shovel and carried away the offending matter for burial. Gaby stood on the porch looking at the horizon, awash in the pale lemon light of the rising sun. Where was Rayne now, she wondered, and when would he return? Soon, she thought, willing him home. Shivering from a chill that came from within, she clutched her arms about herself and looked at the wide prairie beyond the ranch. It had never seemed more vast or lonesome to her.

Now their days and nights passed uneasily. As their fright faded a little, Billy moved his bedroll to the spare bedroom and even left his gun in its holster over the back of a chair, but they never completely relaxed their vigil. When the red-orange orb of the sun began its downward plunge in the west, dread for the coming night would grow in their breasts. By nightfall, they contrived to have all their outside chores done so they could go into the ranch house and latch the shutters and bar the door.

It had been a week since their night visitors and they had begun to breathe easier. One bright, sunny day when Billy was down at the creek doctoring a horse that had cut its leg and Jacinta was in the kitchen making bread,

Gaby gathered up some mending and carried it to the front porch. She sat looking out over the ranch buildings, thinking how lonely and empty they seemed without Rayne and the rest of the cowhands there. Shaking away her melancholia, she set to hemming some curtains for the extra bedroom, taking care that her stitches were small and even as Jacinta had shown her. A movement caught her eyes and she glanced up to see Maria moving across the yard toward the creek, a bucket in her hand. No doubt she'd noticed Billy was there and had thought of a good reason to go there herself.

Gaby smiled as she watched the girl. Maria's skirts swayed provocatively as she moved. Her feet kicked up little sprays of dust. She carried her head proudly. Suddenly Maria stopped and put a hand up to shield her eyes while she peered off into the distance. A plume of dust rose on the horizon as riders topped a rise and moved down toward the ranch. They were riding hard and fast.

Gaby jumped to her feet and stood watching. Could it be Rayne returning? she wondered. He was early. A smile lit her face. How she'd wished him home, and now here he was. Her heart surged with love and anticipation.

Straight on the riders came, riding full tilt, and as they got closer, Gaby could hear their shrill, yipping cries, and it struck terror in her heart. Tentatively she stepped backward toward the ranch house, still unwilling to believe what she was seeing.

"Maria," she screamed. "Billy." The Mexican girl turned as if to run back to the house, but her escape was already cut off.

"Maria, run," Gaby cried, but her voice was lost in the thud of hooves, the whinny of horses, and the men's cries. Gaby strained to see the faces of their tormenters, but they were covered by bandannas. Dust rose about them, obscuring any detail of their clothing.

"*Mi Dios*," Jacinta cried, coming out onto the porch. "Maria, run, run."

Gaby plunged off the porch and ran into the milling riders. She fairly flew to Maria's side and took the young girl's hand. The dust rose around them, choking and blinding them. Gaby could feel the heat of the horses' bodies as they pressed in.

"Maria, come," Gaby said to the terrified girl. "We must run for the porch." Obediently the girl nodded her head and together the two of them began moving back toward the house.

A large roan raced in front of them, blocking their escape. No matter how Gaby tried to dodge the horse, its rider wheeled into their path.

Gaby stopped and looked into the same mocking gray eyes she'd seen before. Even with a bandanna tied around his mouth and nose, there was no mistaking Thad Martin. He laughed, throwing his head back. Suddenly Gaby felt more frightened than she had the night the riders had bombarded the ranch house. Mutely she stood staring up at the ruthless man who took delight in frightening helpless women. She wasn't sure if safety lay in confronting him or in remaining silent.

"Mama!" Maria screamed, and breaking away from Gaby, darted off one side toward the back of the house. Gaby made to follow, but once again the roan cut off her escape. Another masked rider galloped after Maria, swerving his horse so it brushed against her and knocked her off balance. Maria fell to the ground and rolled face down in the dust and lay still.

"Maria," Gaby cried. The report of a rifle filled the air and suddenly the rider who'd chased Maria sagged in his saddle. The other men drew their guns and looked around, trying to locate the direction of the shot. Again the rifle cracked, and this time, Thad Martin grabbed his shoulder. For a moment he swayed in his saddle, but stayed mounted.

"Let's get out of here," he yelled to his men, and spurred his horse away. The other riders followed.

"Wait," called the wounded man, who sat hunched in his saddle. Slowly he gathered up the reins, all the time looking around fearfully, as though expecting another shot to finish him off.

"Maria," Gaby cried, racing to the fallen girl's side.

Slowly Maria raised her head and looked around. "Have they gone?" she asked, and at Gaby's nod, leapt to her feet. "I am not hurt," she cried triumphantly.

Billy came running across the yard from the barn, a smoking rifle still in his hand. "Did they hurt you?" he asked.

"We're fine," Gaby reassured him.

"I couldn't get here any sooner. I was down by the creek."

"You came just in time. Thank you, Billy," Gaby gave him a quick hug. Jacinta was cradling Maria in her arms, crying out her thanks to God in a mixture of Spanish and broken English. They were all trembling and uneasy that they'd been caught so off guard. The daytime attack had been a surprise.

"I'm going to ride into town and get the sheriff," Billy said.

"Billy, you can't," Gaby cried. "Those men might be out there just waiting for you to come riding by." They all turned fearful eyes back toward the rise over which the riders had disappeared.

"I'll take a roundabout route," Billy said. "I'll take you all into town until Mr. Elliott gets back. You'll be safer there."

"If we make it," Gaby said. "They'd know what we were trying to do. They probably have someone watching us right now." Again they glanced around fearfully.

"The sheriff won't help us anyway. He's too scared," Jacinta said, and spit into the dust at her feet.

"We won't leave the ranch unprotected," Gaby decided. "We'll stay, and when one of us has to come out and feed the animals, another will go with him to carry a gun and keep an eye out. If we see anyone approaching the ranch, we run for the house." For the first time she saw the practicality of a ranch sitting out in the open. There was little cover for anyone who might want to creep up on them.

"We'll keep someone on watch at all times," Gaby continued.

"*Sí*, I will shoot the first person who sets foot near the ranch house," Jacinta said, and stomped back into the house.

"Billy," Gaby said, "I want you to teach me how to shoot a gun."

"It takes practice, Miss Gaby, lots of practice." He

glanced around as if seeking some source of help besides three women. Two of them didn't even know how to handle a gun. He felt sick and scared.

"I know I won't be able to do it well," Gaby said, "but I want you to show me how to load a gun and how to fire it. I may need to know before this is over."

"All right," Billy agreed. "I'll go down and get the mare from the stream and be right back."

"I'll go get a gun."

The rest of the afternoon, Billy showed her how to load the rifle and sight along its barrel, how to release the catch and fire it. Her shoulder grew sore from the recoil, but stubbornly she kept on practicing. He also showed her how to use a handgun, and when she was satisfied she knew how to fire one, she set about practicing her accuracy while Billy showed Maria. Perhaps neither woman would become a fine marksman, but in the kind of encounters they'd endured, they might hit someone and help scare off their attackers. Doggedly Gaby kept on firing until her arm was leaden with the weight of the gun and Billy finally murmured something about saving their ammunition.

Now their days were an extension of the tension-filled nights. As they went about their chores, their gazes often lifted to the horizon for reassurance that no riders were silhouetted there. They wore guns strapped to their waists and Gaby found the unaccustomed weight reassuring. No one ventured far from the house alone. One of the women always accompanied Billy when he went to feed the animals. The list of chores Rayne had left for fence mending and line riding were set aside. The four of them took turns sitting up, often falling asleep slumped over a chair at one of the windows.

The marauders returned one night with blazing guns and fiery torches. One of the sheds was set afire, but the barrage of gunfire from the ranch house scared them off. When Billy and the women were sure the attackers were gone, they hurried with pails to put out the blaze.

"I think I got one," Jacinta said when they stood observing the smoldering timbers. They'd managed to contain the blaze, and the damage was minimal.

"At least we showed them we're not helpless," Gaby

retorted. In the light of early dawn they looked at each other's sooty faces and bedraggled clothing and grinned.

Their lightheartedness was short-lived. The tension grew and tempers shortened. The days were growing colder now. The sky was often gray with heavy, dark clouds sitting low and threatening over the ranch. They were a week into November and still Rayne hadn't returned. Now Gaby lifted her gaze to the dirt road as much to look for Rayne as to check for marauders. She began to build a knot of worry which she mulled over time and again. She thought of all the things that could have happened to him.

Then early one morning before dawn, her worst fears came true. She was awakened by the sound of hoofbeats. Anger suffused her as she listened to them come, riding hard and fast as they had before. They were only men, and barely that, if they found pleasure in terrorizing three women and one untried boy. Anger carried her from the bed and to the gun rack. She didn't stop to throw a gown on over her long nightdress or to put on shoes. She grabbed up a rifle and hurried to peer out a window. Jacinta was seated in a chair. She nodded and sat up, angry with herself that she'd fallen asleep at her post. Then the sound of approaching riders penetrated her drowsiness and she sprang up.

"They're back," she cried, and picked up her rifle.

The dawning light lay in long, pale fingers through the slats of the shutters. Gaby hoisted her rifle to one shoulder and took aim, her finger resting on the trigger. She could hear Billy entering the room behind her and taking up a rifle station himself at one of the other windows. The riders had gained the far edge of the corrals now and were coming fast. Gaby sighted one of them and tightened her finger on the trigger. She might still miss from this distance. She held her breath and waited for them to come closer.

"It's Rayne!" Billy cried. "They're back."

"Rayne!" Gaby cried, and dropping her rifle from suddenly nerveless fingers, ran to open the door. Heedless of her state of undress, she ran out onto the porch. "Rayne," she called. He leapt off his horse and was up the steps almost before the horse had stopped. His strong, hard arms closed around her, molding her to him. He buried his face in her flowing, sweet-smelling hair, which lay around her in a dark cloud. He could feel her body unfettered by undergarments beneath the thin lawn nightgown.

"Gaby," he sighed over and over, rocking her sweet body in his arms. God, how he'd missed her. He felt her tremble. In alarm he held her away from him and looked into her eyes. They were shiny with tears. Even as he watched, they spilled over and rolled down her rounded cheeks, while her lips trembled into a smile that was touching and beautiful. He clasped her to him again.

"Gaby, girl, don't cry," he crooned. His amused gaze caught sight of the people standing in the doorway. Jacinta and Maria were smiling and Billy was looking sheepish. Rayne's gaze swung back to Billy. What was he doing in the ranch house? Rayne took in the bare chest and feet. His pants had been pulled on hastily; one suspender was twisted into place and the other dangled down his back.

"What the hell are you doing there?" Rayne demanded of the boy. Gaby pulled back and stared up into Rayne's face as if he were demented, but he paid little attention to her.

"Speak up," Rayne roared. "What are you doing in the ranch house?" Billy's mouth worked to explain, but no sound came. In dismay Gaby looked at Rayne and then at Billy, and as the realization of Rayne's suspicions dawned on her, joy at seeing him again turned to anger.

"He was up here protecting us, Rayne Elliott," Gaby snapped. "We've been attacked several times by a group of outlaws who've come at all hours of the day and night."

"Sí sí, it's so," Jacinta said.

Rayne's face registered shock as Gaby spoke: "We've been shot at, ridden down, and had all manner of filth thrown at us."

"When did this happen?"

"It started soon after you left. If you'd taken the time to look around a bit, you would have seen that the shutters are closed and barred and you'll find all guns loaded and at the ready. Even Maria and I have stood watch at the windows. When we heard you riding hard and fast like that, we thought the riders were back."

"Slow down, Gaby," Rayne said, grasping her arms and giving her a little shake as if to bring her to her senses, but Gaby couldn't stop talking now. Rayne was back and she didn't have to be brave anymore. "I was so frightened . . ." She began to sob. Behind her Maria began to wail, and even Jacinta joined the cacophony, tears streaming down her brown cheeks as she rolled her eyes heavenward and sighed.

"Gracias a Dios," she said, crossing herself. Then she launched into a detailed explanation, all of it in Spanish. Rayne looked at the weeping girls and helplessly turned back to Billy.

"For God's sake, what happened?" he demanded.

"It's true, sir," Billy said, having gained his voice at last. "We wounded two of them, but they got away each time."

"Who were they?" Rayne demanded through clenched teeth.

"I don't know for sure, sir. They came at night, and during the day they wore masks over their faces. They came from that direction." Billy pointed to the west.

"Dusty, Slade," Rayne called. "Get the men and come with me." He sprang back on his horse.

"Rayne, don't go alone. They're armed," Gaby cried.

"You're not going to believe all this malarkey, are you?" Cole demanded. "They're just making it up to hide what they been doing here since you been gone. Any fool can see that."

"If that's the case, we'll soon know it, won't we?" Rayne snapped. "Are you coming with me?" He put his heels to his horse and galloped off. Cole fell in behind the other riders.

"Wait for me." Billy ran back in the house to grab the rest of his clothes.

"I'll make some coffee," Jacinta said, and headed for the kitchen. Gaby went to her bedroom to dress and wait for Rayne's return. She no longer felt a happy glow over his homecoming. Her mood wasn't helped any by her worry for Rayne. The hours dragged and she imagined him and his men wounded and left to die out on the prairie the way Cook Avery and his son had.

Round and round her thoughts went until Rayne and his men rode back to the ranch. By then Gaby was limp with worry. She hurried to the front porch and watched as the men dismounted and led their weary horses toward the barn. Rayne cast a guarded look in her direction before going to tend his exhausted horse. Troubled, Gaby went back into the ranch house.

They hadn't found the raiders. That had been evident in the slumped shoulders. Did Rayne believe they even existed? Billy had replaced the burned cross beams in the shed, and there were only a few scorched timbers to show there had ever been a fire.

Gaby paced from one end of her room to the other. Her concern was that Rayne believe her reasons for having Billy in the house were innocent. She reached the end of the room and with a swirl of skirts turned impatiently, her hands clasped in front of her. Rayne stood in the doorway, his face haggard. His glance avoided hers.

"We found their campsite," he said wearily, crossing to the pitcher and bowl and pouring water for himself.

"Were they still there?" Gaby asked. She would never know now whether or not he had needed that proof of the raiders' existence.

"No, we tracked them back toward Fowler and lost them there. No way of telling who was involved." He looked so disheartened that Gaby longed to rush to him and tell him of her certainty that it was Thad Martin. Only her fear that she was aiding Thad in his plan kept her silent.

"Perhaps they won't return now that you're back home," she said.

"I wish they would, Gaby." His blue eyes pinned her. "I'd like a chance at those cowards for frightening you women."

"At first I was frightened," Gaby admitted, "but Billy fought them off the first few times and then I learned to use a gun."

"You shouldn't have gone through something like this," Rayne said, tossing the towel down on the stand and moving closer to her. "I should have been here." Restlessly he moved past her and out into the parlor. Crossing to the table that held the whiskey, he poured a half-glass.

"You had to go on that drive," Gaby said. "Besides, other women manage while their men are gone. This time I did too."

Rayne downed the whiskey and turned to look at her. "Yes, you did at that," he said, and smiled tiredly.

"I believe I'm becoming a real Texan," Gaby said softly. "Just you wait and see. I'll make you proud of me yet."

"I've always been proud of you," he said, and suddenly his long legs were carrying him across the room to her. He swept her into his arms and his chin rested against her temple.

"Forgive me, Gaby, I should have taken better care of you," he whispered in her hair. There was so much anguish and love in his voice that she nearly forgave him for his earlier suspicions. She clasped her arms around his hard waist.

Their separation had been much too long. She could feel the desire building between them and wasn't ready for it yet, not until she was sure he believed in her innocence. She drew away and paced across to the mantel, twisting her hands as she sought a way to begin.

"How did the cattle drive go?" she asked, casting about for something to say. After their long separation it seemed incredible that they were suddenly strangers.

"We had some trouble, but we finally got the cattle sold." He poured himself another drink and looked around the room. He'd felt the tension between them too. Damn, he thought, he hadn't ridden all through the night to get back to her for this coldness between them. He tossed down the drink and studied her slender back.

He knew his reaction to Billy earlier had upset her, and he could imagine the fearful time she'd had during his absence. Billy had given him a full account of the attacks made on the ranch. They'd virtually been under siege.

Again he cursed himself. He should have foreseen this, what with all the trouble some of the other ranchers were having. He should have left more men to guard the

ranch, and made do with fewer on the trail. He should
have done something to protect Gaby.

He glanced across the room at her. She sat watching
the fire burning on the grate. Her dark hair gleamed in
the firelight and the pale ivory of her skin took on a
burnished glow. He longed to touch her.

Gaby glanced up and saw the lines of fatigue in his
face. "You must be tired too," she said softly, unable to
keep the concern from her voice.

"Some," Rayne replied, and an awkward silence fell
between them. He glanced around the room, looking for
something that would break the restraints between them.

"You've done a lot of work in here," he commented.

"Do you like it?" She glanced up at him.

"It's beautiful," he answered, and watched a small
smile play across her lips, then fade. It wasn't the kind of
smile he was used to seeing on Gaby. Her smiles usually
lit up her face and made you smile back. His gaze flickered away as if he were embarrassed to be caught looking
at her. He studied the thick woven rug, the bright curtains, and the new dishes gleaming on the sideboard.

"Did you charge things at Caleb's store?" he asked,
not really caring.

"He said I could until you got back with the cattle
money, but I knew you wanted to buy the Avery land
and increase your herd, so I . . ." She paused. Now that
the time had come to tell him, she wasn't sure she'd done
the right thing. She took a deep breath. "I sold the little
music box Maddie sent me."

Rayne's gaze was riveted on her now. "You loved that
box," he said. "I used to watch you when you played it."

"I did like it, because it reminded me of New Orleans.
It helped me get over being homesick, but this is my
home now and I wanted to make our home prettier."

"Didn't you think I could provide the things you
needed?" Rayne demanded. His pride was hurt. This
seemed to him another example of how he was failing
her.

"It doesn't matter which of us provided the money,"
Gaby said. "Let's forget about the box and enjoy the
ranch now that you're home again."

"It matters to me," Rayne snapped, and in his fatigue

and irritation was unaware of how harsh his tone was. "Who bought the box?"

"A man named Aaron Spencer," Gaby answered reluctantly. She bit her lip so it wouldn't tremble. "He had a scarred face."

"I know the man," Rayne said, setting his glass down on the table with a snap. He gathered up his hat.

"Rayne, where are you going?" Gaby cried.

"I'm going to Spencer's ranch to get back your music box," he answered, striding toward the door.

"Please don't," Gaby hurried toward him. "The music box in unimportant to me. Besides you need the money to pay for the Avery land. Stay here, Rayne, please. I haven't seen you for more than two months."

He pushed away her hands. "I'll be back," he said grimly, "and then we can talk."

"I don't want the box, Rayne," she cried, but he couldn't let go of his tattered pride.

"I won't have people think I can't take care of you, Gaby," he growled, and tore away from her.

Cole Elliott was standing on the porch and Gaby couldn't bring herself to beg Rayne in front of his father. Even now he'd already heard some of their angry words and his eyes gleamed with a grim kind of triumph.

"He's learning, missy," Cole said. "You can't hide from him the kind of woman you really are."

"I'm not trying to hide anything from Rayne," Gaby cried, rounding on her attacker. The day had just been too much for her. Now she stood facing Cole, her hands on her hips, her eyes snapping with fire.

"Don't do you no good to pretend anymore," Cole replied.

"I've never pretended to anything other than what I am," Gaby replied. "That's enough for Rayne. He knows how much I love him."

"Women like you don't know about loving," Cole spat out. His blue eyes had grown thin and watery-looking over the years and now they regarded her intently. "Rayne knows you ain't gonna stay. It's just a matter of time before you leave and take up with some other man."

"In the meantime, you intend to fill him with all the bitter suspicions you can," Gaby snapped. "Did you ever stop to think maybe the problem lies with you Elliott men? You're too proud and unbending. You make it too hard to love you. No wonder your women run away from you." Her voice broke and she hurried back into the house. She felt shaken that she'd uttered the unthinkable. She would never leave Rayne, never, she consoled herself. Standing in front of the fire, she clasped her hands to her bosom to still their trembling.

The evening was long and nearly unbearable. The ranch grew quiet. The tired cowhands had bunked down early. Jacinta and Maria went up to bed and still Gaby sat on, waiting for Rayne's return, although she was certain it would take him most of the night to ride to the Spencer ranch and back again. Why had he done this? she wondered. She wanted to weep in exasperation.

A coyote's howl awakened her and she lay staring into the darkness. Tomorrow seemed bleak and unpromising. She dozed and was awakened at the first flush of dawn by the sound of Rayne's footstep in the other room, at first sharp and clear on the wooden plank floor, then muffled by the woven rug as he crossed to the hearth. His steps, tired and dragging, turned toward the bedrooms.

"Rayne?" she called softly when he paused outside their bedroom door.

"It's me, Gaby," he said wearily, and walked on down the hall toward the spare bedroom, the one where Billy had slept. Gaby lay stiff with shock and hurt. What had happened to them that they could no longer share a room? How had it gone so wrong? she wondered helplessly. She lay and watched with tearful eyes the morning light spilling through the window.

11

The music box sat on the mantel, a hateful reminder of the estrangement between them. Gaby worked quietly at some needlework while Rayne slept. At times she longed to rush into the spare room and throw herself at him, begging him to talk to her so they could work out their differences.

She was in the kitchen and didn't hear him rise and leave the house. It was only when she took him a cup of coffee that she discovered his absence and was hurt anew. All day she watched the men come and go, hoping to catch a glimpse of him.

Rayne didn't return to the house until late. Silently, as if sensing the tension between them, Maria served the meal and scurried back to the kitchen, where Jacinta's scolding voice could be heard. Gaby and Rayne sat across from each other, their eyes not meeting.

"You mentioned last night that you had some trouble on the cattle drive," Gaby began tentatively. "What happened?"

"We got chased by outlaws on the trail and had to trade off some of our cows to the Kiowa for safe passage through their territory, and when we reached Kansas, they had vigilante posses to stop the herds from passing through their state," Rayne answered, and glanced up with a grin. "No trouble out of the ordinary."

Gaby couldn't repress a grin. "What did you do?"

"We took them west and then headed north. We finally sold them up there. It ran the meat off them, so we didn't get as much as we'd hoped, but it was a fairly successful drive."

"I'm glad you had no real problems and everyone is safe."

"You might say we were luckier than some," Rayne said, and his jaw tightened. "Jim Loving and some of the ranchers were captured and horsewhipped by the vigilante groups."

"Did they bother the Rocking E cattle?" Gaby asked.

"They tried," Rayne said grimly, "but we got away and left a few less members of their little clan."

"Now what will you do?" Gaby asked. "Where will you sell your cattle?"

"There's a market in the North for us, Gaby. We're going to make it with these ugly longhorns that have been running wild on the plains. There's a fortune on the hoof out there, and no one's going to stop us. I didn't make much money on my cattle this year. Neither did Clarence, although we did better than a lot of men did. A good many of them returned home busted, their cattle stolen by the Indians or the rustlers or run to death on the trails looking for a way to market, but there are too many Texas cattle and the demand for our beef is great. Every year more and more are going to get through. This ranch . . ." He paused and looked around the squat sturdy room with its graceless beauty, then turned back to Gaby. "This ranch is ours, Gaby. We can make it what we want it to be."

Watching him, seeing the light in his eyes, Gaby believed he could do anything. But then, she'd never doubted Rayne. He was a man who would never bow to defeat. There'd been no mention of her part in his plans. As usual, Rayne walked alone in his dreams. She could follow and share the dream if she wished, but she could do little to help make it a reality.

Some part of her wanted to cry out a denial of what she saw so clearly. Rayne Elliott would take care of her, he would coddle and pamper her. He would love her and give what he could of himself, but she would always occupy a small corner of his life. Blinking her eyes to hold back the prickle of burning tears, she rose from the table and began to clear the dishes; then another thought came to her.

"You said you didn't make much money on the sale of your cattle, and yet you bought back my music box. You should have saved your money for the ranch and to buy the Avery ranch."

"It doesn't matter," Rayne said, grasping her hand so he could run a rough hand up the smooth contour of her arm. "I wanted you to have your trinket back."

"I'm surprised Mr. Spencer sold the music box back to you," Gaby said slowly. "He seemed so taken with it."

"Maybe he was more taken with you," Rayne said, eyeing her thoughtfully. Gaby met his gaze candidly and he read the innocence in her eyes.

"How could he be? We spoke only briefly in the store while he examined the box."

"You have a way of making an impression," Rayne said, and Gaby flushed beneath his gaze. The words seemed more an accusation than a compliment. "Spencer's quite enamored of you. He wanted to return the box to you as a gift."

"That was kind of him," Gaby said. "But then, he impressed me as being a kind, gentle man. Did you express my gratitude to him?"

"It wasn't necessary," Rayne answered, and his voice was a low growl in his throat. "I paid him back his money. I always pay for things that are mine." He stood up and stalked away from the table. His words cut more deeply than he could ever have known. Gaby stood still, as if wounded, remembering how he'd had to pay for her time back in New Orleans. It seemed that neither of them could forget the past, though it caused them pain and misunderstanding. It was time to put the past behind them and make a new future for themselves. Gaby took a deep breath.

"Rayne, I want to get married," she blurted out. He turned to look at her and she could see the consternation on his face. The thought had never occurred to him, she realized.

"Married?" he echoed blankly.

"Married," she repeated. "Is the idea so outrageous?" Her eyes glinted with angry lights, but inside she felt frightened. She kept remembering Maddie's warning that men didn't marry women like Gaby and her.

"I have to confess I haven't given it any thought," Rayne said, stalling for time. His eyes didn't quite meet hers.

"That's apparent," Gaby said, "since it is I who must ask." Her words made him flush with anger, and he wasn't sure if it was for her or himself.

"You and I aren't the marrying kind, Gaby. Why pretend we are?"

His words wounded. Her wide eyes studied him. His expression was closed, his eyes cold. He seemed a stranger to her. "I didn't realize you felt this way," she said stiffly. "Otherwise I might not have come to Texas with you."

"You came on your own, Gaby," he said, forgetting in his anger and embarrassment how happy he'd been to find her on the ship. "I made you no promises."

He was right, of course, He hadn't. "I see I've presumed too much."

He'd hurt her and he hadn't meant to. Helplessly Rayne tried to make amends. "We've been happy," he said. "Let's leave things the way they are."

"And how are things, Rayne? What am I to you—your own private 'angel'?" Her tone was cynical, derisive, and it angered him.

"You tell me, Gaby. Have you been even that?"

She paused, uncertain of what his words meant, and then understanding washed over her. She gasped and whirled away from him, running blindly toward the bedroom before the explosion of angry tears erupted. In her haste, she forgot the step down from the dining area and went sprawling. The sobs she'd tried to hide burst forth.

"Gaby . . ." Rayne sprang forward. Gently he turned her, taking care not to cause her more pain. He saw the tears, saw the hurt in her eyes, and knew it was not all from the fall. He swept her up in his arms, cradling her, rocking her while he crooned to her and planted soothing kisses on her brow and temple.

"I'm sorry, Gaby," he cried hoarsely. "Forgive me."

Try as she might, she couldn't hold herself aloof from him. This was the Rayne she knew, not that hard-eyed stranger with the bitter, cruel words. Her arms stole up around his shoulders and she buried her face in the warm hollow of his neck. The sobs came, harsh and uncontrolled, sobs of loneliness and fear and anger. They sat on the floor holding each other, forgetting all the trials they'd endured for the past few months. They thought only of each other and the hurt each had caused the other.

At last Gaby's sobs quieted and Rayne raised his head to look down at her. Tendrils of hair clung damply to her cheeks, and her eyes were red from weeping. She'd never looked more beautiful.

"Give me some time, Gaby," he pleaded softly. Tenderly he pushed back the hair from her forehead. "I have to get used to the idea of marriage. I don't want to go through what Pa did. Marriage didn't help things between my parents."

"But we aren't your parents," Gaby protested.

"Shhh, I know we're not. They rushed into things without being sure of each other and what they wanted. Let's not do that, Gaby. Let's take our time. Just give me a little more time."

The hollow feeling fluttered in her stomach and she was tempted to cry out that they had less time than he imagined, but then the fluttering was gone and she remained silent. He wanted time. She would give it to him. His hands continued to smooth and caress her skin and hair.

"Gaby," he groaned, catching her to him, "I missed you so much."

"I missed you too, Rayne," she whispered. "I love you more than you can ever know." The soft light in her eyes showed him the truth of what she said. He scooped her up in his arms and headed toward the bedroom.

"You're in for a night of it," he said with a wicked gleam in his eyes. "I hope you're ready."

"At times I thought I couldn't take another breath until you were back," she whispered. Her eyes were dark pools of desire, reflecting the fire of his own passion.

"Show me," he whispered hoarsely. "Show me how much you missed me." The blue eyes beneath the widow's peak blazed with an intensity that inflamed her senses.

Gaby laughed, a soft husky sound in the breathless night, and pulled him down beside her. Lying across his chest, she entwined her fingers through his hair. The vibrant strands caressed her fingertips. Her lips lowered to his.

They tried to go slowly, tried to savor and enjoy, but their separation had been too long. They coupled and paused, eyes widening as the familiar pleasure washed through them; then body plunged and rose to meet body, muscles strained to reach and touch more and more.

They were spinning too fast. She called out Rayne's name and he was there for her. Together they reached their destination.

Later Rayne watched the dawn light steal into the window. He should get up and be about the ranch business, he thought, but Gaby lay in his arms. He watched the shadows move on her face. There were tired circles under her eyes. He should let her sleep, but his body was already sending its message to her. She woke, turning to him blindly, her mouth already seeking his before her eyes were fully opened. Her skin was warm and satiny. They made love sweetly.

When Rayne awoke again, the sun was already climbing high in the morning sky. With an exclamation he sprang out of bed and began pulling on his pants.

Gaby murmured sleepily and rolled over. "Where are you going?" she asked.

"I've got work to do, woman," Rayne cried. "I'm a rancher. I can't lie in bed all day." The bed sagged under his weight as he sat on the edge to pull on his boots. His broad, bare back was exposed to her view and Gaby gasped at what she saw.

"What happened?" she cried in horror. Rayne turned to look at her. He'd forgotten the condition of his back and the stripes it bore.

"You were one of the ranchers captured and whipped," Gaby cried accusingly. "Why didn't you tell me?"

"They got Pa. He's too old to take some of the things they would have done to him. They were trying to convince him to sign over his herd. I stormed their camp and got Pa out. They took me prisoner and tried the same tactics on me. I was able to hold out until Dusty got the rest of the men and found us."

Gaby watched his face. "You must love your father very much."

"You and Cole are all I have," he answered. "I couldn't let that gang torture him. His pride couldn't have taken it." He paused. "I don't think Pa's ever been happy about anything," he said softly. "I'd like these next years to be good ones for him."

Gaby sat watching as he finished dressing, her thoughts on the bitter old man who was Rayne's father. Cole was part of the reason why Rayne wouldn't talk about marriage now, but no matter how much the old man hated her, she must strive to overcome the bitterness between them. She had to make peace with him for Rayne's sake.

Gaby resolved to do that in the days that followed, but no opportunity presented itself to her. Cole stayed away from the ranch house, eating and sleeping in the bunkhouse with the other hands as he had before the drive.

The weeks that followed were quiet ones on the ranch. No longer did riders thunder out of the hills to attack and harass them.

Now that the cattle had been sold, Rayne turned his attention to other problems on the ranch. He had only a few hands to winter over; the rest had taken their pay and departed. They would hole up in town or at one of the larger ranches for the winter. Come spring, they would reappear, broke and eager to work again. Dusty and Billy, Slade and Little Finger would winter over, as well as Ramon, who was especially adept at breaking horses.

The days were growing shorter now, and a threat of colder weather hung in the air.

"We've been lucky this year," Dusty said one day, standing on the porch drinking a cup of coffee. Gaby had noticed his sudden fondness for Jacinta's coffee, but said nothing. "I've seen some years when we've had a real norther blow up by now."

"A norther?" Gaby asked. "What is that, a storm?"

Dusty chuckled. "Well, Miss Gaby, there's some folks back east that might call it just a winter storm, but once you've seen a norther, you'll know the difference. It's mean as a sidewinder.''

Later in the week, Lorna Blake rode out to the ranch. She didn't come to the house, but sat on her horse out by the corral talking to one of the hands. Gaby watched from the porch. It looked like the Texas woman was talking to Slade Harner. Gaby wondered what the two had in common. True, Slade was good-looking in a slick kind of way, but Gaby couldn't imagine Lorna interested in a mere cowhand. She had her sights set on Rayne. On an impulse, Gaby wrapped a shawl around her shoulders and walked across the yard to greet Lorna.

"Good morning," she called as she neared them. Slade turned a sullen face to her, then walked away toward the barn. Lorna smiled down at Gaby, her eyes challenging.

"Would you like to come up to the house for some coffee?" Gaby invited.

Lorna raised her head and looked around. "Is Rayne here?" she asked, ignoring Gaby's invitation.

"No, he's out somewhere checking on his herd," Gaby replied stiffly. She was growing tired of the woman's rudeness.

Lorna glanced at the sky. "Then I won't stay," she said. "I just rode out to tell you there's a dance Saturday night at the schoolhouse in Fowler. Are you coming?"

"I'd like to." Gaby said, pleased at the prospect of a social. She was grateful Lorna had taken the time to ride out on such a day to tell her about it. Maybe the woman wasn't so bad after all. "I'll check with Rayne and see if he wants to come."

"I'm sure you can persuade him," Lorna said. "I'm looking forward to your coming to this dance."

What made this dance so special? Gaby wondered. "We'll be there," she said. "That is, if the storm holds off." She hugged her shawl to her and tried not to shiver.

"It will," Lorna said, and wheeled her horse around. "Tell Rayne I'm saving a dance for him," she called over her shoulder, and galloped away. Gaby watched her departing figure, once again envious of her horsemanship.

Sighing she turned back. The prospect of a dance loomed before her and she picked up her skirts and ran toward the ranch house.

"Jacinta, Maria," she called. "We're going to a dance." Happily she thought of all her gowns, trying to decide which one to wear. It would be her first chance to meet many of Rayne's friends and neighbors. She wanted to look very special.

"Rayne, I want to talk to you," Cole said the next morning.

"I'll leave you alone." Gaby rose.

"That's not necessary," Cole snapped. "It don't make me no never-mind if you're here when I say my piece." Gaby sank back down in her seat and looked at him.

"I've come to tell you I'm leaving today," Cole said, dropping his news between them like a hot coal. Rayne's head snapped up and Gaby drew in a breath and let it out slowly. Her gaze flitted from one lean, tanned face to the other.

"You can't mean that," Rayne said.

"There's nothing holding me here anymore," Cole answered, and Gaby saw the pain flit across Rayne's face before he smoothed it away.

"Is it the ranch?" he asked quietly. "I'll back off it, give it back to you."

"I don't want it," Cole said, shaking his head. "I nearly walked away from it during the war, but I stayed in case you came back and wanted it. It's your ranch."

"Then why leave?" Rayne demanded. "I need every hand I can get. Stay here and help me build the ranch into something we can both be proud of." Gaby was touched that Rayne was willing to share his dream with his father.

"You don't really need me now," Cole's eyes flashed to Gaby and the unspoken message was all too clear. With her there he wasn't staying. He turned toward the door. "I'll get some grub and a bedroll and be on my way," he said.

Rayne stood up and looked at his father for a long minute, then stalked out of the ranch house. Cole watched him go and prepared to follow.

"Cole." Gaby walked across the room to stand before him, her fists clenched in anger. "You still don't play fair, do you?"

"I don't know what you're saying."

"You know perfectly well. You've given him a choice, you or me. As long as I'm here, you won't stay."

Cole looked at her coldly. "That's about the size of it."

"Then go," Gaby cried, calling his bluff. "Go, old man, because I'm not going. I'm staying here with Rayne."

Cole worked the brim of his hat in his gnarled brown hands, then glared at her, his blue eyes a weaker version of his son's. "I'll go, all right," he said, and Gaby's heart sank. "Either way, I win."

He was right. If he left now, the day would come when Rayne might blame her for his leaving. Cole put on his hat and flipped the brim slightly; a grim smile flitted across his features. He glanced around the room, taking in all the details she'd labored over so long. His gaze came back to her.

"I expect I'll be coming back," he said, and walked out.

"Do you really hate me that much?" Gaby cried, following him. "Do you hate me enough to do this to Rayne?" Cole didn't answer. He continued to walk across the yard toward the bunkhouse. "You're as bad as his mother," Gaby called, and his footsteps halted. He turned around and looked at her quizzically.

"How's that?" he asked warily.

"You're abandoning him too," Gaby said, "at a time when he's trying so hard to make the ranch work. He needs you. He needs your experience. He needs your hands. He needs his father beside him."

"Why should he need me? He's got you," Cole answered stubbornly.

"Yes, he has me for as long as he wants me," Gaby answered. She couldn't back down from him. She had to make him understand there was a place for both of them in Rayne's life. "You're his father."

"He's a growed-up man. He don't need to cling to me like a baby."

"No, and he never would. He'd go right on doing what he's done most of his life, standing on his own two feet, pretending he doesn't need anyone. He's got too much of that Elliott pride to ever show that he's hurt or that he needs anyone. Go ahead and leave like his mother did.

When he's thinking about you, which do you think he'll come to hate first?" Cole swung away from her, his body stiff as he stalked across the yard. "You're going to lose, Cole," Gaby cried after him. He walked on as if he hadn't heard her, and Gaby went back in the house, her shoulders sagging in defeat.

"What did you say to Pa?" Rayne asked that night at supper.

"Nothing much," Gaby replied. "I just tried to convince him to stay."

"Whatever you said worked, because he's staying," Rayne said, smiling at her. "Thank you, Gaby. I know he's been pretty difficult around you."

"Nothing I couldn't handle," she answered. "He's your father."

Rayne gripped her hand, his appreciation plain on his face. "He may not come around. He's pretty set in his ways."

"I'll win him over," Gaby said lightly.

"If anyone could, you're the one to do it. Just don't be disappointed if you can't."

"I won't be, as long as I know you love me," she said.

He grinned and carried her hand to his lips. "Do you need convincing of that?" he asked, a note of laughter in his eyes.

"It wouldn't hurt," Gaby answered, feeling the slow kindling of flames.

Rayne came around the table and picked her up in his arms. "It'll be a pleasure," he said softly, carrying her to their bedroom.

The day of the dance the sky was even more threatening. Maria came to help Gaby dress, her eyes shining softly.

"We are going to have a dance in the bunkhouse," she said. "Ramon will play for us and Billy is going to stay here for the dance."

"That's wonderful, Maria," Gaby said. "I'm almost tempted to stay here as well." She crossed to the pegs that held her gowns and took down a pale pink cotton gown that was too large for her. "I want you to have this."

Maria's eyes glowed. "*Gracias*," she said, hugging the gown to her. "I've never had anything so fine."

"It will look beautiful on you," Gaby said.

"I will never look as beautiful as you," Maria said, looking at Gaby with adoring eyes. Gaby had chosen to wear the white satin gown with the pink trim that she'd worn the first night Rayne came to her at the Court of Angels. Her hair had been swept up high on her head and arranged in soft curls. Her cheeks were pink with excitement and her eyes gleamed with happiness. Rayne caught his breath when he saw her.

"You look like an angel," he said, and a trickle of fear cut through him. What if he lost her? She was so much a part of his life. He couldn't bear it if she went away now.

"If you please, sir," she said prettily, curtsying to him.

Rayne held the warm cape and wished he had a fine carriage to escort her to the dance. He helped her up on the wagon and watched as she settled herself on the seat. Suddenly he felt lighthearted. He climbed up beside her and whistled at the horses. Dusty and Slade, mounted on their horses, fell in behind. Happily Rayne began to whistle a tune, and felt Gaby's small hand creep into the crook of his elbow.

12

The streets of Fowler were quiet except for the sound of music and laughter at one end of town where the schoolhouse sat. Rayne pulled the wagon as close as he could and helped Gaby down. Dusty and Slade had already drifted away to find their own pleasures. Likely they wouldn't be seen again the rest of the night. With morning everyone would drift back to the ranch at his own pace and spend the day resting up. When Texans gave a dance, it was no tame affair and often lasted all night long. Dances were few and far between, and the ranchers and their wives made the most of them.

Rayne and Gaby walked up the steps and entered the schoolhouse. The large room had been cleared of its desks and blackboard and the teacher's long flat board desk had been covered with a cloth and was now laden with dishes of food. Rayne took Gaby's cape and she moved forward to place the dish she'd brought with the rest.

People were milling about greeting each other with shouts of laughter. Gaby was aware of nearly everyone glancing at her. Suddenly feeling shy, she nodded her head at one or two women and offered a tentative smile. They did not return her greeting. Gaby looked around for Rayne. He was making his way through the crowd, nodding and greeting the people he knew, and he seemed to know nearly everyone. The men slapped him on the back and the women smiled.

"Well, I see you made it," Lorna said, and gratefully

Gaby turned to her. Friend or foe, at least she was someone Gaby knew. But Lorna's words were for Rayne, who had finally reached Gaby's side. "You've been a stranger lately," Lorna said, looking at him. "I expected you to ride over and tell me how the drive went."

"I've been busy at the ranch," Rayne said. Absently he looked around. He was surprised at the turnout and felt a growing uneasiness that none of the women were approaching them to be introduced to Gaby. Only Lorna had come. Gratefully Rayne turned back to her. "You heard we had some trouble."

"Pa told me," she answered. "He said you saved his life."

"Not really." Rayne shrugged. "We were all in hot water for a while, but we managed to escape with our herd intact. We were lucky." The band started tuning up and Lorna turned to Rayne once again, a sparkle in her eye.

"You owe me the first dance," she cried, gripping his arm.

"I'm sorry, Lorna, but I can't leave Gaby. We've just arrived," Rayne said.

Gaby stiffened at his words. "Don't let that stop you," she said coolly. How was it that the minute Lorna came around, she and Rayne were at odds with each other?

"Nonsense," the Texas woman said, "Gaby's a big girl." She turned to Gaby with a bright smile. "You don't mind if Rayne dances with me, just this once, do you?"

"Of course not," Gaby said with feigned graciousness. "As far as I can see, there's nothing to be afraid of."

"That's what many a greener thought," Lorna said, and tugged on Rayne's sleeve, leading him out onto the floor. Gaby stood watching, aware of the buzzing that was going around the room. Few people were making any attempt to hide their amusement now.

The dance ended and another started, but Rayne didn't return. Gaby could see him on the other side of the room talking to a group of people. Lorna clung to his arm possessively while she laughed at something he'd said. Gaby fought down a wave of hurt and disappointment. She'd come expecting to make new friends. Instead, she felt isolated and abandoned.

"You must be the woman Rayne's got for himself," a raspy voice said, and Gaby turned to find a woman with graying red hair and a layer of freckles across her leathery skin.

"Howdy," said the woman, holding out her hand. "I'm Jessie Walker."

"I'm Gabrielle Reynaud," Gaby said, smiling in gratitude at the woman.

"Well, are you Rayne's woman or not?" the woman demanded, and although her manner and words were brusque, her smile was genuine and Gaby found herself returning it. The woman meant no insult. It was just her manner.

"Yes, I'm with Rayne," she said.

"Umm, the Elliott men always had an eye for beautiful women," Jessie said. "Well, you're a little bit of a thing. How are you surviving out there at the ranch?"

"Well enough," Gaby answered, glad to have someone care enough to ask. "Your country is very beautiful."

"It ain't all that beautiful," Jessie snapped. "It can be downright mean to you if it takes a mind to, but it gets to growin' on you. I can't think of any other place I'd rather be than right here. It sure beats back east."

"Have you lived in Texas long?" Gaby asked, warming to the crusty old woman.

"Just about my whole life," Jessie said. "I come out here as a bride when I wasn't hardly older'n you, and not much bigger, though that might be hard to believe now." The woman slapped at her ample hip. "But I made a wrong choice of husbands, so I run off. I was goin' back east, but someone offered me a job housekeeping. I decided to stay and give Texas another chance. I've been just about all over this state at one time or another. I was at San Jacinto when they fought the Mexicans there, and I saw Santa Ana and his troops makin' a beeline back for Mexico. I've been poor and I've been rich and I'll tell you now, there ain't no place more unforgivin' than Texas if you're poor and down on your luck." The woman paused for a breath and fanned her flushed face. Bewildered, Gaby thought back over all she'd said. A hundred questions came to mind, but before she'd had a chance to ask even one, the woman took off again. Gaby relaxed and let her talk, listening with amusement as she told tales of Texans and their state. No wonder they were such a proud lot, Gaby thought.

The time passed quickly. So enthralled by Jessie and her earthy conversation was Gaby that she was unaware that Rayne had disengaged himself from Lorna and returned, only to find Gaby preoccupied.

"Come have a drink with us," someone said, slapping Rayne on the back, and with a last reassuring glance back at Gaby, he followed the men outdoors, where the real drinking was done.

"May I join you?" a gentle voice asked, and Gaby looked up at Aaron Spencer. His gray eyes were warm and friendly as he looked at her.

"Hello," Gaby said, then, remembering all the fuss Rayne had made over the music box, flushed guiltily.

"It's nice to see you again, Miss Reynaud," Aaron said. Gaby noticed he made no attempt to hide his disfigurement.

"Likewise, Mr. Spencer."

"Please call me Aaron."

"Aaron," she repeated dutifully. "I'm terribly sorry about the music box. Thank you for selling it back to us."

"It was not my intention to sell it back. I meant it as a gift to a beautiful woman. Mr. Elliott didn't agree. I can't say I blame him. He left behind a bag of gold which one of my men is returning to the ranch even now. I knew Rayne wouldn't be there to object a second time."

"That's very kind of you," Gaby said, "but now I must object. The amount is much too large for me to accept as a gift."

"It would please me if you would," Aaron said so gently that Gaby was loath to argue further. Rayne would be furious with her and they'd had too many disagreements lately. She wanted to avoid more. Aaron saw her distress and guessed at the reason.

"I was just telling Gaby here about some of those early years in Texas before she become a state," Jessie said.

"We do have a colorful history," Aaron agreed, "as do most of the people who've settled here. Most of them came to find a better future than they had back east, some were running from the law or scandals. Most of us felt like we were moving toward something as much as we were running away."

"I see," Gaby said.

"Not sure you do," Jessie interrupted. "If you did, you wouldn't let anything any of these people do tonight bother you. Like Aaron said, most of these people came here looking for better than they had before, and most of 'em found it, rough as life is out here. They found a better way of life or they'd be heading back across the plains as fast as they could."

Gaby looked at Jessie wide-eyed. The older woman had seen the way the others had ostracized her and had done her best to smooth over the hurt.

"There's been an ugly rumor floating around right now, but it'll pass," Jessie continued. "People forget about what you were. It's what you are right now that counts out here, not what happened back east."

"You know about my background?" Gaby asked in amazement.

"Just about everyone in this room knows about it," Jessie said. "Lorna Blake made sure of that."

"She doesn't like me," Gaby said miserably.

"You're darn tootin' she don't like you, girl," Jessie said. "You took her man from her. She's fightin' back. 'Course, she ain't fightin' as fair as she ought to, but then, that never stopped Lorna nor her ma when she was alive. The question is, what are you going to do about it?"

"I'm here to stay," Gaby said. "Lorna can't drive me away as long as Rayne wants me."

"Good for you!" Jessie cried. "Now, Aaron, I think Gaby here wants to dance. I ain't seen her out on that dance floor all evening. It's about time something brought that man of hers back around here to check on her."

"I quite agree," Aaron said. "Would you do me the honor, Miss Reynaud?"

"Please call me Gaby," she said, feeling she'd made two friends.

The band broke into a lilting waltz and Aaron swung her out on the floor. Because of his limp, they moved around the floor slowly. Gaby knew people were watching them, but she held up her chin and smiled prettily at Aaron. She had no idea what that smile did to his insides.

They'd made one circle around the floor when Aaron suddenly halted. "I'm sorry, Gaby," he said. "I'm afraid I'm of little use at something like this." A look of embarrassment crossed his face. "I'm afraid I've pulled something the wrong way," he said diffidently.

"Can I help you?" Gaby asked anxiously. She felt sorry for him. He was too kind a man to have this happen to him.

"I don't think so," Aaron said. A trickle of sweat appeared on his forehead and for the first time Gaby realized he was in real pain and trying hard not to show it.

"I'm much stronger than I look," she said, and taking hold of his hand, laid his arm across her shoulder. Together they made their way off the floor. To onlookers it seemed merely that they were getting overly cozy with each other. A few clucked their tongues in disapproval, wondering what a young girl of her background wanted with a crippled, scarred older man like Aaron Spencer, unless it was his money. None thought to wonder what he might want from her. They all thought they knew.

Once they were back on the sidelines, Gaby helped Aaron into a chair. "I'll be quite all right now," he said gratefully. "I'm sorry we weren't able to finish the dance."

"Don't give it a thought," Gaby cried. "Can I get you something for the pain, a drink, something?"

"I'm fine just sitting here," Aaron assured her. "You should go on and have some fun for yourself." He glanced around and saw that Charley Jepson was already bearing down on them, his intent evident in his eyes.

"May I have this dance?" Charley asked, and without waiting for Gaby's response, whisked her out on the floor. Although the band played another waltz, the man's enthusiasm made him swirl her around the floor in double-quick time. Gaby was breathless by the time the dance had ended, but by then there was another man introducing himself and leading her out onto the floor, and after that, another. Gaby danced with nearly every man there.

She was thankful when the band took a break and went outside to eat and drink some whiskey.

"Come sit by us," Jessie called as Gaby stood looking around for Rayne. He was nowhere in sight, and neither was Lorna. Gaby tried not to be bothered by that, but resentment rippled through her as she turned toward Jessie and Aaron.

Rayne came to join them soon after, as they sat with their plates on their laps. Pulling up a chair, he straddled it, his blue eyes bright with anger. "I see you've been amusing yourself this evening," he said, without even looking at her. His gaze was pinned on Aaron. It was obvious he'd been drinking and it occurred to Gaby that she'd never seen Rayne drunk before. She felt annoyed at him but strove for an easy smile.

"Jessie's been telling me all about her early years here in Texas. She's led an exciting life."

"And what has Mr. Spencer been telling you?" he asked, his tone offensive. Gaby flushed with anger, embarrassed by Rayne's bad manners. Aaron and Jessie had befriended her when no one else in the room would.

Gaby laid her plate aside and stood up. "I'm tired, Rayne," she said. "I'd like to start back to the ranch now."

"So soon?" Rayne sneered. "You haven't danced with all the men yet."

Gaby blinked against the sting of tears. She would not cry here in front of everyone. "Have you missed any of the dances with Lorna?" she asked. "And what were you doing when you weren't dancing with her? You certainly weren't here by my side." She bit back the rest of her angry words, aware that people were glancing at them with undisguised interest. The band members returned, and picking up their instruments, began to tune them. Gaby was grateful to see the crowd's interest turned back to the band. Perhaps she could slip quietly away, but Rayne had other ideas.

"You haven't danced with me yet," he said. He led her out onto the floor. Once again attention was riveted on the two of them. Some of the onlookers snickered at the way the tall rancher was treating his Creole woman.

Pride helped her hold her head high and smile brilliantly. Only Rayne could see how twisted and pathetic it was.

She moved into his arms and they glided around the floor. The music wove a wall around them, closing them off from the others. Rayne's eyes held hers and slowly the anger in him began to seep away. What she'd said was true. He'd left her alone too much this evening, but each time he'd come to check on her, she'd seemed happy and occupied with Jessie Walker and Aaron Spencer. At first he'd been happy to see her making new friends, but as the evening wore on and he began to hear the rumors floating around, he'd grown more on edge. He knew the rumors weren't true. People might whisper "New Orleans whore," but he knew of her innocence the first night she'd come to him. One rumor in particular, elusive and maddening, linking Gaby and Thad Martin, had infuriated him. He'd returned to the dance ready to confront her about it, only to see her leaving the floor with Aaron Spencer's arms draped around her. He'd wanted to fling himself across the room and strangle the man. Instead he'd gone back outside for another drink, several in fact. He wasn't a drinking man and the raw whiskey hadn't helped. Now he glanced down at Gaby, seeing her in her pretty satin dress, and the pride he'd felt earlier seemed like ashes in his mouth.

They danced, each automatically fitting to the other in a rhythm that was too familiar to ignore in spite of their anger with each other. They were so enclosed in the misery of their own making that they were unaware of the handsome couple they made gliding around the floor. Rayne towered over Gaby's small, dainty figure; she arched and swayed toward his taller, stronger one.

The music ended and they stopped moving, looking at each other for a long second. He would ask her to explain the rumors about Thad Martin and her, he decided. It was probably something quite innocent.

"Gaby," he began, striving to keep his voice even and noncommittal. He wanted her to know he was trying to be fair. There was a flurry of conversation around them and someone laughed. Rayne raised his head and scowled.

Gaby was all too aware now of the whispers. She saw how they had hurt Rayne's pride. His woman was being laughed at behind his back, and the Elliott pride couldn't take that. She whirled away from him and made her way toward the door, her eyes straight ahead, her head high. She was shaking so she feared she might begin to weep.

Rayne watched her leave and with a curse stumbled back outdoors to the pocket of men who carried bottles of whiskey in their hip pockets. He needed a drink badly, he thought. At the last minute he veered away, coming to rest in the dark recesses of the steps. His head was reeling, and somewhere in his mind he acknowledged that the whole evening had gone wrong.

The laughter and talk of the other men floated to him on the night air.

"How'd you know she was one of them angels, Slade?" someone asked, and Slade Harner took another pull from the bottle and laughed.

"I was in New Orleans during the war. One night me and some of the others took off and went to this here Court of Angels. Whooee, I tell you it was the finest calico palace I ever been in. They had women in there of all colors, sizes, and shapes."

"Is that where you seen her?"

"Shee-et, I spent the night with her. She's sure something. She's been grateful to see a friendly face since she come to Texas, I can tell you." Slade hitched his thumbs in his belt and feigned nonchalance.

"I hear she had that young kid sleeping there with her in the house when Rayne got back."

"Yeah, well, what could she do, boys, I wasn't around." Slade smirked. "She's been right content since I got back."

"Hey, Thad, what's this talk about you and her down in the stables?"

Thad Martin got out a paper and some tobacco and began rolling himself a cigarette. "Yeah," he acknowledged, "we had some business." His remark was followed by ribald laughter.

"What's she look like under all them frills and petticoats?" a man asked, and giggled drunkenly.

Thad struck a match and lit his cigarette, drawing leisurely while he waited for the tension to build. He cast a quick glance at the shadows near the steps. Rayne

Elliott was still there. Thad could almost feel the rage emanating from him. He blew a smoke ring.

"She's got about the prettiest set of tits I ever seen," he said. Some men turned away, disgusted by the turn the talk had taken; others pressed closer. "She's got this little red star on one of them. Dangedest thing you ever saw."

"Imagine that," a man said.

"I kinda figure she came stamped prime meat and she earned the rating." Thad didn't see the black shadow looming up at him. He heard the roar of anger and then a lean hard body slammed into him, sending him sprawling across the schoolyard. He fell against a rope swing and felt it wrap around his arm and shoulder as he hit the ground. He jumped to his feet, flinging the broken seat to one side, but the weight of the man carried him backward once again, this time into the watering trough.

The breath went out of Thad's body with a whoosh. For a moment he lay limp, trying to get his breath, his face barely out of the water. Iron fists fastened around the front of his shirt and he was jerked out of the trough. Something slammed into the side of his head and it took him a moment to realize it was a fist.

This wasn't the way he'd planned it. Where the devil was Jed? Rayne was coming at him again and Thad swung a fist, feeling some pleasure in the pain as it connected with Rayne's jaw. Rayne fell backward, sprawling in the dust, and Thad took the time to glance around for Jed. His man stood to one side, his hand on his gun as he looked for a chance. Thad nodded at him. All he had to do was back Rayne up that way.

The rest of the men had formed a circle and were placing bets among themselves. Women were streaming from the schoolhouse and across the yard. That was the last thing he had time to see before Rayne was back on his feet and charging him. Thad was surprised to see how fast the man could move.

The two men stood spraddle-legged, watching each other warily, their fists clenched before them, ready to deliver a blow when the other dropped his guard. Rayne's eyes were feral, his teeth bared. Thad maneuvered around so Rayne's back was to Jed. He could see Jed glancing around surreptitiously as he drew his gun and aimed it. Just a few more seconds and Rayne Elliott would no longer be a stumbling block to Thad's plans.

There was a blur of movement at one side, and warily Thad darted a glance away from Rayne. Aaron Spencer was moving toward the concealed gunman. Thad wanted to cry out a warning but there was no time. Aaron already had his gun in his hand.

"Drop it, Jed," he said quietly, and the gunman looked around, surprised that anyone had known he was there in the bushes. "I said drop it." Aaron put the barrel of his gun against the man's side and felt him stiffen. Slowly Jed released his hold on the gun and it fell to the ground.

Gaby came running from the cloakroom, her shawl already clutched about her. She'd been about to ask Dusty to take her home when she'd heard the commotion and seen the women hurrying out-of-doors. Something told her Rayne was involved. Frantically she pushed to the front of the crowd and halted. Rayne and Thad Martin were rolling on the ground.

"What are they fighting about?" one of the women asked.

"They're fighting over the Creole angel," a man called gleefully.

"We might have known." Lorna Blake's voice rang out clear and condemning on the night air. "When you bring a woman like that among decent folks, there's always going to be trouble."

There was a chorus of agreement. Gaby wanted to cry out to them the unfairness of their condemnation, but it would do no good. Her shoulders slumped in defeat. Strong arms circled her waist, and rough, freckled hands took hold of hers.

"Hold your head up, girl. You need to now more than ever," Jessie told her. "You've got your share of unfairness, and that's a fact, but do the best you can with it." With Jessie's wiry old body beside her, Gaby found the strength to straighten her shoulders.

Thad took a punch and slid to the ground, doubled over, gasping for air. Coughing as if gagging for air, he slipped a knife from his boot and waited, cradling the knife against his stomach as if he'd been hurt worse than

he really was. His line of vision took in Rayne's boots as
the man towered over him. Rayne moved away as if
willing to end the fight there. His back was to Thad.
Thad stood up and in one quick movement brought the
knife up.

"Rayne!" A woman cried out and he swerved to one
side. The knife buried itself in a tree. Fury burned in
Rayne's eyes as he turned back to Thad. He launched
himself at the man, knocking him over. This time there
was no letup. Thad felt his consciousness slipping as blow
after blow of Rayne's powerful fists landed on him. He
clawed at Rayne's face, but the powerful hands closed
around Thad's throat, cutting off his breath.

"Rayne, don't," Gaby cried. "You're killing him."

"Rayne, that's enough," Dusty said, dragging him off
the inert body. "He's not worth killing."

Chest heaving, Rayne stood up and looked down at
the battered man. "Stay out of my way, Martin," he
snarled. "Next time there may not be anyone to stop me
from killing you." He took his hat and gun, which Dusty
had retrieved, and limped toward Slade Harner. The
man waited, his eyes darting around the circle. He'd
always been a little afraid of Rayne. Rayne's fierce glance
held him for a moment and then Rayne's fist slashed out
and Slade was sprawled on the ground.

"Don't come back to the ranch," Rayne ordered. "Dusty
will bring your gear to town and leave it at the saloon.
The next time you step foot on my property I'll kill you."
He limped away. People made room for him, stepping
back, their eyes not meeting his.

"Rayne," Gaby cried, running to touch his arm.

Weaving slightly, he looked down at her lovely face.
"Get to the wagon," he ordered. "We're going back to
the ranch." She bit back her humiliation and meekly
walked to the wagon.

"It's all over, folks," Dusty called. "Go on back to the
dance."

They rode in silence all the way back to the ranch.
Rayne had hardly pulled the wagon to a stop before
Gaby jumped down and ran into the house. She could
hear him leading the horses to the barn.

The house was quiet. Jacinta and Maria had retired for

the night. Gaby drew in a shuddering breath, remembering how happy she'd been at the start of the evening. Wearily she moved away from the door and crossed to the mantel, her hands automatically reaching out to touch the delicate little jeweled music box. Her hand brushed against a leather bag. She picked it up and weighed it in her hand. Aaron Spencer's messenger had returned the gold coins. Sighing, Gaby carried the bag to the bedrooom. It was something else for Rayne and her to quarrel about.

A scrape of boot leather made her whirl. Rayne had taken time to splash water over his face. His thick black hair was still damp from it. With the dirt and dust gone, the bruises on his face stood out in ugly relief. Gaby hurried to him, her hand going out instinctively to offer him comfort.

"Leave it," he said, turning away from her touch.

"You're hurt. I'll get something for your bruises."

"Don't bother." Rayne gripped her hand, staying her. His eyes were nearly black as he looked at her. "Tell me about you and Thad Martin in the stable."

"It's not what you think, Rayne," Gaby said, imploring him with her eyes to understand and give her a chance to explain.

"Isn't it? He knew about your birthmark, Gaby. What am I supposed to think?"

"You're supposed to think I'm telling the truth." Her voice was a whispered plea. "You would if you really loved me."

"Love? What's your idea of love, Gaby? You hand it out freely to any man that comes along with the price. Martin, Slade, Billy, perhaps even Aaron Spencer."

"Billy?" Gaby cried, aghast that he could think she would seduce an innocent boy like Billy. "You can't believe this," she said, heartbroken.

"Can't I? Why not, Gaby? Prove it isn't true. I want to believe it isn't, but there's too much evidence that what everyone is saying about you is true. Slade knew about the Court of Angels."

"Maybe Dusty told him," Gaby said.

"I asked him not to."

"Why?" Gaby demanded. "Were you ashamed of me and what I was?" Rayne's eyes dipped away from her for an instant. "Maybe that's the real reason you don't want to marry me."

"I was trying to protect you."

"If you really wanted to protect me, Rayne, you would have married me, but you can't forget my past."

He looked back at her, his eyes unrelenting in their anger. "I could live with your past, Gaby, if it didn't keep intruding in our lives here. You seem to be the one who can't put it behind you and start over. I always find you with men around you."

"And what of you and Lorna Blake?" Gaby demanded. She'd grown angry now. "Don't you think that woman might be behind some of the gossip that was making the rounds tonight?"

"Lorna?" Rayne asked in astonishment. "Lorna tried to stop it. I heard her myself."

"I'll bet she did, after she saw it was well spread. She'd do anything to get you back."

"Lorna and I are just friends."

"But that wasn't always so," Gaby cried. "Once you were lovers." Rayne was astonished. How had she known?

Gaby watched the guilt play over his face.

"That's in the past," he said lamely. "I came back from the war and she was waiting for me, but it's over. It has been ever since I got back from New Orleans."

"So you say," Gaby cried. "How am I to believe you? From the way Lorna acts, I wouldn't think so. Your past is intruding in our lives as well."

"Don't try to change the subject," Rayne shouted. "Don't try to excuse what you've done by pointing a finger at me. I saw how Spencer looked at you tonight. I saw how he had his arm around you on the dance floor. Is he your next conquest?"

"No," Gaby cried, goaded to anger. "He's my present conquest. I forgot to tell you. Aaron Spencer sent this back." She held out the bag of ten-dollar gold pieces, allowing the coins to spill into her hands. "It's for services rendered."

In his anger, he believed her. His hands slashed out to knock the gold pieces from her hands. They fell to the floor with a dull, heavy thud and rolled around at her feet. Rayne's teeth were clenched together as if he could barely restrain his fury. Involuntarily Gaby took a step backward, but his hand grasped her arm, pulling her toward him. One hand came up to catch her hair at the back of her head.

"Is that what you want, pay for what you do so well?" he demanded. "I never understood before." He flung her across the room. As she fell back on the bed, he was on her, his long legs pinning her, his hands holding her still, while his mouth swooped down to claim hers in a punishing kiss. "Is this what you want, Gaby?" he hissed. "No love, just cold, hard passion?"

"Rayne, please," she whispered, growing frightened of him. She'd never been treated like this by him. He wasn't listening to her plea. His hands gripped the front of her gown and pulled, ripping it from her in shreds.

"Rayne, don't do this," she sobbed. The light in his eyes was cold and implacable. The beautiful gown she'd donned with such anticipation that evening now lay around her in rags. Rayne's body fell heavily on hers, his knees bruising her thighs as he forced them apart.

At first Gaby resisted him; then, sobbing softly, she wrapped her arms around him and clutched him to her, hoping the love between them would still save them from this dreadful mistake.

He took no time with her, made no attempt to prepare her, and still she tried to follow, tried to respond lovingly. She tried to give when nothing more was demanded of her than that she submit herself. With her love she tried to take away the sting of his loveless invasion of her body. Rayne felt her tremble beneath him and knew it was from pain and not desire.

His fury and passion were quickly spent and he rose from the bed and stood looking down at her. She lay in the remnants of her tattered gown, her pale breasts still bearing the imprints of his hands, the tiny star birthmark mocking him. Her face was smudged with tears, her lips swollen from his kisses. There was a wanton look about her that fired his blood while it outraged him more.

"Cover yourself." The disgust in his voice was for himself more than for her. He turned away from the sight of her and heard the whisper of bedclothes as she pulled a coverlet over her shivering body.

"Tomorrow we'll leave," he said woodenly. "I'll take you back to Galveston and put you on a ship to New Orleans."

"Rayne . . ." Her voice broke. He turned back to look at her. She lay propped on one elbow, the lamplight casting shadows on the ivory of her arms and shoulders.

"There's nothing more to say, Gaby. This is best. Take the gold. It's yours, for services rendered."

Her head bowed, the dark, glossy hair fell forward in a curtain over her face. "If you say so," she murmured from its shadows.

He'd hurt her. He sensed that. Not physically. Even in his anger he'd been careful of her fragile body. The hurt had gone deeper than any physical pain, but then, he'd been hurt too. He looked at her huddled on the bed and turned away. It was over. It had been a mistake to bring her here.

A great pain rose in his chest, and turning, he blundered out of the bedroom into the cold night air. Tears stung his lids as he gulped in great breaths of air. His chest felt tight and painful. He glanced back at the ranch house. The light in their bedroom window burned warm and welcoming, but there was no welcome for him not now, not anymore. Never again. He made his way to the bunkhouse and found an empty bed. The night seemed cold and bleak, and none of his tomorrows looked any better.

13

Gaby lay where he'd left her, her body convulsed with sobs. Rayne had shamed her. It seemed her heart had been torn into pieces. The way he'd looked at her before he left. As if she were a stranger, or worse, a woman of the streets who'd pleasured him for a moment and would soon be forgotten. The bright promise of their love seemed nothing more than a fantasy now.

At last her sobs slowed and she lay staring into the lamplight thinking of all that had transpired that evening. She thought of Lorna Blake and the way Rayne had defended her. He'd not been so quick to defend Gaby's good name. Thinking of it, Gaby grew angry.

How dare he treat her this way? she stormed. How dare he think he could bring her here and then ship her back to New Orleans when he was finished with her? Gabrielle Reynaud was not a woman to be so easily moved around. She had plans of her own, and right now she intended to stay right here in Texas. She wouldn't be run off by a little gossip. And she wouldn't stay here at the Rocking E Ranch, dependent on Rayne and his father's reluctant charity.

Gaby drew on a gown of dark serge and pulled on her heavy boots. Throwing a warm cape around her shoulders, she made her way to the barn. The sky was black, the stars hidden behind dark clouds. A cold wind tugged at her cape, but Gaby was not to be deterred. She would ride to town and stay with Jessie Walker. She felt sure her new friend would offer her asylum at least until she

could decide what to do with herself. Perhaps she would
hire herself out as a housekeeper the way Jessie had
done. She'd go all over Texas working as Jessie had, and
someday she'd have her own wealth of stories to tell
young people new to Texas.

Awkwardly Gaby saddled a horse, and leading it to a
mounting block, climbed on. Suddenly, with the reins in
her hands and the cold wind moaning around the sides of
the barn, she felt frightened, as if she were about to take
a step into an unknown future. Rayne wouldn't be at her
side now. At the thought of Rayne and the way he'd
looked at her earlier, Gaby found her courage and prodded the horse with her boot.

She held the horse to a walk until they had cleared
the corral; then she urged it to a gallop. The temperature
had dropped and the warm cape felt thin and inadequate.
Gaby shivered and pulled it around her more tightly. She
wouldn't be stopped by a little wind, she told herself, and
pushed on.

A half-hour later she was huddled miserably in the
saddle, her cape plastered to her body by the cold rain
that had begun to fall. Her horse seemed less and less
inclined to move in a direction away from his warm stall
and feed bag. The rain had turned to sleet. It hit against
her face and washed down the collar of her cape.

Ahead, she could see the bridge. Town was still several
weary miles beyond that.

The rain beat a tattoo on the wooden planks, blotting
out any sound of her passing. The river swirled and
roared below the bridge, its waters swollen by the sudden
deluge. Gaby shivered when she reached the other side,
happy to be off the bridge.

The temperature had fallen considerably now and Gaby
trembled inside her stiff, wet cape. Each breath she drew
seemed laden with icy vapors, cutting and stinging the
back of her throat. The rain slanted against her, blinding
her. She'd heard of the blue northers that swept down
out of the Rockies and had thought them exaggerated,
but now she felt a tremor of fear. What had Dusty told
her? Get to shelter as fast as you can. She was far out in
the middle of nowhere and she had no shelter. She de-

bated turning back to the ranch, but pride kept her moving forward.

"Giddap," she cried furiously to the horse, and leaned forward in the saddle. She had to get to town quickly or she might not make it at all. Fear prompted her to kick at the mustang's sides, and suddenly he leapt forward, nearly throwing her. She clung to the wet, slippery reins, forcing her stiff knees to clamp harder. The mad gallop caused her to wobble precariously. She sawed at the reins, trying to bring the horse to a stop, but to no avail. He raced over the icy ground, and the sage and bushes rushed by in a blur, their shapes looming up frighteningly before falling away behind her.

The horse left the road and ran along the side, blundering too near the trees so Gaby was in danger of being unseated. She clung to the pommel as tightly as she could, while her teeth jarred and rattled together with each movement of the horse. She didn't see the low-hanging branch. She sensed something was there and bent low over the horse's neck, and still the branch swept her out of the saddle, stunning her with a blow to the head. She landed on the ice-slicked ground, gasping with pain. Sleet pounded down on her unprotected body as she lay curled in a ball, cradling her aching head. For a moment she feared she might faint. Only the greater fear that she could die before the night was out made her fight the darkness that threatened to engulf her.

She had to get to town before the weather made another shift. She searched for her horse, but free of his burden, he had turned back toward home. She had little choice but to walk. At least it would warm her, she thought grimly, pulling her cape closer about her. It was half-frozen and stiff, but it still provided some protection from the rain.

Gallantly she set out, concentrating on Jessie and what she would tell the old woman when she saw her. She couldn't bear to think of Rayne. That part of her life was behind her.

She heard carriage wheels and was sure it was Rayne come to find her, but the sound came from the direction of town, not the ranch. A solitary buggy came into view. Its top and sides had been pulled forward to protect the

driver from the weather, and Gaby feared he might not
see her. Her pulse fluttered in her throat. Stepping into
the middle of the road, she held up her hand and waved.

"Help," she called. "Please help me."

"Whoa," the man called to his horses, and the buggy
came to a halt. Gaby ran forward, relieved that she was
not alone out here.

"Please, can you give me a ride?" she called, and the
driver leaned out to regard her with his quiet gray eyes.
She didn't need to see the face to know it was Aaron
Spencer.

"Climb in here," he called, holding out a hand to her.
Gaby took it and was surprised at the strength of the man
as he pulled her up onto the platform.

"Where's Rayne?" he shouted above the noise of the
rain on the buggy top.

"He's back at the ranch," Gaby said, and suddenly felt
reluctant to discuss their problems with anyone else. As
if sensing her reticence, Aaron let it drop.

"Get under here and get warm," he ordered, flinging
aside the buffalo robe that covered his legs.

"I'm all wet." Gaby stayed where she was. She could
feel the water drip off her nose and chin and trickle down
her back. Aaron reached out to touch her cape. She
shivered uncontrollably, her teeth beginning to chatter
together.

"Take that off," Aaron ordered, and took off his own
cape.

"I . . . I can't take yours," Gaby protested, but it was
too late. The heavy woolen garment settled around her
shoulders, enveloping her in its heavenly warmth. "N-now
you'll g-get c-cold," she stuttered as he took her shoulders and nudged her down on the seat.

"I'll be all right," he dismissed her words. "I'm dry
and warm already and the robe will keep me comfortable." He was busy tucking the robe around her legs and
feet, and Gaby lay back, happy to be pampered for the
moment. When he saw she was completely covered except for her eyes and nose, he drew the other end of the
robe over himself, and picking up the reins, urged his
horses forward.

"What are you doing out here in this kind of weather?" he asked.

"I didn't know it would turn this fast," Gaby said lamely, avoiding the real question. "My horse stumbled into a tree branch and unseated me."

"It's a good thing I left town when I did," Aaron replied. "A lot of folks are going to weather out the storm in Fowler. I decided to try to make it back to my ranch."

Gaby shivered at the thought that she might yet be trudging along the road if not for him.

They took the road back the way Gaby had come. It lay like a wet gray ribbon that was fast turning slick. Now and then the buggy wheels skittered sideways and the horses seemed to have some difficulty in keeping their footing.

When they reached the fork in the road that led off to the bridge, they could hear the river water churning and slapping high on the pilings. Aaron brought the buggy to a halt and they sat silent, closed in by the rain drumming on the taut canvas. The world beyond the warmth of the buggy was gray and indistinct in the pale dawn light. Gaby shivered.

"We have to get out of this," Aaron said. "I don't trust the bridge. It's been swept away before, and the Rocking E Ranch is too far on the other side. My ranch is closer. I'm going there first."

"All right," Gaby said calmly, but she sensed the urgency in his voice. Her own apprehension grew. As Aaron picked up the reins again, a movement in the gray landscape caught her eyes.

"Wait," she cried. "There's my horse." She leaned out to call to her mount. "Come, Sandy. Come on, boy." Her voice was swallowed up in the beating rain. Helplessly, she watched as the horse worked his way toward the bridge. Just as he was about to cross, a loud rending sound split the monotone of the downpour. Whinnying, the horse backed away, rearing and rolling his eyes in fear. Then all was silent save for the steady downpour of the rain.

"The bridge is going," Aaron said. "We'd better move on."

"What about my horse?" Gaby cried, concerned over the poor frightened creature she'd brought out into the night.

"He's too spooked now to catch him," Aaron said. "We'll have to leave him."

"Will he be all right?"

"I hope so." Aaron hated to leave her with false hope, but his primary concern was for their own safety now.

With the light growing in the east, they could see that the water had reached the bridge itself and was even now working at the log foundations that held it in place.

"It's getting worse," Aaron said, and as if to confirm his statement, the rain turned to hail, hitting against the backs of the horses with such fine cutting stings that they whickered and moved restlessly. Aaron slapped his reins and turned the buggy down the fork of the road leading to his ranch. He'd have to hurry if they were going to make it before the worst of the storm hit. He hated to think of what could happen to them if they didn't get to some shelter soon.

Gaby sat staring straight ahead. If Aaron Spencer was worried, they were in danger. Her thoughts drifted back to Rayne. Had he missed her yet? Was he worried about her? She longed to be back at the ranch. It had been childish of her to start out like this, just as childish as his suspicions, but if she'd stayed, they could have worked things out. Then she remembered the way he'd made love to her, the coldness in his eyes and in his hands when he'd touched her.

Rayne didn't love her anymore. He'd made that clear. He wouldn't care what happened to her now. She was alone in this vast country called Texas. Sobs of self-pity fought their way up to her throat, but she swallowed them back. Aaron Spencer had been kind enough to help her; she wouldn't be a further burden on him with her tears. He needed to direct all his thoughts to getting them to safety. Blinking her eyes, she peered into the sleet, straining to catch the first glimpse of the ranch house.

It seemed they'd been driving for hours. Her muscles felt tense and cramped and she guessed Aaron must feel the same way. Suddenly one of the horses squealed and went down, his heavy body acting as a brake on the other horse and the rolling carriage. They lurched sickeningly and for a moment the buggy leaned dangerously. Aaron was thrown against her. Gaby screamed and gripped his arm. The buggy slid around on the icy road and then they were tipping to one side, going over in a squeal of wood and frightened horses.

Rayne lay in the bunk listening to the rain sleeting against the roof. He'd slept late, later than he'd intended, but there seemed little reason to be up and about. He'd tossed most of the night. The rest of his men and his father still lay huddled in their bunks, loath to get up and face the harshness of a day like this. Rayne heard the rattle of ice on the tin roof.

It looked like a norther, the first of the season. Mentally he checked over everything. His ranch was secure, only some cows out on the south range to be checked. He'd send Slade up to the line camp as soon as the weather let up.

He frowned, remembering he'd fired Slade the night before; then all the angry accusations between Gaby and him came back. He remembered what he'd said and how he'd treated her, and a flush of shame burned in his neck and face. He'd never treated any woman like that before. Even the whores he'd bought for a couple of hours had been treated with more consideration. Yet Gaby, the one person in the world he never wanted to hurt, had borne the brunt of his anger and pride.

Rayne lay thinking of the things he'd heard at the dance. Both Slade and Thad were known to stretch the truth, and he had wanted to say they were liars, but Thad had known about the birthmark on Gaby's breast. How else could he have known? Rayne's fist clenched in impotent fury as he pictured Gaby standing nude before the leering gaze of such men as Thad and Slade. He'd told her he would take her back to Galveston. Well, they couldn't start out in this storm, but he'd avoid her as much as possible until they could leave.

Swinging his long legs over the edge of the bunk, he drew on his jeans and then his boots. He couldn't lie here in bed thinking about her all day. As he'd always done when he was lonely or upset, he'd find some hard physical labor to do. Maybe that would stop him from remembering the soft light in her eyes when he made love to her.

"Come on, you stackwads. I'm not paying you to lie in bed all day." He bumped some of the other beds with his boot as he walked past. Groans and snorts of waking men greeted him. Rayne pulled on his jacket and stepped out on the porch. A rim of ice was already forming in the yellow-and-gray mud puddles.

If the temperature kept on dropping, everything would soon be coated in ice. His eyes wandered to the ranch house. The lamp burned in the bedroom window. Gaby was already up. Perversely he hoped she'd had as much trouble sleeping as he had. He clamped his hat on his head, hunched his shoulders against the rain, and headed for the cookhouse for a cup of Little Finger's black coffee.

Gaby and Aaron lay for a moment struggling to regain their breath, adjusting to the shock of what had happened. The outer wheel made a chirring sound above them as it spun uselessly, and the horses nickered as they struggled to disentangle themselves.

"Gaby, are you all right?" Aaron asked, and she shook her head, one hand going to cover the bump already forming at the back of her head.

"I think so. How about you?"

"Yeah," Aaron grunted. "Can you move?" He'd already backed off her legs and was crawling out of the buggy. When he was clear, he turned back and offered a hand. "Come on." Painfully Gaby got to her feet. They stood looking at the damage. One wheel was bent, raising its useless spokes in supplication to the merciless gray sky. Aaron went to see about the horses. He unhitched them from the buggy and from each other. The big roan struggled to her feet and limped away.

"Easy, girl, easy," Aaron said, stroking her nose and calming her so she wouldn't hurt herself further. When she was free of the traces, he turned back to the other horse, which lay looking up at him with sorrowful eyes. Aaron bent and rubbed her nose.

"It looks bad, old girl," he murmured, and Gaby saw the leg that lay at a crooked angle, the white bone protruding. Aaron hunkered where he was, talking to the animal a few moments more; then with a heavy sigh he rose and walked to the back of the overturned buggy. Rummaging inside, he brought out a rifle and walked back to the horse.

"Goody-bye, girl," he said softly. "You've served me well." The horse looked up at him with pleading eyes. Once a wild creature of the plains, she'd come to depend upon man for everything, and now she looked to him for a surcease of the pain she felt. Gaby turned away.

The shot was loud, its reverberations trapped by the rain and heavy air. Gaby jumped and turned to look at Aaron. For a moment more he stood looking down at his horse; then he put the rifle back in the boot. He hauled out the buffalo robe and wrapped it around him, motioning to Gaby to come within its folds. They stood, their heads and bodies protected from the rain while they considered their options.

"The horse is lame," Aaron said. "The ranch house is still a few miles away."

"We'll make it," Gaby said.

Aaron smiled grimly to himself, his eyes flashing with admiration for this tiny, beautiful woman-child who raised her chin bravely and met his eyes squarely. She knew they were in danger of freezing to death and she made no whimper. But Aaron had seen something in her glance. He glimpsed the feverish bright eyes and flushed cheeks and knew she was on her last legs.

"We'll start out on the other horse," he said. "Can you ride bareback?"

"Of course," she answered promptly. Aaron led her to the waiting horse and boosted her up, then handed up the robe while he clambered up on the broad back himself.

"Lie down against her neck and grab hold of her mane," he shouted, and wrapped the robe around them the best he could.

It seemed to Gaby they rode for hours. Time and place lost all meaning as she gave in to the shivering chills that racked her body. She would never be dry or warm again, she thought. So wrapped in misery was she that she'd didn't at first realize they'd reached the Spencer ranch until Aaron slid off the horse and led it into the barn. Hands came to lift her down. She was carried. The warm horsey smell of the barn was left behind. Rain fell on her face; then she was inside a warm place. There were lights and voices.

"Take her up to the front guest room," Aaron's voice said, and again she was carried, and finally placed on something that was incredibly soft and warm beneath her. Still she shivered as hands stripped away the wet woolen cloak and her gown and petticoats. Warm covers were thrown over her and something warm was laid against her feet. Gaby curled her toes in response to the delicious warmth. She turned into the softness of the down pillow, closed her eyes, and slept.

It was midday when Jacinta went searching for Rayne. He'd already mucked out the stalls himself, a job he hated and usually left for the lowest-ranking cowboy on the payroll, but today he needed to work. He'd stayed busy and had driven his men until he couldn't find anything else for them to do. There was no need to send them out in the storm to check the cattle yet. The storm could pass over without becoming a full-blown norther. He'd seen it happen. Rayne made his way back to the cookhouse, and it was there that Jacinta found him. No doubt Gaby had sent her to get him, Rayne thought, and continued to sip at his coffee, wondering what Gaby would have to say to him.

"Señor Elliott," Jacinta said, looking around the cookhoouse as if searching for someone. "I have not seen Señorita Gaby all morning."

Rayne looked up at her, his coffee and his anger forgotten. "Did you try her room?" he said.

"Sí, she is not there," Jacinta said. "I think she is with you and I do not want to interrupt. On such a day what else is there to do?" She shrugged her shoulders and Rayne realized she had left them alone believing them to be in bed together. He glanced away. "When you did not come out for dinner, I knocked on the door and no one answered. I looked in and the room is empty. Only her gown is on the floor, all torn. I think someone attacked her and took her away."

"No one attacked her," Rayne snapped defensively, and couldn't meet the woman's eyes. Jacinta looked at his guilty face and smiled. The *señor* had been very impatient the night before, she thought, but said nothing. Her worry was eased a little.

"Where is Miss Gaby?" she asked. "She is here with you, yes?"

"No, she isn't," Rayne said, getting to his feet.

"*Señor*, her cape is gone," Jacinta cried, her eyes growing round with alarm now. That same alarm was mirrored on Rayne's face. Without a word he ran back to the house, going from room to room while he called Gaby's name, but she wasn't there. The bedroom was as he'd left it the night before, except that her torn gown lay in a huddle on the floor. Rayne averted his eyes from it and looked around as if she might be hiding in one of the corners, waiting to spring out and tease him for his treatment of her.

"Jacinta, Maria," he called helplessly. "Check all the rooms."

"I have, *señor*," Jacinta said.

"Check them again," Rayne snapped, and ran to look himself, unable to believe she was gone. "Did you check the loft?"

"She is not here," Maria called from the top of the stairs. They stopped searching and looked at each other, dread growing in their eyes as they acknowledged that she was not in the ranch house. The sound of the rain came to them. Surely she wouldn't be out in this, Rayne thought. The little fool should know better. But then, maybe she didn't. He'd never taken the time to tell her about a Texas norther.

"Jacinta, tell Little Finger to round up the men and meet me in the barn," he ordered, and his long legs raced down the porch steps and across the slippery ground. By the time the men got there, he'd taken stock.

"Gaby is gone," he said. "So is that new mustang, Sandy. Did any of you see her ride out of here this morning?"

None had.

"I thought I heard a horse in the middle of the night," Ramon said. "I thought it was one of the boys going to town for a few days."

"Saddle up," Rayne ordered. "We're going after her."

"You want to risk your men like that, Rayne?" Cole spoke up. "This weather could turn meaner than it is."

"Do you want to leave a woman abandoned in it?" Rayne snapped. "*Any* woman?" Cole's eyes dropped.

"Let's go," Rayne said, and his men hurried out to the corrals. No one turned his back on someone in trouble in this kind of weather. Especially not a woman, and especially not Miss Gaby. Most of the men had begun to look forward to her sunny smile and soft-spoken ways. Half of them didn't believe anything had been wrong with Billy sleeping in the main house while they were gone. Sometimes the only way to survive out here on the prairie was to throw conventions to the wind. Most of them had heard Slade's brags and had discounted them as lies. Slade hadn't been one of their favorite people, and they'd never seen Miss Gaby say or do anything that wasn't ladylike. They saddled up and soon were mounted and waiting in front of the barn, oil slickers flung over their shoulders, wide-brimmed hats pulled low over their faces to ward off the sleet.

"Head toward Fowler," Rayne said. "We'll spread out in a wide line as we go. Fire a shot if you see anything."

They rode out across the dun-colored prairie, their hooves throwing up clods of ice and mud. Rayne pushed them hard, making little allowance for the weather. They understood. Men caught out on the plains in a norther had been known to freeze to death. They cast apprehensive glances at the sky and grimly pushed on. How much sooner would a small-bodied woman freeze out here?

She dreamed of New Orleans in the summertime, when sweat lay on your brow and furrowed down your back. She couldn't breathe in the hot, moist air, and she struggled. Why was she back here in New Orleans? She wanted to be in Texas with Rayne. She called his name, reaching out for him, but he stood too far away from her, his face harsh with accusations. Cole Elliott stepped forward, his face wreathed in smiles. She'd never seen a smile like

that before. She smiled back, but then his face changed.
The widow's peak glowed at her like an extra eye seeing
into her very soul, and the wings of hair, so like Rayne's
except that they were streaked with gray, grew into horns.
Cole cackled with glee as he pointed an accusing finger at
her.

"No, no," Gaby cried out, and turned in her sleep.

"It's all right." Aaron's gentle hand nuzzled her face in
the same kind gesture he'd used on his horse. "It's all
right, old girl," he murmured, and she wasn't afraid. She
lay still, letting him gentle her. He went away and Rayne
was there. He held a rifle at his shoulder and sighted
down its barrel at her.

"Rayne," Gaby cried in panic, and he raised his head
and looked at her, his blue eyes sad.

"Good-bye, old girl," he said. "You served me well."
The sound of the gunshot was lost in her scream.

"Gaby, don't be afraid." Aaron's voice soothed her
once more, and she felt a cloth on her face, cooling her
fevered brow. She shivered beneath the covers.

"I think the fever's peaking," Aaron said to someone,
and Gaby opened her eyes and looked into his weary
face. His gray eyes were kind and full of concern as they
met hers. They made Gaby feel safe. She wanted to ask
for Rayne again, but she was too weary to utter the
name. Closing her eyes, she slept.

They made the river. The bridge had been torn away
from its mooring in the muddy banks. The planks and
logs had tumbled and churned in the rapids of the swollen
river and bumped against the banks, catching in the
bushes there.

"She never came this way," Ramon said.

"Maybe she did," Rayne said, trying to fight down his
panic.

"Look, there's Sandy over there," Billy cried, and the
men saw the frightened horse trotting back and forth
along the further bank.

"Let's go," Rayne called and pointed his horse into the
river.

"You can't go across there, you'll drown," Cole shouted
to his son.

"I'm going across," Rayne said adamantly. "Those who want to follow, can. The rest of you head back to the ranch." He cast a final glance over his shoulder at his men. He knew he was asking a lot of them, and of the ones who remained he knew Dusty and Billy would follow. Rayne looked at the young boy. He sat hunched in his saddle, his face pale, his eyes determined. He was so young and untried and yet trying bravely to do what was expected of him.

In that moment something about the boy reminded him of Gaby. Maybe it was the quality of youth they shared.

"Billy," he called. "Ride back to the Martin ranch and raise some help. We may have to search along the riverbanks."

"I want to stay and look for Miss Gaby," Billy said.

"I need you to get some more men for me, Billy. Go on." The boy hesitated, then with some reluctance reined his horse around and galloped off, angling southwest away from the river.

The muddy, ice waters closed around Rayne sooner than he'd expected. The roan lost its footing and only Rayne's firm grip kept it from bolting back to shore. The powerful legs struggled against the current, and still they were swept downstream, man and beast bobbing in the swirling waters like a fallen leaf.

"Steady. Steady, boy." Rayne talked to his horse as, with rolling eyes and great bursts of air jetting from the black nostrils, the animal touched bottom and scrambled up the other side. Rayne gained the high bank and turned back to face his men. While he watched, Cole began his crossing. All the way across, he cursed the dark-haired, dark eyed woman.

"I need the rest of our men from town," Rayne said, and with a nod of acceptance Cole set out for Fowler.

For the rest of the day they searched along the riverbanks. Cole and Dusty and the rest of the men searched the roads to and from Fowler. Thad Martin and his men showed up and searched across the prairie. There was no sign of Gaby. Rayne kept a picture of her face before him. She'd be cold and frightened out here. There would be tears on her cheeks, and her hair would fall in strings across her forehead from the rain, but she would be safe. She'd fly into his arms and he'd hold her and rock her, lending her his strength and warmth. He'd take her back to the ranch and somehow they'd work things out. They had to. He realized now he could never live without her. He never allowed himself the thought that she might be dead, but as the hours wore on and there was no sign of Gaby, a numbness settled over him. His craggy features were bleak and the broad shoulders slumped beneath his poncho. A sick hopelessness settled in his eyes, and his men turned away from it, not wanting to see his pain.

The river waters receded a little and the men searched along the banks again, looking for a small woman's body with flowing dark hair. She might have gotten wedged in among the roots and bushes at the edge of the river.

"I don't think we're going to find her," one of the men said finally. Dusk was falling.

"Keep looking," Rayne ordered.

"Rayne, the men have been out in this all day. It's a wonder we haven't lost some of them," Dusty said. "If we were going to find her, we would have by now."

"Leave if you want to," Rayne rasped. "I'll keep looking until I find her."

"Or her body?" Dusty asked. "She's gone, Rayne. Likely she was washed away when the bridge went. When the waters go down, her body'll turn up somewhere between here and Galveston."

"No." It was an anguished cry, piercing the wintry air. Men blinked their ice-encrusted lashes and looked away. Some of them had known Rayne Elliott all his life. They'd watched him grow to manhood and had even pitied him a little for growing up with Cole Elliott as a father. But they'd learned to respect him as well. Cole had brought up Rayne to be hard and tough even in a land where stoicism was a way of life. Now Rayne sat defeated, slumped in his saddle, his head bowed.

The men milled about, loath to leave him, yet not wanting to spend the night out in the numbing, damp cold. Even now, some of them would have to hole up for the night at the closest ranch house.

"Ho!" someone hailed them from across the river. They looked to see Little Finger sitting uneasily on a

horse. He never rode horseback when he could plant his
rear on a plank wagon seat. Cole crossed the river to
greet him. Rayne stayed where he was, watching, afraid
to hope, afraid to lose hope and thus lose Gaby forever.
Cole reached Little Finger and the two men talked; then
Cole turned back to the river.

"She's been found," he said, riding up to Rayne. "One
of the Lazy S men came over to the ranch. He crossed
south of here a few miles down at the bend. He said she's
alive."

Joy lit Rayne's dull eyes. A smile of disbelief played
over his features.

"She's alive?" he asked. "Is she hurt?" Cole nodded
his head, his eyes steady on his son's face. Rayne sensed
there was more his father meant to tell him, but he didn't
want to hear it now. He just wanted to go to Gaby and
hold her.

"Where is she?" he asked.

Cole's face tightened in the old cynical lines. "She
went to Aaron Spencer's place. She wants her clothes
sent over. She'll be staying there for a time."

Rayne stared at his father as if he'd gone mad. His
eyes turned fierce as he took in Cole's words. "She's with
Spencer?" he asked, and his voice broke. The men around
him shuffled uneasily. A horse stamped his foot against
the frozen ground, another whickered and blew out air in
a billowing cloud of vapor. Rayne sat like a statue, staring into the swirling brown waters as if mesmerized. The
light sank lower in the west.

"I got to get back to the ranch. My woman'll be
wondering where I am," a man said quietly, and turning
his horse, signaled to his men to follow. Slowly the other
men drifted away in small groups, shaking their heads in
pity, remembering Rayne's bereft face as he'd searched
for her. Now he had a different kind of pain. A woman
could sure mess up a man.

Cole waited until most of the men had left, and turned
back to his son. "We'd better head on back to the ranch,
Rayne. There ain't no use you grievin' for her like this.
She ain't worth it. She never was." At his words, Rayne
raised his head and met his father's gaze, and Cole knew

his son wasn't grieving. He glanced away, glad that Rayne
was his son and not his enemy.

"Round up the men and let's head for home," Rayne
said, and without a backward glance crossed the river
and headed across the prairie toward the Rocking E
Ranch.

Gaby woke feeling much better. The fever was gone,
although her chest hurt and her head felt dizzy when she
tried to rise.

"Lie still, you must rest." A tall, gaunt woman with a
stern face moved to the side of the bed and pressed Gaby
back against the pillows. "You haf had a fever," the
woman said in a heavily accented voice. Briskly she moved
about, tucking the covers around the edge of the mattress. With warm, scented water she washed Gaby's hands
and face and then ladled hot soup to her mouth. Eagerly
Gaby drank down a few spoonfuls then pushed the soup
away.

"You must eat it all. It is goot for you," the woman
said.

"Perhaps later. I'm just not hungry now."

Without another protest the woman carried the bowl
to the marble-topped table and left it on a tray. Her
petticoats were so stiff they rustled when she moved. Her
back was ramrod straight, as uncompromising as the iron-
gray hair pulled back in its severe bun.

"Are you Mrs. Spencer?" Gaby asked now, thinking
she'd not heard Aaron mention a wife.

"No, I am Mrs. Schafer. I am Mr. Spencer's housekeeper," the woman said stiffly. "Mr. Spencer is not
married." Gaby felt a little intimidated by the woman's
severe demeanor.

"You've been very kind to nurse me."

"It was my duty," the woman replied, and her words
might have seemed unfriendly if not for the flash of a
smile that crossed her face. She was pleased at Gaby's
comment, but she pulled her face back into its stern lines
and bustled around the room. "Mr. Spencer sat with you
much of the time."

"I remember," Gaby said, and thought of her dreams
and of the way Aaron's tender ministrations had helped

her through the worst of them. She glanced around the room. She was in a beautifully appointed room with soft woolen rugs on the floor and ornate, rich-grained furniture. Heavy draperies hung at the tall, narrow windows. "How long have I been here?"

"Mr. Spencer brought you here three days ago," Mrs. Schafer replied.

"Three days." Gaby sat up. Rayne must be frantic. "I must go," she cried, throwing aside the covers.

"You can't get out of bed. You haf been very ill." Mrs. Schafer pushed her back.

"You don't understand. I must tell Rayne where I am."

"I overheard Mr. Spencer instruct his man to go to the Rocking E Ranch and tell Mr. Elliott."

"Has he come for me yet?" Gaby looked at the door of the room as if he might be waiting on the other side. Why hadn't they awakened her?

"He did not come, but he sent your clothes." Gaby looked at her blankly. "I will haf them brought up for you. You rest now." Mrs. Schafer left the room, while Gaby lay back against the pillows trying to puzzle out why Rayne hadn't come. Perhaps he was still angry with her. Weakly she closed her eyes against the tears that threatened to spill over. Some time passed before she heard a gentle voice call her name. Aaron Spencer stood at the side of her bed.

"I'm sorry if I've disturbed you," he said softly. His gaze took in her pale face and the shadows that lay like bruises beneath her dark eyes. "Mrs. Schafer said you were awake."

"I was." Gaby attempted a smile. "Thank you for coming along and rescuing me. I don't what would have happened if you hadn't found me."

"I'm glad I could help. I just happened to be in the right place at the right time." He dismissed his deed. "How are you feeling?"

"Better." She tried to keep her voice bright, but he could see the weariness on her face. She fidgeted. "Mrs. Schafer said you'd sent word to Rayne."

"Yes, I did, and he sent you some clothes, so you can

dress and join us for dinner as soon as you feel stronger. I've brought up your trunk."

"Was there a message?" Gaby asked eagerly.

"Not to my knowledge. Perhaps there is one inside."

"Yes, there must be," Gaby said. Before Aaron could stop her, she swung her legs out of bed and stood up. For a moment she stood clutching the bedpost while her reeling head righted itself. Anxiously Aaron stood close at hand, ready to catch her should she fall. She looked like a child in one of Mrs. Schafer's austere high-necked gowns.

With Aaron's hand supporting her, Gaby made her way to the trunk. Her heart hammered with frightening apprehension as she raised the lid and looked inside. Her gowns had been carefully folded and packed. Gaby had a fleeting image of Jacinta's gentle brown hands tending to this task. Sitting on top of the gowns was the jeweled music box and beside it, as if flung there by an angry hand, was the bag of gold coins.

Rayne had sent her a message after all. It was very clear to her. He didn't want her back. She didn't know she was weeping until Aaron gathered her up and carried her back to the bed. He tucked her in and stood smoothing the hair from her brow.

"I'm sorry," he said, and Gaby was glad he made no effort to pretend anything was different. He also recognized Rayne's gesture for what it was.

Gaby shrugged, trying to smile through the tears that spilled down her cheeks. "Perhaps it's for the best," she said, although in her heart she didn't believe it.

"What will you do now? Have you someplace to go?" Aaron asked.

Gaby closed her eyes and swallowed against the lump in her throat. "Back to New Orleans, I suppose," she whispered.

Aaron regarded her for a moment, considering his words before saying them. He didn't want to frighten her away. "If you need some time to decide your next move, I offer you my home for as long as you need it. Perhaps with time, tempers will cool."

Gaby shook her head. "You don't know Rayne very well."

"Give him some time," Aaron advised. "A week or two can make a big difference in the way he's thinking and feeling. That will give you time to recover your strength. I would be pleased if you stayed."

"Thank you," Gaby said gratefully. "Perhaps for a day or two more. I'm still so tired."

"Go to sleep. Tomorrow will seem brighter to you." He turned toward the door.

"Thank you again," Gaby said softly. "I don't know how I shall repay you." Aaron understood her words were for more than just his hospitality. He'd been a friend to her. He hadn't asked her any questions about what had happened between Rayne and her. He'd simply offered his help and support. Gaby turned on her side and stared at the gray light at the window. Would the sunshine ever come again? she wondered.

Aaron watched the young woman settle against the pillows, her lids already drooping wearily, and he closed the door and went softly away. In his heart a resentment for Rayne Elliott sprang to life. That the rancher had wounded the girl deeply was all too evident. For him not to even have inquired after her health was unforgivable. Aaron cursed the proud, stiff-necked Texan for his hard-heartedness. How easily the man had tossed her aside. What had happened to cause the rift between them? Surely not those silly rumors floating around at the dance. Aaron thought about his guest long after the house stilled for the night.

One day passed into two, and two into four. Gaby had taken to dressing now and joining Aaron at the dinner table, although a lethargy still claimed her spirits and her physical energy. Aaron was a charming host. For a time he made her forget her situation and sometimes even startled a laugh from her with one of his amusing anecdotes.

The rest of the day, Gaby spent in her room watching with dull eyes the sleet and snow of the winter storm that had brought her to the Lazy S Ranch. She should make plans for what to do next, she thought dismally. Soon this storm would pass, the snow would melt away, but other storms would follow, and if she were not to be trapped here through the winter, she must move on. She would go to Galveston as soon as the roads were passable, and from there she would take a ship to New Orleans. She should leave soon; she'd imposed upon Aaron Spencer's hospitality long enough. Still she lingered, lured by the tranquillity of the large house.

"Don't hurry. Be sure you're well enough to travel first," Aaron urged her when she spoke of leaving, and she was grateful for the reprieve. She knew she was drifting, but couldn't find the heart to take hold of her life again.

"Were you born here in Texas?" Gaby asked Aaron one evening as they sat before a cozy fire in the parlor. Here in this room, as throughout the whole house, there were signs of wealth and good taste in the rich furnishings. Gaby leaned against the tapestry-covered carved back of the love seat and watched as Aaron loosened the tobacco in his pipe.

He glanced up at her and smiled. "Like you, I'm a pilgrim to these parts, although I came here nearly twenty years ago."

"Have you no family?" Gaby asked, and hoped she didn't appear rude in her questions.

"I have a son back in Pennsylvania," he said softly. "He must be . . . oh, a couple of years older than you by now."

"Why isn't he here with you?" Gaby asked in surprise.

"He stayed behind with his mother." Aaron turned away to knock his pipe against the chimney and empty its contents into the fire.

"Didn't your wife like Texas?"

"My wife never came to Texas with me." Aaron hunched his shoulder under the guise of packing a fresh wad of tobacco into his pipe. "We were divorced before I left Pennsylvania. Kevin was one year old. My wife took him away one day and I never saw him again."

Gaby said nothing. She was dismayed that a woman could be so cruel. She was filled with sympathy for the gentle man, yet she knew he wouldn't welcome a display of pity. Quietly she listened while he talked of his early years in Texas. He told of sending east to find a German housekeeper who could take care of his ranch, as his duties took him away from home more and more.

They talked of the politics of the suffering state. Aaron was working with a delegation of men who planned to go to Washington and petition for the right to govern themselves again.

"Martial law must end, and soon, if there's to be any growth in the state's economics," Aaron declared, and Gaby found herself putting aside her own unhappiness as she was caught up in the excitement of a state struggling to heal itself. She listened and learned new sides to Texas.

While men like Rayne struggled for survival, men like Aaron Spencer fought and argued for the rights of all Texans.

The evenings became a bright spot in Gaby's days. She'd been there nearly two weeks now. Aaron had been a wonderful friend to her and Gaby had even learned to relax around the stiff-laced German housekeeper.

"I have to leave," she said one night as she and Aaron lingered over coffee in the dining room.

At her words, he rose and went to stand with his back to the fire, rocking forward slightly on the balls of his feet in a way that was becoming familiar to Gaby. He cleared his throat and pulled at his shirt collar. "You don't have to go," he said.

"I've imposed on you far too long," Gaby replied. "I have to get my life back together and stand on my own two feet again. Obviously Rayne"—she paused and swallowed hard—"Rayne isn't going to change his mind and ask me back."

"Have you got family or friends in New Orleans?" Aaron asked.

"There's Maddie. She took care of me after my mother died. I can go back to live with her and the oth-others."

Aaron looked at her expressive face. He'd grown fond of having her here to greet him when he returned home in the evenings. "Don't go, Gaby," he said.

"You've been so thoughtful and kind. I can't ask you to do more for me," Gaby began.

"I'm asking you to stay for me, Gaby. You've brought joy back into my life. I've been lonely for many years." He paused. "I'd like you to marry me, Gaby. A man needs a wife in politics, someone pretty and smart at his side. It lets people know he's stable, that he's someone to depend on." Damn, he thought. He was making it sound like a business arrangement, and he hadn't meant it that way at all. True, there was so much he could offer, but there were some things he could never give her. Pretty words were one of those things.

"Oh, Aaron," Gaby laughed and reached out a hand to touch his sleeve lightly. "I've never known a kinder, more stable man than you are. But I can't marry you."

"Why not?" he asked, coming to sit in the chair next to hers. His hand grasped hers lightly. His gray eyes regarded her sweet face. "I would do anything for you, Gaby. I think I can make you happy."

"I'm sure you could," Gaby said, "but you deserve more than I can give you. I don't love you, Aaron. I'm in love with Rayne." She hated to hurt him after all his kindness to her, but to give him false hope would be even more cruel.

"I heard you cry out his name when you were ill. I'd be a fool not to know you love him. But he's put you aside, fool that he is, and rather than see you leave to an uncertain future back in New Orleans, I'd be honored if you'd marry me."

Gaby looked at his earnest face, not knowing how to tell him the real reason she couldn't marry him.

He saw her hesitation and misread it. "If it's me and what I might demand of you, rest your mind," he said. Rising from the chair, he paced back to the fireplace. "The same accident that scarred and crippled me also took away my manhood." He whirled to face her again. "I'd never ask that of you, Gaby. You can keep your own room. You can lock the door every night or leave it open. It wouldn't matter. I can neither give nor receive comfort in that manner. But there are other kinds of comfort a man can draw from a woman and she from him. There's the pleasure of sharing our thoughts and plans. I'm a wealthy man. I can protect you and give you a good life here. Unless you'd be ashamed to be seen with me."

"Don't say any more," Gaby cried, springing to her feet and gripping his hand. "You are so kind and dear to me already. I would never be ashamed of being your wife. But I can't marry you when I already carry another man's baby."

Aaron looked at her blankly. In these past weeks he'd noted her listlessness and had never guessed the reason for it. "Does Rayne know this?" he asked, ready to hunt the Texan down and horsewhip him if he had turned his back on Gaby knowing of her condition.

"I was waiting to be absolutely sure before I told him," Gaby answered, "and then we quarreled." She turned away, unwilling to meet his gaze as she remembered the ugliness of her last night with Rayne.

"You have to tell him," Aaron advised. "It wouldn't be fair to return to New Orleans without doing so."

"Do you think I should?" Gaby asked breathlessly, and in that moment Aaron understood that she still longed for the dark-haired rancher.

"I think you must," he answered gently. "Tomorrow I'll have a man drive you. This may be the very thing you need to end this rift between you."

"Thank you, Aaron. Once again you've been a true friend to me." She threw her arms around him and kissed his cheek. A delicate whiff of flowers emanated from her skin. Her eyes were gleaming with happiness as she stepped back.

"You'd better go up to bed now," he said. "Tomorrow is a big day in your life." She skipped away from him. "Gaby," he called as she reached the door, "tell Rayne I think he's a very lucky man." The light in her eyes touched his face briefly, conveying her regrets to him and her joy and hope for what the morrow would bring. Then she was gone, and Aaron sat on in the empty room with its rich furnishings.

The logs burned down and fell apart in glowing embers, and still Aaron sat staring into the orange-red coals while he thought of another time and place, when he'd been a young man with a new wife who'd just told him she was expecting his child. He remembered the poignant joy of the moment as if it were yesterday. Other images crowded in on him. He remembered Abigail's twisted face and the angry words she'd spat at him, words of hate and loathing as she looked at his helpless scarred body. He'd held himself accountable for the bitter end of the marriage. Now for the first time he realized that Abigail had not been all she should have. There had never been the softness and generosity of spirit he'd found in Gaby. If only he were a young man again, he thought. If only he could offer her a whole man, he would fight Rayne Elliott.

Aaron bit down on the stem of his cold pipe, then, sighing, rose and knocked the ashes into the fireplace. Slowly he climbed the stairs to his room. He already missed her, he thought, and she was not yet gone from his house. He wondered how he would endure the lonely days ahead.

14

The next morning Gaby dressed carefully for her trip back to the Rocking E. She wasn't sure of what her reception would be. Her hands fluttered nervously, straightening the high lace collar and cuffs of her otherwise plain gown. Her dark, heavy tresses seemed especially uncooperative as she sought to arrange them into a fetching style. Finally, in exasperation she brushed them into a sleek coil on top of her head and pinned a small dark hat in place.

True to his word, Aaron provided a buggy for her use and a man to drive her back to the Rocking E Ranch. The driver handed her into the buggy and picked up the reins.

"I'll send your trunk over later," Aaron said, standing beside the buggy, gazing up at her.

"I owe you so much, Aaron, how can I ever repay you?"

"You owe me nothing. It's I who should thank you. You made my days less lonely for a while." He gripped her hand lightly. "If you ever need me, I'll be here."

"Good-bye," Gaby said softly.

"Good-bye." Aaron slapped the side of the buggy to signal the driver, and they were off, wheeling away from the elegant two-story ranch house and the sturdy barns and sheds.

The snow and sleet had melted long before, and the days had turned unseasonably warm. The grass was showing starts of green, and tiny wildflowers had poked their heads forward timidly, as if sure this warm, moist weather wouldn't last. The sun burned down brightly, and in spite of the chill in the wind, Gaby grew warm and threw off her cape.

"Looks like they got company," the driver said when they topped the ridge leading down to the Rocking E Ranch. Eagerly Gaby sat forward. At least Rayne would be there, she thought. She'd feared she'd have to wait until he returned from the range.

She peered through the bright sunlight, trying to make out the mounted men gathered near the barns. There were more than usual. Had Rayne hired more hands? She'd understood the ranch work slowed during the winter.

The men were too intent on something to pay much attention to the buggy as it pulled into the yard. As it came to a stop, Gaby was able to see more clearly what was happening, and she gasped. Two men sat their horses, their hands tied behind them. Ropes had been strung from the beams of the barn and encircled the necks of the men.

Clarence Blake and Thad Martin were among the mounted onlookers. There was a sullen rumble of voices from the men, and now and then one raised his voice in angry accusation against the bound pair.

"I say we string 'em up now," a man said. "They been stealing us blind, rustling our cattle as fast as we round 'em up. If we let 'em go, we'll have every cattle rustler in the state down here helpin' theirselves to our cattle."

"You can't take the law into your own hands," another man called, and Gaby recognized Dusty's voice. She shivered and looked around the assembled men, searching for Rayne. Cole Elliott stood near the barn door, the end of one of the ropes in his hand. His eyes were hard and intent.

"I say we leave it up to Rayne, since they're his men and they were caught raiding his cattle."

"Hell, no," another man roared. "We've all lost cattle to them."

"Señorita Gaby!" A girl's impassioned cry caught her attention. Maria ran across the dusty yard and flung herself against the side of the buggy, her dark eyes imploring as they sought Gaby's. "They're trying to hang Billy," she sobbed. Blood pounded in Gaby's head as she looked back at the accused men. One of them was indeed Billy, and she recognized the other as Slade Harner. Horror washed through her. Surely Rayne wouldn't stand by and let these men hang his cowhands, especially not Billy, who'd been a friend to him in every way.

"Where's Rayne?" Gaby cried. Numbly Maria pointed back to the knot of men.

"I say we hang 'em," Cole Elliott was saying. His fists were knotted in the rope he held. "There ain't no excuse for taking something that belongs to another man. They ought to be punished."

"What do you want to do, Rayne?" The men on horseback shifted and Gaby caught a glimpse of him. She could see the conflicting emotions on his face. He hated to see a man lose his life for one mistake. On the other hand, instinct told him Slade Harner had been behind the cattle rustlings for a long time. These men knew the law of the range, and still they'd rustled. Justice might be hard and swift, but it was necessary if the ranchers were to survive.

"Hang them," he said. Cole was surprised his son had agreed. But then, Rayne had been surprising him a lot these last couple of weeks. There was a new hardness to him that Cole approved.

"No!" Gaby's scream filled the yard, startling the men. All eyes turned to her, even those of the condemned men. Tears streamed down Gaby's face as she clambered down from the buggy. Pulling her skirts aside impatiently, she ran toward the men.

Rayne rode forward to meet her and got down from his horse. "What are you doing here, Gaby?" he asked coldly.

"Rayne, you can't do this," she cried. "It's wrong. Billy's been our friend. He protected me when those men attacked us while you were gone. He risked his life to save the ranch. He wouldn't steal your cattle. You know that."

"He was caught red-handed," Rayne said coldly.

Gaby shook her head in denial. "I can't believe that,"

she whispered. "There must be an explanation. Billy's been loyal to you. He doesn't deserve to die like this, without a trial, without someone to listen to his side of the story."

Rayne looked at her tear-streaked face, at the dark, pleading eyes. The sun caught in the dark hair, casting blue lights. His hungry gaze took in the tiny hat perched on her curls, the long graceful neck rising from the prim high collar, and the gentle swell of her breasts beneath the dark bodice. All the things they'd been to each other came back to mock him, and he clenched his fists and stepped backward to keep from pulling her into his arms.

"Rayne, please don't do this to Billy," she begged softly. "Even Slade doesn't deserve to die like this." She saw the flicker of pain in his eyes before his gaze hardened. She'd touched a raw spot, she knew, but she couldn't stop now. "It will be little more than murder if you string them up without a trial."

"Don't listen to her, Rayne," Cole called. He had let go of the rope and crossed the yard toward them. "She's just pleading for their lives because like as not they're in this together." Gaby looked at the old man in consternation.

"Be careful, old man," Rayne grated, but Cole ignored his son's threat.

"It's true," he cried to the other men. "I saw 'em together with my own eyes right here at the ranch, figuring out how to steal your cows and mark 'em."

"I didn't," Gaby cried, thunderstruck at the audacity of his accusation. "I've never had anything to do with Slade Harner."

"Aw, come on, sugar," Slade's lazy drawl interrupted. "You might as well confess. We've been lovers since long before Rayne brought you here."

"You're a liar," Gaby cried, and glanced back at Rayne. This was a nightmare. Once again accusations were pressed on her, and Rayne seemed to believe her accusers over her. Gaby felt her legs trembling and the tears stung her eyes, but she threw her head back and met Rayne's gaze.

"You know the truth of what I was when you met me, Rayne," she said evenly. "There's been no man but you before or since." Her voice was clear, carrying to the men at the barn, but she didn't care if they heard or believed her. It was Rayne she cared about. She saw the lights shift in his eyes and knew he wanted to believe her. Before she could say more, Cole stepped forward.

"I suppose you're going to claim you never helped Slade with the brands he's been using on our cows," Cole pressed. "I saw it myself the day you drew it for him in the sand. It changed the Rocking E to the Circle E."

"I didn't," Gaby paused, remembering a talk with Slade. He'd told her about the branding iron and unconsciously she'd completed the curved line to draw a circle around the letter. A realization of what she'd done and how it must look washed over her and Rayne saw the guilt on her face.

"Rayne," she cried, "it isn't true. I—"

"Are you denying what Pa is saying?" he asked hopefully.

"No," she said helplessly. "I did make the drawing. But I didn't mean it to be used. Rayne, wait, listen to me." He'd swung around and headed back toward the mounted men. "I didn't know what I was doing," she cried.

"He don't believe you, sugar," Slade drawled. "You might as well tell the truth."

"No, Miss Gaby," Billy cried, and Slade slashed out at him with a foot. The boy slumped into silence, but his outcry just seemed to confirm the insinuations Slade was making. Gaby looked around the circle of men. One and all believed she was guilty. Her gaze came back to meet Rayne's, and there was a pleading in the look, this time for more than Billy's life. It was a cry for Rayne's trust and support. Unable to give it, Rayne turned away from her.

" 'Course, if you ain't gonna hang her, it ain't fair to hang us when we was just workin' for her."

Rage flamed in Gaby's heart. To stand here quietly while these men condemned her was more than she could bear. Recklessly she stepped forward, her chin outthrust, her glance bold as it swept around the group of men. Slade's words still hung in the air, making the men uncomfortable. They'd never hanged a woman before and they didn't want to start now. Fists on her hips, Gaby tossed her head and turned back to face Rayne.

"If you've found me guilty, then I should be hanged," she said. "It shouldn't be hard for you. I'm such an evil woman. Think of all the things I've done since I arrived here. Think of the men I've taken as lovers, the lies I've told, the cattle I've stolen. Think of how I've deceived you. I deserve to die as surely as Billy. Why don't you hang me too, Rayne? You let me be condemned, now get on with the punishment." She goaded him, flaunting everything they'd said about her. There was a smile on her face, taunting and derisive.

The sun beat down on their heads, causing sweat to form on her upper lip and in the hollows of her breasts. In a flamboyant gesture, Gaby flung off the demure little hat and loosened her hair. It tumbled around her shoulders in wanton disarray. The wind captured some of the curling tendrils and whipped them around her head. One small gloved hand tore at the buttons at the top of her bodice, ripping them away so she stood with the tops of the pale white mounds visible to the men. She whisked her skirts around with one hand while she strolled haughtily in front of them, railing against their accusations. There was not a one of them who didn't find himself admiring her fire and passion. It was a shame she was what she was, they thought, and sat their horses silently. This had turned into a family matter between Rayne and his woman. They'd stay out of it now, but they'd stay to watch.

"Why don't you hang me too, Rayne?" she taunted. "Why do you hesitate? Is it because you're not sure? Are you asking yourself if you're hanging these men because they stole your cattle or because you think they slept with your woman? Well, hang them, Rayne, and hang me. We're guilty on all counts."

She lashed out at him with words, hardly knowing what she was saying, only wanting to hurt and destroy, as he had done to her and her love for him. She met his gaze boldly, defiantly, forcing him by her very will to meet her gaze. She lied, glorying in the pain that shuddered through him. "Everything they say about me is

true," she said, and winced as his hand swung up and
back. She welcomed his blow. It would mark the end of
all that was between them. They would be forever done
and she could walk away from him and never look back.
In that moment the tears filled her eyes and he saw the
dull ache in them and with it he saw that all her words
were said in anger and were untrue. His hand stilled,
unable to complete its swing downward across her cheek.
He saw her pain and understood all they had lost between them. He turned away and the muscles across his
broad back worked as he drew in his breath, fighting for
control.

"Cut them down," he said tightly.

"Rayne, you don't mean that," Cole cried.

"Cut them down, I said." His face was so fierce that
even Cole was afraid to deny him. A man edged his
horse toward the bound men and began to remove the
ropes.

Without looking back, Rayne stalked off toward his
horse, and mounting, spurred it into a hard gallop. Gaby
watched until the silhouette of man and horse blended
with the prairie and finally was lost in its dips and hollows. It was over, she thought sadly. The look in his eyes
as he'd raised his hand to her had said it all. There had
been denial and hatred in that look. He no longer loved
her or wanted her. She hadn't had a chance to tell him
about the baby, but it no longer mattered. He didn't
want her anymore. He wouldn't want their baby either, if
in fact he even believed it to be his.

The soft thud of hooves against the dusty ground made
her turn back to the men. Billy stood before her, the
reins of his horse held loosely, his eyes grateful. Maria
clung to his side, weeping happily.

"Thank you, Miss Gaby," he said. "I was sure I was
going to die."

"I'm glad I came in time to help." Gaby took his hand.

"I tried to tell Mr. Elliott, but he wouldn't listen to
me. I . . . I never meant to be taking his cows. Slade
asked me to join him and I pretended to. He told me to
drive the herd down to the south pastures for him. I
figured I'd follow along and find out what he had in
mind. Only Mr. Blake and his men came along and

began to chase us. The rest of Slade's men got away, but we got caught. I . . . I sure wasn't tryin' to take Mr. Elliott's cows."

"I know, Billy," Gaby said. "You've been a good friend. What are you going to do now?"

"I don't know," Billy said glumly. "Ride on, I guess," he said. "Only thing is, I got to outrun my reputation now, and that ain't easy. Word carries in cattle country."

"No, Billy, don't go," Maria cried, putting a hand to his cheek. Billy caught it in his and squeezed it, looking forlornly into her tear-filled eyes.

"I can't get a job hereabouts now," he said. "Nobody'll hire me. I'll send back for you, Maria. I swear I will."

"Billy, maybe I can help you," Gaby said. "The Spencer ranch might take you on. I'll speak to Mr. Spencer."

"You'd do that?" Billy asked hopefully. "Even after today?"

"Especially after today," Gaby answered. Poor Billy. He didn't realized he'd been the one done wrong today. He'd bear the scars of today's accusations for the rest of his life, and yet he was willing to take the blame for it on his own shoulders.

"Follow me back to the ranch," Gaby instructed him, and turned away from the sight of the two young people joyously embracing. She'd had such hopes for Rayne and herself today. Now all those dreams were shattered.

Gaby glanced at the men still gathered near the barn. Cole Elliott stood to one side, flipping the grass rope about as he rewound it into a loose lariat over his hand. His hat was pulled low over his eyes, so she couldn't tell what he was thinking, but the slouch of his body proclaimed his disgust over the way things had turned out.

Men were riding away from the ranch in small bunches. Thad Martin and Jed Lager were talking to Slade Harner. The three men cast a quick glance in her direction and laughed among themselves before reining their horses around and riding off together. A quick glance at the horizon showed it was empty. There was no sign of a solitary horseman returning, but then, she'd known he wouldn't return, not as long as she was here.

The driver helped her up into the carriage, and once again they were on the prairie, rolling swiftly away from the ranch and the life she'd known there. She'd never see the ranch again, Gaby thought, and felt a pang of sadness. There was nothing left for her to do but return to New Orleans. She couldn't remain here now. Yet the thought of leaving Texas was unsettling. She'd come to love the vast reaches of sky and prairie, the sparse, unyielding beauty of a land where a single tiny prairie flower assumed great importance. She'd learned to recognize the insignificance of man in so vast a land and to appreciate the bravery and courage it took to survive here. She'd felt it testing her mettle and she didn't want to run away before she'd proven herself. She wanted to stay in Texas, she realized. She'd come here for Rayne, but she wanted to stay for herself.

"I'm sorry," Aaron said. "I'd hoped it would work out." He stood looking down at her, a glass of sherry in his hand. She was seated before the fire, a cup of hot tea on her lap. Billy was already settled in the bunkhouse with the assurance of a job for as long as he wanted one. All the problems seemed to have been whisked away by Aaron upon her return. Now she sat resting, considering her future. The numbing pain and tears that had threatened to spill out were held at bay for the moment by Aaron's gentle care.

"What will you do now?" he asked her, as she'd asked Billy earlier. She read the concern in his eyes.

"I'll return to New Orleans," she said wearily.

Aaron stood silent for a moment; then with a sigh he placed his drink on the mantel and came to squat at her feet. "Am I so repulsive, Gaby, that you can't consider staying here with me?" he asked gently.

Looking into his eyes, Gaby realized the answer meant a lot to him. Surely he didn't believe she was rejecting him because of his scars. She'd long ago stopped thinking about them. Impulsively she reached out to place a soft hand against his puckered cheek, and he saw the compassion in her eyes. At a younger, more unwise age he might have railed against such an emotion from a beautiful woman, but now he calmly accepted it. Compassion was better than nothing from this lovely woman who had

captured his heart and made him look forward to life
again.

"Why do you say such things?" Gaby said softly. "The
scars are nothing to me. You are a caring, gentle man
with so much that is good about you. You have been my
friend at a time when I badly needed one."

"Then continue to be a friend, Gaby," he urged. "Stay
here with me. I'll take care of you and the baby. I'll give
you a home and a name. I know I'm older than you, but
we seem to enjoy each other—"

"Age doesn't matter," Gaby said quickly, "but I still
can't marry you, Aaron." A spasm of pain crossed his
features, and for the first time she knew how much he'd
wanted her to say yes. "If I am truly your friend, then I
must say no. You heard the gossip and rumors flying
around at the dance. Nearly everything they said is true."
She rose and paced the length of the room to where
neither heat nor light welcomed her, then back toward
the warmth of the fireplace and the waiting man. As she
paced, she talked, telling him for the first time of her life
in New Orleans and the Court of Angels. When she'd
finished, she whirled to meet his gaze.

"I make no apology for who I am and where I came
from." He could see the defiant pride. She'd been made
to apologize one time too many for her past, he surmised. She resumed her agitated pacing.

"The things Thad and Slade said about me were lies.
Thad Martin and Jed Lager attacked me in the livery
stable one day. They ripped my gown and would have
raped me, but Billy and Jacinta saved me."

"Thad is a ruthless man," Aaron said. "He's always
victimized the helpless."

"Oh, his attack had nothing to do with me," Gaby
said, her voice shaking with emotion. "He's after Rayne,
and thought to provoke him into a fight. He was using
me for that end."

"That explains why Jed was hidden in the bushes with
a gun, and why Rayne went after Thad."

"I didn't tell Rayne about Thad's attack on me," Gaby
said, and slowed her pacing. Her head was lowered. The
omission of not telling Rayne had cost her something of
her self-pride, Aaron guessed. She wasn't a woman used

to lying even by omission. "When Rayne did find out, he didn't believe me." Whirling, she began to pace again.

"Nothing you've told me has made me change my mind about having you as a wife, Gaby," Aaron said gently. "If anything, it only makes me admire you more." She cast him a slanting glance from under lowered lashes.

"Have you forgotten the accusations Slade Harner made against me this morning?" she asked. "Nearly every man in the county was there, and they believed him."

"If you run away, they will believe him," Aaron said.

"The awful part of it is that I believe Slade was just acting on Thad Martin's orders all the time. Thad's sly and evil and he intends to ruin Rayne. I'm certain of it." Fear and worry clogged her throat.

She still loves him, Aaron thought, although the man had failed her so badly. Aaron felt a stab of envy wash through him. If only Abigail had stood by him like this years ago instead of running away.

Gaby drew a shivery breath and faced Aaron again, her dark eyes still reflecting her pain. "So you see, I can't take your offer. I would only hurt your good name. What would others say of a man who married such an infamous woman as I am?"

"My appointment to Washington would have little to do with the approval of these people around Fowler," Aaron said, "so that's not to be considered. What's more important is you, Gaby, and the way you've been maligned by a series of events and by people who have their own selfish designs. Marry me, Gaby, and we'll overcome the lies and misconceptions that have been started about you."

"In spite of everything you've heard, you still want to marry me?"

"Because of everything I've heard, I only want to marry you more. I'd be honored to have you for my wife." With those simple words he won her over. He saw the surprise, the gratitude, and finally the acceptance on her face. Her smile was like a rainbow after a summer shower, warm and full of hope.

"Thank you, Aaron. The honor is mine."

His large hand gripped hers. "You'll never be sorry,

Gaby, I promise you. I'll do everything I can to make you happy."

"I'll work hard to make you a good wife and I'll never do anything to dishonor the trust you've placed in me." Was it only this morning she'd dreamed of making the same vow to Rayne? She pushed the memory aside. She would be Aaron's wife and she would do her best to forget Rayne Elliott and the passion they'd known. She would close away that part of her life she'd shared with him, and maybe someday the pain would fade.

He'd ridden hard, pushing his horse almost to the end of its endurance. By nightfall, he'd left the plains behind him and was in the foothills, where ridges hid caves and faults in the earth. The first night he made camp in one of the caves, building his fire at the mouth and putting his back against the crumbling limestone walls. It was a cold clear night and the stars looked the size of a man's fist.

Rayne lay looking up at them until the fire burned down; then, piling on more wood and banking it so it would last the night, he crawled back into the welcoming warmth of the cave and settled down to sleep. He wouldn't let himself think about Gaby or what had happened back at the ranch. For now he just wanted to sleep and forget.

He could just keep riding. He'd done that once when he was younger, drifting from one part of the country to another. He could do it again. He wouldn't have to go back to the ranch or deal with Cole and his bitter accusations. He wouldn't have to listen to other men talk about Gaby and he wouldn't have to look into her eyes and wonder if she were telling the truth.

He closed his eyes and willed himself not to think about her. For a little while he had to be away from her, from all reminders of her. The fragrance of her still lingered in his bed and the expectation of seeing her when he came home at night still clung to his mind.

He'd left her behind for a little while. He closed his eyes and slept, huddled against the cold in his single blanket. In the morning he saddled his horse and rode further west, leaving behind the caves and their sketchy comfort. He had no food, no coffee. He drank his fill from the streams and at midday he killed a rabbit, which he tied to his saddle horn, and rode on.

At dusk he halted in a copse of trees along a meandering stream and built a fire. He cleaned the rabbit and skewered it on a stick and hung it over the flowers. It cooked slowly, the juices and fat falling into the fire with angry spits. He was too hungry to wait until it was properly cooked, choosing to eat it while it was still tough. Then, drinking once again from the stream, he checked the hobble on his horse and rolled himself into his blanket and closed his eyes. But once again he was in the open, the sky wide and high above him, and the memory of Gaby's small warm body tucked against his their first night on the prairie came to him bittersweet. She'd been so delighted and awed by everything she'd seen. Then with a laugh she'd gone all soft and yielding in his arms. Rayne rolled on his back and stared up at the stars. She was there too, her face outlined in the sky, her hair reflected in the drift of a dark cloud. The sparkle of starlight was her eyes and mouth; her voice was in the soft night wind. He lay for hours remembering, and when he could bear it no more, he saddled his horse and rode on.

He climbed high into the foothills, pushing his horse toward the distant mountain peaks. They'd sat on the elusive horizon all day and seemed no closer. How many days' ride away were they? he wondered, and decided it didn't matter. He wasn't in a hurry. He had time, all the time in the world. There was no reason to hurry back.

Aaron and Gaby were married quietly in the new church in town, with only a few of the ranchers and their wives in attendance. If some of those men had been at the Elliott ranch and witnessed the things said there, they gave no indication. Stiffly their wives made their way forward after the ceremony to extend their good wishes to the new Mrs. Spencer. Think of her what they may, the fact was that Aaron Spencer was a wealthy and powerful man in Texas. They couldn't afford to offend him.

After the ceremony there was a reception back at the ranch. Sides of beef had already been set to roasting on spits in the yard and barrels of rum and beer left to chill in the well.

Mexican musicians had been employed and the soft strum of their guitars reminded Gaby of the trip across the prairie with Rayne. She pushed away all thought of the tall rangy Texan and smiled brightly at her guests. She danced with every man there and chatted with their wives about everyday affairs. The women played as important a role as the man in making a ranch successful.

In turn the women were surprised at the affection Gaby showed her new husband. There seemed to be no aversion in her gaze when she looked at him, and they laughed together often, as if sharing some special joke. Seeing Aaron's relaxed, happy face, they finally conceded he wasn't so disfigured as they'd at first supposed. Some even allowed as how he must have been a handsome man at one time.

The evening wore on, and thanks in part to Gaby's efforts, everyone danced or ate or talked. No one was left standing stiff and alone in a corner. By the time the band took a break and supper was served, the guests had discovered to their surprise, that they were having a good time.

"I knew you'd bounce back on your feet," Jessie said. "You've set this territory on its ear."

"Oh, Jessie, I'm very fortunate," Gaby said. "I don't know what I would have done these past few weeks if not for you and Aaron and Mrs. Schafer." The two women had helped Gaby with her wedding arrangements.

"Pshaw," Jessie said. "It was fun to be involved in something like this again. Reminded me of when I was young and Walker and me got married."

"You've done a wonderful job," Aaron whispered to Gaby as he ladled her a cup of punch. She glanced around the room. "Everyone's having a good time, even that old gossip Mrs. Johnson. How did you manage it?"

"It's what I've been trained to do," Gaby said. "There's more to being a courtesan than one might suppose. Maddie taught me well."

Aaron looked at her face and found no bitterness or shame there. She was simply telling him something about herself. "I'd like to meet Maddie one day," he said

warmly, and Gaby flashed him a grateful smile. He'd
understood, and his words reassured her that she need
never fear speaking of her background.

He'd reached the mountains now. He hadn't seen a
soul in days except a miner who'd pulled a gun and
ordered him on his way, and an old trader, pushing
southward, looking for Indians.

"They don't come like they used to," the old man said,
smacking his lips over a rabbit leg Rayne had given him.
"They's afraid of us now, you know." He chewed some
more. "Oh, there's some that think it's our armies an'
our guns they's afraid of, but it ain't." He chewed some
more, and Rayne waited, knowing the man would continue when he was ready. Too many years of living alone
out on the deserts and plains had made him slow in his
conversation. The old man threw down his bone and
looked up at Rayne.

"White man's disease," he said, and belched. They sat
together at the fire, both of them quiet and easy, and
Rayne studied the old man.

"You alone," he asked finally, "or do you have family
someplace?"

"Alone," the man replied, then chuckled. "Had me a
gal one time." He shook his head. "She was something
else, though. Whew, could she talk. Talkiest woman I
ever seed." The smile left his face. "Took up with a
sodbuster back in Kansas and had a passel o' kids. Reckon
she wouldn'a been happy a-sittin' back there a-waitin' on
me. Women, now, ain't like men. Got to have them
somebody to love and make over. Take you and me, we
don't need nobody."

Rayne watched Josiah McKinsey for a while, seeing
the old man's unkempt state, the red whiskey nose and
the hands that trembled when he reached for his pipe.
Had he once been young and passionate? Had he had
dreams once? Had he known pain when his woman left
him for a Kansas farmer?

The years had been lonely for Rayne. Little Finger had
been more of a father to him than Cole. It had been the
old cook who had taught him to read and write. His

father had taught him other things. Once when he was very young, Cole had set him on a horse.

"You see this land around you, Rayne," Cole had said. "One day it's yours. If you want to keep it, you have to be tough and hard and mean, meaner 'n anyone else. You have to start learning that now." Cole had whipped the horse's flanks and the animal had bolted around the corral with a frightened little boy clinging to the saddle horn, learning to grip with his legs so he wouldn't fall beneath the pounding hooves. He'd learned and he'd grown tough. He could be hard and mean when he had to be.

But there'd been another side to him, a softer side, a part of him that had needed to give and receive love. Unerringly Gaby had reached that soft core of him and shown him the strength in loving.

Suddenly the memory of that last day at the ranch returned to him. He saw her face lifted to him beseechingly and saw the wince of fear as he'd raised his hand to her. He saw all too clearly how he'd failed her, leaving her alone time and again to face the lies of others. She'd come back to him that day at the ranch. She was returning to him, and once again he'd met her with suspicions and accusations, taking the word of a known liar and thief over hers.

His cry reached upward toward the cold brilliance of the stars and awakened the old man under the wagon. Josiah McKinsey turned over in his sleep and shook his head. The mountains and prairie affected men in different ways. You either learned to survive or you went loco. He vowed he'd ride on alone tomorrow.

"Forgive me, Gaby," Rayne whispered to the prairie wind. "I'll make it up to you. I swear I will." Tears started in his eyes and spilled over, running down the lean, weathered cheeks before he could wipe them away. Self-consciously he glanced around, but there was no one to see his show of weakness. What would Gaby think if she saw him now? Tough, self-reliant Rayne Elliott crying over a woman. Suddenly he knew what she would think and what she would do. He could almost see her before him, her dark eyes warm and full of love and understanding, her small hand soft and gentle against his cheek. He bowed his head against his updrawn knee and wished desperately she were here. He'd never let her go again. Never.

The next morning when the old man woke and climbed out from under the wagon, he found himself alone.

"Plumb loco," he said, shaking his head, and began packing up.

Rayne was well down the mountain slope by the time the sun was high. He chafed at the necessity to stop and rest, to find food and water for himself and his mount. He wanted to rush back to Gaby and beg her forgiveness. He would ask her to marry him, and Cole be damned. What if she did leave someday? He'd ensured that she leave now. He'd driven her away by his actions, but not anymore. Things would be different. He'd be different.

He urged his horse down out of the foothills and back across the prairie, his heart growing lighter with every mile they left behind them. It rained and turned cold the last day out. Still Rayne pushed on. There had grown within him a nagging urge to hurry, a feeling of something about to be irretrievably lost. His horse threw a shoe the last mile or two. Rayne cursed as he walked her home. They limped into the ranch yard late. The place was quiet, a light showing only in the cookhouse. Rayne put up his horse and made his way to the light. Little Finger and Cole sat playing poker.

"Howdy," Little Finger called in surprise when Rayne opened the door and stepped inside. Rayne nodded a greeting and glanced at his father. Cole sat silent, his eyes wary as they met Rayne's.

"I thought I'd stop in and have a cup of coffee, warm myself up before going up to the house," Rayne said, taking off his wet slicker and hanging it on a hook to dry.

"Shore thing," Little Finger said. "I got a fresh pot right here." He poured a tin cup full of the hot, dark brew.

"It's awfully quiet here," Rayne said, looking around.

"Not many men here these days," Little Finger said, cutting a glance at Cole.

"Slade's workin' at the Martin ranch," Cole said, and paused significantly before going on. "And that woman took Billy with her back to the Lazy S." Rayne longed to

ask after Gaby, but he didn't want to discuss her with his
father. He'd heard enough from Cole to last him a lifetime. He downed his coffee and set the cup on the
wooden table.

"Well, I guess I'll go see if Jacinta can rustle me up
something to eat," he said, pushing himself off the bench.

"She ain't here," Little Finger said, and again glanced
at Cole.

Rayne paused, looking from one man to the other.
"Why not? Where is she?"

"She's at the Spencer ranch too."

Rayne waited for a further explanation. The garrulous
old man was strangely silent.

Rayne waited, his alarm growing. "Why did they leave?"
he asked finally.

"They ain't left," Cole spoke up. "They jest went
visiting."

Rayne relaxed a bit. "They'll be back then," he said.
"I'm not too hungry anyway." He turned toward the
door, tamping down the urge to run out of the building.

"Rayne." His father's voice stopped him with his hand
on the latch. Rayne looked back at him. The lamplight
reflected in the old man's eyes. "They went to a wedding
tonight."

"What did you say?" The blood was pounding in Rayne's
temples.

"Your harlot got married today. They're having a party
over to the Spencer ranch right now to celebrate." Cole's
eyes glittered triumphantly.

"No," Rayne cried hoarsely, his voice loud in the quiet
room. "No." The door slammed against the wall and his
howl of denial was lost in the dark, rainy night. The two
men could hear his footsteps running in the direction of
the barn.

Little Finger looked at Cole. "You never once tried to
make anything easier on that boy," he said fiercely.

Cole's eyes blazed as they stared back at his old friend.
"I want him to survive," he snarled. "You ain't no good
as a man if your insides are all knotted up over some fool
woman."

"Are you givin' yourself as an example of that?" Little
Finger demanded.

Cole seemed to sag from someplace deep inside himself. His head sank between his shoulders. "Yeah," he acknowledged. "I'm a good example of that."

Rayne saddled a fresh horse, one of the roans. They were faster and longer-legged than the mustangs. It would cover more ground at a faster pace. The rain had started again and Rayne pulled on his slicker. Thunder rumbled in the distance as he turned his horse toward the south road. The air seemed heavy and caught in his throat, so he had a hard time breathing. He recognized it as anxiety and drew a deep breath, forcing himself to calm down. Spurring the roan, he leaned low in the saddle, his hat pulled over his face to shield it from the rain.

Gaby! Her name was a cry in his breast. It couldn't be true. It was another one of Cole's lies. She'd be there waiting for him. She'd know he was coming for her. She'd know it because she knew how much he loved her.

He crossed the river bridge where he and his men had searched for Gaby's body weeks before. The bridge had been rebuilt, he noted absently. He turned his horse westward away from town and pushed for Spencer's ranch. He could feel the roan tiring beneath him and still he spurred him to a faster gait. The night raced away on either side. Man and beast were gasping for breath by the time they reached their destination. The roan blew air through foam-flecked nostrils. Rayne dismounted and loosened the cinch to ease the horse's breathing. Then he looked around.

The whole ranch house was lit up and buggies and wagons sat around the yard. It was obvious there was a party going on inside. Rayne tried to tell himself it didn't mean a wedding, but his heart had started a slow, painful pounding in his chest. He mounted the porch steps and moved to one of the lace-covered windows. Inside there was laughter and music.

Rayne stood peering into the brightly lit room. Couples moved about in a sprightly dance while others rested on chairs, plates of food in their hands. All seemed to be having a good time. Rayne strained to catch a glimpse of Gaby and found her at one end of the room talking to a group of people. She wore a gown of pale pink satin and lace. Her hair was piled on top of her head in ringlets, and pink satin flowers had been pinned in among the curls. She looked dazzling. Someone spoke to her and she laughed; then the people parted and Aaron Spencer stepped forward. He took Gaby's arm and held it against his side. Gaby smiled up at him. All around them, people raised their glasses in a toast. Eyes glinting with laughter, Gaby leaned forward and kissed Aaron lightly on the lips while everyone clapped.

Rayne turned away. Denial and despair warred within him. And beneath the numbing pain were building anger and the bitterness of betrayal. He staggered to the edge of the porch.

How quickly she'd forgotten him. Their nights together had meant nothing to her. He looked around. The ranch spoke of wealth and ease and comfort. Aaron Spencer had already achieved what Rayne hoped to gain someday. He could give Gaby a great deal. What had Rayne given her? Some whitewash for the dingy walls of the ranch house.

Rayne stepped down off the porch and headed for his horse. Gaby had done what Cole had predicted all along. She'd left him when something better came along. This was the real reason Gaby had left him. Rayne mounted and sat looking back at the lighted windows. Beyond those doors was the woman he loved. He'd been afraid he'd lost her from his own stiff pride, but now he knew better. She'd chosen well for herself. He wished her luck. He gave a mocking salute to the house and the woman inside; then, wheeling his horse, he galloped away.

"What is it, Gaby?" Aaron asked. She stood as if transfixed, her head cocked, her eyes intent.

"Listen," she said. "Did that sound like a horse outside?"

"I didn't hear anything," Aaron said.

"I thought I did," Gaby murmured, and wondered why at that same moment she'd thought of Rayne with such intensity she'd had to look about her to remind herself where she was. For a moment it had seemed as if Rayne were close by. She shivered slightly.

"I guess it was my imagination. Excuse me. I'll ask Maria to bring my shawl." She turned away. Aaron looked after her thoughtfully, then moved to the door and went outside. He stood on the edge of the porch and watched as the fleeting moonlight scudded briefly from behind a dark rain cloud and shone on a lone horse and rider. The moon disappeared a moment, and when it reappeared, the figure was gone. Should he tell Gaby? he wondered, then shook his head. There was no need to upset her. She was his wife now. It was his job to protect her. He went back inside to his wedding party.

15

Rayne had changed. He'd grown quieter, harder. His men could see it and they stayed out of his way. Most of them thought the change was due to what had happened at the hanging party. None of them, except Cole and Little Finger, knew he'd made a wild ride to reach Gaby on her wedding night.

Cole was pleased to see the steely resolve in his son's eyes. In fact he was pleased with the way the whole affair had turned out. The Jezebel had proved Cole right when she ran off to a man with more money. It might be painful for Rayne to bear now, but in the long run he'd be better off for it.

Winter set in with a bitter force as if sorry it had given a short reprieve. The fury of the chinook winds lashed deep into cattle country. The ranchers' worst fears came true. Cows froze in the pastures trying to paw through the frozen snow for food. Men burrowed into line camps, emerging only to try to give aid to the helpless cattle. The best they could do was point them south and hope the longhorns could make it far enough to outrun the storms.

Harbored in the sturdy brick ranch house, Gaby was warm and secure. A fire blazed on the hearth all day long and she never wanted for anything. Her every wish and comfort was seen to almost before she was aware she needed anything.

Every day Aaron rushed home to be with her, bringing an interesting tale of his business dealings or political endeavors. Gaby listened and sometimes offered her advice. Aaron seemed delighted at her involvement.

On the days Aaron was gone from the ranch, the formidable Mrs. Schafer proved to be good company when she could be persuaded to stop fussing about and sit down to talk. Gaby still missed Jacinta's ebullient spirits and warmth. Mrs. Schafer was a different character altogether. Straitlaced and stiffly proper at all times, the German housekeeper seemed too reserved and old-maidish. It was hard for Gaby to imagine there had once been a Mr. Schafer.

Still Gaby was surprised with her wide store of knowledge and her practical, no-nonsense approach to every problem. Her calm, capable air gave Gaby a sense of ease she hadn't felt in a long time.

Jessie Walker came to see Gaby whenever the weather permitted. Gaby was struck by the contrasts among the three women who had befriended her since she'd come to Texas. Surprisingly, Mrs. Schafer and Jessie became fast friends. Mrs. Schafer seemed not to be bothered at all by the crusty old woman's language.

When the winter grew too fierce, Aaron surprised Gaby by whisking her off to the warm seacoast and from there they took a boat to New Orleans to see Maddie.

"*Chérie,* I can't believe it is you," Maddie cried, wrapping her arms around Gaby. The two women clung together. Then Ruby was there and the other girls each wanted to hug her. They had hundreds of questions about Texas and Gaby wanted news about Alcee and even old Mr. Barbieri. Alcee, she learned had run away to sea. They talked all day long while Aaron obligingly took himself off on the pretense of business.

"*Chérie,* you have much to explain to me," Maddie said when the others had finally exhausted the subject of Texas cows and cowboys and had gone off to prepare themselves for the evening.

"What is there to explain?" Gaby hedged.

"All day you have avoided any mention of Rayne Elliott. You left here on a cattle boat in pursuit of him, and you return with another man as your husband. This man Aaron Spencer is very agreeable, very rich, but he does not make you smile as Rayne did. Tell me, Gaby, what has happened?"

"Oh, Maddie, somehow things went all wrong," Gaby cried, and threw herself into Maddie's comforting arms as she had so often in her childhood. How many times had Maddie soothed her and listened to her troubles? Now Gaby gave way to the tears she'd held back for all the months since her marriage. Between great tearing sobs she poured out all the anguish of her breakup with Rayne. When she'd finished she lay back against the chaise, limp from crying, while Maddie brought her a delicate hand-painted cup of fragrant herb tea.

"Thank you for listening to all that," Gaby said sheepishly. "I feel better."

"Of course you do, *chérie*," Maddie said. "A good cry, a little talk, and things look brighter."

"This can't be solved in such a simple way," Gaby said.

"I know, I know, *chérie*," Maddie sighed, and set her cup aside. "I have thought of you often these long months, wondering how you were faring there in Texas. I hoped you'd found a way to make things work with Rayne. Such men as Rayne Elliott and Dusty Simmons are rare in a woman's life. Once I even considered . . . well, no matter. That was another time." Her smile held a lingering regret and once again Gaby wondered what had occurred between the Frenchwoman and Rayne's foreman.

"So you have found another man," Maddie went on. "I think Aaron Spencer would do anything to make you happy."

"He's the gentlest, kindest man. I don't deserve his friendship."

"Oh, my pet, it is not friendship he feels for you," Maddie laughed knowingly.

"I know," Gaby said, and her voice was low. "He knew when he married me that I didn't love him, that I still loved Rayne. I feel so guilty, as if somehow I've tricked him."

"I see," Maddie said, looking at the pale young face. Gaby was obviously seeking her advice. What could she say? Maddie wondered, and then offered the only words possible: "It is time you put aside the feelings you have for Rayne. You must give your love and loyalty to your husband."

"Oh, Maddie, I know that. I would be so happy if I could forget Rayne. It's not that simple."

"Why not? He has betrayed you. He has not trusted you or protected you from the slander of others. Such a man doesn't deserve your love."

"I haven't told you everything, Maddie," Gaby said, and raised her haunted eyes to her friend's. "I'm going to have Rayne's baby."

"Gabrielle," Maddie cried, her voice registering a mingling of joy and concern. How difficult the young made their lives, she thought sadly.

"Have you told Aaron?" Maddie asked, thinking of the shock it would be to the kind man who had brought Gaby back to her.

"He knew before we were married," Gaby explained.

"Before?" Gaby nodded. "And he married you anyway? You are very fortunate, *chérie*."

"I know," Gaby said. "I want to repay Aaron for all his kindness. I want to do everything I can to make him happy. It's true, my life with Rayne is over. I'll just have to accept that."

"It would be wisest, *chérie*. But what of Rayne? Have you told him about the baby?" Gaby's downcast eyes told her the answer long before the single smothered word came.

"I tried, though," Gaby hurried to explain. "I went to the ranch to tell him, but men were there who made horrible accusations against me, and Rayne believed them. He just rode off and left me there."

"Do you plan to tell him?" Maddie asked gently. Inside her breast, her heart beat angrily over the treatment Gaby had received at the Texan's hands.

"Do you think I should, Maddie?" Gaby asked wistfully.

"Yes, although he doesn't deserve it. You cannot keep a secret such as this, Gaby. It will come back to hurt you someday."

"I suppose I must, but not yet. I don't want to hurt Aaron."

"Don't delay too long, *chérie*. The longer you put it off, the easier it will be to justify not doing it at all. It might come out someday in a way that will cause unhappiness for you and your baby.''

"Oh, Maddie, what would I do without you?" Gaby cried, and threw her arms around the New Orleans madam who had given her more love and help than anyone else she'd known in her life.

Long after Gaby was gone, tenderly settled into a carriage by Aaron and whisked off to one of the best hotels in the city, Maddie thought of her and the turn her life had taken. Gaby would always carry the image of the tall Texan in her heart, Maddie knew, for hadn't she done the same with Dusty? Twice Dusty had ridden out of her life, and both times she'd wondered if she'd made the right choice in not going with him. For the first time she felt certain she had.

The fortnight passed too quickly, and before Gaby had gotten used to being back in New Orleans, they were leaving. She was returning to Texas with trunks laden with new gowns, shoes, hats, and parasols for herself and a layette for the baby. Aaron had been more than generous and seemed to delight in showering her with expensive presents. Tucked away in a special valise, for which Aaron had hired a bodyguard, were enough jewels to make Gaby a wealthy woman. Aaron's generosity had taken her breath away.

Maddie and the rest of the girls came down to the dock to see them off. They were dressed in their brightest gowns, looking like lush tropical flowers against the barrels and boxes of cargo stacked around the wharves.

"Who are those women down there?" a lady standing at the rail sniffed and peered down her nose at them. Gaby glanced at the dour-looking woman, then back at the colorful figures on the dock. For a few weeks they'd made her laugh and forget her woes. They'd been generous and funny and Gaby was grateful to them. She was returning to Texas lighterhearted because of them.

"Surely they aren't what they appear?" the woman said archly.

Gaby laughed. "Yes, ma'am, they are," she said. "Angels, every one of them." Aaron's laughter rumbled with hers and the woman turned to peer at the scar-faced man and the beautiful young girl. Still laughing, the two walked away arm in arm. A gust of wind blew against the girl's slender body, outlining for a moment the rounding contours of her figure. The girl was pregnant. Why, she was just a child herself, the woman thought, and that man was old enough to be her father. Sniffing her disapproval, the woman turned back to watch the wharves of New Orleans disappear.

The spring winds came, blowing and nodding the heads of the prairie flowers newly bloomed. The delicately veined leaves of the pasqueflowers heralded the gentler season and gave a promise of the wild blossoms that would follow. The browns and grays of fall and winter gave way to a riot of color, as if the earth itself understood that the wet season was here for only a short while and must be put to full use. Phlox, primrose, Indian paintbrush, milkweed, and fringed prairie orchids delighted the eye at every turn. Patches of bluebonnet bloomed along the streams.

Gaby took long walks, happy to be free of the house and the smothering administrations of Mrs. Schafer. Jacinta and Maria traveled often to the ranch, now that the roads were passable. By mutual consent Jacinta and Gaby never spoke of Rayne. When Jacinta learned of the baby, she was ecstatic, and Gaby made no mention that it was Rayne's. As the months passed, Jacinta's face bore a look of puzzlement, and then puzzlement turned to certainty and Gaby knew she had guessed her secret.

"You mustn't tell anyone," Gaby said one day as she watched Jacinta climb into the wagon for her trip back to the Rocking E.

"I do not tell what is not mine to tell," Jacinta said, and turned a disapproving gaze on Gaby. "What you are doing is very bad. You should have told Señor Elliott. He is a good man. He deserves to know about his child."

"I tried," Gaby cried. "I came the day they tried to hang Billy, but Rayne wouldn't listen. He wants nothing to do with me."

Jacinta studied the young girl, noting the circles beneath her eyes and the lingering sadness in their dark shadows. Neither of them was happy, Jacinta thought, and contemplated telling Gaby of how Rayne had changed and why. Then she shook her head and glanced off down the road. It would only be speculation on her part. Besides, Gaby was married now. Whatever was between Rayne and her must be put aside once and for all.

Gaby salved her conscience by buying the Avery land with the bag of gold coins Rayne had sent over in her trunk. By rights the land was his and she would find a way to give it to him.

Aaron continued to dote on Gaby, taking pains to see that her every craving was satisfied, laughing with her when her wishes seemed silly or outrageous, but providing for them nontheless. Patiently he held her head through morning sickness, listened to her crying moods, and massaged her feet when her ankles swelled. Sweetly he reassured her when she felt horribly fat and misshapen. In his eyes she could never be anything but beautiful.

In truth, Gaby was exceptionally small for the number of months of her pregnancy. That was brought home with startling clarity one day when Aaron had taken her to town. As he helped her from the buggy, Rayne and Dusty rode by. Gaby glanced up to see the shock on Rayne's face as he noted the swelling of her stomach. Shock turned to anger and he looked away without acknowledging her presence.

He thinks the baby is Aaron's, she thought in surprise, and in that instant hundreds of reasons for not telling him the truth came to mind. Only Jacinta knew her secret, and she wouldn't tell.

Aaron's political work increased as good weather descended upon them. Often he had gone late into the night, attending meetings or inspecting area ranches. Several times he traveled to Galveston and to San Jacinto to meet with representatives sent by President Johnson. As her time drew close, Gaby stayed behind, preferring not to travel over the bumpy roads. Now when he must travel, Aaron returned home with an anxious look in his eyes, afraid Gaby might have given birth when he wasn't there. He intended to be at the birthing.

Daniel Spencer impatiently pushed his way into the world on a clear June day when the prairie sky was high and blue and hot winds were already sweeping across the plains in prelude to one of the driest summers in a decade. Streams slowed to a trickle; rivers moved, sluggish and muddy, deep within their banks. The hot winds seared the prairie blossoms so they shriveled and died upon their very borning; then, having defeated the plants that would have held the soil to the ground, the capricious winds scooped up great mounds of prairie dust and whirled it in the air, so the sky grew yellow and hazy from it.

Daniel—or Danny, as he was quickly christened by the indulgent household—drew his first breath of the dirt-tainted Texas air and bellowed his first command. The speed with which his admiring subjects rushed to fulfill that command set the pattern for the long days and nights that followed. The household delighted in the sound of a baby's presence.

Maria, who had agreed to come to the ranch and become nanny, guarded him jealously, indulging his slightest whimper of discontent. Aaron rushed home early from his meetings to hang over the edge of the crib cooing and making funny faces.

Jessie came to see Gaby and declared in her brusque way that Danny was indeed a fine fellow and a true Texan. For a childless woman who declared herself undomesticated in all ways, she showed a surprising skill in handling the small baby. Even Mrs. Schafer unbent when she was around Danny. She never complained if he spit on her spotless bodice, simply sponging it away so she could hold him again. Once, upon hearing singing, Gaby went into the nursery to find the housekeeper cuddling the baby against her shoulder while she crooned a lullaby, a look of wonderment and joy on her austere face.

Shamelessly the whole household vied for Danny's attention, and as the hot summer days passed into weeks and he learned to smile and coo at the adults who wooed him, Gaby sometimes wondered if he knew which of them was his mother. Then he would fuss and squirm so that only she could take him, and would burrow against her shoulder and breasts so she would take him back to the privacy of her room and nurse him, marveling over the sweet roundness of his head and the perfection of the tiny fingers. The glossy dark hair was already forming into a widow's peak on his tiny forehead. When she was alone with Danny, Gaby would allow herself to think of Rayne. At these moments the bond between them still seemed strong and unbroken. Sometimes Gaby longed to bundle Danny into one of the buggies and ride across the prairie to the Rocking E and show Rayne his tiny son. Loyalty kept her where she was. She was Aaron's wife now. She must put Rayne out of her mind.

At such times she held her son to her, cuddling him into the curve of her neck, finding comfort in his soft warm body and the baby smell of him. He was so helpless and he needed her. She'd never been needed by anyone. Always before, people had taken care of her. Each day the need to tell Rayne about Danny grew dimmer, and was nearly forgotten in her joy.

Gaby accepted the role of mother with a steadfast concentration that made Aaron smile. It seemed to him that she was growing happier in their marriage. The hollow grieving look was gone from her eyes and she smiled more often now. But Danny's birth and Gaby's slimming body brought Aaron concern for another area of his marriage. He'd told the truth when he'd spoken of his impotence. He'd already dealt with the crushing emotional scars of that loss. Now he must deal with the problem all over again and consider how it would affect his young wife. During Gaby's pregnancy it hadn't been important, but now he sensed the time would come when she would need a man's touch to still her natural passions. He could not meet her needs in the usual acceptable way, but he could offer her some satisfaction. There were other ways to give pleasure to a woman. So Aaron waited for the first sign of restlessness, the look of longing that he knew must inevitably return to her face. Perhaps then she might welcome his touch and the only comfort he could give her. He waited and worried. Would it be enough for Gaby? he wondered, and knew in his heart it wouldn't be.

June melted into July and the winds of July blew hot across the prairies, burning away what grass had previously escaped. July turned to August and there seemed to be no relief. Then one day when the air was so heavy that heat waves danced on the horizon, a cloud drifted across the hot blue sky and with perversity dumped its precious moisture on the scorched earth before hurrying eastward to the coolness of the Gulf. Earth and sun raced for their share of the rainfall, and within an hour there was little evidence of rain left. The humidity made everyone cranky, especially Danny, who screamed his displeasure to one and all. When at last he'd nursed and fallen into an exhausted sleep, Gaby changed her clothes, donning a riding skirt and shirtwaist.

"I'm going for a ride," she informed Mrs. Schafer.

"Yah, is goot idea. You stay cooped up too much. I vatch Danny while you go."

"Maria can watch him," Gaby said, taking down a wide-brimmed sombrero to shield her face.

"Maria needs a rest too," the housekeeper said. "I vill vatch Danny."

"I'm not tired. I will watch him. It is my job," Maria declared, and Gaby left it to the two women to settle. For the first time since his birth she felt a need to be away from her small, demanding son. She would have to make it a short ride, because all too soon it would be time to nurse Danny again. She didn't know who was most uncomfortable when she was late with his feeding, herself or her voracious son.

Billy saddled a horse and helped her mount. "Do you want someone to ride with you?"

"No, I'm not going that far," Gaby reassured him. "I'll take it easy." She kicked her mount into a sedate trot, her thoughts on the young man she'd brought to the ranch before her marriage. Billy had been grateful for a second chance and had once again proven himself hard-working and trustworthy.

This past year had been a long one, filled with surprising changes. Gaby's thoughts turned to Aaron and his political work. Lately he seemed worried and preoccupied, and she'd noticed he was traveling with two of his hands as escorts at all times. She'd meant to ask him about it, but the two of them always seemed to spend their time together discussing Danny. There was little time or room for anything else. Now Gaby wondered about Aaron's precautions. She'd ask him that evening, she vowed. She'd been neglecting him lately. After all his kindness, he didn't deserve that.

She rode along the river and turned northwest along one of the streams that cut away from it. An hour passed and she didn't notice, she was so engrossed in the landscape. She thought of her first trip across the flat rangeland. It had seemed monotonous and uninteresting to her. Now she was aware of the teeming life beneath the sparse sun-yellowed grass. Small prairie dogs built their homes in such profusion upon the flat land that they were a constant menace to unsuspecting riders. There were small lizards and scorpions burrowing into the ground that once would have sent her screaming. She accepted them as part of the prairie. Even her way of viewing the vast rolling land had changed. Now her eyes caught the shadows of dips and hollows and she'd come to find beauty in the sage and prickly pears that clung tenaciously to life in the unwelcoming soil. Clumps of evergreen oaks and mesquite broke the monotony of the plains, while post oaks and pecan and other trees rimmed the streams that popped up unexpectedly, carrying the rivers' waters to a wider lay of dry land. It was these streams that made the land suitable for raising cows.

Gaby paused beside the stream she'd followed, dismounting to sit in the grass while her horse drank his fill, then munched contentedly on the sweet green grass along the banks. Soon she would have to return, Gaby thought. She could already feel the milk flowing in her breasts. Danny would waken from his nap and want to be fed again. Still she lingered, enjoying the peacefulness of the afternoon and the warm breeze blowing across her face. Lying back in the grass, she stared up at the sparse canopy of hardwood trees.

The sound of hoofbeats on the hard-baked ground roused her. Jumping to her feet, she gathered up the reins and stood peering through the heat waves toward the riders who breasted the horizon. Aware suddenly of her helplessness if they should prove unfriendly, Gaby mounted her horse and turned it back the way she'd come. She cast a short glance over her shoulder and saw that the riders had veered now and were following the stream, much as she'd done earlier, all save one. He had spurred his horse after her, and Gaby could see by the set of the broad shoulders that it was Rayne.

Was he riding to catch her? she wondered. She hadn't seen him in months. The thought of doing so now left her trembling. Digging in her heels, she set her horse to an all-out gallop back toward the Spencer ranch. She could hear staccato hoofbeats behind her. Rayne was pursuing her, she thought with dismay, and urged her horse onward.

He was gaining and there was little she could do. Still she tried, her heart beating wildly, her eyes tearing from the wind rushing against them. Her mount topped a rise of land and floundered down the back side of it, stumbled, and regained his footing to race onward, but Gaby had lost her seating, and inexperienced as she was, bobbed unevenly in the saddle, one booted foot striving vainly to find the stirrup again. She was about to fall, she realized, and rather than suffer that indignity, reined up and swung to face her pursuer. With a rattle of pebbles Rayne brought his horse to a halt near her own. His eyes were nearly black as they looked into hers.

"What's wrong, Gaby? Why are you running away like this?"

"Why are you chasing me across the prairie this way?" she demanded.

"I wasn't chasing you." He paused, studying her intently. He *had* been chasing her, and he wasn't sure why. He'd done it on an impulse. "I wanted to talk to you," he said lamely.

"We have little left to talk about," Gaby said, and wheeled her horse about, but she could feel the saddle slipping beneath her and feared she would be pitched to the ground. Impatiently she swung down and began tightening the cinch. Rayne dismounted and came around to stand by her. He made her nervous. He seemed bigger, broader, harder-boned than before. What did he want from her? she wondered. Had Jacinta told him about Danny after all?

She didn't see the look on his face as he watched her gleaming dark head, or see him bend forward slightly to catch a whiff of her fragrance. The memory of it had stayed with him all these months.

She fumbled with the straps. "What do you want from me, Rayne?" She stiffened as she felt his hand on her arm. Slowly he turned her to face him, and she couldn't deny him.

She could feel the heat of the horse at her back and the heat of the man in front of her. She felt overpowered by Rayne's tall, lean body. She had to get away from him, she thought, but stayed where she was, mesmerized by the blue-black lights of his eyes, the line of his bottom lip, the dark head silhouetted against the sunlight as it dipped down toward her.

Their lips met and clung, and Gaby wasn't aware she'd gone up on tiptoe to meet him. The masculine scent and feel of him was filling her senses, so she forgot time and place and stood on the hot prairie clinging to the rawboned strength of him. His arms drew her tighter, molding her body to his with aching, bittersweet familiarity. His lips parted, demanding the same of her, and helplessly she complied.

Her body remembered what her mind and heart had tried so hard to forget. It remembered and responded to him wantonly. She felt the hard ridge of his muscles flattening her soft breasts, the unyielding steel of his belt buckle, and the equally unyielding hardness below the belt. Her body opened to him. A flare of passion, hot and pulsating, ignited deep within her. This, this was what she'd yearned for these past few weeks. This was the root of her restlessness. She was a passionate woman and she needed to be loved as only a man like Rayne could love her. She grew pliant and submissive in his arms and Rayne took her hands and drew her away from the openness of the prairie toward the trees and grassy banks of the stream. His eyes were dark with the promise of passion to be shared.

The horses stood meekly, heads down, cropping at the vegetation while Rayne laid her back against the cool green bed of grass, then settled his long body over hers. She felt the weight of him and was devastated by it. She strained upward toward the exquisite feel of him.

"Gaby," he breathed against her cheek. "I've been in agony without you." His lips burned her face with kisses; his hands moved downward, cupping her breasts. Impatiently he opened the buttons of her shirt. The thin material clung to her damp skin. He pushed it aside so his hand could touch the softness of her. His tongue rasped against the warm, smooth rise of her breasts, nuzzling as Danny did for a nipple. The thought of her child made her stiffen in Rayne's arms.

"Please don't," she cried, pushing against him.

Rayne raised his head and stared at her in surprise. "You can't mean that," he whispered, trying to recapture her lips, but she turned her head aside. The kiss landed at her earlobe and slid downward.

Gaby closed her eyes against the surge of feeling. "Let go of me," she ordered, deliberately making her voice cold.

Rayne captured her chin, gazing down into her eyes, trying to measure which to believe, her words or her body.

Gaby glared up at him. His long, lean body still pinned her. "You forget I'm a married woman now," she said scathingly.

The words cut through him. Silently he let his gaze roam over her face and throat, and over the pale, half-bared breast, and his look turned derisive. "I hadn't forgotten," he said grimly. "I guess I just figured it didn't make any difference to you."

"You figured wrong," Gaby told him, pushing against his shoulder. "Aaron's my husband. I've made my vows to him."

"Why should that matter to you, Gaby?" he asked, not budging from his superior position over her. "You made vows to me, vows of love and fidelity, but you never kept any of them. Were they just lies, spoken in the heat of passion?"

"Yes," she told him, still trapped beneath him and hating it. Her eyes blazed into his. "And why not? Passion is all that ever existed between us."

"I loved you, Gaby." He held her wrists in his hands, pinning them to the ground above her.

"Loved me," she scoffed. "There was never any love between us, Rayne. Love doesn't believe in the lies of others. I'm loved now by a man who knows how to take care of me. Aaron's been kind to me."

"You mean he's been generous to you," Rayne accused. "Don't confuse the two, Gaby. You've got what you want now." He had misconstrued her words, as usual, Gaby thought wearily. They'd never be able to understand each other.

"Yes, I have what I want now," she said softly. Her answer angered him. He'd wanted her to deny his words. He'd wanted some other reason for her going to Aaron. He didn't want to know that some other man could provide her with more than he could. He threw back his head and laughed mockingly, his face twisting into bitter lines that reminded her of Cole.

"He takes such good care of you that you lie here beneath me writhing with desire like a bitch in heat," he growled, and his lips closed over hers in a hard, demanding kiss that bruised her tender mouth, but bruised her pride even more. She struggled against him, flailing out at him with her nails, but he caught her small wrist in his large hands. She couldn't fight against him, Gaby thought. His strength was far superior to hers, but she couldn't bear to be taken by him in the same loveless manner as the last time they were together. Instinctively she used the only weapon left to her. Her body went limp and passive beneath him. He felt the fight go out of her and released her mouth to stare down into her eyes.

"If you continue with this," she said coldly, "it will be rape."

Rayne released her hands and braced himself on his palms on either side of her head. He grinned down at her, but there was little mirth in the act. "No one would believe it," he said flatly, and rolled to one side, releasing her.

Gaby sprang to her feet and brushed ineffectively at her grass-stained shirt. In the struggle her hair had fallen down her back and now she tried to pin it back into place. Rayne lay watching as the thin material of her shirtwaist grew taut over her full breasts. They'd grown bigger, he thought in amazement.

Gaby gave up on her hair and clamping her sombrero on her head, walked to her horse. Catching at the reins, she turned to face him again. He was retrieving his own hat. She watched the long, clean limbs as he moved. Even now, her body cried for him.

Rayne glanced up and caught the anguish on her face. She looked so vulnerable with her trailing hair and bruised mouth that he took a step forward as if he would take her in his arms again and soothe away the defeated look in her eyes.

"No," Gaby cried, holding out a hand as if to ward him off. "Don't come any closer." She took a deep breath. "Don't come around me anymore, Rayne," she said raggedly. The plea in her eyes cut through him. "Whatever was between us has to end here today. I'm married and I have a baby. I want to be a good wife and mother."

"Gaby . . ." he began, and took another step. He had to hold her in his arms and erase the pain he'd caused her by this meeting.

"No," she cried again, her hand slashing the air angrily. The movement tightened the thin cloth across her breasts and he saw the dark stain. Had he injured her? he thought in alarm, his gaze flying back to her face for some clue.

He glanced at her bodice again and saw the circle of dampness grow at the peak. Suddenly he understood. He'd tried to deny the baby's existence, but now he couldn't. He blinked against the stinging in his eyes. Gaby, his sweet Gaby, was a mother now. She carried within her body the nourishment that kept another human being alive. He pictured her cradling a small body in her arms, baring her breasts, and placing one rose-tipped nipple in a small gaping mouth. There would be a look of love on her face, the same look she'd worn when she looked at him. Gaby, the light-hearted girl who'd sparkled with laughter and glowed with love for him alone, was forever gone from him, and in her place stood a woman who gave life and nourished it and loved someone else more than she'd loved him.

The pain he'd known when Gaby first went to Aaron was nothing compared to what he felt now. Gaby had loved another man enough to give him a child. Now that child was a reality, binding her to her husband with more than words on a paper or the need for his wealth. Rayne's eyes turned bleak, his lips thinned to a bitter line. He clenched his fists in despair and rage. Fear ate at him. He couldn't fight a small baby. He'd never be able to win Gaby back. He'd lost her for good.

"I mean it, Rayne," Gaby cried, and in spite of the tremble in her voice it was compelling and sure in its intent. "I don't love you anymore. I love Aaron and our baby. I don't want whatever is left between us."

"Go on, then," he growled from between clenched teeth. "Get out of here." She looked startled, then frightened at the ferocious look on his face. Quickly she mounted her horse, but before she could ride away, he leapt forward and grabbed the reins.

"Don't ride on Elliott land again, Gaby," he said, low and menacing. "Not if you want to be safe from me." His eyes held hers in a dark, hungry gaze that said the feelings between them would never be ended. For the first time she saw him as his enemies did, a tireless stalker who seldom relinquished what was his. He'd let her slip away from him, but she was still his. She read it in his face and in his eyes. He must never know about Danny, the thought came to her, and she felt fearful of this man she had loved so well.

Kicking her horse, she bolted away. She didn't slow down until she'd gained the river, and even then she pushed the horse, not allowing him to stop for water and grass as she had on the ride out. She rode with the sun beating down on her bare head, for in her haste she'd left her sombrero behind after all.

They limped into the ranch yard, the horse winded and foaming, trembling with fatigue; Gaby windburned and red-eyed. Billy ran out of the barn to catch the reins and help her dismount.

"My God, Gaby, what happened to you?" Aaron cried as she wearily climbed the porch steps. His eyes took in her disheveled state and she could see the mounting alarm. "Who did this to you?" he demanded, taking in the smudged face and bruised mouth. The bodice of her shirtwaist gaped, showing the soft rounding tops of her breasts.

Gaby could see the dread growing on his face, and she uttered the lie: "I fell off my horse." It lay between them, a mean, ugly thing denoting the destruction of the trust they'd held for each other.

"I'm all right," she said lamely.

"Who were you with? Was it Rayne Elliott?" His voice was quiet, his gaze more sad than accusing.

"Nothing happened, Aaron, you must believe me," she cried, and wondered why he should, when she'd lied to him once already. She could see the pain and disappointment washing over his face. His gaze took in her hair and the grass stains on her riding skirt.

"I know how it looks," Gaby began, "but I swear to you I've not been unfaithful. I couldn't repay your kindness that way." Aaron said nothing. Gaby took hold of his arm and peered into his face. "Please, believe me." She couldn't bear to have him hurt.

"I believe you," he said, but she knew he didn't. There was a hurt look in his eyes, and she'd put it there. She could reassure him that she hadn't made love with Rayne, but she could never hide the fact that she'd desperately wanted to. The passion she still felt for Rayne lay between Aaron and her like a dark shadow marring the easy friendship they'd found with each other. Gaby sighed and turned toward the house. She needed a bath, and even from here she could hear Danny's piercing wails. He was hungry, and impatient with waiting for his dinner.

"Gaby?" Aaron called softly, and she turned to face him, a hopeful look on her face. She was willing to do anything to resolve this sudden unease between them.

"Thad Martin has decided to seek the appointment as representative to Washington."

"Thad Martin?" Gaby cried in disbelief. "He can't be serious."

"Oh, he's quite serious. He's after the power he thinks he'll gain with such a position. He's challenged me to a debate in Fowler next week. I'd like you to be there with me."

"Of course I will be," Gaby said, glad that he wanted her. She hesitated, the hatred and distrust she felt for Thad Martin welling to the surface. "If he receives this appointment, he'll never represent the other ranchers fairly. He'll turn this territory into an outlaws' haven. Can't you stop him?"

"I'll try," Aaron said, but he looked tired and worried. Gaby realized anew how beleaguered he'd looked lately. She thought of the extra bodyguards he traveled with now.

"Is Thad Martin threatening you?" she asked, and was startled at the closed look that settled over his face.

"Of course not," he said.

Danny's cries ended any chance for further conversation.

"You'd better tend to your son," Aaron said gently.

Gaby hurried up the stairs, thinking of all he'd said. "Of course not," he'd answered too readily. Now we've both lied to each other this day, she thought.

It was only later, when Danny was again sleeping and she was soaking in a tepid bath, that she remembered something else Aaron had said. He'd called Danny *her* son.

Suddenly Gaby felt bereft, as if she'd just lost something she'd valued very highly.

16

The saloon had been turned into a meeting hall, and on the night of the debate it was full. Texans loved their politics with the same passion they embraced everything else. Men and women alike settled themselves down for a stimulating evening of eloquent discourse. Which of the two opponents they preferred was not yet clear. Many of the men were afraid of Thad Martin and his strong-arm tactics, while others secretly admired him for his success and forgot the means of it. At a time when the law sided with the strongest, some ranchers feared Thad Martin gaining any more power.

On the other hand, Aaron Spencer was a German, and everyone knew they were Unionists. Resentments ran high against anyone of German background. The Texans hadn't forgotten how some of the Germans had spied against the South. More than a hundred of them had been hanged for treason. Yet no man there could remember ever being cheated by Aaron Spencer in a deal. He'd always dealt fairly with them.

Aaron and Gaby arrived early and were surprised to see the hall already filled. Torches had been lit outside, and bunting strung across the front of the building. There was an air of expectancy in the buzz of the crowd. It had been decided by the town council that no drinks would be served before or during the debate, but the saloon-keeper was expecting the onlookers to make up for lost time once the debate was over. Nothing whetted a man's thirst like a hot debate. The talk would go on for most of

270

the night. The hotel had been booked for weeks by the owners of far-lying ranches. The womenfolk had planned a little sewing circle of their own in the hotel parlor. All in all, the enterprising Texans were making the most of the event.

A path was made through the men on the porch who'd come too late to find a chair inside the crowded saloon, and Gaby and Aaron were gallantly escorted to the front of the room. A makeshift platform had been set in front of the bar and chairs had been placed on it. Thad Martin was already seated, his lip curling in derision when he saw Gaby with Aaron. With averted eyes and trembling knees Gaby followed Aaron to their place on the platform and chose the seat farthest away from Thad.

"Ladies and gentlemen . . ." The mayor stepped forward and with a surprising lack of pomposity introduced the speakers. Thad Martin was the first to speak. He stood and bowed to Aaron and Gaby with exaggerated politeness.

"Ladies, gents," he began. "I'm glad to see Mr. Spencer has seen fit to bring his . . . er . . . wife tonight." His pause and tone of voice were sheer effrontery, although his words were innocent enough.

Rayne Elliott was in the audience and he listened to what Thad Martin had to say. That the man thought he could represent the other ranchers in Washington was ludicrous; that anyone else might seriously consider supporting him for the position was frightening. Much as he hated the idea, Rayne had no choice but to throw his support behind Aaron Spencer.

"I was born here in the heart of Texas. My daddy fought for Texas independence. The Bar M Ranch has been in my family for two generations and will be for generations to come. Aaron Spencer, now, is a relative newcomer. He's one of those German immigrants who came here and snatched up a big chunk of some of our best land. Mr. Spencer got hitched recently to a woman who just came out here from New Orleans. She was a . . . uh . . . working woman there." Some men laughed at his words, as if on cue.

"We all know which way the sympathies of these immigrants ran during the war. We strung up a bunch of them during the war for their dirty spying. I say it's a shame we didn't get 'em all. But here sits one, claiming he'll go to Washington and represent our best interests. Now, I ask you, how many of you believe that?" He paused while some men at the back of the room booed. It seemed too well-rehearsed to Gaby. "I surely don't want a crippled, scarred Unionist representing me as a Texan."

Thad continued with his speech, attacking his opponent with such tactless remarks that even the most tolerant man was tired of hearing him and called out for more specific information on what Thad himself could do if he were sent to Washington. His speech ended soon after that and it was clear to Gaby that Thad Martin had little idea of the kind of help the Texans needed from the federal government. He had attempted to hide his lack of knowledge in a barrage of complaints, insults, and bravado.

Aaron was introduced and Gaby gave his hand a quick supportive squeeze as he got to his feet. Unlike Thad, Aaron was well-versed in the Texans' needs and he had very clear ideas about how he'd approach the lawmakers in Washington. His listeners were struck by the quiet, yet knowledgeable way Aaron spoke. He wasn't flamboyant the way most Texans liked their leaders, but he made sense, and that was almost as good.

Aaron's speech was drawing to a close and it was obvious he'd made important points. "We have to convince the federal government to give Texas back her right to govern herself," he concluded. "Then, and only then, can we begin to recover from the war and go forward with the growth of this great state."

A commotion in the back of the hall drew the crowd's attention.

"What do you care about this state? You ain't a Texan," a man called out.

Aaron turned to answer, but another voice shouted, "How do you know what the small ranchers in this county need when you're sittin' on one of the richest ranches in the country?"

"I came to Texas nearly twenty years ago," Aaron said. "I bought my land and built up my ranch from scratch just the way most of you are doing."

"What about your wife, Spencer? Is she going to Washington with you?"

A woman raised her voice. "We don't want a New Orleans prostitute in Washington representin' us Texans." Murmurs ran around the makeshift hall. Angry and frustrated men called derisively. Gaby heard her name repeated over and over. "Creole Angel!"—the chant began in the back and built as more voices joined in. Gaby looked at Thad Martin's smirking face and knew he'd planned carefully for this debate. His men were scattered throughout the audience, stirring up things. Aaron hadn't had a chance against such tactics. He stood in the middle of the platform trying to calm people, and failing. He was losing the crowd.

They'd used her name to humiliate him. Tears of anger and determination sparkled in her lashes as she leapt to her feet. "Give me your gun," she demanded of a man standing at the end of the platform.

"Huh?" he asked, uncertain whether to comply or not. Whom was she planning to shoot, Thad Martin? He gave her the gun.

"Listen, please . . . won't you listen to what I have to say?" Aaron called out to the crowd. "You are wrong about my wife. She's a good and virtuous woman." No one was listening.

Going to the front of the platform, Gaby lifted the gun above her head. It was heavier that she'd expected and wavered in her hand. Still she found the trigger and pulled it twice. The sound of shots reverberated around the room, and the quarreling men and women ceased their fighting and turned startled faces toward the platform.

Gaby still stood with the gun held high above her head, eyes screwed shut, face grimacing from the loud report.

Her hat had been knocked askew. At first the ranchers and their wives weren't sure whether to laugh or roar their disapproval, and in that split second while they stood indecisively, Gaby opened her eyes and peered around at them. Seeing that she had their attention, she lowered the gun and took a deep breath.

"I've listened to these two men talk tonight," she said. "One of them spent his time hurling insults and half-veiled threats. He made little effort to tell you how he can help you if he goes to Washington. If Thad Martin goes to Washington, he will be going for the benefit of one person. Himself." Gaby's voice shook as she spoke, but so intensely did she engage her audience that they couldn't look away from her.

"My husband has told you what he can do for you. I believe him. He'll do his very best for all of you. He's told you his plans, what he hopes to accomplish. He's given you solid proof of his intentions."

"What would a Creole angel know about it?" a man called from the back of the room, and the audience murmured in agreement.

"What would a Creole angel know about it?" she repeated musingly. "I know the way he's helped me and stood by me. He gave me his support and kindness when others would not. Aaron Spencer is a compassionate, caring man."

"And you're a New Orleans whore. We don't want your kind here or in Washington," a man yelled.

"Yeah, that's right," someone seconded him.

"You've heard that I came here from the Court of Angels in New Orleans," Gaby said, and paused, while everyone waited for her denial.

"You've heard right." There were murmurs at her confession. Gaby raised her chin and paced across the stage toward them and looked them square in the eye, her gaze moving from one to the other unflinchingly.

"I was born in the Court of Angels," she cried, "to a Creole mother of fifteen. My father was the son of southern aristocrats who had his way and refused to marry her. Her family disowned her. She was taken in and befriended by a woman who ran the Court of Angels. That woman raised me, loved me, and cared for me. I never knew anything but love from her. When I was old enough, I became an angel too."

Gaby's sweeping gaze had caught a glimpse of a familiar face. Rayne Elliott stood in the audience listening to her, his head thrown back, his blue eyes brilliant as they watched her.

"I had many debts to repay," Gaby said softly. Her gaze held his. Raising her chin, she glanced around the room again. "Then I came to Texas to begin a new life," she said, and her voice changed. The room was quiet, the people intent on the tiny girl on the stage.

"How many of you or your fathers came to Texas for a new beginning?" she asked them, and suddenly their gazes shifted, feet shuffled uneasily. "And you found it." Gaby was unrelenting. "Am I to be denied what each of you found here?" Her gaze raked around the room.

"Well, I'm here to stay in Texas," she continued, "and I won't let any man drive me away." Her gaze went back to Rayne. "I've been called a Creole angel here tonight. Well, I was at one time, but now I'm a Texan, and if you want to call me names, call them right. I'm not a Creole angel. I'm a Texas angel." Unconsciously she lifted her hand above her head, the gun still clutched in it. To the Texans who'd always loved the flamboyant, she was magnificent. One and all, they took her to their hearts in that instant.

Pandemonium broke out in the room. Men who'd heretofore jeered her now cheered her. "Texas angel!" they shouted at her, and Gaby stood stunned at their reaction. She glanced at Rayne. Through a blur of tears she watched as he moved toward the platform, and she knew he was coming for her. She wanted him to.

"Darling, you were wonderful," Aaron said, and took her in his arms. He pulled her against his chest for a quick hug, and over his shoulder Gaby watched the expression on Rayne's face slowly fade, his feelings carefully hidden, and she wanted to cry out. Helplessly she watched the stiff sway of his shoulders as he made his way to the door. Don't go, my darling, she wanted to cry, but Aaron was holding her away from him, laughing triumphantly down at her.

"Why, Gaby, you're crying," he said in surprise.

"It's just that I'm so happy things turned out well for you," she said. "They like us."

"Of course they do," Aaron said, as if he'd known all along it would work out. "They just had to get to know us a little."

*   *   *

Now Gaby traveled with Aaron as he went around the country getting to know the ranchers better and offering his help and support.

Everywhere they went, Gaby charmed them. Tales of her exploits had been greatly exaggerated, so that by the time they arrived in town she was often greeted with hails of "Texas angel!"

It was little surprise to anyone when Aaron was appointed to represent Texas on Washington's special committee. Thad Martin had not distinguished himself before or after the Fowler debate.

"I'm so proud of you," Gaby cried when Aaron came home with the news. "When do we leave for Washington?"

Aaron's face grew still. "Gaby," he said hesitantly, "I want to go by myself this first time."

"I see," she said, and tried not to show her hurt. He was ashamed of her after all, she thought. But as if reading her mind, he hurried to grip her shoulders and shake her slightly. "It's for your own safety."

"Is there danger for you?" she asked.

"Probably not," Aaron hastened to reassure her. "It's just that rumor has it that Thad Martin is not pleased with the appointment. It's feared he might plan some sort of 'accident.' "

"Surely Thad wouldn't do anything now. It would be too obvious."

"I don't think I have anything to fear from him," Aaron said, "but I'd rather not take a chance with you and Danny. Ben and the other men have already been instructed to keep a close eye on things while I'm gone. You're not to leave the ranch without an armed escort."

"Don't go to Washington now," Gaby cried, feeling a shiver of premonition. "Wait until Thad gets over this and goes on to someone else."

"You know I can't do that, Gaby. We can't let men like Thad Martin dictate how we live our lives. That's not living. We can't knuckle under to his fear tactics. That's how he gets away with his bullying anyway. The only way to disarm him is to show him we're not afraid of him."

"Then let Danny and me go with you. Let us make a stand beside you as we did at the debate."

Aaron smiled again at the defiant quiver of the small

body. "Not this time, Gaby. If Thad does come after us, I don't want to have to worry about you and the baby."

"What if something happens? What if you're killed?"

"I'm taking extra guards. If anything should happen, Gaby, I've made arrangements for you and Danny. Just see Jeremy Wallace. He'll take care of everything."

"If anything happens to you?" she repeated, startled, all her fears born anew. "Then you *are* worried about Thad Martin."

"I made these arrangements nearly a year ago when we were first married. I just wanted you to know that if I'm not there, you and Danny will be well-cared-for."

"Not the way we are when you're here," Gaby cried. "Money and property can't replace the love and care you give us."

He'd known those where the words she'd choose, but it pleased him to hear them nonetheless. Perhaps he had won a little of Gaby's love after all. "I'll be very careful," he said, gripping her arms. "So must you. Don't take any chances."

"I'll stay right here at the ranch, waiting for your return," Gaby vowed, and remembered a similar vow she'd made to Rayne the year before. Thad Martin had loomed, a menacing shadow over her world then too.

Aaron left on a September morning that was crisp and cool with the first hint of autumn in the air. Gaby stood shivering in the predawn chill watching him load his bags into a carriage. His bodyguards were mounted and ready to follow.

"I'll be back well before Christmas," he said, and she thought of the autumn morning she'd stood just so bidding Rayne good-bye.

"Be careful," she whispered, going up on tiptoe to drop a light kiss on his lips.

Aaron tried not to show how startled he was by her show of affection. Instead he gave her a quick hug and climbed up in his carriage.

"Hurry back," Gaby cried as he picked up the reins. "Danny and I will be waiting for you." Her words warmed him.

The rest of the household stood on the porch waving until Aaron's carriage had driven out of sight down the lane toward the main road. Maria came to take Danny, and Gaby stayed where she was, her eyes straining to catch one final glimpse when she knew there was none. At last she went inside to find Danny and hug his fat little body to her, more for her own comfort than his.

"We won't let Thad Martin bother us, Danny, sweet," she said lightly, tickling his fat chin until he gurgled out loud. Her hand stilled and she stared out the window, suddenly aware of how much she feared Thad Martin.

"Do you want me to take Danny now?" Maria asked so eagerly that Gaby had to smile.

"No, I'm going to give him his bath." She noticed Maria's crestfallen face. "I could use your help, though." Maria brightened and hurried away to tend to the hot water.

The day passed with all of them finding things to keep busy so they wouldn't miss Aaron. He'd been gone before, but this time it would be weeks and weeks before they saw him again.

Late in the afternoon dark clouds scudded across the flat blue sky and a cold, driving rain pelted the dusty ground. Gaby ate supper in the kitchen with the rest of the women. She hated the thought of eating alone in the dining room. Lightning zigzagged across the sky, filling the black square of kitchen window with blazing color.

Gary wondered if Aaron had reached his lodging before the storm hit. She hoped so. She felt moody and jumpy at the evening wore on, and blamed her nervousness on the storm. A shiver of apprehension dogged her, making her peer around the nursery door several times to check on Danny. He lay curled in a ball, sleeping peacefully.

The next day dawned bleak and rainy. All day it continued, until Gaby was exasperated. She didn't mind sticking close to the ranch, but to be trapped in the house was too much. Finally she threw a shawl around her shoulders and went to stand on the porch and watch the gray, sleeting rain. She'd felt uneasy ever since Aaron left, and the feeling was growing.

Impatient with her own morbidness, she dragged herself upstairs to bed, where she lay staring into the black shadows. She was almost relieved when she heard the hoofbeats pounding against the earth. The riders swept down the road and into the ranch yard. At first Gaby lay stiff in her bed, wondering if that dreaded nightmare were beginning anew; then a voice called out and she was released from the cold numbness that held her captive upon the bed. She sprang up, and drawing on a robe, hurried downstairs.

Mrs. Schafer stood in the downstairs hall, staring out the open door, her body rigid. Her long, gray braid hung down her back and she wore a robe hastily tied over her nightclothes. Her normally calm face looked haggard.

"What is it?" Gaby cried.

"I . . . I'm not sure," the older woman said.

Gaby paused on the bottom step, her eyes, like Mrs. Schafer's, fixed on the open door. There was the scrape of leather against the porch step and footsteps hurrying, as if they carried a burden of some sort. Gaby remained where she was.

Rayne and another man appeared in the doorway carrying a body between them.

"Aaron!" Gaby cried. Lightly she touched Aaron's cold brow and looked up questioningly at Rayne. "He isn't dead?"

"He's still alive," Rayne said grimly. "He's been shot." Two other men held Aaron's legs, and between them all they carried him to the parlor and laid him on one of the sofas.

"Maria, get Billy. Send him to town for the doctor. Hurry."

"Sí, señora," Maria said, and disappeared.

"Mrs. Schafer, have the cook put on some coffee for the other men."

"Yah," the German woman said, and hurried from the room. "Bring hot water when you come back," Gaby called after her.

"I vill."

"Aaron, say something to me." Gaby knelt beside the sofa, wiping the rain and mud from his face with the edge of her robe. He made no answer. He lay still and white. Her frantic gaze settled on the blood-soaked front of his shirt and she began to weep quietly.

"He's lost a lot of blood," Rayne said. "He was con-

scious when we found him, but the ride here was hard on
him. Let's get some whiskey down him. That might re-
vive him." Rayne wasn't sure if it would or not, but he
had to give Gaby something to do. Her face was too
pale.

It seemed to Gaby that Aaron took some of the whiskey she held to his lips, swallowing weakly, although his
eyes remained closed, his face deathly pale.

"Tell me what happened," Gaby asked, never taking
her gaze from the injured man's face.

"We were coming back from our cattle drive," Rayne
began, "when we heard shooting. We went to investigate
and came upon Aaron's carriage. Men were firing at him.
They took off when we rode up. He was wounded but
conscious."

"Where were his men? They were supposed to protect
him."

"They're all dead, I'm afraid," Rayne replied quietly.

"They can't be," Gaby cried in disbelief. Had it been
only yesterday that they'd all set out? The men had
looked so grim and capable with their guns strapped to
their hips. And now they were dead.

"From what Aaron said when we found him, they'd
been ambushed sometime yesterday afternoon. They were
outnumbered but they turned the carriage over and took
shelter behind that. During the night, they tried to escape, but the killers picked off his men one by one." He
paused considering her distraught face. "He's in bad
shape, Gaby," he said finally, as if to prepare her.

The man on the couch stirred and moaned in pain.
Gaby turned back to him, her eyes wide and anxious.

"Aaron," she said softly. "My poor sweet Aaron." She
laid her cheek against his, the tears spilling down her
cheeks to fall against his face. "I knew something was
wrong," she whispered brokenheartedly. "I sensed it. I
kept praying he'd be all right."

Rayne looked at her grief-stricken face and listened to
her words. He felt as if someone had hit him a staggering
blow. He pushed the feeling aside. Gaby loved this man,
and Aaron Spencer was a decent man. He'd made Gaby
happy. She'd worried over him and prayed for his safety.

Jealousy thick and hot ran through Rayne, so he drew back from the couple on the sofa.

Aaron's pale eyelashes fluttered against his waxen cheeks. His eyes opened and he stared at Gaby. Slowly recognition returned and he smiled, a pitiful shadow of the warm smile he usually gave her. "Gaby . . ." he whispered.

"Don't talk, Aaron. You've lost so much blood. The doctor's coming. Just lie still." Her voice lowered to a soothing croon and she patted his shoulder gently so as not to hurt him more.

"I have something to tell you," Aaron said. "I tried to make things right for you."

"Shhh! Don't talk. Save your strength."

"I tried to make sure you and little Danny would be safe."

"We are, don't you worry, darling," Gaby cried, and Rayne heard the endearment and drew back more, feeling awkward at witnessing the intimacy between them.

"Beware of . . . of Thad M-Martin," Aaron began again.

"He can't hurt you anymore. You're safe back at the ranch. I'll keep you safe, Aaron. You'll be all right." Tears washed over her cheeks and she held the dying man tightly, as if she would will the life back into him.

Aaron smiled gratefully. "I love you, Gaby," he whispered.

"And I love you, Aaron," she said, and realized she'd never told him those words before.

He lifted a limp, muddy hand as if to touch her cheek, but he hadn't the strength. It fell back against his chest. "When Danny grows up, tell him I wish . . . I wish he really had been . . ."

Alarmed, Gaby glanced at Rayne, but Aaron didn't finish his words. His hand fell lifeless and his head lolled to one side.

"Aaron!" Gaby cried, and looked beseechingly at Rayne. He stepped forward and felt for a pulse, then slowly shook his head.

"No! No, Aaron," Gaby cried, burying her face against his neck. There were so many things she wanted to tell him. She wanted him to know how grateful she was for his love and support. She wanted to explain about the day she returned from the river, so he wouldn't think she'd been unfaithful. She wanted to tell him she loved him, truly loved him, and she wanted to see him smile with that gentle light in his eyes. "Please don't die," she cried, "don't die. I couldn't bear it."

"I've got the wa . . ." Mrs. Schafer paused in the door when she saw Gaby crying, and the pan of warm water slid from her hands, spilling down over the rug. Throwing her hands over her face, she turned blindly back down the hall toward the kitchen. Her loud wails drifted back to them. Other people came into the room: Maria and the cook and Billy and the foreman. The women clung together, weeping quietly, while the men turned away and rubbed at their eyes.

Rayne glanced back at Gaby where she sat grieving, rocking the dead man against her shoulder. He felt helpless in the face of that grief. He was an outsider to Gaby. It wouldn't be seemly to offer her his comfort. Quietly he left the room and gathered his men and began the journey back to his ranch. Nearly every step of the way he kept hearing Gaby's voice as she whispered her love to another man.

17

With Mrs. Schafer's help, Gaby bathed and dressed Aaron in his best suit, then sat by him for the rest of the night. The tears finally dried on her cheeks and a steely resolve formed in her breast. One day she would pay Thad Martin back for all the grief he'd brought her.

When dawn lit the eastern sky, she stirred herself and sent Billy into town for the sheriff. When he arrived she had him sent to her in the parlor. Beside her dead husband's body she told him of the threats Thad Martin had made against them and of Aaron's last words.

"Rayne rode into town to talk to me about this already, Mrs. Spencer," the sheriff said, nervously twisting his hat in his hands. "It's like I told him. We don't have any witnesses that Thad shot your husband, and he was in town most of the time these past few days. He got pretty drunk and shot up the saloon before his men took him over to the hotel to sleep it off. He's got an alibi."

"But he threatened my husband," Gaby cried.

"What reason would he have for killing your husband?"

"He was furious that Aaron was appointed to go to Washington instead of him."

"Yeah, he was right upset about that," the sheriff conceded, "but that ain't hardly a reason to kill a man."

"In Thad Martin's way of thinking it would be."

"Now, Mrs. Spencer, I know you and Martin never got along well, but you oughten to slander a man."

"He threatened my husband," Gaby cried, frustrated.

"Did you actually hear the threats?"

"No, but Aaron told me so. Before he died, my husband named Thad Martin as his killer."

"Exactly what did he say, Mrs. Spencer? Did he say Thad Martin shot him?"

"No. He said, 'Beware of Thad Martin.' "

"There, you see," the sheriff said with obvious relief. "He never really claimed Thad shot him."

Gaby drew herself up, her gaze glacial as it settled on the sheriff. "As always, I want to thank you for protecting the decent people of Fowler, Sheriff."

"Now, Mrs. Spencer, you're just distraught. You've just lost your husband and you ain't seeing things too clearly."

"I see one thing very clearly, Sheriff. You're protecting Thad Martin, either because you're on his payroll or because you're too frightened to go after him. Either way, we don't need a man like you as sheriff of Fowler, and I'll do anything in my power to have you relieved of your duties."

"Now, Mrs. Spencer . . ." the sheriff began placatingly. Too late he realized that she now held all the considerable power that once had belonged to Aaron Spencer.

"Get out of my house, Sheriff," she said coldly, and the look in her eyes told him he'd better comply. He clamped his hat on his head and stalked out, unable to see what all the fuss about this woman had been. She was little and mean-tempered and not a woman he could admire at all.

The autumn rains had let up by the day of the funeral. The sun burned down in a bright yellow light that couldn't warm the sting of the northwestern winds or the cold emptiness in Gaby's heart. Friends and neighbors came to bid a last farewell to a man they'd little understood but had instinctively trusted. They came, as was their custom, to bring their sympathy and dishes of food.

Rayne had come. He stood to one side of the rest of them, as if not sure he wanted to be a part of it. Yet his eyes constantly sought out the small black-clad figure. He was there to help Gaby if she needed him.

They buried Aaron on a high hill overlooking the ranch house. All the hands were there, hats in hand, their heads bowed. The preacher came out from town to say some words over Aaron's grave. Gaby listened to his reading of the Scriptures and tried not to be bitter toward a God that could take a good man like Aaron Spencer and allow a man like Thad Martin to live.

Almost as if summoned by her bitter thoughts, three horsemen rode up the hill and dismounted. The preacher stopped his sermon and people swung around to look at the late arrivals who'd had the bad manners to interrupt the funeral service. When they saw it was the man rumored to have killed Aaron Spencer, they gasped and looked away. Thad seemed not to notice their disapproval. He left one of his men holding the reins of his horse and leisurely walked to the foot of the open grave and peered down at the coffin, a half-smile on his face.

Rayne eased himself forward, motioning to his ranch hands to do the same. Casually he brushed aside the tail of his coat to clear the holster and gun strapped to his hip. There'd be no trouble at this funeral, not if Thad wanted to walk away from it on his own feet.

The grin on Thad's face broadened.

The preacher cleared his throat nervously and resumed his sermon. Gaby glared across the open grave at the man who'd killed her husband. That he should show up like this only pointed out how little he feared the law. Catching her gaze on him, Thad smiled, his eyes arrogant as they swept over her face and then deliberately dropped downward to stare at her breasts. Gaby refused to be intimidated. Her gaze was unwavering and full of all the hate and fury she felt for this man. He was untouched by it.

"Ashes to ashes, dust to dust," the preacher intoned, and let some of the yellow prairie soil fall through his fingers onto the coffin lid. Then he turned to Gaby. "Perhaps the departed's wife would like to say something," he offered solemnly.

"Yes, I would," Gaby replied, her gaze never breaking with Thad Martin's. "I swear by the grave of my dead husband that I will get the man who killed him, and when I do, I will kill him without mercy, as he has killed my husband. I swear it!" Her voice rang out tragic and clear on the air, and for the first time Thad Martin's smile vanished from his face.

"Now, Mrs. Spencer, the sheriff told me that you accused me of doing this. I came here today to pay my respects to the dead and to assure you I wouldn't have anything to do with such a deed. I always respected your husband." His declaration was made more for the benefit of the other people assembled there than for the widow.

Rage tore through Gaby. "You tormented and hounded my husband the last weeks of his life," she cried, "with the same tactics you used on so many other men who were left no choice but to sell out or be killed. You made him afraid for his family. You'll be paid back in kind, Thad Martin. I swear it. You can't gun down innocent people and get away with it. Now, get off this land and don't ever set foot on it again or I'll have you shot for trespassing."

"Now, that's right unneighborly of you, ma'am," Thad began in an aggrieved tone. He made no move to leave. "I just come here to offer my condolences to my neighbor's widow and to tell you if ever there's anything I can do for you—"

"Yes, there is," Gaby cried. "You can stay away from me. If you ever try to come near me again, I'll have you killed. Now, get off Spencer property. You're not wanted here."

"You heard her, Martin," Rayne said, stepping forward. "Get back on your horse and ride out of here."

"Well, lookee who's here. Rayne Elliott." Thad sneered. "What're you up to, Rayne? Couldn't you even wait until the body cooled before you came around here?" Thad hooked his thumbs in his belt and swiveled around to glance at Gaby before facing Rayne again. "What is it, Rayne? You want her back again? Maybe you figure your whore's worth more to you now, or did you two work this out between you? She'd marry the old man and you'd gun him down."

Rayne's fist knocked Thad flat. He fell on the hard ground and for a moment it looked as if he might teeter and roll down into the grave itself. He lay where he was, glaring back at Rayne with hate in his eyes. One hand rubbed his jaw while he remembered the beating he'd received from Rayne on their last encounter. Gritting his teeth, he smiled up at them.

"This don't hardly seem like the way to behave at a man's funeral," he said, and slowly got to his feet and with careful strokes brushed off his clothes. His hand strayed near his gun and he thought of drawing it and firing at Rayne. Maybe he could catch him unawares, but a glance around the circle of people told him it was a bad move. All the Lazy S ranch hands had moved forward, their hands at the ready near their gunbelts. Some of them had circled Thad's men, so there was no question of who had the upper hand. The Lazy S hands would like nothing better than to get the man who'd killed their boss.

"Get out of here, Martin, before I kill you myself," Rayne rasped. His chest heaved with the effort not to attack the man before him. Thad turned toward his horse. The men parted, letting him through, staring at him as if he were a deadly snake.

Thad mounted and from the safety of his horse once again grinned down at Gaby. "I'll be seeing you again, Mrs. Spencer," he said, and put his spurs to his horse. Silently the congregation watched until Thad and his men were indistinct blurs on the horizon.

"Be careful of Martin, Gaby," Rayne said. "He won't hesitate to kill you if you get in his way. The fact that you're a woman will mean little to him." Gaby turned to look at Rayne and he was startled at the gauntness of her face. She'd been through hell, he realized, and longed to take her into his arms and comfort her, but her words stopped him from any display of sympathy.

"Are you growing afraid of Thad Martin as well?" she challenged.

"I'm always afraid of a snake when it's coiled and ready to strike."

"Then heed your own warning, Rayne. Thad is out to destroy you as well."

"There's nothing he can do to me," Rayne answered.

"He's already done it, and you're too big a fool to see it." She turned away, but her words left him puzzled. On the long ride back home, Rayne thought about what she'd said. Thad had taken nothing from him yet. He still had the ranch and his herd. The only thing he'd lost in the past year was Gaby.

Rayne drew his horse to a stop as he thought back over the events that had led to Gaby's leaving. Surprisingly, Thad figured in nearly every misunderstanding they'd had. Even that day the men had meant to hang Slade and Billy, Thad had been there, and although he'd said nothing, his man Slade Harner had made the accusations against Gaby. What a fool he'd been, believing Slade and Thad's lies, letting Cole's bitter accusations blind him to Gaby's innocence. It had cost him the woman he loved.

Rayne kicked his horse forward, the events at the funeral running through his mind. On the way here today, he'd thought about Gaby. She was free again. He'd wondered if he would have a second chance with her. But now Thad's words mocked him, insinuations that he was interested in Gaby only for the money she would inherit, and the hint that they might have deliberately planned Aaron's death. Rayne had given no thought to Aaron Spencer's money, but who else would believe him? He'd have to stay away from Gaby for a spell, go slowly, until the mourning period was over. Then he'd go to her and beg her to come back to him. The money would be damned. Next time, it would be different, Rayne vowed.

"So, as you can see Mrs. Spencer, he's left the bulk of his estate to you."

Gaby sat in the parlor staring at Jeremy Wallace, Aaron's attorney. "That can't be," she said. "We were married only a short time. Surely there was someone else my husband intended to have his estate."

"You must have made him very happy in that short time," Wallace said. "You are the only beneficiary of his will. You're a rich woman, Mrs. Spencer, probably one of the richest in Texas. Besides the ranch, which is of considerable value, there are large herds of cattle, and there are holdings in Galveston and along the east coast. I believe he has stock in some railroads as well. He worked very hard to persuade the railroads to establish spur lines to certain towns to enable cattlemen to get their cattle to market. When those tracks are built, the stock will skyrocket."

"Please, I feel quite breathless from all this," Gaby said.

"You and your son have a very secure future, thanks to your husband's farsightedness."

"I hardly know what to say," Gaby said, looking at the pattern in the woolen carpet. Then a thought came to her and she raised her head. "What about his other son? Did he leave nothing for him?"

"He made no mention of another child in his will."

"He has another son, by a first marriage, and although he hasn't seen him since he was a baby, I know Aaron thought of him often."

"Since Aaron made no provision in his will, there is nothing I can do."

"We must do something," Gaby cried. "I couldn't bear to think he'd been left with nothing. My conscience wouldn't allow me to rest if I made no effort on his behalf. Isn't there some way we can locate him and see that he shares in his father's estate?"

"I could hire some detectives to look for him," Jeremy began hesitantly, "but these things are not always fruitful."

"We must try," Gaby insisted.

"Aaron came from Pennsylvania, didn't he?"

"Philadelphia, I believe," Gaby replied. "I remember Aaron called his first wife Abigail, and his son's name is Kevin."

"I'll write to a friend of mine back east and get someone on it right away—that is, if you're sure this is what you want to do?"

"My husband was a very generous man, Mr. Wallace. He was kind to me when others were not. This is one way I can repay him for that kindness."

A warm, approving smile crossed the lawyer's face. "There was one trait of Aaron's that I admired very much," he said, snapping his case shut. "The ability to unerringly choose the right people. I'm glad to see that carried over into his personal life as well."

Gaby returned his smile, feeling comforted by his comment. Perhaps in some way she had made Aaron happy during the last year of his life. She hoped so.

"I'll let you know as soon as I have some information," Jeremy Wallace said before stepping into his buggy. Gaby stood watching the buggy bounce over the dirt lane on its journey back to town. She stood remembering the day Aaron had brought her here. He'd tried to protect her then, and he was still doing it. There was little comfort in the thought of that wealth. She would gladly give it all up to see Aaron driving his buggy back down that road toward the ranch.

She sighed. Another part of her life was over. It was time to put aside her grief and loss and go on. Soon it would be Christmas, Danny's first Christmas, and although it would be a sad affair without Aaron, Danny would make it bearable.

After Christmas, the winter set in harsh and bitter. The killing winds drove more cattle southward into Texas, and even there they couldn't escape the bite of the northers. In spite of the harshness of the winds, there was little rain and snow. Spring was a welcome sight. It brought relief to the spirit as well as the body. The relief was short-lived, as the sky continued to hold its moisture through the spring months. The blooms that normally covered the prairie floor at this time of the year shriveled and died, their flower buds hard and black. Now men looked ahead to the summer months and worried about droughts.

There'd been no word of Aaron's first wife and son. As the months passed, Jeremy Wallace was ready to give up the search, but Gaby insisted they keep trying. Somewhere there was a young man who needed to know his father had thought of him often.

One day as Gaby left Caleb's store, Rayne rode into the square. Caught off guard, she couldn't hide even from herself how glad she was to see him. It had been months, and for a moment she feared she wouldn't be able to look away from him. Her hungry gaze took in the details of his appearance, the lean cheeks and square jaw, the brilliant blue of his eyes and the lines radiating from each corner. He looked spare and tough as whipcord. The line of his mouth softened as he looked at her.

"Hello, Mrs. Spencer," he said, touching the brim of his hat. His words were polite and impersonal.

"Mr. Elliott," Gaby said coolly. Her gaze darted away from him and then back again. Their eyes met and Gaby felt rooted where she stood, as if one of the northers had swept down over the plains and frozen her in her tracks. She'd thought all the feelings she had for him had died; now here they were again, full-blown and just as tumultuous. She glanced away from him. She would do nothing by look or word to sully Aaron's memory. She was his widow and she would observe the proper mourning.

Rayne's voice, ragged and husky reached out to her and she shivered in the heat. "How are you doing, Gaby?" he asked softly.

"I'm fine," she said abruptly, afraid of the way he made her feel.

"If there's ever anything I can do . . ."

"No, thank you. I have Ben and the other cowhands, and Maria and Mrs. Schafer. They're all quite capable." She knew she was babbling, but couldn't stop. She felt brittle and vulnerable standing here on the walk in front of the general store. Surely her feelings must show, she thought wildly. She longed to tell Rayne to ride away and leave her, but remained silent, afraid he would do so anyway.

A voice broke the spell between them. "Well, ain't this a pretty sight." Gaby turned to glare at Thad Martin and Slade Harner. They'd brought their horses to a stop near the buggy and now they sat slouching in their saddles, contemplating first Gaby and then Elliott.

"Yessir, Slade, you got to admit that Rayne Elliott is a real go-getter. He don't let any opportunity slip by him to get ahead. It's just like I've been telling folks. He's after the widow Spencer."

"You devil," Rayne swore. His hand slashed downward as if he might grab his gun from its holster.

"Rayne, don't," Gaby cried, and Rayne's hand stayed itself. His eyes were icy and dangerous as they stared at Thad. "Don't you see that's just what he wants you to do? He's looking for an excuse to kill you."

"Or get killed," Rayne said coldly, without taking his gaze from Martin's face.

"Ain't that sweet?" Thad goaded further. "She's trying to protect her lover. The lady blamed me for killing her husband, but maybe it was you what killed him. You're the one who brought him home that night. Maybe you killed him yourself so you could get your woman back. Or maybe she was in on it from the start and the two of you worked it out to kill Spencer and get his land." Thad continued to talk, while Slade slowly edged his gun from its holster. Gaby watched fearfully. Wildly she looked around, but there was no one in sight. As usual when Thad Martin came to town, the sheriff managed to occupy himself elsewhere. Ben and the rest of the hands who had ridden to town with her would still be in the saloon at the end of the street. Her frantic gaze fell on the whip in its socket and she snatched it up.

Thad continued to goad Rayne, his tone languid, his eyes narrowed and watchful. "I can't say I blame you for wanting her back, Rayne. Especially now that she has all that land. 'Course, she was something special before, wasn't she, Slade?" Slade Harner nodded his head, a smile twisting his lips.

The movement came faster than Thad had anticipated, the hand slashing downward, then up, with the dark bore of a gun pointed squarely at his chest, while his own gun hadn't cleared the holster yet. Hurry, Slade, get him, Thad silently urged, and I'll finish him off. The crack of a whip followed by a yelp of pain brought Thad's head around. Slade sat nursing his face and arm. His gun lay in the dirt of the street. Gaby stood on the high plank walk, her head thrown back, a whip clenched in her fist, pulled back and ready to swing again.

"You and your gunman are right. She *is* a special lady," Rayne said, smiling. His gun never wavered from its target. "And I don't think she liked what you had to say. You and your man had better ride on down the street before she takes another swing at you."

Thad looked at the smiling face, the narrowed eyes with their deadly message, and knew he was defeated. Slowly he relaxed the hold on his own gun and slouched back in his saddle. "Come on, Slade," he growled. "Let's leave him and his whore alone."

Gaby cracked the whip again and it sang through the air, leaving a red welt along Thad's cheek. Rayne couldn't stop the chuckle that erupted at the look on Thad's face.

Along the boardwalk other people had stopped to watch. They'd seen Gaby strike Thad Martin with the whip, and even now some of them were hurrying to tell others.

"You two don't seem to be in the lady's good graces," Rayne drawled. "I think you'd better move on."

Slade slung a leg over his saddle, meaning to dismount and retrieve his gun, but Rayne's cold voice stopped him. "Leave it," he ordered, and with a last quick glance at Thad, Slade eased back down in his saddle.

"You'll pay for this," Thad spit out, his eyes venomous as he glared at Gaby.

"That's only a small portion of what you deserve," Gaby retorted, flicking the whip tauntingly. She longed to draw it back and strike the man yet again.

"Get going, Thad," Rayne said, and pulled back the hammer on his gun. With a last menacing look over their shoulders, the two men rode off. When they were out of sight down the street, Rayne turned to Gaby with a grim smile on his face.

She stood now with the whip clenched before her, all her bravado gone. "Why can't the law do something about him?" she cried.

"He'll get caught eventually," Rayne said.

"He's out to get you."

"Or you," Rayne said quietly. "Maybe both of us."

"Why?" Gaby asked. "What have we done to him?"

"You've just humiliated him in front of the whole town, for one thing. As for me, well, it's a long-standing feud." He looked at Gaby and drew himself straighter in the saddle. "I'll be wishing you a good day now, Mrs. Spencer."

"Rayne, wait," Gaby cried. "We need to talk."

Rayne cast a look up the street, then pulled his hat brim lower over his face. "It's best we don't talk anymore, Gaby. Right about now, Thad is up there in the saloon spreading his lies about your husband's death. If you don't want people to start believing him, then keep away from me."

"Since when have you become concerned about what other people think?" Gaby cried, hurt by his rejection and yet knowing the words he spoke were wise and true.

"I don't care much what anyone says about me. It's

you and your son I'm thinking about. Rumors can get pretty wild. The next thing you know, they'll be saying he's my son and not Aaron's."

Gaby glanced away, uncomfortable that he'd come so close. Something urged her to tell him the truth about Danny then and there, while another part of her urged silence.

"I'll be wishing you a good day, Mrs. Spencer," Rayne said, going all stiff and proper again. He doffed his hat.

Gaby stood on the boardwalk watching him ride away, and realized that Thad Martin was once again destroying her chances to be happy with Rayne.

She would wait. She had time. It was barely six months since Aaron's death, and she would give him the year of mourning he so richly deserved. Then she would fight Thad Martin and anyone else who interfered with Rayne and her.

18

In the weeks that followed, Thad did spread his rumors, and there were some who considered them to be the truth, but when there was no evidence of Rayne and Gaby being together again, the speculations died away. Nearly everyone had heard how she'd horsewhipped Thad in the middle of town, and so his accusations were put down to revenge.

Gaby's life spoke for the kind of woman she had become, and there were some who didn't want to hear the rumors about the "Texas Angel." After a while, Thad saw the advisability of keeping his mouth shut, and the rumors died away.

With the return of summer came the nemeses of all ranchers: the cattle rustlers. Once again the small ranchers were targeted. Barns were burned and cattle run off in raids. There was an outcry among the more prosperous ranchers, who gave the sheriff an ultimatum: do something, or else. There was talk of forming a vigilante group, but cooler heads prevailed and the ranchers joined the posses that rode out nearly every day, roaming the countryside, chasing down any lead. Once in a while they got lucky and rode up on a rustlers' campsite hidden in some valley, but the rustlers usually pushed their stolen cows westward, where they were lost among the cross timbers with the rest of the renegades and the Comanche.

Gaby did her share, participating freely in the fund-raising dinners for the burned-out ranchers. She also donated large sums of her own money. When a poor

rancher lost some of his hands, or his cattle were stolen,
Gaby often sent over a few of her own hands to help out.
It was commonplace to see a Spencer-branded cow being
skinned and butchered to provide meat for a ranch family
that might not otherwise have made it through the harsh
winter. Now, with the advent of the dry spring, Gaby
opened a trail across Spencer property to the river, where
the thirsty cattle could water.

"Tell the Texas Angel we're mighty grateful," a cowman might say as he herded his cattle down to water.
Gaby tried most to help the families of ranchers who
were still holding out against Thad Martin. A wagonload
of supplies—flour, salt pork, and even some calico—might
appear at a rancher's door just when he was ready to give
in. As proud as the Texans were, they accepted what she
sent them. She was one of them, and Texans took care of
their own.

Word spread, and the name that had been intended as
ridicule so many months before took on new meaning as
people spoke of the Texas Angel with affection. She was
fast becoming a legend. Still living in quiet seclusion, as
befitted a widow mourning the loss of her husband, Gaby
was little aware of the effect she was having on the
country around. She'd sought only to give aid where it
was needed and to help the other ranchers hold out
against Thad Martin.

Rayne had heard of her deeds, and he heard the pride
and respect when Texans spoke of Gaby. She seemed
more unattainable now that when Aaron Spencer was
alive.

Lorna had taken to visiting the Rocking E Ranch more
often now. Nearly every day she rode over from the
Blake ranch with a pie or cake or bread she'd baked
herself. Rayne was at first surprised and then alarmed at
her domesticity. He was accustomed to seeing her in
pants working the ranch like a cowhand. Now she began
to appear in lace-trimmed calico gowns.

The drought continued through the spring and into
early summer. The corridor to the river became well-
marked, the grass scoured away and the ground packed
hard by a thousand hooves. It became a watering hole for

several ranchers close enough to get their cattle there and back in a reasonable amount of time.

The prairie grass withered and died, the grazing lands grew arid and brown. Cows were eating the leaves and bark off the post-oak trees. Cowhands burned the needles off prickly pears so their cattle might eat them and not die. And every day the ranchers lifted their eyes to the cloudless sky and wondered when it might rain again.

One day when Jacinta had come to visit them, Gaby overheard her telling Mrs. Schafer and Maria that the wide stream that had watered the Rocking E Ranch was drying up.

"Each day there is less water for the cows," Jacinta complained, "and each day I must make do with less water to wash and clean with. It is bad, very bad." Jacinta stopped talking and looked up guiltily as Gaby entered the room.

"How is Rayne?" Gaby couldn't help asking.

"He's very tired. I never see him," Jacinta said. "All day he is in the saddle riding, riding, looking for water, trying to find food for his cattle. He comes home at night tired, his face gray, too tired to eat. He sleeps a few hours and then he's up again." Jacinta's bright, dark eyes watched Gaby's face. When would this stubborn girl realize that Rayne needed her and come back to the ranch where she belonged?

"He need you," Jacinta said.

"I hear he has Lorna Blake now," Gaby said. The rumor of the two of them together had hurt more than Gaby wanted anyone to know.

"Bah!" Jacinta replied. "That one. She is not good for him. She does not make him laugh and forget his cares for a while. You are a widow now, why don't you come back? Take his son to him and tell him how you feel."

"I came back to him once and he rejected me. This time he must come to me."

"He is too proud," Jacinta said.

"So am I," Gaby cried, and at Jacinta's disapproving look, asked defensively, "Am I not allowed my pride as well, or am I suppose to swallow it once more just because I'm a woman?"

"It is because you are a woman that you can do this.

Pride is an important thing to a man. Besides, you are a fine lady with a rich ranch. He cannot come to you. It would appear he wants only your money."

She could not go to Rayne yet. It was too soon after Aaron's death. Rayne would have to wait for her.

She could do something for his drought problem, though. She dug out the deed for the Avery property which she'd had Aaron buy with the gold Rayne had included in her trunk of belongings. She'd bought the land with the thought that one day she would give it to Rayne. It had access to the Brazos River and would increase his grazing land greatly.

Gaby signed the deed over to Rayne and sent it back by Jacinta. She felt better knowing it was at last in his hands.

She heard him ride into the yard that evening and she had no doubt it was he. Her heart leapt in anticipation. Not to appear too eager, she waited in her room, impatiently twitching her gown into place, smoothing back her hair, and trying to still the flutter of pulse in her wrist and temple until Mrs. Schafer came to announce his arrival.

Calmly Gaby descended the stairs and swept into the parlor. Rayne stood at the mantel, much as she'd pictured him, hat in hand, his hair flattened at his temple by the hatband. His boots and jeans were dusty from the long ride over. His blue eyes swung to meet hers as she entered the room, and she thought he'd never looked more masculine.

"Hello, Rayne," she said lightly. "Can I get you a drink?"

"No." His tone was tense, his glance stern. He reached inside his shirt and pulled out the deed to the Avery land.

"I can't take this," he said without preamble.

Gaby looked at him in surprise. In her imaginings, she'd never thought he'd refuse the land. It was his. "Why not?" she asked softly.

"I'm not one of your charity cases," he growled.

"Of course not," Gaby said. "This land is yours." She stopped speaking at the flare of temper in his eyes.

He took a step toward her, the paper crackling between them. "Did you think I would take this from you?" he demanded. "What is this, Gaby? A gift or an attempt to buy me?"

"Of course not," Gaby cried, growing angry herself. Hadn't he bought her back in New Orleans, and now his precious pride kept him from allowing her the smallest gesture. Here he stood in self-righteous indignation that she'd even dared to believe she could buy him. She swallowed against her anger and tried again. "Of course I'm not trying to buy you," she said. "This land is yours. I bought it for you—"

"With some other man's money," Rayne interrupted her.

"I didn't use Aaron's money."

"You had nothing yourself," Rayne insisted. "I brought you here, remember? You had no money, no gold, but the minute you married a rich man, you rushed out and bought the land you knew I wanted."

"Is that why you can't accept it from me?"

"I don't like duplicity, Gaby."

"I never hid the fact that I'd bought the land."

"You never told me, either. I thought Martin had it."

"Would you rather he did?"

Her question left him floundering for words for a minute. "Where did you get the money, Gaby?" he demanded.

"I earned it. This money was given to me for"—she paused significantly—"services rendered."

There was no flicker of understanding in his eyes. He'd forgotten the painful words he'd hurled at her nearly two years before. His face was pale and he stepped forward to grip her arms. "You haven't a decent bone in your body," he snarled. "Even a good man like Aaron Spencer didn't really change you. Oh, you may dress like a lady and do good deeds. People may call you the Texas Angel, but underneath it all you're still that little whore I picked up in New Orleans." His words cut through her, leaving her cold and barren. Rayne flung her arm away from him as if he couldn't bear to touch her anymore, and tossing the deed to the floor, he stalked out of the ranch house.

Mounting his horse, he sent it at a headlong gallop out of the ranch yard, back toward the Rocking E. Her mocking words sang in her ears. She'd earned the money and she made no secret of the way she'd earned it. Rayne gritted his teeth and cursed her soundly.

Gaby stood listening to the fading hoofbeats and the echoes of the ugly words that had been spoken in this room. She drew a quivering breath. She'd had enough of Rayne and his anger and jealousy and suspicions. Even now, after these years apart, even after she'd built a respectable life for herself, Rayne could sweep it aside as if it were nothing and believe the worst of it.

"Rayne Elliott, I vow that you'll rue this night. You're going to learn once and for all just what the Texas Angel is all about."

She dried her tears—the last she would shed for Rayne, she vowed—and wearily mounted the stairs. She'd find some way to bring Rayne to his knees if she had to spend every nickel Aaron had left her.

The summer deepened. The drought worsened. The sun beat down on the hot, dry land mercilessly. The days grew long and oppressive. Tempers, already short, flared. Neighbors who had once cooperated over roaming cattle now fought with each other. Accusations of cattle rustling were made, pride was offended, and fights erupted, sometimes ending in the exchange of gunfire.

One day as Gaby was riding the range, trying to assess the damage to her own grazing land, she noted a herd of cattle being driven across Spencer land toward the river. The wide, tall silhouette of one of the cowhands made her rein in her horse and peer closer.

"Ben, whose cattle are those?" she asked her foreman.

"Looks like the Rocking E brand," he said.

"When did they start using the river to water their cattle?"

"A couple of weeks ago. Their springs went down to a trickle."

"That's too bad," Gaby said, her mind racing. After a moment she tapped her heel against her horse's sides and they rode on.

The next day she set some of the Spencer hands to patrolling the borders that led down to the river, with clear instructions. Rocking E cows were not to be allowed to water.

"You can't do that, ma'am," Ben said. "Without water, them cows are gonna die on Elliott."

"Trust me, Ben, Rayne Elliott won't let it come to that," Gaby said, and spurred her horse on. Ben cast a glance of distaste after her. Normally he held his boss's widow in high regard, but today she'd not made a wise decision. People in Texas helped one another. He'd thought she understood that, since she helped so many people. Still, she was the boss. Trust me, she'd said, and he guessed he'd have to. He hadn't minded working for a woman like the Texas Angel, but he sure wasn't going to like his duties for the next few days.

Gaby was there the next day when Rayne's cattle crossed the prairie toward the Spencer land. Ben and his men were spread out in a line along the boundaries, waiting for them. Ben hesitated, reluctant to make a move in case his boss had changed her mind, but she simply raised an arm and waved him on. The Lazy S men rode out to stop the advancing herd. From her vantage point Gaby watched as Ben and Rayne rode toward each other on the blazing prairie. The two men talked briefly, and even from where she sat, Gaby could see Rayne's head come up with a jerk and feel the heat of his angry gaze. Deliberately she rode forward so he would see that she was there and indeed that it was her decision that his cows be turned back. He sat staring at her, and his gaze was more scorching than the prairie sun. As his men and the first cows reached him, he swung his horse around.

"Head 'em back the way they came," he shouted. With a look of consternation Dusty and the other men began to turn the thirsty, bawling cattle in a circle, heading them back to their home range. They could smell the water and resisted being led away from it. Gaby stayed and watched, now and then catching a glimpse of Rayne's tall figure through the dust and confusion, stiff and unbending in his saddle. Proud to the end, she thought, and prayed that of the two of them, the one who must bend this time would not be her. Let's see how proud you are in a few days, Rayne Elliott, she thought, when your cows are in desperate need of water.

Spurring his horse across the prairie, Rayne drew up

302   PEGGY HANCHAR

before her. "What is this, Gaby?" he demanded. "What games are you playing now?"

"It's not a game, Rayne. I'm simply exercising my right to decide who goes across my land to the river."

"What is it you want from me?" Rayne demanded.

"I want nothing from you," Gaby replied smoothly. "I'm just trying to understand how a man who is so proud he won't take the land that is rightfully his can swallow his pride enough to go across my lands to water his cows at my river."

"There's a world of difference and you know it," he shouted.

"Perhaps to one of your advanced moral development, Rayne. To me there is little difference. You can take your cattle across my land to water," she said finally, "but you'll have to do it my way or not at all."

"Not at all, then," he snapped, and wheeling his horse, galloped away in a cloud of dust.

He came at night, right after supper, when the hands had settled down in the bunkhouse and Mrs. Schafer and Maria had already gone to bed. Gaby was just thinking of peeking in on Danny and retiring herself when she heard the sound of a solitary horseman. She knew it was Rayne.

"Come in," she said, meeting him at the door and leading him back to the study with its massive desk and thick carpets. "What can I do for you, Rayne?" she said, settling herself so the desk was between them. Her expression was cold and aloof. She wouldn't make it easy for him.

"You win," he said, and his eyes couldn't quite meet hers. He wasn't used to being bested, and never by a woman. "I'll accept the deed for the Avery land."

"It's no longer offered to you," Gaby said. "I don't give away valuable pieces of land, Rayne. It wouldn't be good business."

His head came up and he glared at her. "Then what's this all about, Gaby?" he demanded. "Why am I here?"

"You're here because you want to water your cattle at the river on my property. You want something from me."

"You know I'll lose my cattle if I don't get them to water soon," Rayne flared.

"Of course." Gaby rose from her seat and crossed to the bottles of liquor. "May I pour you a drink?" she asked, waiting for his answer, her hand poised above the bottles. Rayne understood what was required of him.

"Yes," he said, and his tone was clipped.

Gaby smiled and poured a glass of whiskey and took it to him. She stood close to him, letting him breathe in her perfume. Oh so slowly she put a hand on his chest. She could feel the heat of his body beneath her flat palm. "You can take your cows across my land, Rayne," she said softly. "I've never meant for you to do otherwise." She stepped closer to him, letting her body brush against his. She could feel the hammering in his chest increase in tempo. One large, roughened hand came up to catch hers. "All you have to do," she whispered throatily, "is make love to me."

The look in his eyes had an edge of panic now. Gaby smiled softly, arching her body against him so her breasts brushed against his chest. One hand wandered upward to encircle his neck and pull his head down to hers.

"Gaby," he said hoarsely. She read the denial in his eyes, but it was never spoken. He didn't halt the downward plunge of his mouth to hers.

Lightly she kissed him, touching the corners of his mouth softly with the warm, moist tip of her tongue. She kissed the lean, spare lines of his cheeks, the firm, stubborn chin, and the warm, brown hollow of his throat. Then she pulled back and smiled up at him. "Make love to me, Rayne," she said softly. "That's all I want from you."

"Gaby," he groaned, trying to deny her request at the same time he felt himself giving way to it. She raised herself on tiptoe, swaying like a reed in his arms. Wantonly she offered him her mouth. His tongue tasted the sweetness of her lips and explored the smooth edge of teeth. His arms wrapped around her, molding her to him. He'd been hungry for her for so long, too long, and now here she was, his Gaby, soft and pliant in his arms. He forgot all the anger between them and lost himself in the beauty and passion of her. His tongue thrust against hers time and again in simulation of the love act that would follow.

"I've missed you so much," he whispered. "I've wanted you so."

"I'm here now, Rayne," she whispered. "I'm here. Make love to me, Rayne. Make love . . ." Her words caught in her throat and turned to whimpers as he molded her to him so tightly a sweet fierce aching began somewhere deep and spread to her own body. They kissed, clinging to each other, hands rushing to touch first here, then there, in a wild abandon. Familiar, so familiar and dear was the feel of the other's body. How long the senses clung to their memories, and now those memories were being reawakened.

He bore her to the floor, cradling her gently so she wouldn't be hurt. She felt the thick carpet beneath her and the weight of the man above her, and she reached out greedily for the passion he brought her. It had been too long. Revenge lost itself in the fury of their passion.

He took her there on the floor, so great was their need that clothes were left half-buttoned; only those that hampered the meeting of their bodies were impatiently pushed aside. She felt his first thrust, hot and strong within her, and couldn't still the wild cry that escaped her lips. Her hands tore at his shirt, her nails finding the smooth flesh of his broad back, and she urged him on to greater efforts. Together they rode their passion higher and at last reached the pinnacle they'd never been able to reach with anyone else. Rayne felt the blood roaring in his ears, and Gaby cried out exultantly.

They lay spent and sweating on the floor, their limbs entangled amid petticoats and his gunbelt. Rayne lay on his back, still gasping in air. Gaby sat up and looked around. This was madness. What had happened to her plan to break Rayne Elliott's pride? She glanced down, and a smile lit her face.

"What's so funny?" he asked, gazing up at her.

"I've never made love to a cowboy with spurs on before," she said, making her voice and expression lascivious.

Rayne laughed with her; then his face sobered. "We

shouldn't have done this," he said softly, and reached out a hand in such tenderness it nearly undid her resolve.

"I wanted this to happen," she began, then bit her lip. Not yet, she thought, not yet. She didn't have to end it yet. They could have the night. She glanced at him and saw the same thought in his eyes.

"Gaby, I don't want to start talk about you," he said.

"Then come up to bed with me," she answered. "We wouldn't want to scandalize poor Mrs. Schafer."

They stared into each other's eyes and without more words rose and gathered up their scattered clothing and mounted the stairs. At the door of her room, Rayne paused. "Gaby, I can't share the same bed as another man," he began.

"Shhh," Gaby reassured him. "Aaron never slept in this room with me."

Closed in the soft darkness, they took off their clothes, then met again, naked flesh to naked flesh, cool, shivery skin warmed by the touch of the other. Slowly they touched and explored. They had time. The night was long and they were together again. Through the night they loved each other and fell asleep wrapped in each other's arms.

The pale gray light in the east heralded the dawn as Gaby lay with Rayne's dark head cradled against her pale breast. Their night together had ended; now she lay steeling herself for what she was about to do. She had pledged herself to do this, and she would not back down. She perceived that she'd been far too softhearted in her dealings with Rayne. He was a hard man in a hard land, a tough and single-minded man in many ways. It took such men to survive the rigors of ranching in Texas. Such a man required a special kind of woman, who could be tough when she had to be and soft when it was needed. Gaby wanted Rayne, but she wasn't willing to have him on his terms alone. In the long run she would lose him if she bent too often to his will.

"Rayne, it's time to leave," she said softly.

"Ummm." He rolled away from her. Her body felt bereft without the warmth and weight of him. She watched him stretch lazily, long, sinewy arms reaching toward the ceiling, fists lightly balled. A strong, muscular body slowly coming awake. She turned away and got out of bed. Wrapping a robe around her, she turned to face him again.

"Good morning," he said softly. There were lights in his eyes, warm and compelling, luring her back to him.

"It's time for you to go," she said. "Soon it will be daylight and I don't want anyone to see you sneaking away from here."

"I won't sneak."

"Before you go," Gaby went on as if he hadn't spoken, her voice cool and brisk. "I want to tell you that you may bring your cattle to the river to water today."

"All right," Rayne said warily. He studied her closed expression, then smiled at her as one would a child who must be humored. He reached for her.

Deftly Gaby sidestepped him. "That's my pay to you for your night's work." She paused, casting a glance at the bed he'd just left. "For services rendered."

"What do you mean?" he demanded, all six-feet-plus of him quivering with injured male ego.

"Last night you were my whore, Rayne. I told you what I would pay if you made love to me, and you did. A good job, I might add."

"What are you talking about?"

"I'm talking about services rendered," Gaby answered, one eyebrow rising as she uttered the words. "See how easy it is to compromise yourself and your honor, Rayne? We do what we must to survive. You need to take your cows to water, so you did as I bade you. It's an amicable arrangement, don't you think? I can grant you favors, and in return you render certain services. It's a system that's worked for centuries. You did a good job, Rayne, and I may require your services again. I'll let you know when."

"All right, Gaby," he said quietly, his rage barely leashed. "You've got your revenge, haven't you? Is that all last night meant to you?"

"Is that all any of our nights ever meant to you?" she cried, her anger getting the upper hand.

"It's not the same," Rayne snapped.

"Isn't it?" Gaby laughed. "What's wrong, Rayne, does

it hurt that mighty Elliott pride to find your honor has a price just like everyone else's?"

The question hung between them, making him pause.

"I found out what your price was, Rayne, and I was willing to pay it. I bought you just like any one of the whores at the Court of Angels, and I shall treat you accordingly as long as you continue to please me."

"You devil," he whispered.

"Not a devil, an angel, remember?"

In tense silence they stared at each other, both wounded by the words uttered between them now and in the past. Gaby could feel the tears stinging her lids but willed them away. Her lips were trembling and her chest rose and fell as if she'd run a mile in the prairie heat. For a moment more their eyes locked in combat, and then he swung around and jerked on his pants. With long angry strides he made his way down the stairs and out the door, leaving it to bang behind him. His boots and shirt were clutched in his angry fists. Her words pounded in his brain, mocking him like a thousand demons on the long ride back to his ranch.

19

At first Rayne was too angry to think of anything but putting his hands around her throat and throttling the life from her. Once again she'd angered him beyond endurance, but this time she'd gone too far. Mighty Elliott pride, indeed. Well, she'd done her best to humble him today. He cursed her and felt no better for it.

Gaby listened to the door slamming behind Rayne and bit back the tears. She would not cry out. She would not call him back. She'd decided on this course of action for a reason, and if she and Rayne were ever to have a future together, he had to view her differently than he had in the past. She was entitled to some pride too.

Sleep was out of the question, so she dressed and sat in one of the window seats, watching the sun rise over the prairie. The plains seemed empty and desolate in the early-morning light, as empty as her life would be if Rayne didn't come back to her.

"Think about the things I said, Rayne," she willed him. "Think about them and come back to me. I need you."

The sun pried itself away from the edge of the earth and steadily rose in the azure sky, already scorching the earth with its heat. Belowstairs, Gaby could hear the cook in the kitchen making coffee, and Maria in the nursery. The gleeful gurglings of her son came to her and she hadn't the heart to go play with him.

At midmorning she heard horses in the yard and the front door opening. Rayne had come back, she thought joyfully. She didn't take time to don shoes or brush her hair up. Her cheeks still bore traces of tears.

"Rayne," she called as she ran down the stairs, then paused halfway down, her skirts caught up in one hand, one slender bare foot halting on the edge of the step. Her dark eyes widened and filled with disappointment as she looked at her visitors.

A young man and an older woman stood in the hall below. It was obvious from their dress that they were from the East. Just as obvious was the fact, from the similarity in coloring and features, they were related. Two pairs of gray eyes turned to gaze at her, one pair friendly and sparkling with good humor, the other dour and disapproving.

"Hello," Gaby said, somewhat breathless from her hurrying. Her bright smile of welcome had faded but the color on her cheeks was still high. She looked like a Gypsy, the man thought, with her bare feet and tumbled hair. He smiled up at her and felt his mother stiffen in disapproval.

"I am Mrs. Aaron Spencer," the woman said, and Gaby was so startled she couldn't speak at first. Before she could find her voice and introduce herself, the woman had turned away, moving with arrogant assurance along the entrance hall. Removing her gloves with precise movements, she cast a censorious eyes upon Mrs. Schafer. The housekeeper stood with her mouth gaping in surprise, staring from one Mrs. Aaron Spencer to the other.

"And who are you, if I may ask?" the woman inquired in starched tones. Mrs. Schafer gulped and introduced herself.

"I see," the first Mrs. Spencer said. "Well, Mrs. Schafer, you will find that I am an exacting taskmistress. I demand that things be done well." She strolled about the hall, swiping at objects, checking for dust. Disapprovingly she held up her finger to show what she'd found.

"In these barbarous wastelands, it is too easy to grow lax in one's duties, Mrs. Schafer, but now that I'm here I expect things to be done in their proper order. You can start by having the furniture dusted immediately."

Mrs. Schafer cast one quick, frantic look back at Gaby,

who still lingered on the stairs; then she hurried away as the newcomer made her way to the parlor.

"Ummm hum," she said, and Gaby was left to wonder if she approved or disapproved. The woman swept through to the kitchen, where Gaby heard raised voices and the crash of a bowl. The woman made a quick exit back into the main hall, and Gaby smothered a laugh. The first Mrs. Spencer had just met their fiery cook. The woman pinned Gaby with a gaze meant to send her quaking for cover.

"Have you seen to my bags yet?" she inquired imperiously. "Why are you still standing about? And for heaven's sake, where are your shoes? This may be a heathen country, but people can dress properly."

Gaby was torn between amusement, irritation, and relief as she looked at her visitors. The young man smiled at her again, obviously trying to soften his mother's highhanded tactics. He had a nice face, Gaby saw, and although he favored his mother greatly, possessing her sandy coloring and jutting chin, Gaby could see a resemblance to Aaron as well. It made her feel close to the young man immediately.

"You must be Kevin," she said.

"Yes, I am. How did you know?"

"Your father spoke of you often, and of course you look like Aaron."

"Aaron?" the woman repeated with exaggerated outrage, her eyes going wide. "How dare you be so familiar with your employer?"

"Aaron was my husband," Gaby said, trying to be polite in spite of the woman's attitude. "I thought they would have told you about me when they contacted you."

"They did nothing of the sort," the woman snapped.

"I'm sorry. This must be a shock to you," Gaby said with sympathy. "I'm Gabrielle. My friends call me Gaby. You're Abigail."

"You're a child," Abigail said, ignoring even the merest civilities. "You couldn't have been Aaron's wife."

"I'm twenty years old and I was indeed his wife. Welcome to the Lazy S Ranch." Gaby held out a hand to the young man, who sprang forward to shake it. Abigail ignored it. "We hadn't had word from the detectives in such a long time, we'd given up hope of ever finding you."

"When we heard of my husband's death, we came immediately," Abigail said, and Gaby refrained from telling her she was no longer Aaron's wife. "My son and I came to claim our inheritance." Gaby was dismayed at the woman's boldness. She'd hardly stepped foot in the door and she was already concerned about getting money from her ex-husband's estate. She hadn't even inquired about Aaron's death. Gaby felt her patience with the woman fast slipping away.

"I'm afraid there is no inheritance to be claimed," she said, and took some pleasure in the look of shock that etched its way across Abigail Spencer's face.

"The detectives told us there was. Obviously Aaron did not die a pauper." Abigail glanced around the elegant hall, noting the chandelier and the curved stairway with its rich-grained balustrade. The woman's blatant greed and her assumption that Aaron's estate would naturally go to her rankled, but Gaby tried to be tactful.

"When Aaron died," she began, moving forward so she could face them directly. Her flowing hair and hesitant, gentle air made her seem childlike. Her beauty captivated Kevin, who found he couldn't tear his gaze away from her. "When Aaron died, he had no way of knowing where Kevin was or even if he wished to come here to Texas. I'm sure those were the reasons for writing his will as he did."

"Are you telling me that Aaron did not put his own son in his will?"

Gaby let her silence be answer enough for the outraged woman.

"I suppose he left everything to a little slut who's hardly more than a child."

Again Gaby remained silent, careful to keep her growing dislike of Aaron's first wife under control. She owed Aaron for his kindness, she reminded herself.

"Mother!" Kevin cried, moving toward Abigail as if to take her arm and so still her vicious tongue that way. It was obvious he was embarrassed at her rudeness.

"Can you believe the outrage, the effrontery? Oh!"

Words failed the woman as she glared first at Kevin, then at Gaby.

"She's explained why Father didn't put me in his will," Kevin said reasonably, "and we can hardly blame her, or father."

"Whom should we blame if not the two of them? She's contrived to steal your inheritance. As for your father's behavior, this is just one more cruelty in the many your father has heaped upon me. He never loved us, Kevin, dear boy." She laid a loving hand along his cheek, her eyes going all teary and helpless-looking. Her voice was that of a martyr. "Now he shows the whole world how little we meant to him. He always was a cruel and selfish man."

"That's not true," Gaby said, her face flushing. "Aaron was one of the kindest, gentlest men I've ever known. He spoke of you often, wondering where you were and if you were well and happy. He longed to see you."

"He ran away from us," Abigail cried. "He came here and lived like a king while we struggled to stay alive. We'll challenge the will, have it overturned."

"Mother, I don't think we should," Kevin began, and Gaby found herself warming to the young man. "If it's Father's wish that his estate go to someone else, then we should accept that."

"Nonsense," Abigail cried. "Obviously there was something in the will for you or those detectives wouldn't have searched for you. We can't go on just the word of this woman. We'll see a lawyer ourselves."

"That's a good idea," Gaby replied. "Perhaps it would make you feel better. I'll send for Aaron's lawyer immediately. In the meantime, you can rest and refresh yourselves." She turned to Maria, who was holding the baby. "Give Danny to me and go tell Billy I'd like him to ride into Fowler."

"Yes, ma'am." Maria handed over the chubby baby. Danny sat on his mother's hip, cooing and chuckling to himself.

"He's a beautiful baby," Kevin said, holding out a finger to Danny.

"Thank you," Gaby said proudly. Abigail sniffed her disapproval.

"Is he yours?" Kevin asked, jiggling a fat little foot until Danny giggled in response.

"Yes, he is," Gaby answered, smiling at Danny's happy response.

Kevin stopped playing with the baby. His face sobered. "Then he's my half-brother," he said softly.

"Oh, Kevin," Abigail said in disgust.

"He would be," Kevin insisted. "Wouldn't he?" He turned back to Gaby for confirmation, and she sensed his desire to learn more about his family here in Texas. Her gaze flickered from one face to the other. One was hopeful and eager, the other cynical. She couldn't risk having Danny hurt, and Abigail's demeanor said all too clearly she considered Gaby an impostor in every way. She hated lying to Kevin about something so important, but she must.

"Yes, he would be your brother," she said firmly.

Abigail turned away with a dismissive shrug.

Lunch was a stiff, silent affair. Abigail's animosity was a tangible thing in the house, despite Kevin's attempts at some warmth. After the meal Gaby offered to show them around the ranch. Abigail professed a headache and the need for rest. Kevin leapt at the offer. Gaby took Mrs. Schafer aside and instructed her to attend to Abigail's needs while she was gone.

"Don't vorry," Mrs. Schafer said grimly. "I'll keep a goot eye on her." Gaby was sure the housekeeper meant far more than she'd intended, but said nothing. She didn't trust Abigail Spencer either.

Away from his mother, Kevin proved to be a lively, curious young man with a natural kindness and courtesy much like his father's. Gaby wondered how a woman like Abigail had ever been able to produce a son like him.

By the time the lawyer arrived, Gaby felt that Kevin was eager to accept her friendship.

"So it's true. He's left us nothing," Abigail stormed.

"I'm afraid that's so, Mrs. . . . er . . . Spencer," Jeremy Wallace replied calmly. "Everything was left to Aaron's second wife and their son."

"I am the *only* Mrs. Aaron Spencer," Abigail snapped. "My husband and I were never divorced."

Gaby's face registered her shock. It had never occurred to her that Aaron had not been free to marry her, so great had been her trust in him.

"That's an interesting claim," Wallace said in his mild voice, and Gaby felt like laughing at the absurdity of his understatement. "Of course, we have only your word for it."

"Are you calling me a liar?"

"No, I'm simply saying we'll have to verify your claim. Gabrielle Spencer has legal documentation proving her marriage to Aaron Spencer."

"It isn't worth anything," Abigail fairly crowed with triumph. "Aaron's first marriage is the one the law recognizes. So verify anything you want. In the meantime—"

"In the meantime, the will must stand as read. Mr. Spencer named Gabrielle and his son Daniel as his heirs."

"That baby is no more Aaron's than a man in the moon," Abigail sputtered. "You only have to look at that black hair to know it isn't Aaron's child."

"You seem to forget, Mrs. Spencer, that his mother has black hair," Jeremy pointed out mildly. "And to make such slanderous statements could leave you open to a lawsuit."

Abigail's glare swept over Gaby once again, and she sniffed. "Yes, well, perhaps I was wrong," she conceded, taking the lawyer's warning to heart. "Still, my son is entitled to my husband's estate, or at least a large portion of it. After all, he is the firstborn, and legitimate."

"I'd be very careful what I said, Mrs. Spencer," Wallace reminded her. Each time he said her name, he hesitated.

"Well, Kevin is the firstborn, and the law says that—"

"Those old laws of the firstborn receiving everything don't apply here in this country, Mrs. Spencer." He closed his briefcase. "No, I believe Aaron Spencer made it very clear in his will to whom he wished to leave his estate."

"We'll fight it," Abigail flared. "That woman can't steal my son's inheritance and get away with it."

"If not for that woman," Jeremy Wallace said, "you would not be here. It was at her instruction that we made the search for your son. Mrs. Spencer"—Wallace nodded toward Gaby, stating the title firmly and with obvious relish—"Mrs. Spencer is generous enough to want to share her inheritance with Kevin. She is not required by law to do so."

"Are you telling me that we are here under this woman's auspices?" Abigail huffed.

"That's just what I'm telling you," Wallace replied.

"Thank you, Gaby," the words were spoken quietly, and all three turned to look at the young man who had sat pale-faced and silent until now. "It was kind of you to think of me, even though my father didn't."

"That's what I've been trying to tell you, Kevin," Gaby cried. "He thought of you so much, especially after Danny was born. I'd watch him play with the baby and I'd know he was thinking of you and of how he'd missed all the years with you. He was saddened by the thought he'd never known you."

"That wasn't my fault," Kevin said angrily.

"No, it wasn't," Gaby replied, and wanted to tell him it was his mother's fault. "It wasn't his either."

"He could have come back. He could have found me if he'd wanted to. You did."

"Yes, I suppose he could have," Gaby said, "but he was afraid to."

"Ha!" Abigail sniffed. "Aaron Spencer always was a coward about things."

"He wasn't a coward. He was a brave man, but he was afraid of how you might respond to him, of what you might think about a scarred and crippled man for a father."

"He'd been injured?" Kevin asked, and Gaby felt like hugging him for the love and concern she saw in his face.

"Yes, it happened long ago, when you were just a baby—" she began.

"Well, you have us here, what happens next?" Abigail broke in, and Gaby was certain she didn't want Kevin to hear of his father's injury or of her behavior. "We've traveled here at our own expense with money we could ill afford. Not all of us have been fortunate enough to have found an old fool with money."

Gaby bit back an angry retort. She was fast tiring of Abigail's insensitive remarks. "You will be reimbursed for your traveling expenses," she said. "If we'd known you had been found, we would have sent traveling money to you immediately."

"Humph. Now that we're here, what do you want with us?" Abigail demanded. "What part of the estate are you giving to my son?"

"I don't know," Gaby stammered. "I hadn't thought that far ahead. I just thought perhaps Kevin could stay here at the ranch and help me run it."

"Here at the ranch with you?" Abigail echoed. "A young man and an unmarried woman? What would people think? If you have no sense of propriety, I assure you I have."

"I meant for you to stay as well," Gaby said smoothly, and Jeremy Wallace marveled that she didn't cringe as she made the offer.

"Well, if my son is to get what rightfully belongs to him, then I suppose I must. If I'm to stay for any time at all, I must have a bigger room. I'll want my things moved into the large bedroom at the end of the hall, and Kevin will take the one next to it."

Gaby breathed deeply to calm her anger. While she had shown Kevin the ranch, obviously Abigail Spencer had done a little exploring of her own. If they were to live with any kind of harmony, Gaby realized, she would have to establish now just who was mistress of the Lazy S Ranch.

"I'm sorry," she replied, keeping her voice and smile gracious. "The bedroom at the head of the stairs belonged to Aaron. It's far too masculine for a woman of your . . . sensibilities. I'll have Kevin's things moved there." She saw the light of gratitude leap into the young man's eyes.

"As for the room next to it, that has always been mine. Since it is near to the nursery, I will stay there." She heard Abigail's hiss. "However, there is a lovely room facing mine, which is every bit as large and has its own dressing room. I'm sure you'll be quite comfortable there."

Abigail's mouth opened and closed a couple of times as if she meant to protest, but Gaby had spoken to her with such friendliness that the woman had nothing left to complain about. She snapped her mouth shut and glared at the lawyer, who bit his lower lip to hide his smile. It looked as if the first Mrs. Spencer had just met her match.

"Do you think she was telling the truth about the marriage?" Gaby asked later when she and Wallace were alone.

"I don't know, Gaby," the lawyer responded truthfully. "A lot of men leave behind families when they head west. Once here, they establish new lives for themselves and forget old ties."

"That didn't happen with Aaron," Gaby said. "He was devastated by the loss of his son. Is there some way to check on Abigail's claim? I want to do right for Kevin at any rate, but I don't trust his mother."

"Neither do I," Wallace said. "I'll start a man digging into the records back east. There's bound to be a record of a divorce somewhere."

"Thank you, Jeremy," Gaby said, holding out a hand. "You've been a good friend since Aaron died. I can see why he placed such trust in you." She smiled, and Jeremy Wallace took the memory with him of sparkling eyes and flashing teeth and thick black hair pulled into an impossibly severe knot.

It was a funny thing about words, Rayne reflected. They came back to haunt a man for days after, burrowing into his mind like an infernal prairie dog. Deliberately he drove himself, trying to work himself to the edge of exhaustion that would allow him to lapse into sleep the moment his head hit the bunk mattress, but too often he lay awake remembering the silk of Gaby's skin and hearing the pain in her voice as she'd hurled the hateful words at him. Often he was driven from his bed to sit on the porch watching the moon rise full and bright over the prairie. And in those lonely night hours—the witching hours, the cowmen called them—he began to find some answers, and he didn't like what he found.

He'd been a fool, he decided, and now he must pay the fool's price. With unerring clarity Gaby had shown him how one-sided he'd been, how biased, how foolish. He saw how he'd driven her away and how he'd held her at arm's length ever since Aaron had died. He'd been afraid to become involved with her again, but not for the reasons Gaby thought. He wasn't sure he could bear the pain again if it didn't work out. It had been agony without her. The night he'd spent at the Spencer ranch was still in his mind, and he realized the misery he felt now would never get better, not until he had Gaby back again. He felt a great urge to throw a saddle on his horse and hurry back to the Lazy S to tell Gaby that everything she'd said about him was true and to offer her his heart, his soul, and most of all his body for whatever price she was willing to pay. But she wasn't alone now. He'd waited too long. Rayne cursed his pride.

The household help and hands alike made every effort to stay away from Abigail, the woman who once had been married to Aaron Spencer and had through the years somehow changed from the lovely young girl he'd chosen for his first wife into a pinch-mouthed, unpleasant woman intent on getting her hands on his estate.

As the days turned to weeks, Abigail began to feel her isolation. However, pride kept her from making any effort at friendship with the German housekeeper, the Mexican nanny, or a mere cook of questionable pedigree. Making friends with the woman who had robbed her son of his inheritance, and would now be intent upon seducing him if not for the presence of his mother, was out of the question. Even Gaby's friends met with little approval from Abigail. She found Jessie Walker, with her rough talk and ways, too ill-bred for her own fastidiousness.

Finally loneliness forced her to ask Gaby about their neighbors, so Gaby took her into Fowler and introduced her to some of the townspeople and began planning a party to introduce her guests to other ranchers.

Kevin, on the other hand, took to the ranch and its ways with surprising ease. He was an excellent horseman and quickly learned to handle the more fractious mustangs the Texans rode. When he was given a particularly spirited horse and was bucked off, he just brushed himself off and remounted to the good-natured cheers of the rest of the cowhands. Since he and Billy were close in age, they quickly overcame the disparity of their backgrounds and became friends.

Everyday, he was outdoors with the other hands, learning to rope and brand cows with the same enthusiasm he displayed while mending corral fences or mucking out the barn stalls. He took everything in stride. Each misfortune that befell him seemed to become an adventure, so lightheartedly did he greet it.

Kevin had a way about him that soon charmed every woman who spent much time around him, and the nice thing was, he didn't try. That charm was a natural part of his makeup, and the longer he remained on the ranch, the happier he seemed to be.

Even Mrs. Schafer was won over. "He is a fine young man," she said one day as she and Gaby sat resting on the wide front porch. Mrs. Schafer had brought Gaby a cool glass of tea and lingered to chat.

"You're beginning to like him," Gaby teased her gently. The other women of the house had long since fallen under the spell of Kevin's charm, but Mrs. Schafer had been holding out.

"Yah," she replied warily. "I like him."

"I like him too," Gaby replied and saw some of the tightness leave the housekeeper's face.

Mrs. Schafer had been worried. She loved Gaby, but Kevin was the son of the man she'd served ever since she'd come from Germany. Her loyalties had been sorely tested in the past few weeks. "Kevin has many ways like his father," she said with a knowing nod of her head.

"Yes, he does."

"He likes the ranch," Mrs. Schafer said wistfully. "Having him here is almost like having Mr. Spencer back. I'll hate to see him leave."

"Perhaps he'll stay here on the ranch and help me run it," Gaby said. "Aaron would have liked that. The ranch is big enough for both of us."

"It vould be goot," Mrs. Schafer decreed, and with her customary briskness got to her feet. Many of her concerns had been put to rest. Humming, she rustled away to continue her duties.

*　　*　　*

"When were you and Aaron married?" Abigail asked on one occasion, and probed to find the exact date. Then she asked when Danny was born. Her eyes narrowed speculatively when she figured the difference. Gaby said nothing, trying to maintain an easy air toward the woman and all her snooping, but Abigail worried her. If she guessed the truth about Danny, she wouldn't hesitate to use the information to her own good and no one else's. Gaby found herself checking Danny often when Abigail was prowling around the house.

"Poor Aaron," Abigail said one day to the cook. She didn't know Gaby was in the side pantry.

"Yah, poor man," the cook agreed. "Very sad to see him die like that, and him so happy with his young wife and baby."

Gaby could see the frown that crossed Abigail's face; then the woman smoothed away the flush of anger and settled her features once again in lines of sympathy and understanding.

"I understand poor Aaron was behaving strangely before he died," Abigail probed.

The cook raised startled eyes to her. "I hadn't noticed, ma'am," she said. "Was he ill?"

"I've been told he wasn't himself. He'd grown forgetful and begun to imagine things. He even thought people were out to kill him."

"Somebody did," the cook said laconically.

"But he had suspected everyone of wanting to do him harm," Abigail persisted. "Even those who professed to love him."

"Is that a fact?" The strong arms never faltered as they turned bread dough out on a board and began kneading it. The cook didn't like Abigail. The conversation made her nervous, as if she were being asked to tell secrets about Mr. and Mrs. Spencer. She thumped the bread dough with a little extra vigor.

"Some seemed to be worried that he was beginning to lose his mental faculties. It must have been so hard on poor Gaby at the end, to see Aaron deteriorate the way he did."

"It wasn't hard at all," Gaby said, leaving the pantry to face down the woman and her hateful insinuations.

The look of astonishment on Abigail's face gave her a moment of pleasure. "Aaron was a remarkable man, loving and caring up to the day he was murdered. It will do you no good, Abigail, to continue in this line. Aaron had just been appointed to a position in Washington. That wouldn't have happened if he were suffering a mental illness, as you've tried to insinuate. No one would believe you. Aaron was loved by all who knew him."

"Not by all, my dear." Abigail had recovered from her surprise. "Someone killed him. Rather profitable and convenient for you, I'd say." At the stricken look in Gaby's eyes, she swept triumphantly from the room. The girl was hardly more than a simpleton, and no match for Abigail Spencer. She'd find a way yet to recover what rightfully belonged to her and Kevin, she vowed. Given enough time, she'd find a way.

20

As the long, hot summer passed, Kevin spent less time inside the ranch house with the women and more of it out on the range or in the bunkhouse with the rest of the men.

"He's getting to be one of the best hands I've got," Ben said one day as Gaby rode out to the range with him.

"That's wonderful news," she said. "I think one day Kevin may even want to take over the running of his father's ranch."

"He's going at it the right way. He's determined to learn everything and to do it himself. He may not have been born here in Texas, but he's making up for lost time."

They turned their horses eastward along the river. Its depths were falling dangerously low and most cattlemen were looking toward the winter, hoping its precipitation would bring the water levels back to normal. It seemed they'd all given up on rain for the summer.

"Are the Rocking E cattle still watering here?" Gaby asked. Rayne had started driving his cattle back to the river after his night with her. It must have been hard for him to swallow his pride, but no rancher would let his cattle die of thirst if he could help it.

"Yes, ma'am, they are," Ben said. He cast her an apprehensive glance. He didn't know why she'd changed her mind again, but he was glad she had. Rayne Elliott was a respected man in these parts.

Gaby hadn't seen Rayne since that night.

Despite Abigail's unrelenting hostility, Gaby continued with her plans for a welcoming party. She did it for Kevin more than for his mother. She had grown quite fond of the young man and knew Aaron would have been proud of his son.

The shindig was set for two week later. Summer was drawing to a close and soon everyone would be too busy with fall roundups to attend any social functions. Gaby took special care to see that the Elliott ranch received an invitation. Jacinta would be there, so would Dusty and most of the cowhands, but she wasn't sure if Rayne would come. She knew he'd been avoiding her. To keep herself from dwelling on it too much, she threw herself into the preparations.

The party would begin in the afternoon and continue most of the night. She'd place tables and chairs out in the yard under the shade trees and on the wide porch. The barn, with its wide plank floors, was made ready for dancing. Some of the cowhands wouldn't know how to behave in the stiff formality of the drawing room. Their dancing could become pretty rowdy.

"You mean you aren't having the party in the parlor?" Abigail stormed when she found out the arrangements. "Why, I've never heard of anything so outrageous."

"Many of the ranchers and their hands will come," Gaby explained. "There's more room in the hayloft. Besides, it will be cooler dancing there than in here. We can open the doors at either end and let the breezes blow through."

"Humpf," Abigail declared. "I won't attend a gathering that must be held in a barn."

"I'm sorry you feel that way," Gaby said patiently. "Of course I'll make arrangements for tea and refreshments here in the parlor for the older ladies who don't wish to dance. I'm sure you can have a lovely visit with them." Gaby allowed herself a glimpse of Abigail's outraged face before she fled. The woman would at least make an appearance in the barn, Gaby was sure, for she was vain enough not to want to be flocked with the grandmotherly old women who'd take their ease in the parlor, away from the rowdiness of the dance.

The day of the party dawned hot and sunny, without a cloud to mar the pristine blue. Gaby had expected little else. She wasn't sure it was ever going to rain again. Sides of beef had been suspended over open fire pits roasting since dawn. Jacinta had come over two days before to help make bread and pies and a variety of other dishes. Everything seemed ready.

The ranchers started arriving in the middle of the afternoon. Invitations were seldom turned down in this lonesome cattle country. They came, most of them riding horseback beside their ranch wagons, which were filled with wives, children, and bedding as well as their best party clothes. They would wash and change once they reached the Spencer ranch. They came with a spring to their step and a sparkle in their eyes, and with each new arrival the air of festivity grew. They ate and drank their fill between laughter and talk, all of it about cattle.

Gaby watched as the ranchers warmed immediately to Aaron's son and suffered Abigail with cool politeness. Abigail didn't seem to notice or care about their reticence. She in turn felt irritation with these rough-talking ranchers and their women. How had Aaron ever decided to settle here among them? she wondered, and her pinched expression and darting eyes told the ranchers all too plainly what she thought. She was a chaparral fox, they decided privately, a title conferred on someone who was mean and treacherous. The Texas Angel would have to watch out for this one.

Lorna Blake arrived with her father and after a few stiff words to Gaby went off to join a group of ranchers' wives. After Gaby's marriage to Aaron, Lorna had been less hostile, but they would never be close friends. Gaby noticed that Lorna often glanced around as if searching for someone. It was obvious she was looking for Rayne.

The sun had set by the time the crowd had eaten and visited to their fill. Shadows had crept across the prairie and lay in dark pools around the buildings. Lanterns had been lit around the barn, and the fiddlers were tuning up. The ladies retired indoors—to freshen up their spit curls and check their noses, as one rancher put it. His remark was greeted with laughter. There was an air of well-being and anticipation among the guests. It was a good party—but then, most of them had never seen a bad one.

Gaby had given up on Rayne coming when she saw Billy leave Maria's side and hurry across the yard to greet Dusty and the rest of the Rocking E ranch hands.

Rayne handed his reins to one of his hands and glanced around. Gaby knew he was searching for her. Even as their eyes met and clung, Lorna moved between them, twining her arm in Rayne's as her head moved close to his shoulder. She whispered something to him and laughed lightly. Gaby turned back to her other guests, but she had the comfort of knowing Rayne had looked for her first.

The musicians broke into their first dance and couples flocked to the center of the floor and moved energetically in a foot-stomping dance. Everyone seemed to be in high spirits, and even the old-timers made their way to the floor to stomp a little.

"Would you care to dance, Gaby?" Kevin was at her elbow. He was dressed like the other cowboys, in clean but worn pants and a plaid shirt with a bandanna knotted neatly around his neck. He'd chosen not to wear one of the fancy eastern suits he'd brought with him. Gaby had to smile at his determination not to appear a tenderfoot. Even the leather boots he wore, though not very old, had been made to look well-worn. She found his efforts endearing.

"It would be my pleasure," she said, and went into his arms. They danced around the floor and Gaby was surprised anew at the changes in Kevin. He'd filled out in the first few weeks on the ranch, his shoulders broadening with a newly acquired ridge of muscles. The lines of his body were already growing lean and hard and his once pale face was tanned up to a line on his forehead where his hat rested. The Texans seemed to wear that line like a badge, Gaby thought, remembering the first time she'd noticed it on Rayne.

Kevin swung her around the room and Gaby noticed several ranchers' daughters cast him a flirtatious eye. She was unaware of the picture she and Kevin made as they whirled gracefully around the room. She was dark and exotic in her beauty, he was fair and sleek, and both were unusually handsome in their youthfulness. Knowing looks and whispered speculations began to circulate the room. Only Abigail, by the forbidding, jealous nature of her, saved them from scandal, but many onlookers were prone to a little matchmaking. Gaby was nearly ready to shed her widow's weeds, and not many there believed she'd remain a widow for long. Few women did in this harsh land. A woman needed a man to take care of her, and unattached females were still too scarce to be neglected. It seemed fitting to many of them that Kevin and Gaby might get together. Their sentiments were not lost on Rayne, who tightened his lips and swung Lorna around the floor.

Men took turns bringing drinks to the fiddler, and the music continued throughout the night with hardly a pause. The later the hour grew, the more energetic the dances became. Gaby walked along the sidelines, watching the flying feet and wondering where Rayne was, when suddenly he appeared before her.

"Gaby," he said, his eyes dark in the lantern light.

She felt her blood stir within her. Dimly she heard the band start another tune, this time a lilting waltz, and she thought of the night she and Rayne had danced on the prairie beneath the stars. His eyes flashed and she knew he was remembering too.

Without a word she went into his arms and they went out on the dance floor. They moved together, their bodies betraying the easy familiarity that had once existed between them. Rayne cradled her in his arms as if she might break, and Gaby rested there, feeling secure and happy for the first time in weeks. They had eyes for no one else. As one, they swayed in time to the music and were unaware of the glances they drew. Those who'd speculated about Kevin and Gaby now discarded their previous notions. This was the man for the Texas Angel!

As she watched them, Abigail Spencer's eyes narrowed speculatively. She saw dark hair sweeping away from a peak, and suddenly she smiled. She would have it all.

Reluctantly the fiddler drew his bow across the last strains of the song and lifted his chin, caught in the spell of romance he'd helped create. Rayne and Gaby stopped moving and stood, their hands still clasping, their gazes

locked. The shuffle of couples breaking apart and re-
forming for the next dance broke their reverie and they
drew apart. The fiddle sang out again, this time calling
the dancers to a faster, easier mood. Rayne escorted
Gaby back to the edge of the room .

"I'm glad you came tonight," she said breathlessly.
She wanted to say so much more, to tell him she was
sorry for the things she'd said to him.

"I figured it was time we buried our differences and
tried to be good neighbors," he said.

"I'd like that too," Gaby replied. Only she wanted
more. At least this was a beginning.

"Rayne, I'm truly sorry for what I said that night you
came."

"It doesn't matter, Gaby, forget it."

"It does matter. I turned your desperate situation against
you. I shouldn't have."

"Isn't that what I did to you? Isn't that what you were
trying to show me?" he asked gently.

Surprise widened Gaby's eyes. He had understood.
Why hadn't he come back to her, then?

"I shouldn't have tried to destroy your pride," she
said.

"The mighty Elliott pride?" he asked, and laughed.
"Seems you were right. It needed to be taken down a peg
or two."

"Not the way I did it," she said miserably.

"Forget it, Gaby," he advised, turning away.

"Rayne, wait. There's something I've been wanting to
talk to you about."

"What is it?" His gaze held hers.

The noise and gaiety swirled around them. This was
not the time to tell him about Danny. "Not here, not
now," she said.

Rayne nodded in acceptance. "I'll be seeing you, Gaby,"
he said, and was gone, striding through the dancers while
she stared after him with mingled frustration and foreboding.

There had been in his eyes a look of resignation.

Don't give up on us now, Rayne, she thought. It's time
for us to try again. We can make it work. We're wiser
now. We won't make the same mistakes. She should

have told him that, she thought, and looked around the hayloft searching for him. She'd tell him now. But there was no sign of Rayne. She caught a glimpse of Lorna Blake just leaving, her shawl thrown over her shoulders. Clarence Blake still stood talking at the other end of the dance floor. Lorna would leave the dance early for only one reason. Gaby's legs moved automatically toward the barn door. She hurried outside and saw Rayne climbing into a carriage. Lorna was seated beside him, and his horse was tied on behind. His name on Gaby's lips died unuttered as she hugged her arms around herself and miserably watched the carriage pull away.

At last the dance drew to a close. The fiddler was given a final drink and persuaded to play one last tune. It would be a stag dance. The ladies stood on the sidelines well out of harm's way and clapped their hands to the music. These final dances had a way of becoming rough free-for-alls as men competed to do the most spectacular steps. These jigs had been known to end in wrestling matches.

Such was not the case now. The men cavorted and kicked up their heels in wild abandon, making the plank floor shudder under their feet until they were too exhausted to go on and the fiddler could not be bribed for another tune. At last they all trooped toward the porch, where the cook had put out big pots of strong black coffee.

"Whewee, my feet feel like they've wintered on some mighty hard pasture," one rancher said to another as they stood sipping the hot brew. All seemed to agree the Spencer jamboree had been a success. It had been just the break most of them needed before starting the business of gathering and branding their cattle. Gaby was pleased with the outcome of the party. Kevin had done his father proud, and even Abigail seemed to have found a friend or two, although the women were not to Gaby's liking. They had too much love for gossip.

The weary ranchers bedded down for a couple of hours' sleep before beginning the journey back to their homes. Wearily Gaby climbed the stairs to her bedroom. She lay thinking of the dance she'd had with Rayne and of his strange mood. When she woke later, the sun was already high and every wagon of the visiting ranchers was gone. Little sign was left of the party.

The roundups started. As before, several ranches set up a central location where they gathered to sort their cows and brand them. For the drive they would pair off, for they'd found there was greater security from rustlers and Indians. Some of the bigger ranchers who couldn't spare the time away from their ranches were hiring drovers to oversee getting their herds up the trails to market. Ben had already made arrangements to join Rayne and Clarence Blake.

The first day of the roundup Gaby and Kevin followed the chuck wagon out onto the prairie. Kevin planned to stay, sleeping out under the stars with the other cowboys, and he was boyishly eager.

"Just think, Gaby," he said enthusiastically, "if I were back east, I'd be sitting in a stuffy law office someplace. This is the kind of life for a man."

"Are you thinking of staying on here in Texas?" Gaby asked.

"I'd like to," Kevin said. "There's nothing back east for me."

"I don't think your mother is happy here."

"She just needs a little more time," Kevin said blithely. "If she could get out and see the prairie the way I've been able to, she'd love it as much as I do."

Gaby smiled at him, remembering how she'd fainted at her first roundup. Of course, she must have been pregnant with Danny then and hadn't realized it, for she hadn't fainted since. She'd come to accept the branding and marking as a necessary part of ranching.

The ranch was quiet without the hands there. Gaby found herself impatient with the woman talk and chores. Although she had taken over a heavy portion of the ranch supervision after Aaron's death, the roundup was one area in which she couldn't help, except with peripheral decisions. She should have relaxed and enjoyed the extra time with Danny, who was taking his first toddling steps, but it was impossible. The other women of the household vied with her for his attention. Surprisingly, even Abigail had begun to take an interest in the little

boy, holding out a toy to him while she chatted to Maria
and Mrs. Schafer.

"His eyes are such a bright blue," she would say. "I
don't remember Aaron's eyes being blue."

"Ah, he's a baby. Baby's eyes are always blue," Mrs.
Schafer would say.

"Aaron must have been very proud of his son," Abigail remarked on another occasion.

"He was, he was," Mrs. Schafer agreed. "He used to
rush home to see him and make plans for him. Mr.
Spencer was happy the last year of his life, happier than
I'd ever seen him before."

"How nice," Abigail would say, and stroll out on the
porch.

Then: "What is that thing on his forehead?" Abigail
inquired one day.

"What?" Maria ran to look at Danny's forehead, fear-
ing he'd fallen and bruised himself.

"That thing, that tuft of hair."

"It is a widow's peak. It is very handsome, don't you
think?" Mrs. Schafer asked.

"He looks deformed," Abigail replied, and both Maria
and Mrs. Schafer turned their backs on her and refused
to speak to her for several days.

"Doting idiots," Abigail would mutter under her breath,
and sweep her skirts aside when Danny's uncertain steps
carried him in her direction.

Gaby saw the woman's hostility toward her son and
knew she must never admit the truth of his paternity. She
must protect him. As it was, Danny hardly noticed the
grumpy woman with the sour face, so surrounded was he
by loving, admiring females. The person who gave him
the greatest delight was Kevin. From the first, the young
man seemed to take a special liking to the baby he
thought was his half-brother. He always took time to pick
Danny up and toss him high in the air. While the women
cried out in disapproval, Danny would cackle with glee.
Very soon the baby got so he looked for Kevin's return
and would hold out his arms to be taken. Held high in
Kevin's strong young arms, the baby would shove his
chubby little hands into his shirt pocket. Kevin, Danny
had discovered, always had a surprise there for him.

Sometimes it was something to eat and sometimes it was something exciting and funny like a prairie flower or a little brown frog that jumped in his hands.

Kevin was the first one to take Danny on a horse, lifting the baby up and settling him on the saddle in front of him, carefully cradling him while he walked his horse slowly around the ranch yard. Was it any wonder Danny loved Kevin? Gaby thought, watching the two of them together. But Abigail Spencer was incensed that her son should show such generosity to a rival for Aaron's money.

Jeremy Wallace rode out one day. Abigail, bored with the dull ranch life, had taken a buggy and driven herself into town to visit one of her friends. Kevin had spent the night at the roundup site and wasn't expected home until late. Gaby led the lawyer to her study.

"Tell me what you've found out," she said.

"It seems Mrs. Spencer was right when she said she had never divorced Aaron. A request for a divorce was made and then withdrawn some twenty years ago."

"That's why Aaron thought he was divorced," Gaby said, and was glad to learn he hadn't deliberately lied to her.

"Umm, yes," Wallace said, studying some papers he'd brought. "Apparently Abigail didn't notify him she'd changed her mind. But there was something else here that you'll be interested in hearing." He sounded triumphant. Gaby sat up straighter in anticipation.

"It seems that a few years later, Mrs. Spencer took it into her head to remarry." Gaby's eyes widened at this information. "And not being able to find her husband, she had him declared legally dead. She married a man named Orin Peterson. Mr. Peterson was some years older than Abigail and died a year later. She claimed all his inheritance, a rather modest sum, but it kept her and the boy in some comfort for these past years."

"That must have been why Aaron couldn't find her later when he searched for her. He didn't know her married name."

"Yes, and maybe he didn't search too hard. She's a veritable dragon lady." The comical expression on the lawyer's face made Gaby smile, which was what he'd intended. He'd been shocked by the dark circles under her eyes and the tight, drawn look of her face.

"How are you doing?" Wallace asked. "Is the dragon lady getting to be too much?"

Gaby smiled wanly and shook her head. "No. Kevin's worth the trouble Abigail causes. You should see him. He's so happy here, and he's taken right over in learning the ranching business."

"Is it wise to let him assume so much authority around the ranch?"

"I don't feel threatened by Kevin," Gaby said. "He means me no harm. In fact, he's changed so much since he's come here. He's not so bitter about not having known his father. He seem genuinely happy."

"You're a special sort of lady," Wallace said. "Not many women would take in their husbands' first wives and sons."

Gaby shrugged away his words. "Why shouldn't I? Abigail Spencer is no longer a threat to me, thanks to this information." She held up the papers he had given her.

"Don't underestimate that woman, Gaby. She's ruthless in getting what she wants."

"Her hands are tied and she knows it," Gaby said. "She just doesn't know yet that I know it as well. Let's keep what you've found out a secret for a little while."

"All right," Wallace agreed, and stopped, his head turned toward the door. Gaby glanced over her shoulder. Kevin stood there, his gray eyes wide and uncertain as he looked from her to the lawyer. Had he heard her final words? There was a flash of suspicion and mistrust in his eyes, and then it was gone.

"Hello, Kevin," Gaby said. "You remember Mr. Wallace."

"How do you do, sir?" Kevin said, stepping into the room to shake hands.

"Fine, thank you, Kevin. I see what Gaby's been saying is correct. You look like one of the other cowboys." Wallace stressed his words deliberately, as if to remind the young man of his true position on the ranch.

Kevin glanced down at his dusty working clothes and suntanned hands and nodded. "I suppose that's true," he agreed. Normally he would have smiled with pleasure at the observation, but now his face remained passive. Gaby knew Jeremy had been looking out for her interests, but she wished he'd take it easy on the young man. Kevin's troubled expression bothered her.

"How do you like Texas? Quite a change from what you're used to back east."

"Yes, sir, it is," Kevin said, his gaze going from one to the other. Gaby could almost read the questions in his eyes. "Is there anything you needed me for?" he asked the lawyer.

"No, I just had some business to discuss with Gaby. And since we've concluded that business, I'll be going."

"Thank you for coming out, Jeremy," Gaby said, sliding the folded paper into a pocket. She could feel Kevin's gaze following them as she accompanied the lawyer to the door. She would have to try to explain things to him, Gaby thought, and felt unsettled over the things she'd heard today. Kevin knew his mother had been married before, and yet he'd said nothing. She was bothered by his deception.

She stood on the porch until Wallace's buggy pulled out of the yard, then turned back to the study, wondering what she could say that would dispel the mistrust between Kevin and her. She didn't want him to think she'd been plotting against him and his mother, and she didn't want to feel Kevin was a part of Abigail's schemes.

Kevin wasn't in the study when she returned. She found him down by the barn saddling up a fresh horse.

"Are you going back out to the roundup tonight?" she asked.

"Yep," Kevin said, tightening a cinch.

"I thought you'd intended to spend the night here."

"I changed my mind."

"Abigail will be disappointed she missed you." He made no answer. "Kevin, how did you and your mother get along all those years you were growing up?"

He glanced at her, startled and wary. "Mother had a little money. When that ran out, she worked as a housekeeper for an old man. She sent me to boarding school. It was a bad year for both of us, but then a distant relative died and left us some money. It happened at a good time, for the old man died at about the same time, so Mother would have been out of a job. She didn't have to work after that."

Gaby listened to his story, gauging the truth of it, and felt relief. Abigail had not even told her son of her marriage. How convenient for Abigail that the old man had died when he did. Gaby pushed the thought away. Even Abigail couldn't have been enough of a monster to murder her helpless old husband. Gaby looked at Kevin's innocent face and decided to wait awhile longer before revealing the information she had. It would only hurt Kevin to find out his mother had lied to him.

The roundups were drawing to an end. Every day some rancher cried "Hiah up!" and started his herd along the northern trail. Gaby rode out to see how the Lazy S herd was doing. Extra men had been posted as lookouts, she saw, and guessed there must have been some trouble with rustlers. They sat on their horses on the distant rises, their rifles at the ready, their eyes squinting against the sun as they scanned the horizon. One rode out to meet Gaby and her escort and turned aside when he saw who it was.

Gaby rode over the rise and halted, gazing at the milling, chaotic scene below. It was much the same as the first time she'd reviewed it two years before, only this time she had a better understanding of what was going on. She watched the range-hardened men work with the cows. These lean, self-sufficient men had found their place in the scheme of things. Take them from this land and they would be lost, their rugged independence would fade. They were Texans, a special breed of men. Gaby felt a thrill of pride and instinctively looked for Rayne.

She could see his broad-shouldered silhouette across the valley. He sat straight and tall in his saddle, hat in hand, waving and calling to the stubborn cows that tried unsuccessfully to resist the flow of movement toward the branding fires.

"Quite a sight, isn't it?" Lorna Blake said at her elbow, and Gaby turned in surprise. She might have known the woman would be somewhere around. She never seemed to let Rayne very far out of her sight.

"Hello, Lorna," she said wearily. "What are you doing here?"

"I might have asked you that question," Lorna returned. "I seem to recall you have difficulty in watching a branding."

"Things change," Gaby said, trying not to sound defensive.

"Yes, things do change," Lorna repeated significantly. "I'm here to see Rayne myself. I miss him when he's gone night after night like this." Startled, Gaby glanced at the woman, trying to read the truth behind the words. There was a sleek, satisfied look to Lorna, and she smiled languorously at Gaby, her glance triumphant. She'd won, she seemed to be saying. Gaby bit the inside of her lip to keep from crying out a denial.

The men were drawing near. Ben had joined them. They looked tired and they were covered with dust. It lay in thick layers in the fold of their clothes and caked itself in their eyebrows and the lines of their faces.

"Hello," Lorna called.

"Hello, Lorna, Mrs. Spencer," Rayne said, touching the brim of his hat.

"How are things going, Ben?" Gaby asked her foreman.

"Better than expected." He took off his hat and wiped at his forehead with a shirt sleeve. "We're going to have a bigger herd than I thought this year."

"Good. When do you leave for the North?"

Ben glanced uneasily at Rayne. "Well, ma'am, as you know, I'd thought to join the Rocking E and the Bar B ranches for our trail drive, but Rayne wants to head west."

"West?" For the first time Gaby looked at Rayne. "The markets are in the North."

"Not all of them, Mrs. Spencer," he said, and Gaby hated the formal sound of her name on his lips. Why was he playing this charade? Lorna grinned. "New Mexico has a better market for us right now. We can take the old Goodnight-Loving trail up over the Pecos."

"That's desert country, long stretches without water, and through Indian Territory," Gaby said, and he wondered how she'd come to know so much about a part of the country she'd never been. Even Lorna seemed surprised at her grasp of the problems.

"That's true," Rayne agreed, "but Goodnight got his cattle through last year by driving them at night as well. We can make it. As for the Indians, we have to go through Indian Territory on the trail north, plus we have to contend with the rustlers and outlaws who patrol the Kansas borders." His voice turned bitter and Gaby knew he hadn't forgotten the beating he'd taken at the hands of the vigilantes.

"I hear a man named Joseph McCoy has opened up a cattle yard in Abilene," Gaby said stubbornly. "The train can ship them east from there."

"It sounds good, but we don't know for sure how it's working out. Don't forget, Kansas imposed a ten-thousand-dollar bond for each herd against damages. That's pretty steep, especially in view of the drop in cattle prices."

"It's better to take our cows where we can sell at any price rather than lose them in the deserts or to the Comanche. And once you get to New Mexico, you don't even know if you can sell them."

Rayne studied Gaby's set face. She was putting up more resistance to the idea than he'd expected. Her arguments were valid and well-thought-out, but there was something more than concern for her herd that kept her eyes from meeting his.

"I already have a contract to deliver three thousand head to Fort Sumner."

"Three thousand head!" Gaby exclaimed.

"The government's got Indians on reservations out there. They need to feed them or the Indians are going to leave and start fighting again. They'll pay us top dollar."

"But if we lose cattle on the way . . ."

"You always lose some cattle. It's a gamble. I'm willing to take it." His voice had a note of finality to it.

"Is it fair of you to expect the rest of us to risk our cattle just because you want to get rich faster?"

"Maybe not," Rayne said slowly. "You can always join up with some other outfit heading north." Now that he'd offered her the option, Gaby didn't want to take it. She couldn't allow her personal anger to jeopardize her fall drive. Everything he'd said about the Kansas market was true. There were many ranchers who didn't trust McCoy and his promise of an Abilene market. Kansas hadn't been kind to the Texas ranchers, and now they suspected a swindle.

Gaby sat considering the things said. Rayne waited quietly, making no more argument in his favor, and perhaps it was that which decided her. She'd bank on Rayne any day. If anyone could get the herd through the western trail, Rayne could.

"We'll drive with you," she said.

The hard lines of Rayne's face relaxed a little. "You won't be sorry," he said, but Gaby barely heard him. She'd already wheeled her horse and was riding away from him.

At first she didn't hear the hoofbeats behind her and when she did, she knew it was Rayne.

She'd run from him once before, she thought, and remembered how they'd nearly made love by the bank of the stream. It would be different this time, she thought and turned to meet him. He nearly ran her down before he brought his horse to a stop. Their legs brushed against each other for a brief moment. His was hard and muscular.

"Gaby, what's wrong? Why are you running away like this?"

"Our business was concluded, Mr. Elliott. I saw no reason to linger."

"I was afraid I might have said something to anger you."

"Would it have mattered?" she snapped impatiently.

"Of course it would have," he answered. "I want to put the past behind us, Gaby, and at least be friends."

"I'd sooner be friends with the devil himself," she cried, and spurred her horse away. Once again she was galloping over the prairie, but this time there were no hoofbeats following her.

Friends, he had said. How dare he speak to her of friendship after all they'd been to each other? Maybe now that Lorna was in his life and his bed, friendship was all he wanted from her, but she wasn't ready for friendship from Rayne Elliott, not yet anyway. Maybe in fifty years, when she was too old to think and feel and remember.

21

Gaby's eyes felt dry and scratchy by the time she'd reached the ranch, as if some of the prairie dust had blown beneath the lids and now scoured against her eyes. Wearily she dismounted and gave her horse to one of the hands and headed for the ranch house. What she needed was a hot bath and some time alone away from all the vexations of the ranch and its problems.

Abigail Spencer met her in the hall. "There you are," she said sweetly. "We'd begun to worry about you. Kevin said you left the roundup ahead of him. We were afraid you'd been thrown or something."

"I'm fine," Gaby answered shortly, thinking Abigail probably wished she *had* been thrown. Tonight, however, Abigail seemed in amiable spirits. She smiled at Gaby warmly.

"I'm having the cook prepare a special supper, since Kevin is here. It's his last night before they leave."

"They're starting the drive tomorrow?" Gaby asked.

"That's what Kevin said," Abigail replied cordially. "Now, dear, you have just enough time to bathe and dress before dinner. I'll have Maria bring you bathwater." She turned toward the kitchen, leaving Gaby to stare at her in openmouthed astonishment. She'd never seen Abigail Spencer be accommodating to anyone. This new sweetness made Gaby uneasy. Thoughtfully she climbed the stairs to her room.

Kevin had taken time to bathe away the prairie dust and had donned one of his eastern suits. He sat at the dinner table, silent and tense, his gaze never meeting Gaby's, ill-at-ease in a suit that no longer fit the breadth of his shoulders. Now and then a sun-browned, work-roughened hand came up to tug at the stiff white collar that dug into his brown neck.

Gaby glanced at him, trying not to give away her amusement. He looked so ridiculously out of place in the dandified suit. The metamorphosis was nearly completed. In a few short months Kevin had grown from a boy to a man, with new dimensions to his physique and his character that he might never had reached in the East. He tugged at the top button of his collar and Gaby thought of suggesting he loosen it, but knew Abigail would disapprove. Kevin glanced up and caught her smile, and as if reading her thoughts, unfastened the collar and gave a deep sigh of relief. Gaby's tinkling laughter was joined by his baritone, and suddenly the tenseness around the table seemed to dissolve.

"Goodness, I fail to see what's so humorous," Abigail said, piqued at being excluded from their private joke.

"It's nothing," Gaby said, pressing a napkin to her lips to still her laughter. Her merry glance flew back to Kevin. It felt good to laugh after the anger and frustration of the afternoon.

"Kevin, I want you to be very careful on this drive. Men get killed."

"I know, I know," he said, casting a quick glance at his mother. He was surprised at Gaby's maternal tone.

Abigail's brows were drawn together. "Perhaps you shouldn't go, Kevin," she said.

"It won't be that dangerous, and I'll be careful."

"Oh, Kevin, do you promise? I will worry about you every moment you're gone. You are my only child. What would I do without you?" Her voice wavered threateningly and Kevin groaned silently. He'd seen his mother's tearful demonstrations before and didn't want to cope with one tonight.

"He'll be safe, Abigail," Gaby replied. "He'll be with Rayne." They weren't exactly the words Kevin would have liked to hear from her. As if sensing this, Gaby hurried on. "I've seen Kevin shoot, and he's one of the best. There will be extra trail hands from every ranch.

Rayne Elliott and Dusty Simmons are two of the best
men in the country."

"You should know, dear," Abigail said with narrowing
eyes, and Gaby caught the double meaning. Unperturbed,
she smiled. She'd known Abigail's sweet mood wouldn't
last for long. Actually, she preferred Abigail this way,
spewing out her nasty innuendos. At least this way Gaby
didn't have to guess what was going on in the woman's
mind.

Kevin sensed the hostility between the two women and
laid his napkin beside his plate. "There's a full moon out
tonight, Gaby. Would you like to step outside and see
it?"

To escape Abigail's company and because she knew to
do so would anger the woman further, Gaby accepted.
"Excuse us, Abigail," she said sweetly, and taking Kevin's arm turned toward the front porch.

To her surprise, Abigail's voice, sweet and falsely maternal, called after them, "Have a good time, children."

Gaby was shocked to realize she was included in Abigail's blessing. What did the woman have up her sleeve
now? Gaby wondered, and stepped out into the moonlight.

It was a beautiful night, the sky velvety black, twin-
kling with the brilliant light of Texas stars. The round
moon looked too perfect. It cast a glow over the ranch
buildings, gilding the edges of the corral fence and the
sagebrush growing on the distant hills. A hush of expectancy lay over the land, and Gaby felt herself caught up
in the beauty of it.

She pressed her hands together and sought to still the
wild, yearning cry that rose within her breast. Where was
Rayne right at this moment? Was he even now lying in
Lorna's arms, saying his farewells before leaving on the
drive? She remembered their last night together before
that first trail drive. How poignant and beautiful it had
been. Gaby had thought she and Rayne would be together forever. Now she knew that forevers didn't always
last.

Kevin moved beside her restlessly and she turned to
him with a smile.

The soft light cast a golden glow on her cheekbones
and lips and along her rounded arms. The scent of her

rose to him on the night air and Kevin wiped his sweaty palms against his trousers and cleared his throat. "Gaby, . . ." he began tentatively.

"Do you know how much I envy you?" she said before he could speak. "Here you are in Texas for only a few months and you can ride and rope and shoot as well as any Texan, and tomorrow you begin a great adventure, going on a trail drive. Sometimes I wish I were a man." Her words shocked him a little.

"I'm glad you're not," he began. "You're much more beautiful as a woman."

"If I were a man I wouldn't have to worry about looking beautiful. I could just worry about doing my job the best way I could. I should try to be like Jessie Walker."

"But she's old and coarse. You could never be like that, Gaby. Besides, you handle the ranch very well."

"As it is now, I can only work from the ranch. I can't go on the trail drive or stay out on the prairie for the roundups."

"You could," Kevin said, somehow feeling guilty and not sure how or why. "You could come on this trail drive. After all, you are the boss."

"That's right, I am," Gaby said, as if considering it; then her shoulders slumped. "It would be wiser if I stayed here. It's what's expected of me."

"You never do the things that are expected of you, though," Kevin replied, thinking to soften his way with a little flattery. "That's one of the things I admire the most about you." He paused and took a deep breath, then forged ahead. "In fact, I admire everything about you, Gaby. I . . . wondered if you . . . you could ever think of me in a kinder light than . . . than . . ." He stammered and paused, stuck on what to say next. Should he plunge in and tell her how he felt about her? Should he go down on one knee and beg her to marry him? He had no prospects and she might think he sought only the ranch. How could he convince her he would ask her to marry him if she possessed nothing except herself and Danny?

"I care a great deal for you, Kevin," she said softly, placing a hand on his sleeve. He could feel the slight weight of it through the worsted. "You know you'll always have a home here. This was your father's ranch and he would be so happy to know you were here."

"Do you think you'll come to love me someday, Gaby?" Kevin stammered.

"I love you now," she answered. "How could I not? You are so like Aaron. You remind me of him in many ways."

"Gaby," Kevin began again, realizing she had misunderstood the import of his words, "I don't want the ranch. No matter what happens with the will, I want us to always be together here on the ranch."

"I want that too, Kevin," Gaby cried happily. "Your father would have wanted you to have your share. There's no need for us to think of the will or abide by it. We can share the ranch. It's big enough to meet all our needs." She paused and smiled at him warmly. "I'm happy we've had this talk, Kevin. It's something I've wanted to tell you from the beginning, but I haven't known how you felt about the ranch. Now I can see that you love it as much as I do. I hope we can always remain as we are, the best of friends."

Kevin felt his heart sink. She hadn't understood what he'd tried so ineptly to say to her. Before he could try again, she moved away from him and stood staring morosely out over the yard. One foot tapped restlessly against the wooden floor.

Friends, Rayne had said. As if they could ever be friends. Gaby's hand gripped the railing. Had he forgotten so quickly the passion between them? Had it meant so little that he could set it aside and turn to another woman? Her foot tapped faster. She thought of the night Rayne had come to the ranch to ask for the right-of-way to take his cattle to the river. She remembered the hunger in their first mating and the passion-filled night that followed. Had Rayne forgotten all that, pushed it aside for the lukewarm emotions of friendship? She would have to remind him, she decided.

She'd waited long enough. Her period of mourning was over, her time for widowhood ended.

Gaby drew back and grinned conspiratorially at Kevin. "I'm going on the trail drive with you," she cried.

Kevin looked at her with gaping mouth. "Are you

sure, Gaby?" he asked tentatively. "You said yourself it's a dangerous trip."

"I'm sure," she answered. "I'll be riding with the best of men. I'll be safe enough. I'd better get ready. We'll have to leave by daybreak to make it to the camp before they leave."

With a final hug, she was gone, and Kevin could hear her running lightly up the stairs. He stayed where he was, watching the moonlight and shaking his head. He couldn't figure Gaby out.

Suddenly he smiled. He'd failed in his attempt to propose to her, but on the trail he'd have weeks, even months of being with her. The opportunity would appear again for him to press his suit, and next time he'd be more successful. He broke into a cheerful whistle and headed for the bunkhouse.

"Gaby, are you coming?" Kevin called. She'd been a whirlwind of activity all morning, but now she dawdled and he couldn't understand why. Loyally he stayed behind to ride with her. The men would have moved the herd out by now, but Kevin felt confident they could still catch up with them. By early afternoon they could see the dust on the horizon, but each time he tried to hurry, Gaby seemed to develop a problem. First she was sure her horse had thrown a shoe. Kevin had gotten off his horse to check, and found that all were intact. Then the horse seemed to have picked up a pebble, so they were forced to walk for a spell, although Kevin could discern no limp. Then, when it seemed they might reach the herd soon, Gaby became ill from the sun and they were forced to pause in the shade of a tree while she slowly sipped water from her canteen and fanned her face with her hat. Kevin was fairly beside himself with impatience. Still, if Gaby were ill, he couldn't leave her alone, and her face *was* flushed and her eyes feverishly bright.

They were forced to ride slowly and stop often for the rest of the afternoon, never able to make any real gains on the herd. The cows had already been bedded for the evening and the campfires lit by the time Kevin and Gaby caught up with the rest of the men. The smell of cooking food assailed their nostrils as they rode into camp. The cookfire was blazing beneath a big pot of stew, and men were hunkered down on the ground eagerly spooning down their portions. They glanced up at the sound of horses.

"Hey, Kevin, where've you been? We've been expecting you to catch up with us all day long." Their questions halted as they caught a glimpse of Gaby riding behind him. Kevin saw one of the men lay aside his plate and get to his feet, his face stern and forbidding in the flickering firelight. He recognized Rayne Elliott and just as quickly recognized that all their problems in getting here had been delaying tactics on Gaby's part. The farther they were from the ranches, the less likelihood there was that Gaby would be forced to return. He might have known, Kevin thought, and barely hid his smile.

"What the devil are you doing here?" Rayne demanded before they'd had a chance to alight.

"Sorry to be so late," Gaby said reasonably, as if there were nothing untoward in her appearance. "We had some trouble with my horse, but he seems to be all right now."

"Gaby—" Rayne began sternly.

"What is that on the fire? It smells delicious. We did without our noon meal and we're both famished, aren't we, Kevin?" She slid out of her saddle and crossed to the fire.

"I sure am," Kevin said uncomfortably, aware that unwittingly he'd been made her accomplice. "I could eat a whole cow by myself."

Rayne glared at him, then followed Gaby to the fire. "What in hell are you doing here?" he demanded of her. He wasn't going for Gaby's act, Kevin could see, but Gaby seemed unperturbed by his anger.

"I'm going on the trail drive," she said offhandedly, and shrugged. "Little Finger, may I have a cup of that coffee?"

"Yes, ma'am," the old cook said, and cackled with glee for no reason at all that Kevin could see.

"It's too dangerous for a woman to go on a trail drive. What are you thinking of in coming out here like this?"

"It's no more dangerous for me than it is for you or Kevin or any one of the other men," Gaby said equably, accepting a plate of food and a tin coffee cup from Little

Finger. Someone cleared an upturned keg for her and Gaby sat down as regal as a queen.

"I forbid it," Rayne said. "You'll have to ride back in the morning." He rounded on Kevin. "And you'll have to take her back, since you were fool enough to bring her out here in the first place." Rayne's blue eyes were icy enough to cut as he pinned his gaze on the young man.

Kevin blanched in spite of himself. "Yes, sir," he said miserably.

"Now, just a minute," Gaby said. She was on her feet, the cup and plate set aside, her hands planted on her hips, eyes glaring with fiery determination. "First of all, you can't forbid me anything, Rayne Elliott. You have no say-so over me, and as for Kevin, he didn't bring me here. No man takes me from one place to another. I take myself. I allowed Kevin to ride with me so he wouldn't be riding across strange country on his own. Last of all, I intend to stay with this cattle drive all the way to Fort Sumner. One-third of these cows are Spencer cows and I intend to see to my investment."

"You can't," Rayne began again.

"I can and I will," she replied firmly, her head thrown back, her small chin thrust forward. Kevin thought he'd never seen a more magnificent woman. Rayne thought he'd never seen a more stubborn one. He towered over her, staring at her with the same icy blue gaze that earlier had intimidated Kevin, but Gaby never flinched.

For the first time Kevin was aware of the sparks that seemed to fill the air between the two of them, and not understanding them, he took the horses away. He led them to the makeshift corral of ropes and began unsaddling them. Gaby didn't need him. She had things well in hand, he thought, and suddenly felt out of his element.

Word of a woman on the drive spread quickly around the campsite, and the hands went one at a time to the coffeepot just to get a glimpse of her. It was the Texas Angel, all right. They'd seen her out at the roundup site, but they'd never dreamed she'd be accompanying them. Somehow her presence made this drive even more special. It was true that women didn't normally go on trail drives, but the men had no objections to her.

Rayne sensed the mood of the men and was surprised.

On a trail drive men could be spooked almost as easily as cows over some things. Some men might have thought it bad luck to have a woman on the drive, but if any objected to her presence, none came forward to say so.

Once Rayne was over his anger at her unexpected appearance, he had to admit he didn't really object either. He lay in his bedroll watching the tiny mound that was Gaby, asleep in her own tumble of blankets, and found himself smiling. She never ceased to amaze him. Suddenly he felt lighthearted. For the next few weeks he'd get to see her every day.

In the days that followed, Gaby settled into the routine of the trail drive, rising at daybreak to drink strong black coffee and eat a hearty breakfast of sourdough bread and potatoes.

Every morning the cowboys got the cattle moving, stringing them out in an unbroken line so they wouldn't injure one another with their horns, yet keeping them close enough to let them feel each other.

"Hiah, hiah," the men called to keep the drags moving. Gaby noticed the men constantly changed positions, sometimes riding at the side of the herds and sometimes at the back. Soon she learned that only the best riders were allowed in the front, riding point, while the others must take their turns riding at the rear, a position not to be envied, for the man who drew drag position rode in the dust of the whole herd all day long, urging on the lazy, uncooperative steers.

Gaby learned about the cows too, finding out that they had their personalities and their order of importance and rank. She learned that steers had traveling companions, and when they were separated, they raised their heads to get wind of each other and bawled plaintively until they were together again. She learned that certain cows had followers, and a good lead steer was worth saving and taking back to the ranch for the next trail drive.

She came to recognize the flighty two-year heifers, which were the most difficult to handle on a trail drive and sometimes ended up in the stewpot if they couldn't be settled. She identified the muleys, which where born hornless and were never quite accepted by the other cows, and the loners, which wandered up one side of the herd and down the other, looking for the never lost, and she sympathized with the outcasts, which were rejected by all, even the muleys, and usually ended up at the back of the herd with the rest of the drags.

The days were hard from the moment they rolled out of their bedrolls and splashed cold water on their faces until they spread their oil slickers and gratefully lowered their weary bodies onto them again at night. They slept in their clothes and ate in shifts. They rode six hours from breakfast to their first stop at noontime. After the noon meal they picked fresh horses and rode for another five or six hours. In the beginning they made thirty miles a day, but as cattle, horses, and men tired and the trail worsened, they were grateful for whatever progress they made.

Sometimes they made only ten or fifteen miles a day beneath the burning sun, and Gaby began to lose all sense of perspective. It seemed they had always dragged their weary bodies into the saddle to push the bawling, recalcitrant cows a few miles before falling onto the ground to sleep a few precious hours. But as tired as she was, she knew the men were feeling even more tired, for it fell to them to bed down the cows each night, seeing they were watered and given fresh grass, then riding in shifts through the night in case they were spooked and stampeded.

Gaby seldom saw Rayne during those days, although he seemed to be everywhere, tending to all details, pushing himself harder than he pushed his men. He was avoiding her. Patiently she bided her time.

Early in the drive, Gaby became aware of one practice that she would never be able to accept. Each morning the cowboys moved among the herd shooting the calves born during the night. The newborns couldn't keep up and they weakened their mothers. Each morning Gaby sat gulping her coffee and flinching at the sound of gunfire.

One morning Rayne came upon Gaby as she sat with tears on her cheeks, listening to the shots that spoke of the ending of life for still another baby calf. His blue eyes searched the pale face and the lips clamped tight to keep from making a sound. "It's not as easy to be a rancher as you thought, is it, Gaby?" he asked quietly.

She raised her tearstained face to him. "I'll manage," she said stonily.

Rayne swirled the coffee in his cup, remembering how she'd once fainted at the roundup. She'd changed a lot, but there were some things about Gaby that would never change. He wouldn't want them to.

"I'm getting along just fine," she said proudly, and wiped at her cheeks with her hands.

"I believe you are," Rayne answered, and tossed the dregs of his cup in the fire.

The plaintive cries of the bereft mothers rent the air. The men would have to yoke them to steers to keep them from trying to turn back and find their calves. They made a pitiful sound.

Restlessly Rayne got up, then turned back to the woman huddled before the fire. The tears were rolling down her cheeks again. "Why did you come, Gaby?" he demanded impatiently. "This is no place for a woman."

"I came to keep an eye on my herd," Gaby said, and scrubbed at her cheeks.

"If you didn't trust me, you should have sent your herd north."

"I do trust you." She'd offended him, and was sorry for it. Her dark eyes met his, and in spite of himself, Rayne couldn't look away. His chest felt tight.

"Then what's the real reason you're here?" he demanded, his voice ragged.

Gaby stared up at him and decided the truth was best. "I came because you're here," she said softly. "I came to be with you for a while."

Her answer stunned him. He hadn't expected it, but when had Gaby done what he expected? Wonderment ran though him like an unleashed tide, and he struggled to hold his feelings in rein. "This is no good, Gaby," he berated her. "You shouldn't have come. It will only give people more to talk about."

"Let them," Gaby cried, springing to her feet. "What can they say that will hurt me? I'm a cattlewoman doing what hundreds of other ranchers are doing, looking after my interests. They need never know that my interest is you."

"They'll know. Nothing escapes people like Thad Martin and Abigail Spencer. They make it their business to find out. They'll hurt you with their gossip."

"Are you sure my good name is your only concern? Maybe you still believe all those lies about me and Thad and Slade . . ."

Her words caught him by surprise. "No, I know they were lies." There was no time to hide his true feelings for her. They were all there for her to read at a glance. He couldn't pretend any more, so he chose retreat, heading for his horse and the less complex problems of getting three thousand head of cattle over a nearly impossible trail.

But Gaby wouldn't give up so easily. "Rayne . . ." She hurried across the rough ground toward him, and when she was standing close, too close for his comfort, she pierced him with the unflinching directness of her gaze. "If there is gossip about my coming on this trail drive, if people say the worst they can about us"—she paused and took a deep breath—"I hope every bit of it is true."

He left her then, striding toward his horse, while inside his head a wild, joyous refrain repeated itself. Gaby still loved him. Hope beat in his breast and fear licked at his heels. He had a second chance with Gaby. Should he take it, no matter what the cost to her? Could he bear not to take it? His mind was in a turmoil, but his heart was lighter than it had been for nearly two years.

"Hiah!" he shouted, slapping a cow on the rump with his hat. Then he surprised the rest of the hands by whistling a merry, jaunty little tune.

22

The drive west toward the mountains had been an easy one. The herd had caused no trouble so far. They reached the cross timbers, an area of post oaks and scrubby pines. Now the men stayed alert. They were in Comanche territory.

"They know we're here," Dusty said grimly, and Gaby glanced around at the unrevealing canyon walls. Were there really Indians skulking there behind boulders and trees? Try as she might, she could catch no glimpse of movement. Still, she could feel the tension mounting among the crew, and they seemed to prod the cows a little harder.

Rayne came riding up, his face grim and worried. "Gaby, I want you to go back and ride with Little Finger," he ordered in a tone of voice that brooked no argument.

"Are they out there?"

"Probably. I don't want to take chances."

Before she could turn back to the chuck wagon, one of the line riders galloped toward them. "Rayne, look up yonder," he called even before he'd brought his horse to a stop.

All eyes turned to the western slopes, where a line of Indians sat like sentinels on the rim of the horizon. Fear made Gaby's heart leap. The men around her automatically gripped their guns.

"Tell the men to keep their rifles ready, but don't fire

350

unless they attack," Rayne ordered. "Keep the cattle moving."

"Yes, sir," the cowboy said, and spurred his horse into a gallop back along the line.

"Will they attack?" Gaby asked breathlessly.

Rayne never took his gaze from the slope. "I don't know," he replied. "Let's not give them an excuse."

All day they were stalked by the Comanche. As the herd moved, the Indians would ride forward and line themselves up again, so their number seemed greater and the line stretched for miles across the hills.

Supper that night was an uneasy affair. The weary cowboys, their nerves stretched taut from the uncertain danger of the day, ate quickly, casting quick glances over their shoulders at the dark plains. With few words they emptied their plates, gulped down their coffee, and saddled fresh horses for extra night duty. Some settled themselves into bedrolls on the ground.

"How can they sleep at a time like this?" Gaby exclaimed to Kevin.

"You do what you have to," he replied. "We may not have a chance to sleep later."

"Kevin's right," Dusty said. "You should try to get some rest while you can. You may need it later on."

"Make sure there are extra men on the remuda," Rayne said to his foreman.

Dusty nodded. "Those Comanche have a love of horseflesh, especially if they've stolen it from someone else."

"Why do they steal when the plains are full of wild horses?" Gaby asked.

"They want to steal them. They count coup against their enemies. It brings them great honor among their people," Rayne replied.

"D'you reckon that's Quanah out there?" Dusty asked.

Rayne shook his head. "I hope so."

"They say he ain't as bad as the others. He's more civilized and don't kill and scalp like some of them other Comanche."

"So I've heard," Rayne answered. "It may be because he's half-white." His glance flashed across the fire to Gaby, and for a sickening moment he imagined her captured by the Comanche, her dark hair torn from her scalp, or worse yet, her sweet body used by some savage warrior. She was too little and fragile. She couldn't endure the kind of abuse the Comanche were said to heap on their white captives. He should have sent her back when she first showed up in camp. Cursing, he rose from the fire and walked away, Gaby's startled gaze following him.

"It'll be all right, Gaby," Dusty said, and rising from his haunches, headed for the remuda.

"The Comanche took about a hundred head last night," Rayne said the next morning as he crouched before the fire.

"A hundred head?" Gaby cried. "Are you going after them?"

He shook his head. "I don't intend to tangle with half the Comanche nation over a few head of cattle."

"It isn't just a few head of cattle," Gaby said. "Those hundred cows would have brought us five thousand dollars at Fort Sumner. That's a lot of money."

"I expect I know that better than you, Gaby," he replied quietly. "It's hard to see five thousand dollars ride off across the prairie. I need every penny I can get to keep the ranch going, but it's not worth risking the lives of my men."

"You're right," Gaby conceded. "I wasn't considering the danger the Comanche pose for us."

Rayne's eyes softened as he looked at her. "We'll probably lose more cattle before the Comanche are through with us," he said abruptly, and turned away quickly to toss the contents of his cup on the ground. "Stay near the wagon today." He was gone so quickly she could think of nothing to say that might hold him there.

All day they were stalked by the Comanche, who stayed within sight but never approached them. Again nerves grew frazzled from the strain. As if sensing the unrest of their handlers, the cattle grew fractious as well, requiring a more diligent effort from the cowboys to keep them moving forward. At midday the men took turns stopping at the chuck wagon for a quick meal. It was while Rayne and Gaby and a few others had paused to eat that the Indians rode down on them. Coffee cups went flying as the men scrambled for their guns and dropped behind any available cover.

"Don't fire," Rayne shouted, and prayed the men with the herd wouldn't get trigger-happy. He stood in the clearing near the chuck wagon, his shoulders square, his head high and proud. There was no sign of fear about him. It was the only way to meet a Comanche.

"Gaby . . ." Rayne called her name, but his voice was calm. He never took his eyes from the approaching Indians. "Get under the chuck wagon," he ordered, and his tone held such authority that she did as he bade.

From her hiding place Gaby watched as a dozen or so Indians rode into camp. The rest of the tribe sat in full view back on the rim of the hill, their very presence a reminder to the cowboys of what would happen if their leader were harmed. With morbid interest Gaby studied the Indian warriors.

They were dressed in buckskin leggings and calico shirts. Their long black hair was held back by twisted bands of rawhide around their foreheads. They wore no war paint and in fact looked somewhat ragged. Their weathered brown faces, even those of the younger men, looked tired and worn. How had they gained such a fierce reputation? Gaby wondered, but then she noted the pride with which each man held himself and the ease with which he sat his horse. She remembered that someone had said the Comanche were excellent horsemen. They rode into camp at full tilt and brought their horses to a halt scant inches from Rayne. He could feel the steam of the horses' breaths and didn't even flicker an eyelash.

"I am Little Horse," the leader spoke.

"I am Rayne. We are friends to the Comanche," he continued.

"The Comanche also wish to be friends," the Indian said smoothly. "That is why we let you travel through Comanche land."

"You do us a great service. How may we repay you?"

The Indian looked off into the distance at the line of cattle moving forward. Soon they would be out of Comanche land. "You have many cattle," Little Horse said finally. "The cattle eat our grass, drink our water—

grass and water that feed the buffalo. Without these things the buffalo will not come to our hunting grounds."

"I know the importance of the buffalo to the Comanche people," Rayne replied

"The white man's cows do not give the Comanche the things he needs, the way the buffalo do. There are no warm hides to make our lodges, or robes to protect us from the winds of winter. The cow's meat does not sustain us or give us courage and strength as the wild buffalo does."

Rayne waited patiently while the Indian spoke his complaints.

"Still, we try to live in peace with the white man. We let him cross our lands safely and we ask only a few cows in return."

"I will pay what Little Horse asks, for I have heard he is a fair man," Rayne answered, and the Indians relaxed in their saddles.

"It is done," Little Horse said with a flourish. He gave Rayne a magnanimous grin that revealed gaps in his blackened teeth.

"I'll have my men cut out the cattle you want," Rayne said, and turned to his horse. Together the men rode out toward the herd.

"Whooee! Let's get out of here while the gettin's good," Little Finger said, and kicked dirt over the cookfire. He began packing things. He would have to ride long and hard through the afternoon before setting up a place to stop for the night. He hoped fervently they'd be out of Indian country by then.

Gaby mounted her horse and trailed along behind Rayne and Little Horse, still curious about the fierce-looking Indians. The braves rode into the herd, picking out prime steers. For not thinking much of cattle, they certainly had a good eye for the best ones, Gaby observed. Again and again the Indian braves rode into the herd, and at times it seemed they were deliberately chousing the herd, trying to stir them up into a stampede. Adroitly Rayne and his men settled the cows and kept them in a line moving relentlessly forward.

Little Horse remained on the side watching the proceedings with bright, expectant eyes. For a while it seemed as if the men would never stop cutting away cows, but at last they had gathered a satisfactory number and some of the braves headed them out across the hills. Their shrill cries rose on the air. Little Horse raised his hand in a final farewell and he and his men rode after the others.

"They must have taken another hundred head," Gaby observed.

"At least," Rayne said, eyes narrowed as he stared after the ragtag band.

"Another five thousand dollars lost on the prairie," Gaby said.

Rayne glanced at her. "If it'll make you feel any better, just think of where those cows are going. Like as not, hidden somewhere back in those hills and cross timbers is a tribe of half-starved women and children. Winter's coming on and they have no place to go except to a white man's reservation. They won't go there because they've seen how even more of their people die of starvation."

"I didn't realize," Gaby admitted. They rode together in companionable silence, each thinking of the ragged condition of the Indians and their ponies, and of how the shrinking prairie had less and less room for the Comanche as the white men moved in. Sympathetic to their plight, Gaby glanced at the horizon where Little Horse and his men had disappeared. With a start she realized that for the first time in days, they were without the menacing presence of the Indians.

"They've gone," she said.

"They're still there, just out of sight," Rayne said, and seemed untroubled by the thought.

"Will they be back?"

"Tonight." Rayne looked at the sky and the land around. "Tonight they'll come back to steal some more cows."

"We've given them what they asked for," Gaby cried in outrage. "Why would they steal more?"

"Because it's the way of the Comanche, to steal cows and some of the horses if they can."

Rayne's predictions were right. That night they lost another hundred head to the Comanche, but the Indians never revealed themselves to the trail drivers again and by the end of the following day the herd was well away from Comanche territory. Everyone breathed a sigh of relief. Rayne was glad they'd gotten through with so little loss. Gaby consoled herself over the loss of fifteen thousand dollars with the thought that small children would be able to survive the cruel winter months ahead.

Only Kevin seemed to take everything in stride and with an endless amount of enthusiasm. Every day, no matter what his duties on the trail, he came to ride beside Gaby for a while and talk to her about the drive. This had been his first encounter with Indians, and his eyes glowed. He told her of the Comanche's past deeds of bravery and honor. She was surprised at how much he'd learned about them and about trail driving in a few short weeks.

She enjoyed his company. Often he made her laugh with his observations. Sometimes as they sat around the campfire chatting about the day's events, Gaby would glance up and find Rayne's gaze fixed on them, his expression tight-lipped and bleak. When he saw that Gaby was watching him, he would glance away again, but the angry, unhappy look seemed etched on his face.

She didn't realize the cause of that anger until one night Kevin and she walked away from the campfires and strolled along the edge of the stream. The moon was huge in the black sky and Gaby lifted her face to it, welcoming its gentle light after the harshness of the prairie sun. Kevin fidgeted beside her. He cleared his throat several times as if he were about to say something, then fell silent again. Gaby didn't prod him. She was content to stroll along in silence. It had been a tiring day.

Suddenly Kevin swung around and gripped her shoulders tensely. "Gaby, Gaby . . ." he repeated, and swallowed.

"My goodness, Kevin, what is it?" she asked, glancing around. Before she could guess his intentions, he pulled her forward and planted a kiss on her unresponsive lips. Gaby was so stunned she stood still in his arms. Her silence further encouraged Kevin in his advances.

"Gaby . . ." he said. His voice was high and tense, but he felt more confident. She hadn't pushed him away or slapped his face as he'd expected. "I have something important I want to ask you," he said.

Before she could answer or make any protest at his embrace, a deep voice disturbed the hushed, expectant silence. "It's too dangerous to be walking out here alone." Rayne stepped out of the dark shadows.

Kevin sprang back. Even in the dark, Gaby could feel the heat of his embarrassment.

"You know better than this, Spencer," Rayne went on. "We're still close enough to Indian Territory to practice some common sense. You shouldn't have brought Gaby out here."

"Yes, sir," Kevin gulped. Gaby felt sorry for the stammering young man.

"Hadn't you better get back? Dusty's looking for you. You're to ride first shift tonight."

"Yes, sir," Kevin said, his eyes darting from Gaby to Rayne and back again. "Will you see Gaby back to the fire?"

"Yes, go along now," Rayne ordered, and the boy hurried away. In the shaft of moonlight, Gaby watched Rayne's face and for the first time understood his stiffness toward her and Kevin on the trail. Rayne was jealous of Kevin. After Kevin's actions tonight, Gaby conceded, he might have reason. Kevin was growing far more serious than she'd realized.

"You'd better get back," Rayne said gruffly, and without offering an arm led her back toward the firelight.

"Rayne," Gaby began hesitantly, "about what you saw back there. It meant nothing to me." She saw his lips tighten. "I didn't realize Kevin felt that way about me. I don't return his feelings."

"That's too bad," Rayne said. "He seems decent enough to me. You might want to reconsider. It would be a good match."

"Not if I don't love him."

"Folks are speculating you two will get together."

"They're wrong," Gaby replied, putting a hand on his sleeve to still his long strides. She was breathless from trying to keep up. "It's you I love, Rayne." She saw the fire leap in his eyes; then he turned away, his long legs carrying him the rest of the way to the campfire, but she heard his groan, low and desperate-sounding.

The mood had lightened since they'd left Comanche

territory. The two chuck wagons kept the men fed well, and everyone did his job.

Their first trouble came one night when they'd halted in sight of the first mountain range. Rayne expected to take the cattle through the pass the next morning and down into the salt valleys beyond. There would be little water there. The trail would grow more difficult from here on.

The air was sultry as they bedded down the cows. The more experienced cowboys cast a wary eye at the ominous sky. Rayne seemed worried too, and posted extra men to ride night guard.

Gaby made her bed under the chuck wagon and settled down beneath her oil slicker. She fell asleep to the rumble of thunder as it crept closer. She woke to a tumultuous sound that set the earth to trembling beneath her. Thunder, she thought, and looked out from under the wagon. Jagged lightning rent the blackness of the sky, illuminating the prairie with an eerie blue light. What Gaby saw in that moment made her heart quake with fear. A tangled mass of bodies and flashing horns surged across the prairie.

Stampede!" someone shouted, but the sleeping men had already thrown aside their bedrolls and were pulling on their boots. Other men worked frantically saddling horses. Rayne raced by on his horse shouting at his men; then he was lost in the blackness of the night. Lightning scored the ground again, and the aftermath of its zigzag path hung in the air like a warning of danger.

"Turn them away from the camp," Rayne yelled, and Gaby could see that the crazed cows had veered and were heading in her direction.

Instinctively, she moved, scrambling from beneath the wagon. There was no time for her to get to her horse, so she fairly leapt into the chuck wagon, praying the tough bois-d' arc wood of which it was made would be strong enough to withstand the onslaught of stampeding cattle.

The cows thundered into the campsite, trampling the abandoned bedrolls beneath their hooves. The pot hook and coffeepot clanked in protest as they were knocked to the ground and trampled beyond recognition. The squat, solid wagon rocked wildly as the maddened cows brushed against it. Gaby screamed and hid her head in her arms, envisioning herself trampled as the coffeepot had been. But the wagon remained upright and the whistling, shouting men managed to turn the cattle yet again so they raced away from camp, back over the open prairie they'd just traveled.

"Gaby, Gaby . . ." She could hear Rayne's frantic voice and crawled to the front end of the wagon. "I'm here," she cried. "I'm all right."

Rayne raced to the wagon, his eyes terror-stricken. When he caught a glimpse of her, he climbed up on the wagon seat and pulled her against him, cradling her against his chest. "My God, I thought you'd been trampled," he said raggedly against her hair.

Her cheek rested against his heart and she could hear its wild, erratic pounding. Her arms wrapped around his lean middle. Everything had happened so quickly she'd hardly had time to think, and even now the aftermath of fear hadn't hit her. She lay against Rayne, taking comfort in the nearness of him, wondering if he'd realized yet just how much of his feelings he'd revealed.

"Are you all right?" she said softly, one small hand patting his back soothingly.

His hands gripped her head gently to pull her away from him so he could look into her face. "I don't know what I would have done if something had happened to you," he whispered, and his mouth lowered to hers in a desperate kiss. "I love you, Gaby."

Gaby answered him with sweet, joyous kisses. Her heart seemed about to burst with happiness. He loved her. He'd said the words. He pressed urgent kisses on her cheeks and throat and mouth while lightning crackled above.

Common sense returned to him. "I have to see to the cattle," he said, reluctantly pulling her arms from his waist. "We'll be rounding them up for days if we can't get them stopped. Stay here with Little Finger. You'll be safe. When I get back, we'll talk."

"I'll be here."

Where could she go—but they both knew it was a pledge of something more between them. Rayne climbed back on his horse while Gaby sat on the high seat watching him. Another shaft of lightning lit the night.

"Get back in the wagon," he shouted, worrying over all the things that might befall her while he was gone. Gaby watched him ride away. Raindrops fell on the wagon canvas, then picked up in intensity until the hills and mountains were obscured by a thick curtain of rain. Gaby huddled back under the canvas, feeling undaunted by the gray veil of rain that isolated her. Rayne had said he loved her. The world beyond the wagon seemed as bright as the sunniest day.

Impatiently she waited for the men to return. The night gave way to day, although the rain continued to fall. The hours passed and the waiting grew harder. Now and then a man brought in a small bunch of cows, grabbed a bit to eat, and headed out again, but there was no sign of Rayne and the main herd.

"Them cattle's probably scattered from here all the way back to Waco," Little Finger said glumly.

Late in the afternoon Gaby wandered down to the stream and in the privacy afforded by the thick bushes stripped and bathed. Then she washed out her riding clothes and hung them to dry on the bushes. She sat on a patch of grass in her lacy bloomers and camisole, letting the afternoon sun dry her hair. Rayne found her there. She sprang up, a joyous cry of greeting falling silent on her lips as she took in his weary eyes and dust-encrusted face.

"Did you get the herd back?" she asked quietly.

"Most of them," he answered wearily, and slapped his hat against his pants leg. A cloud of dust rose. "The men are bringing them back now." He paused, not meeting her eyes, and Gaby's heart sank. Instinctively she knew what was coming. "I've talked to Dusty and he's agreed to take you back to the ranch."

"I won't go."

"You have to, Gaby. Last night proved how dangerous these trail drives are. You were almost killed. I shouldn't have allowed you to stay in the first place."

"You had no choice. I made my decision then, and it still stands. I'm staying."

"Gaby, don't be so god-awful stubborn about this. The

trail gets rougher now. There's no water; there're snakes and Indians and there's no guarantee that the cattle won't stampede again."

"There are no guarantees about anything," she said. "I could be killed on my way back to the ranch. We'd be traveling back through Comanche territory."

"There's less danger there than here. You'd travel light and fast and at night. The Comanche wouldn't bother you. It's cattle they want."

"I'm not going," she answered implacably. He looked at the stubborn tilt of her chin and knew it was useless to argue. "If there's danger for you, I want to share it," she said softly, and the look in her eyes undid his resolve. How could she do that? he wondered briefly. His mind had been made up to send her home whether she wanted to go or not. Now once again she was to have her way.

Gracefully she moved around a fallen log and walked toward him. He was aware of her slim, perfect body in its scanty attire. He could see the shadow of her nipples through the thin chemise, and the sight stirred his blood. He looked away, but she wouldn't let him ignore her. She took the hat from him and tossed it on the ground, then turned to the buttons of his shirt.

"You look exhausted, hot, and dirty," she said softly, and her voice was as soothing as her hands. "You're going to bathe in this stream and rest for a while." Her soft hands were sliding across the bare skin of his chest, pushing the shirt over his shoulders and down his arms.

Rayne felt a stirring in his loins and knew he was too tired to act on it. He groaned in his chest. "Gaby . . ." he protested weakly.

"Shh, my love, my darling," she crooned. "You're just going to bathe, that's all." Her hands went to the buckle at his waist. He felt the weight of his gunbelt leave his hips and heard the thud as it hit the ground at his feet. Now his pants were loosened, and soft, gentle hands glided them down his hips. He could feel the brush of her cool hands against the feverish skin of his hard thighs and his shaft quickened with desire.

Gently she pushed him back against the grass, still crooning to him in half-snatches of words, their meaning unimportant, for it was the soft singsong of her voice that

lured him with her siren's song. His body shivered in the
hot air and he knew it was from anticipation, but Gaby
seemed not to notice. She knelt above him, her hands
tugging at his dusty boots and pulling his pants down
over the long legs and feet until he lay nude before her.
He watched her face as she looked at him, saw the desire
growing in her eyes, but now she took one hand and
pulled him back to his feet. Willingly he followed. He
was her slave, here to do her bidding, without a will of
his own.

Gaby led him to the water and waded in beside him,
mindless of the dampness that crept up the cloth of her
bloomers, making the thin material cling to the curve of
her thighs and buttocks. She turned him about in the
water, urging him in her crooning voice to swim, and he
struck out across the shallow, narrow stream. The water
was cold, washing down from the mountains, and it re-
vived him. Side by side they swam; stroke to stroke she
matched him, and then they swam back, floating on their
backs, staring up at the innocently blue sky. They clambered out and Gaby led Rayne back to the grassy bed
where she'd lain before. Gently she pressed him back.

"Sleep now," she crooned. "Rest, my darling." She
hovered above him, the tips of her wet hair brushing
against his chest, the outline of her small, perfect breasts
visible through the shimmering wet chemise. Desire surged
through him hot and urgent, and the slave turned and
became the master.

His hand reached out to her, pulling her down on top
of him. He could feel the coolness of the wet cloth
between their heated bodies. His mouth claimed hers,
urgent and demanding, and after the first startled moment she made no resistance to him. He held her against
him, his questing hands exploring the tiny, womanly shape,
gliding over the firmness of her buttocks, the curve of her
hips, the daintiness of her rib cage, and finally to the
fullness of her breasts. Grasping her at the waist, he slid
her upward, feeling her body slide along his hardened
shaft. Now her breasts were at his mouth, and he sucked
the taut nipples through the wet cloth. Gaby moaned and
writhed on him, her slender legs parting to fall on either
side of him. Now the moistness he felt against him was

not the coldness of the cloth, but the hot, throbbing sweetness of Gaby herself.

Impatiently the wet cloth separating them was pushed aside. He thrust upward into the moistness and heard her sigh of delight. He suckled the other nipple, holding her captive above him, and then his body quickened and he began to move against her. Gaby sat up, arching her body, her face lifted to the sky, her teeth flashing in a smile of ecstasy.

Too soon. It was going much too quickly, he thought, but the pulsating warmth of her demanded its own response and he couldn't refuse. He felt the whirling giddiness take hold of him and felt the answering passion that exploded between them, carrying them for a time beyond the mountains and prairies before leaving them to drift slowly back to the small patch of grass beside a mountain stream.

Gaby lay across him, gasping for breath. Gently he stroked her wet hair and soft, smooth shoulder, and finally they slept. When he woke later, Rayne could hear the sound of the herd in the distance and the clank of metal against the pot irons as Little Finger called the men to eat. Rayne hadn't eaten all day but the hunger he felt now was not to be assuaged by food. He looked at the sleeping girl who still lay across his chest and gently kissed her awake. He wanted to see her eyes darken with passion again in that moment before she lost touch with the earth and soared. He wanted Gaby warm and giving as she had been earlier.

It was as if the time they'd been apart had never existed. Her eyes opened and she smiled and stretched languorously. Her sleepy gaze widened as she felt his throbbing arousal. Her eyes met his and she smiled. Rayne rolled over, cushioning her against the soft grass, and gently lowered his body to the flowerlike sweetness of her.

"Gaby," he breathed, "I love you."

"I love you too, my darling," she whispered, and pulled him down to her.

23

Gaby opened her eyes and looked around. The sound of water running swiftly over stones brought her wide-awake. She was still by the stream, rolled in Rayne's bedroll, but he was gone. She glanced around. He must have gone to check on his men and the cattle, she thought, and lay back, snuggling beneath the blankets. They still carried the warmth of his body. She lay dreaming of Rayne until a restlessness to see him claimed her. She leapt up and pulled on her clothes.

As she approached the camp, she could see men gathered around the fire and could hear the low murmur of their voices. She placed Rayne's bedroll on the front of the chuck wagon and walked to the fire.

"We lost one of the water barrels," Little Finger was saying. "Musta fallen off when them cows brushed against the wagon, and they trampled it to smithereens."

"Is the other one all right?" Rayne asked. Lines of worry creased his face.

"It 'pears so," Little Finger said.

"Fill it," Rayne ordered, "as much as you can. Fill all the pots and pans that'll hold water. Tell the men to make sure their canteens are full. We're going to need every drop of water we can carry out there." He turned his gaze in the direction of the Middle Concho, the harsh salt desert. Despite the Indians and the stampede they'd experienced thus far this was the most dangerous portion of the journey, for it was out there on the hot, white dust plains that the sun leeched men and beasts of their sanity and their lives. The rest of the hands remained silent as their eyes followed the direction of Rayne's gaze. They were all aware of the danger. Most of them dreaded this portion of the journey.

"Little Finger . . ." Rayne turned back to the short, wiry cook. "Make sure you have enough food cooked up for the next three days. We won't be stopping until we have to, and then only for a short while. Most of the time we'll eat in the saddle."

"I'm way ahead of you," the old man said. "Gaby and me cooked up a batch yesterday. We're ready to roll."

"That's all for now." Rayne dismissed his men and walked across the clearing to stand before Gaby. "Are you sure you want to go?" he asked. "It's going to be tough and dangerous out there."

"I'm sure," Gaby replied. "Don't worry about me. I'm tougher than I look."

Rayne smiled and couldn't resist brushing a finger against her rounded cheek. It pleased him just to look at her. His hand fell to her shoulder.

Gaby could feel the heat of his touch through her shirt. It was strong and reassuring. "I'm not afraid when I'm with you," she said softly. The grim lines in his face lifted as he smiled. Then with a final squeeze of her shoulder he was gone. Gaby watched him walk away and all the love she felt was there on her face. Kevin stood watching her and she knew he had seen the little exchange between Rayne and her.

"Kevin . . ." she began helplessly. She hated to think she'd hurt him.

"It was him all along, wasn't it?" he demanded. "He's the reason you came on this cattle drive." The truth of his words was so evident she couldn't deny them. Without waiting for any further explanation, he whirled and ran to his horse.

Regretfully Gaby watched as he mounted and rode away. He was hurt, but he'd get over it. Sighing, she went to wash up and brush her hair into a braid.

Creosote bushes and greasewood gave way to yucca, ocotillo, and cactus as they moved away from the foothills and down into the barren desert basin. Soon all sign

of vegetation disappeared, unable to survive in the white
alkaline dust. Strong winds picked up the dry, powdery
dust and flung it against them as if to drive them back
along the trail. They rode with heads down, their bandannas knotted over the lower parts of their faces. Still
the gritty dust crept beneath their clothes, mingling with
their sweat and burning their skin. Gaby pulled at her
dust-laden shirt and longed for the stream where she and
Rayne had bathed.

The white dust settled over horse and man and lay
across the backs of the cattle so they took on a ghostlike
appearance as they plodded across the wasteland. Wearily Gaby clung to her saddle, determined not to make a
complaint. The men had their hands full trying to keep
the herd moving forward. The thirsty cattle tried vainly
to turn back to the last watering hole they remembered,
but the line drivers were there prodding them in place. If
any of the cattle wandered away now, they would be left
behind. The men couldn't risk the delay to look for
them. They had to make the Pecos River before they all
died from lack of water.

As hot as the days were, once the sun had set, the
nights turned cold. They rode hunched in their saddles,
traveling straight through the nights, grateful for some
surcease from the heat of the day. Rayne allowed them
to rest only a few brief hours before he prodded them
onward.

The second day out, they began to pass small sluggish
streams and stagnant watering holes so poisoned by alkali
that the cows would have died if they drank. The cowhands worked untiringly to keep the cows in line, but
now and then a few broke away and ran to drink. They
were left lying on the banks among the bleached bones of
other unfortunate beasts, their sides heaving for air as
they waited for death to claim them.

"How are you holding up?" Rayne asked, riding close
to Gaby. He was covered with a layer of white dust. It
lay in the weary creases of his face and lightened his dark
hair. Gaby knew she must look the same. Lurking in the
dark blue depths of his eyes was worry for her.

"I'll make it," she reassured him. His hand reached for
hers and for a brief moment they clung together, riding

side by side, remembering the night they'd shared so recently. The contact was comforting. Rayne's strength flowed to her through his hard, lean hand.

Mercilessly Rayne pushed the herd onward, and on the third day, the bawling cattle picked up their pace.

"Must be getting near the Pecos," Dusty said. "Cattle can smell water nigh on to ten miles away." The pace quickened more, and by the end of the day they were nearing the deep banks of the river.

"Hold 'em back," Rayne called, and Gaby wondered why he didn't allow the poor thirsty cattle to drink at will. As if reading her puzzlement, Little Finger explained, "Them banks is steep, and if them cows have their way, they'll plunge over the banks too fast. We'll have drowned cows on our hands."

Gaby watched as the men worked to maintain their control over the frantic, thirst-crazed cattle, whose bellows drowned out the whistles and cries of the cowboys.

Rayne and Kevin sat their horses on the riverbank overlooking the milling, chaotic scene.

"We made it," Gaby said.

"Yes, we did. I think the worst is behind us." Rayne's gaze held hers and Gaby flushed with pleasure, reading the reassurance in his face. The worst was over for them as well. Her eyes were bright with love; then she noticed the hot anger in Kevin's eyes. Her smile faded. What could she do to end this impossible resentment Kevin showed her now? He hadn't spoken to her since they crossed the Middle Concho.

The noise and confusion of the scene below caught her attention again.

"Watch the lead cows," Rayne shouted. "They're heading out too deep. Turn 'em." His horse paced as if he were readying himself to ride down the bank and help turn the cows.

"I'll go down," Kevin shouted, and with a last glance at Gaby, spurred his horse forward. Clearly he meant to impress her.

"Kevin, come back here," Rayne shouted, but the young cowboy guided his horse down the sandy, steep slopes. "Kevin!" Rayne shouted, standing up in his stirrups in an effort to be heard. There was an urgency in his voice that frightened Gaby.

"He'll be all right, won't he?" she asked as Rayne yanked at his reins and headed his horse down the embankment.

"He'll get trapped in the middle if he's not careful. He's still too new at this," Rayne snapped, and digging in his spurs, slid down the sandy bank toward the cattle.

Kevin had already entered the water and was leading his horse to the head of the frightened, confused cows. The lead steers had sensed the depth of the river and its current and now were frantically looking for a way back to shore.

"Hiah!" Kevin shouted at them, flapping his hat. For a moment it seemed as if the cattle were unmoved by his presence; then a steer turned, surging back toward the riverbank. His followers turned after him. Kevin pressed his horse in closer to tighten the circle, and the cows flowed around him, encircling him. Even from where she sat Gaby could see the surprise on his face as he realized the danger of his position.

"Head 'em upstream." Rayne was there on the outside, trying to turn the cows away from their leader, but they were too panicked. Gaby saw Rayne caught up in the maelstrom of flashing horns and rolling eyes and her breath caught in her throat. Bit by bit he edged his way toward Kevin. Gaby saw his rope flash across the backs of the surging animals, and Kevin gripped it, clinging to it as he was swept from the back of his horse. How could he survive that press of bodies? Gaby wondered, but her frantic gaze went back to the tall, lean figure on the roan.

"Don't let him be hurt," she prayed. For an instant Rayne lost his seat and half-fell from the saddle. Gaby cried out and was unaware she'd made a sound. Then he was back on the horse, his shirt wet and clinging, his hat lost, but his hand still gripped the lifeline to Kevin.

Kevin made his way through the cows, sometimes slithering over their backs, sometimes darting between them. It was a slow process, for Kevin's right arm hung limp and useless. Time and again the rope caught in the long horns, and with his good hand he tried to unhook the rope without losing his grip on it. Without that precious bit of rope he would be crushed between the cows and pulled under by the current their movement created.

Even Rayne was in danger. In his preoccupation with Kevin's safety he forgot his own. He didn't see a steer as it veered too close to him. One sharp horn caught him in the thigh, ripping a deep gash from hip to knee. He bent forward, cradling his injured leg, while blood oozed through his fingers, staining the churning water.

"Rayne!" Gaby screamed. She kicked at her horse, but Dusty was there to catch the bridle and hold her horse. "Let me go," she cried. "Rayne's hurt."

"Wait, Gaby. He's all right," the foreman said through tight lips. His face was unnaturally pale and Gaby remembered how close the two men were. She darted a quick glance back at the men in the water and saw that Rayne was sitting upright again, although with one hand he tried to hold the edges of his wound closed.

"He needs me," Gaby cried. Her cheeks were wet.

"You'll only distract him if you go down now," Dusty said. "I've got the men turning the cattle away from them."

Gaby knew he was right. There was nothing for her to do but watch helplessly as Rayne struggled for his life and Kevin's. Steadily he pulled the boy to safety, and when at last Kevin was mounted behind, Rayne turned his horse toward shore, weaving around the confused cattle. The cowboys slowly brought the cattle under control.

Nothing could hold Gaby now. She started down the bank, her horse half-sliding on his haunches as the others had done. She reached the edge of the river just as Rayne urged his tired mount up out of the water.

"Rayne, are you all right?" she cried. Leaping off her horse, she ran to help the men dismount. She could barely spare a glance at Kevin for her concern for Rayne. Rayne eased himself to the ground, his hand still gripping the gash. "Oh, Rayne, I was so frightened for you," Gaby cried, throwing her arms around him and pressing kisses on his cheek and ear. She pulled back and looked at the deep gash on his leg. "How bad is it?"

Rayne looked at the angry tear. "It didn't hit a vein."

The bleeding had stopped but the ragged edges gaped. "I'll have Little Finger sew it up later." He took off his bandanna and tied it around his thigh to hold the edges together and yet not tight enough to cut off the blood flow. Gingerly he stood up and gathered up his horses' reins.

"What are you going to do?" Gaby cried incredulously.

"I've got to help with those cows, Gaby, or else we'll lose more than the Comanche took."

"I don't care about the cows. You're injured. You can't go back out there."

Rayne looked down at his thigh and shrugged dismissively. "During the war we fought all day with wounds worse than this one. I'll be all right." A smile softened his face. "You're awfully little to always be taking care of someone. See to the boy. He's injured too." He climbed in his saddle and Gaby saw the bandanna turn red with blood at the movement. Before she could offer any more objections, he urged his horse back into the river.

Gaby turned to Kevin and dropped to her knees beside him. Under his tan, his face was pale and strained-looking, but his eyes were dark with anger. His arm hung limply at his side.

"Are you hurt bad?" Gaby asked, gently touching his sleeve.

"What do you care?" he snarled. "You've got your cowboy back safe."

"No thanks to you," Gaby flared.

"I didn't ask him to come charging down the hill to rescue me," Kevin said. "I would have been all right without his help."

Gaby's small hand flashed through the air, leaving behind an angry imprint on Kevin's cheek. "You ungrateful child," She stormed at him. "You would still be in the river, if not for Rayne. He risked his life to save you from your own folly. Now you sit like a lump of clay making light of what he did for you, and all out of anger and jealousy. He should have left you in the river."

She swung into her saddle and guided her horse along the bank, following the progress of the lead cows and the men trying to rescue them from the water. Somehow they managed to get the cattle headed back to land, and the cows streamed ashore and stood on the banks, heads lowered, legs trembling while their sides heaved with the effort of breathing. The cowboys took little time to rest. They urged the cows up the banks and out onto a field of sparse grass. The crisis was over, and after taking a look at the damage, Rayne determined they'd lost over fifty head of cattle. Some had been trampled under the maddened hooves of those that had followed too closely, while others had been swept away by the currents and drowned in the swift waters downriver. They had lost a few of the horses, and a couple of the hands besides Kevin and Rayne had been injured as well.

"We was lucky, mighty lucky," Little Finger said later as he sewed up the gash in Rayne's leg. Gaby hovered nearby, her arms wrapped around Rayne's shoulders, tears streaming down her cheeks. Every time the silver needle pierced the flesh on either side of his wound, fresh sobs would pour from her throat.

"Gaby, why don't you go away from here until Little Finger is finished," Rayne said, but she only shook her head, tightening her arms around his neck. He wasn't sure which was more uncomfortable, Little Finger's needle or Gaby's stranglehold on him. He took another swig of whiskey and set his teeth, determined not to show by even a flicker of an eyelash the pain he felt. Gaby was beside herself as it was. At last Little Finger was finished and the leg was bandaged. Except for a little soreness, Rayne was able to get around without any trouble. He grinned his thanks at Little Finger.

"Next," the old cook cried, and one of the cowhands who'd been injured stepped forward. Little Finger examined him with the skill of a trained doctor. He'd already set Kevin's broken arm and wrapped a bruised rib cage. Now he listened to the cowboy's complaint.

"Is your leg really going to be all right?" Gaby asked, as if she couldn't trust Little Finger's prognosis.

"It's fine. I hardly feel a thing," Rayne reassured her. They walked back to the campfire, and Rayne was aware of Kevin's glowering gaze on them. He sighed and glanced away. "How's Kevin doing?" he asked.

"He seems to be all right, although he broke his arm," Gaby answered shortly. She was still angry at the young man for acting so foolishly that afternoon.

Rayne took a deep breath and plunged, knowing what he was about to say would hurt, knowing too that it was for her own good. "The other night should never have happened. I was a fool to risk your reputation like that."

"Let me worry about my reputation. What happened the other night was something we both wanted. You can't deny that."

"I'm not denying it," he said. "I'm just telling you there won't be a repeat of it. You'll be better off for it."

"How would you know what's best for me?" Gaby blazed. Her voice had risen in anger and Rayne cast a warning glance at her. The cowhands were openly listening now. But Gaby didn't care. She'd come too far and gone through too much to give up quietly.

"I love you, Rayne Elliott," she said, and her clear voice rang out in the night air. "I'm not afraid to say so. And you love me. If only you weren't so stubborn and mule-headed." She jumped to her feet and with a swirl of dark hair stalked away to the chuck wagon to get her bedroll. The cowhands hid their grins and took up their conversations. This was Rayne's problem and he'd have to work it out.

Gaby carried her bedroll along the riverbank away from the campfire. Still seething with anger, she rolled herself into the covers and lay staring up at the stars. Men and their moods, she thought irately. They were far worse than women.

"Gaby." The whisper woke her. A black shadow hovered above her.

"Rayne?" The air was still and charged between them. She could hear the tremble in his sigh.

"You're right, Gaby. I do love you." He had no time for more words, for her arms were about his neck and she was drawing him down next to her in the bedroll. Clumsily he tried to return her kisses and take off his boots and pants. At last they were together, heart to heart, flesh to flesh.

"I'm sorry," he whispered, holding her tightly while he kissed her sweet mouth. "I always seem to say the wrong thing and hurt you. But I love you, Gaby, and I don't want you to be sorry for coming to me."

"Never, never, my love. My greatest sorrow has been our separation. Sometimes I thought I would die with longing for you."

"I know," he answered between feverish kisses. "It was the same for me." He kissed her long and deeply. "Gaby . . ." he breathed against her mouth.

"Mmm?"

"Let's not talk anymore."

Gaby's laughter was rich and happy, the way he liked to hear it.

The rest of the trip was easier. Although the grass was sparse, there were adequate pastures for the cattle to feed on, and they found streams or small lakes enough to supply them with water. Compared to the hardships they'd endured so far, the rest of the trip took on aspects of an outing. Only Kevin's aloofness marred Gaby's happiness. But at night when she lay in Rayne's arms, she forgot even Kevin's anger. The stars shimmered above them, clear and bright in the cold night air. They lay snuggled close for warmth and for the sheer pleasure of being together.

"Do you ever stop and think how long those stars have hung there just like that?" Rayne asked lazily. "Men come and go, wars are fought, men suffer and die and are reborn into another generation of men who look beyond themselves at the heavens and wonder too."

Gaby lay with her head pillowed on his arms and stared up at the black sky. "What's going to happen with us now?" she asked, and waited breathlessly for his answer. The silence between them grew. "Rayne?" she said softly, and he pretended to be asleep. She could tell by the tenseness of his body that he was not. His evasion made her feel afraid. She moved closer to him, wrapping her arms and legs around him as if she would bind him to her. It will be all right she reassured herself, and lay staring into the dark sky, feeling very alone.

*   *   *

They reached Fort Sumner without further mishap, and the garrisoned troops gave them a cheer as they drove the cattle into pens outside the fort. There'd be fresh beef for all of them that night. Rayne went to have a drink with the commanding officer and collect his pay for the herd, and Dusty and the rest of the men lined up at the bathhouse and settled down for drinks at the town saloon.

Gaby checked into a room at the hotel and ordered a bath. When it came, she soaked leisurely, reveling in the clean, warm water and her own delicately scented soap.

After her bath, she pulled out the gown she'd packed and shook it free of wrinkles. It would be nice to wear something feminine again and to go down to dinner on Rayne's arm. She held the gown to her and whirled around in anticipation. They'd brought their cattle through without losing too many, and she and Rayne had resolved their differences.

Life seemed bright and promising to her. There were only a couple of problems she must attend to. One was Kevin. She felt heartbroken at their continued estrangement. The other problem was Danny. It was time she told Rayne about his son. She would do it tonight after dinner, when they were both snuggled into the big feather bed basking in the afterglow of their lovemaking.

Gaby smiled as she thought of the look on Rayne's face. He'd be surprised at first, and then pleased to find he had a son, especially one as fine and smart as Danny was. She'd tell him of all the sweet things their baby did, and together they would laugh. Perhaps Rayne would want to leave the first thing tomorrow so he could get back to see his son. Gaby missed Danny terribly. Together they would be a family at last. Somehow Gaby sensed Aaron would have been happy for her.

When the knock sounded on the door, she fairly flew to open it. "Rayne," she cried happily, then paused.

Kevin stood in the doorway. He'd bathed and shaved. He wore a suit and it was only slightly wrinkled from being packed in his saddlebags. His hair lay slick and wet in a neat part. He looked uncomfortable in the too-short sleeves and the high tight collar, but his face wore a look of determination that made Gaby's spirits sink. She wanted to talk to Kevin and try to work out their misunderstanding, but not tonight. Tonight was special.

"Gaby," Kevin said, swallowing hard, so his Adam's apple bobbed nervously. "May I come in? I have something to talk to you about."

"I want to talk to you too, Kevin," she said, twisting the doorknob nervously. "But this is a bad time. Can we talk tomorrow."

"I won't take long," he said, looking so crestfallen that she felt guilty. "It's important."

"All right," Gaby said, standing aside so he could enter. "You look quite handsome. Some girl will be lucky tonight."

Kevin glanced down at his suit. "I didn't do this for some girl," he said solemnly, and Gaby wondered where his humor had fled. "I did it for you, Gaby." With a sinking heart she realized he was intent upon a confrontation. She didn't want to hurt him, and instinctively knew she would.

"I know you may not consider me a good catch," Kevin began. "I don't have land or money to offer you, except for the provisions you've made, but I freely give it all to you and pledge my love, Gaby. I ask you to do me the honor of becoming my wife."

He had rehearsed it well. Gaby could only stare at him, wondering how she could handle this without hurting him unduly. "I don't know what to say," she hedged. "I love you, Kevin, truly I do." She saw the flare of hope on his face and hastened to explain. "I love you as a brother." The look in his eyes died away and was replaced by a twisted bitter look on his mouth. She stepped forward to touch his hand. "I see how good and gentle you are, and wish time and again that Aaron were here to see what a fine man his son has become."

"But not good enough," he said bitterly.

"You are good enough for any woman. Any woman would be proud to have you as a husband."

"But not you."

Gaby stared at him helplessly, not knowing what else to say. She didn't want to offer platitudes when he'd just honored her with a proposal. "I'm sorry, Kevin," she said gently, placing her hands on his shoulders. "I was so happy when you came to the ranch and I saw that you loved it as much as I do. But I can't change the way I feel, Kevin. I would if I could, but it's impossible. Don't let that harm what feeling we have for each other." Her words were interrupted by the opening of the door. She raised her head and looked at Rayne. He took in the scene but said nothing. Gaby backed away from Kevin, feeling guilty Rayne had caught her thus when all she'd meant to do was give comfort.

Rayne dropped his saddlebags on the floor. "Have I interrupted something?" he asked harshly.

"Of course not," Gaby cried.

Kevin faced Rayne, his eyes wide and defiant as they took in the rancher. His gaze swung to Rayne's saddlebags flung against the wall of Gaby's room and turned an accusing gaze on her. Gaby felt caught between the two of them.

"Is Rayne the reason why you can't marry me?" he demanded. It was obvious to him that Rayne had planned to share the room with Gaby.

"Kevin, you must understand," she appealed to him. "I came to Texas with Rayne. I've always—"

"I understand everything," he spit out. "The rumors are true, aren't they? You married my father to get his land for your lover."

"You know that isn't true," Gaby whispered, stunned by his accusation. He made no answer, storming out of the room and slamming the door behind him. Gaby moved toward the door, but Rayne caught her arm.

"Leave him," he said. "Let him cool off some, then we'll both try to talk some sense into him."

"He can't possibly believe that about us," Gaby cried in distress. "He's only repeating those ugly rumors Thad Martin started. Won't they ever be forgotten?"

"People have long memories out here."

"But it's all so unfair and untrue." Gaby paced around the room, twisting her hands in agitation. Suddenly she paused, looking at Rayne with troubled eyes. "He asked me to marry him, and in my clumsiness I hurt him."

"He'll get over it," Rayne said tersely. He hated the

thought of any man making a bid for Gaby's attention. He turned his back to her and opened the saddlebags. Talking out a sack of gold, he held it toward her. "Here's the money from the sale of your herd," he said. Gaby made no move to take it, so he dropped it on the bed. "It was a profitable trip for all of us."

"Is that all this trip was worth to you?" Gaby demanded. "What about us?"

"What about us?" Rayne swung around. "You just heard what Kevin said. The rumors about us are still going strong. We can't fight them, Gaby. You should marry Kevin."

"Marry Kevin?" Gaby shouted in outrage.

"He's in love with you."

"He only thinks he is. He'll get over it."

"I don't think so. You're too hard to get over." Rayne's gaze met hers. "He'll make a good husband for you."

"I don't want him for a husband," Gaby protested. "I want you."

Rayne turned away from her words. "We don't always get what we want, Gaby."

"Not if we give up," she beseeched him. "I can't marry another man feeling as I do about you."

"You did before, or are you telling me you loved Aaron Spencer when you married him?"

"You know I only loved you. Aaron knew it too."

"And yet he married you anyway. Why, Gaby? Why did you marry him if you loved me."

"You'd made it clear you wanted no part of me."

"So you married another man with hardly a pause. Why did you do that, Gaby, if you didn't love him? For his money?"

"No." She couldn't believe the words he hurled at her.

"You did it once, you can do it again. There's been speculation that you might have to give up some of what Aaron left you. Marry Kevin and you'll get it all anyway."

"How can you believe this of me? I didn't marry Aaron for his money."

"Oh? You didn't marry him for love or for money. So tell me, Gaby, why did you marry Aaron Spencer? I want to understand. Tell me." His eyes snapped with anger, his tone was disbelieving. Once again he had her pegged and she must defend herself against his unfair judgment. The question hung between them, a thick wall that grew more impenetrable each second. Gaby looked at him beseechingly. She wanted to tell him about Danny, but not like this, not in anger, not as a defense against his jealousy. How could she blurt out to this cold-eyed stranger that the son she'd borne was his and not Aaron's?

"If you could only listen to what I have to say without all this mistrust. I can explain everything, and after you hear, you'll know how much I really love you."

"I'm sure you can explain, Gaby," he said flatly. "I'm not so sure I could understand." He crossed the room and picked up his saddlebags.

Gaby felt afraid. "Rayne, you must listen to me," she implored. Her skirts dragged at her ankles as she hurried toward him.

"It's over, Gaby," he said, slinging the heavy leather bags over his shoulders.

"Where are you going?"

"Back to the ranch. I'll leave Dusty and the rest of my men to accompany you home. You'll be safe enough."

"You can't go like this. We have to straighten this out."

"I don't think we ever can, Gaby. This is the end of it. I can't take any more. I want some peace in my life. I want to start a family of my own." Gaby felt dread growing at his words. "When I get back, I'm going to marry Lorna Blake."

"You can't," Gaby cried in anguish, but he was already out of the room, striding down the hall to the stairs. Gaby ran to catch him.

"Rayne, come back. You must listen to me." He never paused in his headlong rush down the stairs. "You already have a family, Danny and me. We're your family, Rayne." The door closed on her words with resounding finality, and the silence mocked her. "Danny's your son," she called, but it was too late, too late. Gaby clung to the railing, swaying with grief and shock. She couldn't have lost him again. Sobs racked her body and she hadn't the strength to pull herself away from the yawning stairwell. Suddenly strong young arms were there pulling her to safety.

"Gaby!" Kevin was shocked at the bleakness of her eyes. Her face was ravished with tears.

"Oh, Kevin, Kevin," she sobbed. "He wouldn't listen to me. He didn't believe that I love him." So great was her anguish that Kevin felt guilty for the accusations he'd hurled at her. He knew they weren't true; still, in his anger and pain he'd sought to hurt her with them. Now he put his arms around her and patted her shoulder in an awkward attempt to comfort.

24

The trip back was uneventful.

When they came in sight of the ranch buildings, Gaby spurred her horse ahead of the others and galloped into the ranch yard. She held Danny's squirmy little body in her arms and breathed in his sweet baby fragrance. His chubby, dimpled arms went wide in his baby version of a hug, and he buried his head against her shoulder.

"He missed you so much," Maria said. "He said 'Mama' over and over."

"He said 'Mama?" Gaby smiled through her tears.

Maria grinned and nodded.

"Mrs. Schafer, it's good to see you." Gaby turned to the German housekeeper, who was rushing down the steps.

"Yah, me too," the housekeeper said, and surprised Gaby by giving her a quick hug.

"It's good to be home," Gaby said, looking around.

Abigail Spencer stood at the front door, but she spared no attention for Gaby. Her eyes were on the riders as they galloped into the yard and wearily dismounted. Kevin hurried to greet his mother.

"Kevin!" Abigail ran to throw herself in her son's arms. Sobbing, she clung to him. "Oh, my poor baby, my son. I was so worried for you. I was afraid you'd been killed by some savage Indians or trampled to death. I've been sick with worry."

"It didn't affect her appetite," Mrs. Schafer said under her breath, and Gaby bit back a smile. Things hadn't changed much since she'd been gone. With Danny riding on one hip, she mounted the porch steps and entered the house. Under Mrs. Schafer's firm hand, everything was in meticulous order, as she'd known it would be. Gaby looked around. It was good to be home, she thought, and suddenly the finality of all her shattered dreams hit her and she bit her lips to keep from sobbing out loud. She loved the ranch, but it gave her little or no pleasure. Without Rayne in her life, she would never be happy again.

"Are you all right?" Mrs. Schafer asked, coming to stand behind her.

Gaby nodded and tried to summon a smile. "I'm just tired. It was a long trip."

"You need a goot hot bath. That vill fix you up." Mrs. Schafer marched purposefully toward the bath.

An hour later, Gaby lay across her bed bathed and refreshed, Danny lying beside her. They'd spend the past half-hour playing together and now he was growing drowsy. She should take him back to the nursery and tuck him into his crib, but it felt so good to have her baby next to her again. If only Rayne could see him now, she thought, smoothing the fine hair from his forehead. The widow's peak was becoming more pronounced now. Drowsily Danny grinned up at her and stuck his thumb in his mouth.

"I tried, Danny," she whispered. "I tried to bring your daddy back to us, but he wouldn't listen." She lay cuddling her baby while her mind played back over that scene in the hotel room. Would it have helped if she'd told Rayne about Danny? Should she go to him and tell him now? It couldn't be over for them. It couldn't. Tomorrow she would ride over to the Elliott ranch and make one last attempt to talk to Rayne and tell him about Danny. This time she'd make him listen. He'd have to see that they belonged together. They had a son, evidence of the love they'd once shared. Feeling better, Gaby placed a light kiss on the small round head and carried her son off to his bed.

The sun was already high by the time she left the next day for the Elliott ranch. Jeremy Wallace had stopped by with ranch business and she'd had to see Ben about work for the hands. As she came down the stairs, her hat and riding gloves in hand, Abigail came out of the drawing room. Gaby's heart sank. She had no time for the woman this morning, but Abigail called out a greeting.

"Aren't you in a hurry today?" she said.

"I have business to attend to," Gaby answered stiffly. She paused on the bottom step so she could look down on the woman. Tall as she was, Abigail usually had the advantage.

"Business?" Abigail repeated curiously, but Gaby didn't elaborate. Impatiently she slapped her riding crop against her boots.

"I would have thought after that exhausting cattle drive you would want to spend the day in bed."

"Not when there's work to be done," Gaby said pointedly, but Abigail ignored the hint and continued to block her path.

"I had a long talk with Kevin last night. He told me some of the things that occurred on the trail drive. It seems you had yourself quite a time." The woman's eyes flashed with temper as she looked at Gaby.

"We all did," Gaby said, "but we managed to get the cattle through in good shape."

"It wasn't the cattle that worried me," Abigail snapped. "Kevin told me you turned down his proposal of marriage."

Gaby was surprised he had discussed it with his mother. "Yes, I did," she replied finally. "As fond as I am of Kevin, I couldn't marry him."

"And why not?" Abigail demanded. "Don't you think he's good enough for you, or is it the other way round?"

"What happened is between Kevin and me. I won't discuss it with you." Gaby stepped down off the bottom step and brushed past Abigail, but the woman's hand clamped over her shoulder and stopped her short. Furiously Abigail spun her around.

"Don't walk away from me. I haven't finished with you yet."

"I am finished with you," Gaby answered, and thought that Abigail meant to strike her. The woman struggled to bring her temper under control.

"You've spurned my son and hurt him dreadfully, and

all because of your neighbor, Rayne Elliott. Oh yes, I heard how you carried on with him on the trail drive. You've stolen my son's inheritance from him and now you think you're going to marry some other man and share the wealth with him. It won't work. I won't allow it." The woman was working herself into a fury, her eyes flecked with madness.

Gaby backed away from her to the door. "Whether I love Rayne Elliott or not, I could never marry Kevin. I don't love him. If you think so little of me as a person, how could you possibly want your son to marry a woman like me?"

"So we can get what's rightfully ours!"

Gaby stared at Abigail in shock at the thought that Kevin had been part of her shabby schemes. She remembered Kevin's stricken face on the trail when he'd realized she and Rayne were lovers, and some part of her wanted to believe his proposal had been sincere. Still the doubts remained, nagging and ugly.

"I feel sorry for you," she said finally to Abigail. "But I feel sorrier for Kevin for having a mother like you. You have no claim against Aaron's estate. You were no longer his wife. Jeremy's men found proof that you'd had Aaron declared dead so you could remarry. You lied to Kevin about being married to poor old Mr. Peterson. It's very clear why you married him. You wanted his money. Now you're encouraging Kevin to marry me because you know it's the only chance you have of getting Aaron's money."

Abigail's face had gone white and blotched-looking. "So that snoopy lawyer did find out and tell you," she spit out. "That's what I figured when Kevin told me the lawyer and you had been closed up in the study so hush-hush one day. I suppose it gave you great pleasure to tell my son the truth."

"I've told Kevin nothing," Gaby said. "He loves you. He believes you're good and decent." The relief was visible on Abigail's face. Suddenly Gaby wanted to be out in the open air, with the clean blue sky above her and the endless stretches of prairie untouched by man's petty connivings and greed.

"Where are you going?" Abigail cried fearfully, but

Gaby didn't answer. She ran outdoors and toward the barn, wanting only to be away from the hateful woman.

"You come back here. I have more to say to you," Abigail screamed across the yard, her voice strident and angry. Gaby didn't pause.

"Go on, then," Abigail yelled. "Run off to your lover, that no-account rancher, but you won't get away with it. Do you hear me? It's my money. It's mine. I deserve it. It would all be mine now if Aaron hadn't had that accident. I couldn't live with a scarred and ugly cripple for the rest of my life. He cheated me out of all those years when I might have lived like a queen. I'm going to get what's coming to me. Do you hear me, you Texas whore?"

Gaby ran past Kevin, not stopping to acknowledge his white face or the embarrassment deep in his eyes as he started toward the distraught woman.

"Run to your lover," Abigail cried. "Are you going to plot getting rid of Kevin and me the way you got rid of Aaron? Murderess, whore!"

"Mother, stop! That's not true about Gaby." Kevin was at the porch now, an arm around Abigail as he led her back indoors.

Let her say what she will, Gaby thought. I *am* going to my lover. I'm going to beg him to try again and forget the ugly things people are saying. Impatiently she waited while a horse was saddled for her, then she was on its back and pounding across the prairie, the horse running open and free, with long efficient strides. He wasn't fast enough. Gaby felt an impatience to be back on Elliott land.

Her horse was foam-flecked and heaving for breath by the time she reached the Rocking E Ranch. Slowly she walked it around the corrals and barn and toward the sturdy ranch house. She hadn't been here since the day they'd tried to hang Slade Harner and Billy. She had come then to tell Rayne she carried his baby. Now she came to tell him of his son. So much time had been wasted between them. This time she wouldn't allow anything to deter her.

Cole Elliott stopped her halfway across the yard. "What are you doing here, woman?" he shouted, and Gaby brought her horse to a halt and met his hostile gaze.

"I've come to see Rayne," she answered.

"Rayne don't want to see you," Cole said. "Just ride on out of here back to that big fancy ranch of yours and leave him be."

"You can't stop me, Cole. I won't go until I've seen Rayne."

"He ain't here."

"I'll wait for him."

"Won't do you no good."

"I'll take my chances."

A crafty look appeared on Cole's face. "You might as well go on up to the house and wait, then," he said. And Gaby walked her horse to the deep porch and dismounted.

"Hello, Gaby." At the sound of her name, Gaby turned from the hitching post. Lorna Blake stood in the doorway. She wore a calico gown with an apron protecting the long skirt, and held a cloth in one hand.

"Have you taken up cleaning houses now, Lorna?" Gaby asked sarcastically.

"Only for Rayne," Lorna replied. "Can I do something for you?"

"Where is Jacinta?" Gaby hedged.

"I've let her go. She wouldn't work. You know how these Mexicans are."

Gaby bit back an angry retort. She remembered how Jacinta had come and put everything right when she'd nearly despaired.

Lorna moved to the edge of the porch and looked down at Gaby. There was a gleam of triumph in her eyes. "Rayne and I are to be married."

"I heard you were," Gaby said stiffly. Her chin was held high, although her eyes were downcast. She wasn't able to meet the spiteful gaze of the other woman.

"The wedding is to be next week, Saturday," Lorna continued.

Gaby's heart stopped. So soon, she thought in panic.

"I do hope you can attend."

"That's kind of you," Gaby said, and her voice was barely audible. "I'm afraid I won't be able to."

"I'm sorry to hear that. I would have loved having you there," Lorna said sweetly, and Gaby knew the woman had indeed hoped for that. It would have put down once and for all the rumors and speculations about Rayne and the Creole. As it was, Lorna's victory was complete.

"I'm doing some decorating in the house," Lorna continued. "It was so plain and ugly before." Gaby remembered the soft rugs she and Jacinta had placed on the scrubbed pine boards and the beautiful *colcha* Jacinta's mother had spent years making, the freshly whitewashed walls, the simplicity and beauty of the spacious rooms. Now Lorna was changing them, putting her stamp on them. Rayne meant to marry her. Gaby couldn't go begging to him now. She didn't want him just because of Danny. She wanted him to love her as much as she loved him. Rayne had made his decision. Gaby untied her horse and prepared to mount.

"Gaby . . ." Lorna's voice, sharp and angry, made her pause. "Don't try to see Rayne anymore," she said. "It's over between you two. You've lost and I've won."

"You'll never win, Lorna," Gaby cried. "Rayne loves me. He always will. I have proof of that love."

"Do you mean his son?" Gaby's face registered her shock. "Oh, I've known all along that Aaron couldn't have fathered your child. I found out during the war. People let their guard slip a little in times of trouble."

"And you've never told anyone?" Gaby asked in dismay. She couldn't believe Lorna had been kind enough to keep it a secret.

"I saw no need to," Lorna answered smugly, "especially Rayne." Suddenly Gaby realized how devious Lorna really was.

"He'll find out someday and he'll be angry that you tricked him this way."

"I'll never admit that I knew the truth. No, Gaby, his anger will be at you for keeping it from him."

"Aren't you afraid he'll leave you and come back to me when he finds out about Danny?"

"It won't matter, Gaby," Lorna said with great humor. "You see, I'm already carrying Rayne's child myself." Her laughter pealed across the porch, striking at Gaby with a malicious force.

Lorna's revelation was shattering to Gaby. For a moment it seemed as if the spinning ground would rise up and slap her. On wooden legs Gaby mounted and turned her horse back toward the prairie. Rigidly she held herself upright, unwilling to reveal how devastated she felt. She didn't even notice Dusty as he came out of the barn and stared after her with puzzled eyes. Putting down the bridle he'd been mending, he turned toward the house. He was tired of being played the fool by Lorna. It was time they got some things straightened out.

Gaby rode on without direction. Had Rayne known about Lorna's condition when he made love to her on the trail drive? Had he known even then at the very beginning that he was coming back to marry Lorna? Had he let her dream her foolish dreams alone?

She felt confused and battered. Nothing was going the way she'd planned it this morning. First she'd had to deal with Abigail and all the accusations, and then with Lorna. She needed a friendly shoulder right now. Automatically she turned her horse toward Jessie Walker's ranch. The old woman had been a rock for her since Aaron's death. Once again she would seek Jessie's wisdom and strength. But when she arrived at the Walker ranch, she was shocked to find Jessie in bed.

"Why didn't you send word you were ill?" Gaby admonished the old woman. Her own troubles were forgotten as she noted Jessie's condition.

"I knew you was just back from the trail drive," Jessie replied with only a shadow of the old fire she'd once shown. "How'd it go? Tell me all about it. Was it a good trail or did Goodnight and Loving lead a bunch of folks astray?"

"It was a difficult trail," Gaby said with some pride, "but we made it through." She settled herself close to Jessie's bed and smoothed back the tangled gray hair and plumped the pillows.

"Stop your fussin' and tell me more," Jessie scolded.

Gaby did as ordered, forcing herself to a cheerfulness she didn't feel. Her efforts were worth it, for she coaxed laughter back to Jessie's eyes.

Gaby went to see Jessie every day during the next week, taking some of the cook's chicken-and-dumpling soup or rich German pastries that might tempt her friend to eat a little. She was alarmed at the dark circles under the old woman's eyes, the sunken cheeks, and the feverish flush. She sent for the doctor, and after examining Jessie, he met Gaby on the porch, shaking his head.

"It's her heart," he said. "She's just too blamed old for me to do anything. Keep her as comfortable as you can and be prepared for the worst."

"It can't be," Gaby cried, turning tearful eyes back toward the house.

"She's lived a full life," the doctor reminded her gently. "Do the best you can by her."

Gaby stood on the porch for some time after his buggy rolled out of sight, waiting until the tears had stopped, before she went back to Jessie.

"It don't do no good to cry, child," Jessie said one day. "I ain't afraid of dying."

"Oh, Jessie, you aren't going to die," Gaby said. "You're just lying down on the job for a while. You'll get better. You have before."

"This time's different, child. We both know it. I ain't afraid. Except for you and Danny and Molly"—it took Gaby a moment to know she was talking about Mrs. Schafer—"I ain't got a whole lot of people I mind leaving behind. And Walker, he's waitin' for me."

"Jessie, please don't give up yet," Gaby insisted, gripping the old woman's hand. It seemed so frail, and that scared Gaby even worse than her words. Jessie had always seemed so robust, so indestructible. "Danny and I still need you for years and years."

"No, you don't, Gaby," Jessie whispered tiredly. She patted Gaby's hand comfortingly, much like the old Jessie would have. "I've watched you grow up in the past two years into a fine, strong woman. You're the head of one of the biggest ranches in these parts, and you handle it like a man. You're goin' to be just fine, Gaby, just fine."

"You don't know how much I've relied on you, Jessie. I need your good sound advice and your humor and your common sense."

"You've got a good head on your shoulders, Gaby. You're finding your way. You'll make it."

Gaby wiped at her eyes. She mustn't cause Jessie any further distress. She was tiring rapidly.

"Gabrielle," Jessie said, and Gaby was startled to hear her full name said out loud. "Go look in the top drawer of my dresser," Jessie directed. "There's a paper on top marked 'Last Will and Testament.' Bring it to me."

Gaby gave a start and with sinking heart brought the document to the bedside. It seemed Jessie was determined to die, no matter what the effort of those who loved her.

"Now, open it to the second page and read it."

"Jessie, I shouldn't. This is your—"

"My last will. My last chance to say how I want things," Jessie said weakly. "Read it out loud so I can hear it."

Gaby began to read. She could detect Jeremy Wallace's fine hand in the words and phrases that leapt out at her. " 'I hearby decree that all my lands, building, and stock go to Gabrielle Spencer, and in the event of her death, to her son, Daniel Spencer.' " Gaby stopped reading and looked at the old woman. "Why are you doing this?" she asked.

"I ain't got anyone else I want to leave them to," Jessie snapped with something of her old fire. Her eyes sparkled with humor and satisfaction. She'd intended this to surprise Gaby, and it had.

"I can't take your ranch," Gaby said.

"I don't want it to go to no one else. I see how you've come to love this land. This ranch ain't as big as the Spencer ranch, but it's good land. You can graze a goodly number of cows on it and not have 'em go hungry except during drought. The river held during the last drought, not like some that dried up."

"It's too much," Gaby cried. "I can't just take your land. You've worked and fought for this land your whole life."

"And it was worth every minute of it," Jessie declared. "Walker and me, we stood side by side against Indians and rustlers and anything else the good Lord saw fit to put in front of us, but now I'm done with the land and it's done with me. It's best I pass it on to someone else, someone who'll love it as much as Walker and me did."

"I already have one ranch. What will I do with two?"

"I understand you better than you believe I do, Gaby," the old woman said sternly. "I don't want little Danny to be landless. Land makes a man here in Texas or else it breaks him. Either way, he's better off owning a little chunk of it. Take the land for Danny's sake."

"How can I refuse then?" Gaby answered softly. Her hands gripped the older woman's, her dark eyes brimmed with tears of love and sadness. For a moment Jessie studied the young face before her, noting the finely drawn lines. Gaby had been grieving for more than just her.

Jessie sighed. "I figure the Bodine ranch and the Kreutter ranch'll go up for sale soon. Both their husbands have been killed off by Thad Martin and his gang. If you beat Thad to the draw and buy up those ranches, this land'll connect up with the Elliott ranch. Altogether that'd make a mighty big piece of land. You're going to need a big spread to raise cattle. That's where the money is, Gaby."

Gaby had turned away at the mention of the Elliott land. She hadn't the heart to tell Jessie of Rayne's wedding. It was only a few days away now. But it seemed even that fact had not escaped Jessie's attention.

"What are you going to do about that weddin' on Saturday?" she asked abruptly. Gaby whirled around, her face stricken. Jessie had never doubted something would happen to bring Rayne and Gaby back together, but now, seeing the defeat in Gaby's eyes, her own confidence was shaken.

"There's nothing I can do, Jessie," Gaby said, and her voice broke. "He's going to marry Lorna. She's carrying his child. He must have known that before he left on the trail drive. He tried to tell me, but I wouldn't let him. I was so sure I could win him back." The dark head bowed and the slim shoulders shook.

"Come here, child." The old woman lifted a fragile hand and Gaby threw herself on the bed, her face buried in Jessie's shoulder while she sobbed out her hurt and fear.

"It'll work out," Jessie soothed. Her gnarled old hand brushed across the bright dark coils of Gaby's hair. "You

and Rayne belong together." But she'd begun to doubt
her own words. How foolish and full of pride young
people were, she thought, and remembered the fire and
passion of her own days with Walker. The soothing pats
of her hand stilled and she slept. Gaby looked at the
tired old face. The frail chest barely moved beneath the
white cotton nightgown. Rising, Gaby wiped resolutely at
her tears. She must gather her strength. Jessie depended
on her now. Later she would cry, when no one needed
her anymore.

Gaby's days and nights ran together as she traveled
between her ranch and Jessie's, trying to spend as much
time with the dying woman as she could. In spite of the
demands made on her, she remembered Jacinta, so cal-
lously let go by Lorna Blake. She brought her good
friend to Jessie's ranch, where Jacinta coddled the sick
old woman with special dishes she never had the appetite
to eat. Mrs. Schafer also came to the ranch to stay with
Jessie so she wouldn't be alone when Gaby couldn't be
there. They would sit for hours exchanging tales of their
early years in Texas. Under such care, Jessie seemed to
rally, and Gaby began to hope she'd recover completely.

One morning as Gaby was about to leave for Jessie's
ranch, Abigail called out to her. Gaby had rarely seen
the woman since their last unpleasant encounter, and
when she had, she'd simply nodded and hurried on her
way. But Abigail had no intention of being ignored this
morning.

"So you're off again," she said with her usual spiteful
whine. "Are you going to see your sick friend or are you
using that as an excuse to sneak off and see a man?"

Tired from the demands made on her, Gaby whirled
on her tormentor. "I wouldn't have to sneak off and see
a man if that were my desire. I am widowed, remember?
And I've spent the proper time in mourning. I'm going to
see one of the finest women in Texas, who happens to be
dying. I'm sorry you never took the time to get to know
Jessie better, Abigail. Perhaps some of her decency and
character would have rubbed off on you."

"Well," the woman sniffed in an aggrieved tone, "you
can be insulting all you want. I've come to expect little
else of you."

Gaby remained silent. She'd come to realize Abigail couldn't tolerate being ignored.

"It's been simply awful around here the past week, what with that shiftless housekeeper of yours off on a holiday and you gone all the time. All Danny does is whine, and Maria does nothing to make him stop. I finally made her keep him in his room."

"You've kept Danny and Maria in the nursery during the day?" Gaby cried in anger.

"I can't stand his crying and his temper tantrums. He's gotten quite spoiled. You're seldom home to tend to him yourself. Maria never disciplines him. I have to do it myself. He's such an unpleasant baby. Of course, you don't see that. You run off every chance you get. I would too if I had someplace to go, but no, I'm stuck here in this wasteland."

The woman's voice droned on with her complaints, but Gaby was no longer listening. She was bounding up the stairs. "Maria," she called before she'd even reached the top of the stairs.

The maid came out of the nursery, her eyes wide and uncertain. She clutched Danny protectively in her arms. "Yes, Gaby?" she asked softly.

"Get Danny ready. You're going with me today."

"With you?" Maria repeated, and the pinched, unhappy look left her face. "Did you hear that, Danny? We're going with Mama."

"Mama," Danny said, and squirmed to reach his mother. Gaby took her son in her arms. In her preoccupation with Jessie and Rayne, she'd been neglecting Danny the last few days. Now she carried him back to the nursery and helped Maria dress him for his outing. Danny set himself the task of charming the two women, and soon had them both smiling and chuckling.

Jessie was delighted to see Danny again. The baby sat on her bed surrounded by a silver-backed mirror, a music box, and any other item Jessie thought might amuse the baby. Carefully Danny examined each object, his small dimpled fingers poking and prodding every detail. His antics with the mirror brought laughter from Jessie. Gaby was glad she'd brought her son. He was the best medicine for the sick woman.

When Jessie grew tired, Gaby cleared the playthings from the bed and bent to kiss Jessie's cheek. Seeing his mother's action, Danny crawled over to repeat it on the other cheek. Once again Jessie chuckled, her eyes looking brighter, her coloring better.

"It was goot you brought the little dumpling," Mrs. Schafer said, bouncing the baby in her arms, and Gaby wasn't sure which woman had been more pleased by Danny's visit. Maria seemed happier too for her visit with her mother.

On their drive back to the ranch, Gaby decided to stop in town and pick up a few supplies to take to Jessie the next day. She glanced at Danny. It was well past his napping time, and his lids drooped several times. Fearful of going to sleep and missing some of the excitement, he would stir and bat at the air impatiently.

In town, Gaby made her purchases and brought Danny a candy stick, the first he'd ever had. Once he'd tasted it, he refused to give it up, letting out a loud squawk of anger whenever Maria tried.

Gaby smiled as she stowed the packages in the boot, her thoughts on her son.

"Hello, Gaby." Rayne's tall figure loomed between her and the store. Gaby felt herself flush with the increased beating of her heart. She hadn't seen Rayne since the trail drive.

"Mr. Elliott," she said coolly, and would have swept past him except that he gripped her arm.

"Don't run away," he said. "I want to apologize for leaving you back there in New Mexico."

"You needn't apologize," Gaby responded crisply. "I made it back without any trouble. I had Kevin with me."

"Still, it was a dang fool thing for me to do."

"It doesn't matter now," Gaby said. She could hear Maria and Danny bidding good-bye to the people in the store. Soon they would be here, and suddenly Gaby didn't want Rayne to see Danny.

"If you'll excuse me, Mr. Elliott. I have things to do."

"I don't blame you for being angry with me."

"I'm not really angry," Gaby said, gauging the time before Maria would reach them. "Jessie's been sick and I'm taking some supplies out to her. I have to go now."

"Gaby." Still he detained her. "If there's anything I can do for Jessie, let me know."

"Thank you, I will." Gaby pulled away from him and would have hurried back into the store, except that Maria was there bearing a triumphant Danny in her arms. His face was smeared with candy and his eyes sparkled with humor and self-pride. He'd made another conquest.

"He was so funny, everyone laughed at him," Maria said. "He likes people." She stopped talking when she saw Rayne, her face stricken as if she'd been caught in an illegal deed.

"Is this your son, Gaby?" Rayne asked, looking at the little boy. He'd never met Danny, and even now he glanced away, not really wanting to acknowledge his presence in Gaby's life. He was the physical evidence that she'd loved another man. Curiosity got the better of him and he looked at the baby again. The child was Gaby's, and he wanted to pick out the resemblances, to find the familiar and dear nose, the dark eyes. Danny's hair was dark like Gaby's and yet different.

Curiously Danny turned his head and stared at the tall stranger talking to his mother and Maria. The man's broad shoulders seemed to invite Danny. He could certainly see better from there. Gurgling in his best manner, he leaned toward the tall man, his chubby arms reaching out in invitation.

Rayne stared at the boy, shock rippling through him. There was little evidence of Gaby in the boy's face and none at all of Aaron Spencer. Rayne noted the deep blue eyes and the long straight nose and the telltale peak at the top of the forehead. The imprint of his own features was already etching itself on the baby's face. Slowly Rayne extended a finger to his son and felt the soft, warm hand grip it. Danny carried the finger to his mouth and chewed on the end. Rayne could feel the scrape of baby teeth across the callused tip. The boy looked up at him and grinned, a mischievous light in his eyes.

Gaby watched mesmerized as father met son for the first time. So many times she'd dreamed of this moment, but never had she thought it would be like this, in the middle of town where anyone could look up and witness what was happening. She'd envisioned his finding out some other way.

"Maria, take Danny to the carriage," she ordered, and her gaze was drawn to Rayne's face as his eyes watched the baby. There was a look of pride and awe and dawning love. Danny looked back over Maria's shoulder and cried out for the tall dark-haired man, his little arms reaching back. Gaby saw the emotions mirrored on Rayne's face. Maria climbed up on the seat and cuddled Danny into a comfortable position. Diverted by the candy stick, he settled down.

Hungrily Rayne watched his son, then turned back to Gaby, and his eyes hardened with anger. "Damn you, Gaby," he cried, "Damn you to hell."

"Is that all you have to say to me?" she asked, her dark eyes shiny with unshed tears. "More words of condemnation?"

"He's my son. Why didn't you tell me? I had the right to know." Rayne's face worked as his mind sought to accept the knowledge of his son's existence.

"I . . . tried to tell you that day at the ranch," Gaby began, not able to meet his gaze, "but you were too busy listening to Slade's lies about me. Well, I never slept with any of those men, not even with my husband."

"You expect me to believe that?" Rayne's tone was derisive.

"Aaron was injured in an accident years ago," Gaby said gently "He was impotent."

"All this time you let me think Danny was his," Rayne accused. "Did you hate me so much, Gaby?"

"I never hated you." she denied.

"I want my son," he snarled, and his demeanor was so unyielding that she felt fear. In all the times she'd imagined Rayne finding out about Danny, she'd never once thought he'd respond with this rage.

"You don't know what you're asking," she whispered. "I can't give you Danny."

"I know exactly what I'm saying," Rayne snapped. "He's my son. I want him."

"You can't have him. He's my son too." Involuntarily she took a step backward away from the fury she read in his face. "The law says he's a Spencer and you'll never be able to prove differently. You can't have him. The law will never give him to you." She turned toward the carriage, but his hand, hard and painful on her arm held her. His gaze captured hers, making her flinch, pinning her so she must listen.

"I won't need the law." His voice was low and grim and very precise. "Be forewarned about this, Gabrielle. He's my son, and one way or another, I'll have him." He let go of her so suddenly she nearly fell. For a long moment she studied his implacable face. She had no doubt that Rayne meant what he said. And yet she couldn't lose her baby.

"Leave my son alone, Rayne," she cried. "You'll have another. Lorna's already told me she's carrying your child. Leave Danny and me alone. He's all I have left." Her defiant words ended in a whispered plea, but there was no softening of the fierce expression on Rayne's face.

Whirling, Gaby ran to the carriage and climbed in; then, taking up the reins, she whipped the horses so they reared in surprise, then galloped wildly down the street. Maria clung to the seat, her arms tight around Danny. Gaby whipped at the horses again. She had to get back to the ranch. They'd be safe there.

For the first time, she felt a deep hatred for Rayne Elliott.

After that, Gaby left the ranch only to see Jessie. She ordered her foreman to hire more men, and a twenty-four-hour guard was placed around the ranch house, with orders to shoot any trespassers on sight.

Abigail drove over to the Elliott ranch on Saturday for the wedding and returned much sooner than expected with the news that there had been no wedding. It seemed that Rayne and Lorna had fallen out and Lorna was now being courted by Dusty Simmons. Gaby listened to the news with a sinking heart. Why had Rayne refused to marry Lorna when she carried his child, unless Lorna had lied? Gaby held her head in her hands. Had she been sidetracked from telling Rayne about Danny by a lie? She thought of how things might have been if she'd stayed at the ranch that day and told Rayne the truth. He would have been angry, but perhaps not as much as now. Together they could have worked it out. Gaby's nerves grew edgy and her eyes carried a haunted look in them.

And then Jessie died. Although Gaby had been expecting it, the loss hit her hard. She felt alone in the world. She'd never fully realized how much Jessie had meant to her. Kevin was kind and supportive, showing Gaby by a word or glance that he was there if she needed him. More and more she left the running of the ranch in his hands. She attended Jessie's funeral and was surprised at the number of ranchers and their families who came. In her lifetime, the rough-talking, kindhearted pioneer woman had made many friends. After the funeral, Gaby closed up Jessie's house and headed back to the Spencer ranch.

"I'm real sorry about Miss Jessie," Billy said when he took her horse.

"Thank you, Billy," Gaby said wearily. "I'll miss her terribly."

"She was a fine old lady." he said.

"Billy," Gaby called as the young cowhand was leading her horse away. He paused, pushing his hat back on his forehead. "Maria tells me you and she plan on getting married."

"Yes, ma'am. Just as soon as we get a place to stay."

"How would you like to be foreman for me out at the Walker ranch? You and Maria could live in the main house."

Gaby watched as hope flared behind his eyes. "You really mean it?" he asked fearfully, as if she might change her mind.

"Think you'd be interested?"

"Yes, ma'am," Billy said. "But ain't you afraid to try someone so young as me?" he couldn't help asking.

"How old are you, Billy?"

"I'll be twenty-three my next birthday."

"That *is* young," Gaby replied, and for a minute the light died in his eyes. "If it were anyone else but you, I might not consider it, but I know what you can do. You're a good man, Billy, I hope you and Maria will be happy."

"We will, Miss Gaby, and thank you." Billy watched as she trudged across the yard toward the house. Her shoulders seemed weighted down by an impossible burden. He waited until she was inside before he exploded with glee. His wild whoop echoed around the yard, and even Maria heard it up in the nursery. She gave a start and then smiled. Someone had something to be happy about, she thought, and continued rocking Danny while she daydreamed about her life with Billy.

25

The days were growing colder now as winter prepared to pour its wrath down on their heads. Gaby often sat in the drawing room before the fire. Abigail was there too, her eyes watchful and sly, her words whining or baiting. Gaby ignored her as best she could, closing herself in some gray world of her own. Abigail grew frightened, sure that Gaby was plotting some way of getting rid of Kevin and her. Mrs. Schafer worried too, but for quite a different reason. Gaby's nerves were worse, the lines of her face too finely drawn. She began to lose weight and slept badly. Mrs. Schafer often heard her pacing her room late at night.

The young thing had too much responsibility, Mrs. Schafer thought sadly, and urged the cook to greater effort on Gaby's behalf. All to no avail. The snacks and cakes brought to the parlor were left drying on Gaby's plate or were gobbled down by the greedy Danny. The only time Gaby laughed was at her son, and even then it was quickly replaced by melancholia. Only Maria had witnessed the scene between Gaby and Rayne, and her loyalty to Gaby kept her silent.

Late one night, when the household had retired and Gaby lay in her bed dozing, a soft, insistent sound woke her. She jerked awake and peered into the darkness. A dark shadow loomed over her, menacing and frightening. Gaby would have cried out, but a hand clamped over her mouth, cutting off her scream. She was snatched upright and the hand was replaced by lips, cold and savagae.

Rayne! Gaby thought, and her heart hammered in her chest. Yet, even in her fear, her body responded to his nearness, her lips surrendered to his. Her body turned pliant in his embrace. Roughly she was flung against her pillows, while the dark shadow continued to hover above her.

"This is just to let you know that no matter what you do, no matter how many men guard this ranch, I can still get through to you," Rayne growled. "I'll come get my son in time, and you and your men won't be able to stop me."

"Rayne, no," she cried out, but he was already gone, a flitting shadow in the black night. Gaby sprang out of bed and hurried to the window. The ranch yard was dark and empty, only the fading hoofbeats of Rayne's horse a reminder that his visit had been real.

Gaby stood with her arms clutched around her middle, shivering in her thin nightgown. What was she to do? she wondered in despair. How had things come to this impasse, that Rayne and she were enemies fighting over Danny?

After that, Gaby seemed to grow more tense. Even Kevin could offer her no comfort. The only relief given to her was when Abigail spent the long afternoons and some of the evenings away from the ranch. There was a sly, evasive air about Abigail now. She never spoke of where she was going, and Gaby didn't care enough to ask. If she'd wondered at all, she would have assumed Abigail was visiting one of her friends.

One evening Gaby and Mrs. Schafer sat companionably before the fire, watching Maria and Danny playing on the floor. Abigail had gone calling and would spend the night. As the women relaxed and enjoyed their time away from Abigail, Gaby realized just how much tension the woman created in the household.

Suddenly their peaceful evening was disturbed by the sound of rushing hoofbeats. Mrs. Schafer looked startled. "Who on earth would come calling at this time of night?" she asked. "They're riding fast; perhaps something is wrong."

With sickening dread Gaby listened. It was Rayne come to get Danny. She was sure of it until she realized there were too many horses. Rayne wouldn't need that many men to take what he wanted.

Old memories stirred of another ranch when Gaby had been alone and raiders swooped down on them. Was that nightmare happening all over again? Surely not, for this time she was not a helpless woman with only a young, untried boy to protect her. She had several men guarding the ranch. Uneasily she glanced at Maria and saw the same fear reflected in her eyes. Even as the women sought to reassure themselves, the sound of gunshots came to them.

"Maria," Gaby said urgently, "take Danny to the nursery and leave the lights off."

"Yes, ma'am." Maria hurried up the stairs with Danny. Mrs. Schafer crossed to the gun cabinet and opened it. "Ve vill need these," she said matter-of-factly, and began to load a rifle. For once Gaby was grateful Abigail was absent. The woman would have been hysterical by now. The two women lowered the wicks in the lamps, casting the room in shadows. Gaby checked the door to see it was locked; then they waited, listening intently to the exchange of gunfire. It was closer now. A bullet ripped through a window, showering the rug with broken glass.

"Get down," Gaby cried, and the two women crouched behind furniture. Gaby heard footsteps on the porch. Kevin was coming to help them, she thought gratefully, and ran to fling open the door for him. Too late Gaby saw her error. Two men, bandannas pulled high over their faces, stood on the porch.

Gaby tried to slam the door shut, but they kicked it out of her hands and she fell sprawling backward. The gun fell from her hands and went skittering across the floor out of reach. The men entered, their eyes intent on Gaby.

"That's her," one of them said. "Don't hurt her. The boss wants her alive." The men rushed forward and jerked Gaby to her feet, forcing her back toward the door.

"No," Gaby screamed, struggling in their grip. "Leave me alone." A bullet ripped into the woodwork near their

heads and the men turned toward the parlor door. Mrs.
Schafer stood there, a smoking gun gripped firmly in her
hands. The deadly barrel was pointed at the two men.

"Let go of her or the next one won't miss," she said,
but the man holding Gaby twisted her around to act as a
shield while he drew his gun and fired. A bright red stain
appeared on Mrs. Schafer's starched white bodice. Her
face twisted in pain. The gun fell from her nerveless
fingers. The two men jerked Gaby through the door and
the last thing she saw was Mrs. Schafer slowly crumbling
to the floor.

A third man brought a horse around. Gaby struggled
against them as they tried to put her on the horse.

"Hurry," one of the men commanded.

"We can't control her. She's like a wildcat," one of
Gaby's captors gasped. The man got off his horse and
came to help, and Gaby's flailing hand caught in his
mask, pulling it down so his face was exposed.

"Slade Harner." Gaby stopped struggling. Her face
was cynical as she looked at him. "Still doing Thad
Martin's dirty work, I see."

Slade's expression turned ugly at her jeer. "Hold her,"
he said, and the men who held her arms tightened their
grip. She saw Slade's fist coming, but could do nothing to
avoid it. The blow landed at her temple, stunning her. She
felt the pain in her eye and cheek and her knees slumped
beneath her.

"Get her on the horse, if you have to tie her on. Then
take care of the baby."

Danny! No, they couldn't harm Danny. She tried to
protest, but no words come. She couldn't fight off the
blackness that claimed her. They were moving. She could
hear dwindling shots and men shouting, then nothing.
Her captors pushed forward at a full gallop, and long
after the ranch was behind them, they kept their pace.
They must anticipate pursuit, Gaby thought fuzzily.

They rode through the darkness, crossing the prairie
and heading into the cross timbers toward the mountains.
When they'd ridden for a couple of hours through the
post oaks and scrubby pines, they turned north off the
trail. Now their progress was slow as the men followed
each other single file. The reins of Gaby's horse were

held by the rider ahead. The trail led them upward. The impenetrable blackness of the mountains seemed ominous. Still the men pushed on over a trail they knew by heart.

Gaby was exhausted and chilled despite the rough jacket someone had tossed around her shoulders. Her cries of terror and grief had long since stilled. She rode silently, her mind filled with the image of Mrs. Schafer clutching her bloodstained bodice as she sank to the floor. Why hadn't they killed her as well? she wondered. Did they hope to hold her for ransom money? Had they killed Maria and Danny, or had they brought them along? She strained to hear the sound of a baby crying, but the hills were silent.

The horses climbed slowly now, their hooves striking against the rocky ledge as they topped the peak of a low-lying mountain and headed downward again into the valley below. The man in front of her swore and dropped the reins of Gaby's horse as he swung his own horse hard to the right. The horse scrambled on the loose rock and shale, trying to get a better foothold. She was free, Gaby thought, and leaned forward to grab hold of the loose reins. Prodding her horse with the heel of her slipper, she tried to swing back up the path, but the other riders had crested the rim and were starting downward. Frightened by the dark and the close presence of the other horses, her mount whinnied and bolted forward, crashing into other riders.

"What the hell?" a man shouted as his horse reared backward away from the wild thrashing. Behind Gaby other men shouted out.

"Get the woman. She's trying to get away." Hands reached out for Gaby, nearly yanking her from the saddle, while other hands subdued her frightened horse. Slade Harner moved back up the line until his horse was level with hers. Even in the pale moonlight, Gaby could sense the evilness of the man. He looked at her, a half-smile on his face; then his hand slashed out, striking her across the mouth. She reeled backward from the force of the blow and nearly fell from the saddle.

"I might have known you'd try something," he said in

a voice that was too quiet and reasonable. "They don't call you the Texas Angel for nothing, do they?"

"You'll pay for this, Slade Harner."

"Take care, Mrs. Spencer. You're not down on your big ranch now. You don't have Rayne Elliott or a bunch of your men here to protect you. All your power and money don't mean jack shit to me. You try to get away again and I'll make you sorry you was ever born."

"I don't need Rayne Elliott to protect me from the likes of you," Gaby cried. "I've whipped you before, Slade Harner, and I can again." His face turned ugly at her reminder of that day in town when she'd taken a horse-whip to him.

"Things are different now," he snarled. "Now I'm the boss. The high-and-mighty Texas Angel is at my mercy, and don't you forget it."

"You won't get away with this, you know," Gaby said. "You've killed one woman and kidnapped another. The other ranchers will be after you. They've probably already formed a posse and are on your trail now. They'll hunt you down."

Slade cast a quick glance over his shoulder as if he expected to see the sheriff and a posse top the rise. "It ain't gonna happen." He sneered. "Cain't nobody find us up here. You just keep hopin', though." He laughed low and sinister in his throat; then, taking the reins from Gaby's hands, he started back down the trail.

"Let's get moving," he called to his men, and they continued their slow, careful descent toward the dark valley. When they'd reached the valley floor, they rode for a short distance until they came to a stream, its waters glinting serenely in the moonlight. The men dismounted and Slade walked back to Gaby's horse.

"This is it," he said, reaching up to grab her arm. "This is your new home, Mrs. Spencer. 'Course it ain't grand and fancy like you're used to, but I call it home." He yanked her out of the saddle and pinned her against the side of the horse with his body.

Gaby cried out and tried to pull away as his hands brushed up along her waist and settled at her breasts. He lowered his head, and his mouth, hard and brutal, claimed hers. Gaby beat at his arms and shoulders with her fists. He didn't release her until her flailing hands brushed against his holstered pistol. Frantically Gaby tugged at it, but his hand knocked her aside.

"You don't learn very fast," he snarled, and taking hold of her arm, half-shoved her across the uneven rocky ground toward a dark opening in the rocky wall of the mountain. They entered a cave and Gaby was surprised to see how much had been done to accommodate its inhabitants. A rough table and chair held cooking utensils and a few tin plates and cups. Logs and large rocks had been rolled into place around a fire pit. At the back of the cave, rough beds had been knocked together out of post oak and other wood and were covered with bedrolls. Slade shoved Gaby back toward these and her heart lurched with fear. A final push sent her backward across a bed and Slade towered over her menacingly.

"I'm going to have to teach you a lesson, Gaby," he snarled. "You're going to learn how to say 'yes sir' and 'no sir' and 'pretty please.' " He leaned over her, his face scant inches from hers, his eyes glittering with anger. "When I get done, you're going to be a new woman." He grinned evilly and turned away, striding across the cave to give orders to his men.

Gaby lay where she was, drawing in a deep breath and striving to still her thumping heart. For the moment she was safe from Slade Harner and his intentions, but how long would that last? She huddled on the bed, watching as the other men came into the cave, searching for some sign of Maria and Danny. They weren't there, and Gaby wasn't sure whether to be relieved or not. She shivered, feeling tired and chilled. Her bed was against the wall of the cave and its dampness seemed to penetrate her very bones.

"Rayne, where are you now?" she half-whispered. "I need you."

"We gotta stop," George Naylor said. "We can't travel through Indian Territory in the dark. We could blunder into a camp of 'em and get scalped before the sun comes up."

"I've traveled through this area at night," Rayne said. "We can follow the trail."

"What if they left the trail someplace back there?" George objected. The whites of his eyes flashed in the dark. "We'd have to backtrack for miles before we found where they turned off."

"We aren't stopping," Rayne said flatly.

"Sheriff," George appealed to another man.

"Naylor's right, Rayne," Tom Garner interjected. "It won't do no good to push on when we can't see the trail signs. We'll camp here and start again at daybreak."

Rayne sat uneasy and frustrated in his saddle. He couldn't stop now. They had Gaby. He couldn't rest until she was back safe and sound. But the men were dismounting and unsaddling their horses.

"Come on, Rayne. It'll help if you rest a little," Kevin said.

"I can't rest with Gaby out there."

"Then I'll ride with you." Kevin's face was gray with fatigue. The material of his shirt was plastered by blood to his shoulder. He'd caught a bullet back at the ranch when he'd run out of the bunkhouse trying to stop the men who'd taken Gaby. The bullet was out and the wound bandaged, but Kevin looked like he was ready to fall out of the saddle. Billy Fuller and Cole Elliott still sat their horses, waiting to see what Rayne's decision would be. If Rayne insisted on pushing on, he knew these two men would join him as well. His father was too old for this, Rayne thought. Slowly he shook his head.

"We'd better rest. We'll be fresher in the morning." Reluctantly he climbed down off his horse. He was too keyed-up to sleep. He rolled himself in a blanket and sat with his back against a tree watching the night shadows deepen just before they lightened to the pale gray of dawn. All his thoughts were on Gaby. Where was she now? Was she safe?

When he could pick out the mounds lying around on the ground, he stood up and moved among the men who made up the posse, waking each one with a nudge of his boot or by calling out a name. Reluctantly the men rolled out of their bedrolls, rubbing at their eyes and grunting.

They tracked the outlaws through the morning and lost the trail by midafternoon. They rode back to the spot they'd last seen a trace of them and spread out searching for more signs. An old hoofprint of an unshod horse led them in one direction. An unshod horse meant Indians, and white men had attacked the Spencer ranch. By nightfall they still hadn't found the trail, and once more they bedded down for the night, feeling frustrated and depressed.

Rayne sat tense and silent through the night, barely tolerating the delay. Deep lines had etched themselves in his face. Men who'd helped him look for Gaby once before along the flood-swollen banks of a river remembered that look of despair. He was still in love with her, they thought, shaking their heads, and then admitted to themselves it was easy to be a fool over a woman like the Texas Angel.

A second day they looked, and a third, riding into every crevice and canyon they could find. Their coffee gave out and so did their food. Now part of each day was spent hunting for game, and with every shot they vacillated between relief that there would be something for supper and dread at the thought that the Comanche might have heard the shots and were even now tracking them down. They kept moving, both to search for the trail of outlaws and to keep out of the reach of the Indians.

"Look what Thad and me found back there on the trail," Otis said, holding up a strip of material.

"Where? Show me," Rayne ordered, hope flaring where before there had been none.

Thad Martin's lips thinned as the men rushed after Otis. He fell back from the rest and unfastened one of his spurs. After a quick look around, he threw it into the chaparral growth as hard as he could, then galloped after the other men. Otis led them along the trail to a spot.

"You've gone too far," Thad called out. "It was back yonder a ways."

Otis paused and looked around him. "Are you sure?" he asked doubtfully. "I was dead sure it was down here."

"I tell you it was back this way," Thad called. "Come on, men, let's spread out and search the area." He wheeled his horse and headed back up the trail. One by one the other men followed.

Otis looked at Rayne and scratched his head. "Guess I ain't had enough sleep lately," he said. "I was dadburn certain I found this here scrap up toward that ridge there." His words were interrupted by a shout.

"We've found something," a man called, and Rayne spurred his horse back up the trail in the direction Thad and the other men had taken. When he reached them, Silas Flume sat holding a spur aloft.

"One of them's lost his Chihuahuas," he said, holding the Mexican spur aloft. It gleamed wickedly in the fading light. "Whoever lost this don't like his horseflesh none," Silas observed, giving the rowel a spin with his finger.

Rayne's eyes narrowed as he looked at the spur. He'd seen it somewhere before. He took it and examined it closely. The heel band was made of ornately stamped silver. Thoughtfully Rayne tucked the spur into his saddlebag. He'd figure it out later. Right now he wanted to go after Gaby. They set out along the trail, searching for more clues on the hard, rocky soil.

"Where's the girl?" the new arrival demanded.

"She's back there sleeping." Slade nodded toward the back of the cave. Abner Harris looked at the cowboy with ill-concealed contempt. Slade felt a trickle of fear up his spine.

"Martin ain't too happy with you for taking her," Harris said, squatting before the campfire. "You were supposed to kill her and leave the body there to be found." Harris poured himself a cup of coffee. He managed to keep his gun hand free at all times. It made Slade nervous.

"I've got me some old scores to settle with her and Rayne Elliott," he said.

"Martin has his own plans. He's paying you to help carry them out and do what you're told. He's made arrangements with Abigail Spencer to buy the ranch, but the Spencer woman can't claim the ranch if this one's alive."

"What am I getting out of this? I've been wanting her

ever since she stepped off the boat in Galveston. I aim to have her."

The dark-haired man looked over his shoulder. "I hope she's worth the trouble you've gotten yourself into." He stood up. He was a heavyset man, but there was a hardness to him that came from living by his wits on the trail with other men as unscrupulous as he was. Slade had always felt uncomfortable around him. He'd never been able to stare down that hard, black gaze. Instinctively he knew Abner would kill him without a second thought if it suited him or if Thad Martin ordered him to. As fast as he was, Slade was still not sure he could outdraw Harris.

"What's it gonna hurt?" he wheedled.

"Thad wanted her dead," the man said. "That was the deal. You were to kill her and the kid. The only one you killed was a useless old woman. Thad ain't too impressed with you."

Slade swallowed hard and held his hands out placatingly. "It ain't too late. I'll kill her now," he said, taking a step toward the back of the cave.

"It is too late." The man leveled a long, cold stare at Slade. "Thad says to keep her alive now. He may send her back, so he don't want no harm to come to her. That means keep your hands off."

"I ain't touched her anyhow," Slade said quickly.

"See that you don't. Mess up again, Slade, and the vultures will be feasting on you."

Slade swallowed hard, realizing how close he'd come to ensuring his own death. "Look, I'll make it up to Thad. I'll go down to the ranch and take care of the kid. We can kill the woman and leave her down on the trail someplace."

"I said not now." Abner's voice was cold and hard. "Do as you're told, Harner. Martin don't want her harmed. You got that?" His beefy hand reached out for the front of Slade's shirt and pulled him forward like a rag doll.

"Y-yeah, all right," Slade said, shaking his head. "I'll do just what you say. I won't touch her."

"Good." Harris let go of his shirt and with a final warning glare left the cave.

Gaby took a deep breath and eased it out slowly, her

eyes staring at the smoke-blackened wall of the cave. Her mind was whirling with all she'd heard. Abigail Spencer had schemed with Thad Martin to have Danny and her killed, just so she could have the money she'd get from the ranch. Only Slade's lust for her had kept her alive. Something else she'd heard gave Gaby new hope. Slade hadn't killed Danny yet. She pressed a fist against her lips to stifle a sob of relief.

Footsteps approached, and quickly she calmed herself, taking slow deep breaths to feign sleep. Slade walked to the edge of the bed and looked down on her for a moment. Cursing, he left the cave. Gaby let her breath out slowly and opened her eyes. Danny was alive. For the moment she was safe from Slade, but she had to find a way to escape. She had no way of knowing when Thad might change his mind again. Rolling off the edge of the bed, Gaby walked to the mouth of the cave and peered out, her darting gaze seeking some means of escape.

"Where's Martin and the rest of the men?" Rayne demanded.

"They've left. Headed back to town."

"Damn them. They can't quit now. Gaby's still out there somewhere. God knows what those bastards have done to her."

"That's just the point, Rayne," Garner said. "The outlaws have Mrs. Spencer and they've done their worst now. She's either dead or alive."

"She's alive," Rayne shouted hoarsely.

"Maybe she is and maybe she ain't."

"You can't just ride back to your comfortable fires and forget about her."

"That's not what we're trying to do, but we have to be reasonable. The men lit out after them outlaws without taking time to get food or clothing and bedding for the cold nights up here in these mountains. We can't do Mrs. Spencer no good if we're sick and half-starved."

"She may be all those things," Rayne said.

"That's true, but staying out here without provisions won't help find her any faster. I'm going down with the rest of the men. We'll get our gear and come on back. I'll see about getting that half-breed from up north to come down and track for us."

Rayne made no answer. He sat hunched in his saddle, his eyes dark and accusing as they stared back at the sheriff. Kevin, Billy, and Cole waited silently. None of them had taken the time to shave since they'd started the search. They all looked haggard, and Cole slumped in his saddle. Rayne's face was stark and set beneath his beard. His eyes gleamed with purpose. He would not go down the mountain without Gaby. Looking at him, the sheriff wondered what Rayne would do if they didn't find the Texas Angel.

"You should come down and rest," he said persuasively. "Your pa looks in a bad way."

"He can go down. I'm staying," Rayne said flatly.

"I'll stay with Rayne," Cole rasped out. He appeared old and shrunken inside his clothes. His nose and cheeks were red with cold, and he shivered. He wouldn't be able to go on for long.

Rayne turned to the younger men. "Take Pa back to the ranch," he said. "Get provisions and come back."

"No, Rayne," Cole said feebly. "I want to help you find your woman." Rayne's head came up at his father's words. "I know you ain't never got over her," Cole continued. "I don't want to see you end up like me 'cause your woman's gone."

Rayne smiled briefly, a grim flash of teeth in his whiskered face. "We'll find her, Pa," he said. "I need those provisions. Go down the mountain and bring them back to me." After a long moment the old man nodded and followed the sheriff down the trail.

Rayne looked at the two young men who remained. "Go on down," he ordered, but they only shook their heads.

"I owe Miss Gaby something," Billy said. "She saved me from a hanging once. I ain't abandonin' her now."

Rayne turned to Kevin. "I suppose you aren't going down either."

"That's right." Kevin's voice was hard and determined.

"No sense in arguing with a lovesick fool," Rayne snapped.

"I thought you'd understand that," Kevin said, and the

two men stared at each other, rivals who understood all too well.

"Let's go back up the trail," Rayne said, and led the way back to the spot where Otis had first claimed to find the piece of material. Night was coming on. The coldness was creeping in again, biting through the thin trail coat he wore. Bill and Kevin were huddled in their saddles, their sleeping blankets wrapped around their shoulders. Maybe they should stop and build a fire and rest before starting out again. None of them had slept well the last few nights. Rayne shivered with a sudden chill. Gaby might be out there somewhere on the trail, cold and tired, needing help. They had to find her. Without complaint, Billy and Kevin followed him back up the mountain.

She had a gun! It was tied to her thigh beneath her petticoats. She could hardly believe her good fortune. One of the men had been cleaning his gun. Gaby had watched as he polished it and reloaded the chambers. Then he laid it to one side to begin on the other. Someone called him out to the corral and he'd gone, leaving his gun behind. Gaby had moved quickly, covering it with her full skirts, and when no one was watching, scooped it up. Later she'd pleaded a need to relieve herself and in the sketchy privacy afforded her had torn strips of petticoats to tie the gun to her thigh.

The man had come back much later, his eyes overly bright, his speech slurred. When he hadn't found his gun he'd made an outcry. The others had helped him look.

"You're drunk," they accused. "You could have lost it anywhere. Did you look down by the creek?"

The search for the gun had moved outside, and finally all was quiet. Now Gaby moved a little, just to feel the scrape of the gun against her flesh. It felt cold and heavy against her leg, and vastly reassuring. Now she must think of a plan of escape. She lay tense and unmoving long into the night, while her mind raced from one idea to another.

The next morning she approached Slade warily. He sat hunkered down on a stump, a cup of coffee in his hands as he stared into the fire.

"What do you want?" he snarled when she stood beside him.

"I need to wash my face and hands," Gaby said. "I've been closed in here for three days now."

"Now, ain't that too bad?" Slade jeered. "Did we forget to draw the lady's bath?" Gaby made no answer, waiting patiently for his sarcasm to end. "We ain't got no bathtub here,"

"The creek will do," she said.

"I don't want you to go, see?" he shouted, jerking his thumb back at his chest. "Me, I'm the boss, and I say no."

Gaby felt her hopes sink. He wasn't letting her out. She tried again, keeping her voice even. "I overheard one of the men saying how you were afraid to do anything without asking the boss first."

"I make the decisions around here." He glanced at her. "Go on," he said suddenly. "Go down to the creek and wash up. Then get back up here."

"Yes, sir," Gaby said, knowing it would please his ego. She hurried out into the cold mountain air, shivering in the thin jacket she wore. Still she knelt by the stream and scooped up the tumbling icy water and began to splash it over her face and neck. She shivered violently, gasping at the shock of the cold water, then bent again with cupped hands. Huddled where she was, she looked around. They were in a canyon. Upstream a corral of sorts had been built to hold the horses, and behind it was another cave opening. Men were going and coming from it, carrying saddles or hay. The cave must be a storage barn.

Other men sat on rocks, seeking the stingy warmth of the winter sun while they played cards or dice. Gaby glanced around the rest of the clearing, looking for a means of escape. Scrubby pines grew here and there, their growth stunted by the high altitude and the coldness of the winters. Carefully she noted the trail leading out of the canyon and looked for any covering on either side of it. Even on horseback, she wouldn't be able to outrun the men in this terrain.

Glancing around, Gaby noticed Slade Harner watching her and again bent over the stream as if totally absorbed in making herself clean in the icy mountain water. When she could no longer bear the coldness, she rose and walked back toward the cave.

"Well, are you satisfied?" Slade asked, smirking. He hadn't been fooled by her ploy. He knew she was trying to escape. He wasn't bothered by it. Where would she go up here?

"I won't be satisfied until I'm home again," Gaby snapped.

"You ain't goin' home again. And there ain't no way for you to get out of this canyon without our knowing it." Gaby swept past him, her eyes flashing with anger. How she longed to scratch at the man's hateful face, but she mustn't do anything to further arouse his hostility. He might find the gun and he might not allow her out of the cave again.

She walked back to her bed and sat down. The sun had been high, nearly at its apex. It must be midday. The afternoon stretched before her, a wearisome thing to be gotten through before the night and another day dawned. Tomorrow she would insist on going to the stream again, and this time, this time, God willing, she would find some way to escape.

There was no sun the next morning. The wind blew down off the mountains cold and biting. Gaby watched the light grow, pale and unpromising in the cave opening. Finally the men stirred and made coffee for themselves and threw some beans in a pot. Gaby walked toward the fire pit, where Slade Harner sat with the other men.

"I'm going down to the stream to wash," she said, and kept her feet moving toward the cave opening.

"You can't go out there," Slade snapped.

Gaby turned to stare at him. "Why not? You let me go down yesterday."

"That was yesterday, this is today," Slade said. "It's too cold and I ain't going to stand out there and keep an eye on you."

"There's no way out of the canyon. You said so yourself." He didn't answer. Frustrated, Gaby stayed where she was. Maybe she could sneak out when he wasn't looking.

"Looks like a norther is blowing up," one of the men said.

"Could be," another acknowledged.

"Well, when are we gittin' out of here then? I don't want to spend the winter up here eatin' beans and trying to stay warm." Several of the other men raised their voices in support of the man's question.

"We'll be leavin' soon," Slade said. "We're waitin' for someone."

"Martin?" the first man asked, and the others cast a warning glance at him and then at Gaby.

"What are you standin' there for?" Slade demanded. "If you're going to the stream, go on." Quickly, before he could change his mind again, Gaby hurried out of the cave.

"You fool," she heard Slade say to the man. "You want her to know who the boss is?"

"If Martin's the boss, why ain't he here tellin' us what to do?" the man responded. "I'm tired of waitin'."

"You'll wait as long as you have to," Slade snarled.

Once again she squatted on the muddy banks.

Even now a man was watching her from his lookout perch up near the corral. Gaby dipped her hands in the cold water. A rim of ice had formed along the edges where it was shallow. Under the pretense of washing, Gaby once again studied the hillside. A movement high on the stony slope caught her eye. She fixed her gaze on that spot until her eyes were strained and her vision blurred. A man was up there. Was it one of the lookouts?

The man shifted from behind the boulder and moved his hand in a single wave. Gaby blinked her eyes and looked again. It was Rayne. She clamped her teeth together over a cry of joy. Somehow she'd known he would come for her. Was he alone? She bent over the water, scooping up a handful, unmindful of the chunks of ice. She ducked her head as if about to splash the water over herself, and glanced around. She caught a brief glimpse of Billy and then of Kevin. Then they were gone out of sight again. They'd shown themselves only for a moment to let her know help was at hand. She blinked back the tears as she pretended to wash. Her heart was singing with relief. She wasn't alone anymore.

*   *   *

She was alive!

For the first time in days, the tightness in his chest eased a little.

They'd picked up the outlaws' trail the night before, and nearly stumbled into the canyon before they'd realized it.

Only the clink of a gun barrel against stone had warned them of the sentry. It had been easy to slip around and knock him from his perch, and easier still after that to slip over the rim and down into the valley.

Now Rayne lay watching Gaby as she searched the valley for help. Once again her eyes turned back to him, and he eased up enough to motion her to move upstream toward the corral. They'd have to get fresh horses if they were going to outrun the kidnappers.

Gaby nodded in understanding, then crouched where she was, her head bent, her hands working at her skirts. What was she doing now? Rayne wondered. The rest of the men might come out of the cave any minute.

Gaby gave a final glance at the lookout at the corral and stood up, one hand gripping her full skirts, the other pushing aside strands of dark hair blowing in her face. She gazed at a spot high above the cave. The man at the corral glanced up, and seeing her attention riveted on something, moved from his perch to a better spot so he too could look up the mountain wall. Had she seen someone up there? No one could get in that way easily, but it could be done. The man fingered the trigger of his rifle and studied the terrain.

Good girl, Rayne thought, and crouching low, left his hiding place and ran across the valley floor toward the next clump of bushes. He sensed Billy and Kevin moving forward too. Running and stopping to glance at the lookout, they made their way nearer the corral. The man didn't notice them coming. His attention was divided between the girl by the stream and the spot she watched up along the mountain wall.

Now Gaby was laughing and dancing around, one hand still gripping her skirt, the other waving at the ledge above. She'd seen something, the lookout thought, and moved down the path away from the corral. He'd better let Slade know. He glanced back up at the ledge, striving to see what the girl saw. There had to be someone up there, someone she thought would rescue her. He glanced back down at her. She was gone. He stopped in his tracks and looked around. She couldn't have made it to the mouth of the cave. Was she down by the stream? He looked around again, feeling more uneasy.

A sound at the corral made him jerk his head around. There was someone after the horses. He pulled his gun from his holster and took careful aim at the broad back, lining up his sights.

Gaby steadied her gun against the rock where she hid. She'd never shot a man before, but he was going to shoot Rayne. She closed her eyes and fired. The sound of the shot seemed to echo in the canyon, repeating itself over and over.

Inside the cave, Slade and his men leapt to their feet. "What the devil?" Slade cried as they headed for the opening, their guns already out of their holsters. Horses swept down on them as they cleared the cave. One man fell beneath their hooves, while others leapt aside, then ran after the horses, trying to catch them.

Slade stood at the entrance to the cave looking for a figure that would be running low and crookedly. His eyes narrowed as he picked out three men. He raised his gun and fired at one, but missed. Another man slung his long legs over a horse and galloped down the rise toward the stream. Slade took careful aim and waited until the rider was nearer.

Suddenly a shot rang out behind him and Slade felt the impact of the bullet in his thigh almost as soon as he heard the sound. It spun him around and he fell. The girl was behind a rock, and she held a smoking gun in her hand. When she saw Slade looking at her, she ducked down again.

Rage spread through Slade Harner. He should have killed her when he had the chance. He raised his gun and took careful aim. She'd come up again, and when she did, he'd shoot her. The sound of hooves reminded him of the rider. He glanced back over his shoulder, torn between which to shoot first. His indecision gave Rayne the split second he needed to take aim and fire. Slade crumbled to the ground.

Drawn by the gunshots, the other men gave up chasing after the horses and began to fire back at Rayne. Kevin and Billy were thundering down the slope after Rayne. Suddenly Billy slumped forward in his saddle, his hand pressed to his side. By sheer willpower he straightened and began firing again.

Gaby watched Rayne ride down the slope toward her, unprotected from the men who were trying to kill him. Flattening herself against the rock, she began to fire at Slade's men, trying to draw their fire away from Rayne. She heard the ping of a bullet against the rock, and dust flew toward her. It had been close. Gaby fired until the hammer clicked down on empty chambers, then threw the gun aside and huddled down behind the rock, hoping a ricocheting bullet wouldn't hit her. The hoofbeats were closer now.

"Gaby," Rayne yelled as his horse skidded to a stop beside her hiding place. She leapt up and ran toward the horse.

Billy and Kevin galloped toward them, their guns blazing a protective wall of fire.

Rayne caught her up in his arms, keeping her low against the side of the horse. He kicked the little mustang and it bolted away up the trail toward the rise that would take them out of the valley. Kevin and Billy were close behind, turning now and then to fire at the pursuing outlaws. Gaby clung to the saddle and Rayne's leg, her feet scant inches from the rocky ground. She could feel the muscles of Rayne's arms quiver with the strain of holding her thus.

Bullets whizzed around them. It was a miracle they hadn't been hit by one. The crest of the rim seemed impossibly far away, and all of it up a steep incline. They'd never make it, Gaby thought in despair, but Rayne pushed the laboring horse forward. The shouts of the men down in the valley seemed farther away now, and although Gaby could still hear the sound of gunfire, she guessed they were too far away to be hit now. Except by rifle fire. A bullet thudded into a nearby rocky outcropping, scattering pieces of shale.

"Come on, hiah up!" Rayne called encouragement to the mustang. Valiantly the little horse pushed himself up the trail, but he was unaccustomed to the drag of weight at his side. Gaby's feet scraped along the rocky slope and she tried to pull them higher, her muscles screaming a protest.

Rayne brought the horse to a halt beside a flat boulder. "Climb up in front," he shouted, and his arms wrapped around her protectively. Instinctively Gaby knew he'd put her in front to shield her from the bullets.

The horses scrabbled up the loose rock and gained the top; then they were plunging downward. The wild hammering of Gaby's heart stilled a little. They were going to make it!

with a low thump against Rayne's and flat and rolled down the hill herself.

"Gaby!" Rayne called out, galloping downward frantically.

26

They made their way down the outer slope, sliding in their haste. Only fear that the horses might go lame made Rayne slow down a little. They veered from the rough path and into the trees, and Gaby saw the men had left their horses there. They stood with heads hanging. They were too tired to be of much use.

"I'll take the roan," Rayne said, climbing down and running to the other mount. "We'll make better time than riding double."

"It'll take them some time to gather up their horses," Kevin said.

"Not as long as you think. That canyon's small." Rayne fixed an eye on Billy's white face. "Are you going to make it?"

"Don't worry about me," Billy answered valiantly.

"Let's go," Rayne said, and his horse was moving forward even before he had hit the saddle.

Shots rang out, reminding them they weren't in the clear yet. Some of the outlaws had captured their horses and were pursuing.

Rayne led them down the mountain path. It was on the last steep grade that Gaby's horse lost its footing and half-slid down the rocky path, his eyes rolling in fright, his cry of pain rending the air.

"Gaby!" Rayne's cry was one of anguish as he watched her descent. If the horse rolled over, she'd be crushed, but he stayed upright, sliding on his flanks. The bumpy, jarring slide threw Gaby from the saddle and she landed with a hard thump against the rocks and dirt and rolled down the hill herself.

"Gaby!" Rayne cried out again as the small body rolled to a stop and lay still. He urged his horse back up the slope and got down to look at Gaby. The blood roared in his head. She looked so little and lifeless, her body limp and unresisting in his arms as he carefully turned her over, searching for injuries. Her eyes were closed. The small face was pale, and blood oozed from a cut on her forehead. A purple bruise was already forming on one cheekbone. One eye was black, but it was an old injury. Someone had hit her, he thought, and clenched his teeth in rage.

"Is she all right?" Billy called from the bottom of the hill. He held the reins to Kevin's horse as the young man climbed back up the hill. He knelt beside Gaby, calling her name.

Gently Rayne's hands ran over her limbs, looking for broken bones. Dark lashes fluttered against her pale cheeks. Her eyes opened and she looked around in bewilderment.

It all came back and her eyes cleared. Rayne hovered above her. Gaby threw herself into his arms.

"Oh, Rayne, you came for me. I knew you would," she cried, her arms gripping him tightly. He held her head against his chest, rocking the small body, and Kevin turned away from the look on the other man's face, shaken by the love he saw there. He had no place here between these two, he thought, and walked back down the trail.

"Rayne, those men," Gaby said, pulling back to look at him. "Are they still after us?"

"They are. Are you able to travel?"

"I'll be all right," she assured him, and got to her feet. "My horse isn't." She nodded at her mount. It stood with head lowered, one leg held up away from the ground.

"He won't be any use to us now. We'll both ride my horse."

"Ride on without me," Gaby began, but Rayne ignored her, lifting her up and settling her in the saddle.

"I'm not leaving you, Gaby," Rayne said, climbing up in the saddle. "We're leaving together or not at all."

Their progress was slower now. The outlaws were gaining on them. Rayne was surprised at their persistence. With Slade dead, they should have lost interest by now. Grimly he pushed on.

"I have to know one thing," Gaby said over her shoulder. Rayne could feel the tenseness in her body. "Is Danny all right?"

"He's safe. Maria hid in the attic with him. They're both fine."

Relief flooded through her and Rayne could feel her body slump a little. Another thought made her stiffen. "Mrs. Schafer is dead, isn't she?"

"Yes. She died instantly," Rayne said. "She had little pain." Gaby slumped back against him and he knew she was quietly crying.

When the horses could go no further, Rayne slowed to a walk, looking on either side for a place of concealment and protection for them. He nearly missed it. A slash in the rocky walls seemed to offer some protection. A jumble of rocks stood sentinel, blocking the view of the lower trail from those who traveled down.

"Get down and hide over in those rocks," he ordered. "Billy, stay with Gaby. Kevin and I will take the horses on down the trail and hide them, then we'll come back." They had to hide the horses so they wouldn't give their position away. He found a place around the next bend in the trail. A small mountain stream tumbled over the rocky ground, and grass grew sparsely along its banks. They tied their horses, and carrying their rifles and all the extra ammunition, made their way back to the rocks.

They could hear Slade's men coming down the trail.

A cold wind blew against their backs. The sky was leaden above them. If they got out of this alive, they still had to make it back to town before a winter storm hit. Gaby wasn't dressed warmly enough to weather a norther. None of them were. Where were the sheriff and his posse? Rayne could use them along about now. Their chances weren't good. They were outnumbered. He had a badly wounded man, a woman depending on him, and a greenhorn kid to help him.

The scrape of an iron-shod hoof against rock and a man's curse alerted them that their pursuers were close.

Rayne brought his rifle up, balancing it on a rock, lining up his sights on the opening in the rock. The men would have to ride through it one at a time.

This might improve the odds some.

"It don't make no sense," one of the men was grousing. "We ought to be packin' up our gear and gettin' out of these mountains before the storm breaks."

"We will," another man answered. "As soon as we find and kill them. Rayne Elliott has this coming."

Rayne shifted his weight slightly. That voice explained a lot. No wonder the outlaws had continued to pursue them. Slade Harner wasn't dead, and he wanted revenge.

"They can't go on much further anyway," Slade continued. "They're shy a horse, and that's hard riding in this country. One of their horses'll give out soon."

The first man appeared in the opening, and Rayne's finger tightened on the trigger. He hated to kill a man this way, but if he gave them a warning, Gaby and the rest of them would be killed. He waited until another man appeared, then squeezed the trigger. He heard the report of Kevin's rifle, and both men dropped from their saddles. The men behind pulled up, grabbing their guns while they looked around. Rayne squeezed the trigger, and another man fell.

"Take cover," someone yelled, and the men scattered, leaving their horses to run riderless. The outlaws scrambled into the rocks and began to return Rayne and Kevin's fire. Rayne had chosen his spot well. Slade and his men couldn't get through the narrow opening without exposing themselves. If they tried to climb up and around, they were again exposed. They were neatly pinned.

Rayne's rifle was empty and he didn't dare take time to reload it. He took out his pistols and waited. A sound at his back made him whirl, his gun cocked.

"It's me," Gaby cried, and Rayne eased the hammer back in place.

"Go back, Gaby. You'll be safer back there."

"I'm here to help you," she answered. Rayne cursed her stubbornness.

"The best help you can be is to stay out of the way. I don't want to have to worry—" A high shot made him duck down.

"Then don't," Gaby said. "I'll load your rifle." Before he could object, she had moved forward and picked up the rifle and saddlebags of ammunition. Expertly she proceeded to load both rifles. When she'd finished, she picked up one of Rayne's pistols and moved into position between him and Kevin.

Rayne looked at her and made up his mind. "Kevin, I want you to take Gaby and Billy and make your way down the mountain to get some help. I can hold Slade and his men."

"Kevin can go by himself," Gaby said. "I'm not going."

"I'm not going down either," Kevin said, his eyes on the rocks where Slade and his men crouched.

"Gaby, don't be stubborn. Do as I say," Rayne shouted angrily.

"I am. You said we were leaving here together or not at all. That still goes."

"Gaby . . ." Rayne began helplessly. He could see she wasn't going to budge.

Her dark eyes sparkled as she cast him an impudent grin. Her face was dirty and bruised, one eye black, and still she could smile. "Who's out there?"

"Slade Harner," he answered.

"He's not dead then?" Gaby asked with a sinking heart.

"It takes a lot to kill a rattlesnake. He's wounded, though. I put a slug in him."

"I got him in the leg," Gaby said, and Rayne glanced at her in surprise. "How many are out there?" Her eyes were fixed on a black shadow that moved, sliding behind a rock.

"I counted eight," Kevin said. "We got three."

"Five left," Gaby said. The shadow had moved again. A man darted from behind a rock toward the next bit of covering. He was working his way closer. Soon he would have an easy shot down on them. Gaby followed his progress with the sight of her gun.

"Gaby," Rayne began impatiently, "don't waste ammunition. We'll need it later."

"I'm a good shot," she said, not taking her eyes off the rock where the man had last disappeared. The man showed himself again, moving cautiously. Gaby took a deep breath and squeezed the trigger. The man cried out and fell backward. Rayne looked at him in surprise and then at Gaby.

"I've been practicing," she said, and grinned.

The man crawled away. They watched him go. Neither of them wanted to kill a wounded man. The killer crawled back to his horse and pulled himself into the saddle.

"Murphy, you coward, where are you going?" Slade shouted, but the man didn't answer. He kicked his horse into a gallop and headed back up into the mountains. Other men ran down to catch their horses and ride away.

"Come back here!" Slade shouted, and fired at the backs of his own men. Then all was quiet.

Tensely the three in the rocks waited, straining to hear anything that would tell them a man still waited to gun them down. The wind moaned around the steep walls, lonely and forlorn-sounding. Had Slade left too? Kevin glanced at Rayne and Gaby. Rayne looked at the sky. The wind was blowing colder now, a threat of what was to follow. They should get moving soon, he thought. He looked back up the trail at the rocks and boulders. There was no movement and no sound. The canyon walls echoed the emptiness of the mountains.

"Stay here," Rayne ordered, and cautiously stood up, revealing himself a bit at a time. He stood listening to the rocks and mountains, listening for the telltale rattle of a snake about to strike, but all was silent. He glanced down at Gaby. Her face was anxious and questioning.

"I think they've gone," Rayne said quietly. "Give me the rifle." Gaby handed it to him. "Kevin, get Billy and make your way down the trail toward the horses." Kevin headed back into the rocks. "Go on, Gaby. Follow him."

"Are you coming?" she asked fearfully.

"I'll be right behind you. Go on."

With a pistol clutched in one hand and the rifle in the other, Gaby did as he ordered. Rayne put himself between her and the rocks where Slade had taken cover. He walked backward, his gaze raking across the stone outcroppings, his finger firm on his trigger. All was still. When Gaby was around the bend of the trail and shielded by the rocky abutment, Rayne made one last sweeping glance around, then turned and followed her. They moved quickly, making as little sound as possible.

Kevin already had Billy settled on a horse, the reins in his hands. Rayne holstered his pistol and placed the rifle back in its case. His hands were at Gaby's waist, preparing to lift her up on the horse, when he heard a pistol being cocked. He looked around and saw Slade Harner standing on the trail. The left shoulder of his shirt was blood-soaked, as was one leg of his pants, but the gun in his hand was rock-steady and pointed right at them.

"Surprised to see me, Rayne?" Slade asked, taking a step forward. The grin on his face was savage and deadly. "You always did underestimate me. Well, that little mistake is going to cost you. Now you're going to find out which of us is the better man."

Gaby's eyes sought Rayne's. Her hand gripped his, guiding it along her waist to the gun shoved into the band of her skirt. Rayne looked into her wide dark eyes. They were unafraid as they met his. Suddenly Gaby sobbed and sank forward against Rayne, half-turning so her body blocked the sight of the gun from Slade.

"From where I stand, Slade, only one of us is a man, the other is a polecat," Rayne said, playing for time while he eased the gun from Gaby's waistband.

Slade laughed as if in appreciation of a fine joke. "You always did think big of yourself, Rayne. You and that old man of yours. In the army, men used to act like you were such a strong leader, said they'd follow you anywhere, but out here you ain't so much. I have men following me now. I'm the boss. I tell 'em what to do and when to do it."

"Looks like they didn't listen too well," Rayne said. "They ran off on you. You're all alone." He watched Slade's eyes.

The grin faded from the gunman's face. "They don't count for much," he said dismissively. "They were cowards. Besides, I don't need my men to take care of you. I can do that all by myself."

Slades eyes narrowed as he raised his gun and took better aim. Rayne thrust Gaby away, out of the line of fire, and brought his gun up, pulling the trigger almost before the barrel was centered on Slade's chest. As the force of the bullet hit him, Slade stumbled backward, flinging his arms upward. His gun went off, its lead going wild. Slade landed against the rocks and lay still. His gun slid from his hand and clattered down over the rocks before coming to rest. Then all was still.

Rayne remained with his gun trained on the fallen gunman, afraid to make the same mistake twice, but it was obvious from the sightless eyes staring at the cold gray sky that the man was dead.

Hoofbeats scrambled on the trail as Kevin turned back to see what had happened.

Gaby got to her feet and went to stand beside Rayne. "Is he dead?" she asked breathlessly.

"Yeah, this time he's dead," Rayne said, but went to check anyway.

"Is everyone all right?" Kevin asked.

Rayne nodded wearily. "Let's get back to town. We aren't finished with this yet," he answered, and swung Gaby up into the saddle.

They rode hard for town, as fast as Billy's condition allowed. Now there was no threat of danger from behind them, only from the leaden sky. Rayne had gone back up the trail and brought down Slade's horse, so now they rode single. They left the mountains and cross timbers behind them, riding through the foothills and out onto the prairie.

Gaby drew a deep breath, as if able to breathe freely for the first time in days. When they took a few minutes to rest, she told Rayne of the plot she'd overheard in the cave. She didn't mention Abigail's part in it. She couldn't bear to see the hurt it would cause Kevin.

Rayne's mouth was grim. It all fit now: the spur, the scrap of cloth, and the boldness of Slade and his men in kidnapping Gaby.

Rayne had a score to settle with Thad Martin, he vowed. Seeing his face, Gaby began to doubt the wisdom of telling him anything at all.

They rode into town just before dark. Someone ran to tell the sheriff they were back, while others crowded around to help Billy from his saddle and carry him up to the doctor's office.

Cole Elliott came out of the general store. "We was

just gettin' ready to leave again," he told Rayne. "We've had the supplies and men ready all day, but the sheriff kept findin' one excuse after the other."

"It doesn't matter. We made it," Rayne said. "Where's Martin?"

"Thad? He's up at the saloon."

"Rayne, don't do anything rash," Gaby cried. "Let's tell the sheriff and let him handle it."

Rayne didn't answer. He rode down the street toward the saloon.

"Cole, help him," Gaby cried. "He can't go up against Thad Martin and his men alone."

"Come on, men," Cole yelled. "We need some help down at the saloon." Several men swarmed after him.

Gaby kicked her horse into a gallop and headed toward the doctor's office. "Kevin, come quick," she called. "Rayne needs you at the saloon." The young man headed up the street.

Rayne was already at the saloon door. Wait, please wait, Gaby wanted to cry out. Help is coming. She remained silent. She didn't want her shout to warn Thad Martin. By the time she'd gotten to the saloon, Cole and the rest of the men were there. They crowded inside and stopped as Rayne approached the table where Thad and his men sat.

"Well, hello, Rayne," Thad said affably. "I see you came down out of the hills. Hear you found your woman."

"Yeah," Rayne said. "I found her." His lips were a thin line as he looked at the rancher.

Martin leaned back in his chair, feigning a nonchalance he didn't feel. He didn't like the look on Rayne's face or the men who waited at the door of the saloon. "That's good. We won't have to ride out tonight."

"You're not ready to go anyway," Rayne said. Martin looked wary. "You don't have your spurs on, Martin. Could be you lost one back there in the cross timbers."

"I don't know what you're talking about," Martin said.

"I mean this," Rayne said, tossing the silver spur on the table. "I believe it's the kind you wear."

"It might be. A lot of men wear spurs around here. It's cow country, you know."

"Not a lot of men wear spurs this fancy. This is the

spur you claimed to find on the trail, the one that led us away from the outlaws' trail."

"Now, Rayne," Martin began placatingly, "why would I lead you astray?"

"Why indeed?" Rayne said grimly. "Unless you were afraid we'd find the trail that would lead us to the hideout where Slade and his men had Gaby."

The men around Gaby muttered in consternation.

"That's right," Otis said. "It was Martin who claimed we found that scrap on another part of the trail."

"You planted that spur to get us to search in the opposite direction," Rayne accused Thad.

"That's ridiculous," Martin said. "I've never seen that spur before."

"Prove it," Rayne said. "Show us your spurs."

Martin looked around the circle of men, then smiled, opening his hands, palms out. "I'm afraid I can't do that, gentlemen. I'm not wearing spurs." He lifted his booted feet to show them.

"You always wear spurs, Martin," Rayne pressed. "What's happened to them?"

"Look in his saddlebags," someone called.

"I'll look," Cole said. "I know his saddle." He left the saloon.

Martin's gaze shifted from one man to another. "Look, gents, let's forget all this misunderstanding. The woman's back safe and sound. No harm's been done. Drinks are on me. Bartender, set 'em up." No man moved toward the bar. They stood watching Martin, remembering all the ranchers who'd been driven out, the men killed and the lands bought at half-value from their distraught widows. They thought of the cattle rustled, and none of them stepped up to the bar to drink whiskey paid for by Thad Martin.

"I got it," Cole Elliott said, walking to the table. He opened his hand and dropped one spur. The men craned forward.

"It's a match," Cole said, and the saloon filled with angry murmurs.

Gaby stepped forward and the men quieted down to listen as she spoke. "I overheard one of your men talking to Slade. He said you were angry because Slade didn't do

his job. He was supposed to kill me and my baby." The
men behind her muttered angrily. Martin's men looked
at each other with quick, nervous eyes. They hadn't
bargained for this.

"How do you know it was one of my men?" Martin
asked.

"Because I can identify him," Gaby said. "It was that
man right there." She pointed at Abner Harris, seated
beside Thad. The man's guilt was clear on his face.

"You're under arrest, Martin," Rayne said.

"You can't arrest me, Rayne. You ain't the sheriff."

"We just made him the sheriff," the men cried out.

Martin looked from them to Rayne and back again.
Finally he shrugged. "All right, Sheriff," he said, and
stood up.

"Use your left hand and ease your gun out of its
holster," Rayne ordered, and Martin did as he was told.

"This is all a mistake, Rayne." Thad dropped the gun
on the table. "Obviously the little lady heard wrong. I
can't help what my men get mixed up in. As for the spur,
I must have knocked it off when I was riding through the
chaparral."

"You can tell it to a judge," Rayne said, motioning
with his gun. "Let's go, Martin."

Compliantly Martin walked toward the door, but when
he got level with Gaby, his hand swept out and he grabbed
her, jerking her tightly against him, while he whirled to
face Rayne and the other men. He held a small-caliber
gun, the kind easily concealed up a sleeve. He placed the
snub-nosed barrel against Gaby's cheek.

"Put the gun down, Elliott," he ordered, "or I'll kill
her."

Helplessly Rayne dropped his gun. Thad's men had
their guns out now and were stepping forward to flank
their boss.

Martin backed toward the door. "Tell these men to get
out of my way," he ordered, and Rayne nodded them
away from the door. Kevin stood white-faced, his eyes
darting from Rayne to Martin. Thad moved toward the
door, half-dragging Gaby. She let her weight hang heavy,
making it difficult for him to move.

As they reached the swinging doors, Martin paused to

look out into the street. The diversion was what Gaby
had been looking for. She slumped against him, then
jerked backward away from him. The motion pulled him
around, taking his attention off the men in the room.
Gaby let herself fall, carrying Thad down with her. His
grip on her waist broke as they hit the floor, and Gaby
rolled to one side, seeking shelter. She could hear the
room exploding around her as men went for their guns.
Shots were fired between the ranchers and Thad's gunmen. Gaby glanced back and saw Thad Martin raise his
gun and level it at her. There was an explosion, then a
tearing hot pain in her chest, and blackness roared up to
claim her.

"Rayne!" Kevin called, and tossed his gun. Martin was
already on his feet and heading out into the street. If he
got to his horse, he'd be hard to catch. Dodging the
crossfire, Rayne made his way to the saloon door. Gaby,
he noted, lay huddled behind an overturned table. At
least she had some protection there, Rayne braced his
shoulder against the doorframe and peered out, Thad
was just climbing onto his horse.

Rayne fired and Thad fell back.

Rayne watched him for a moment. Thad wasn't dead,
but he was wounded too badly to climb on his horse.
Rayne turned his back and surveyed the room. The gunfire had ceased as men dropped their guns and surrendered. Satisfied, Rayne glanced at the table where Gaby
lay hidden. She was lying just as she had been when he
first looked at her. Fear washed over him as he leapt
toward her, flinging aside the table. Gaby lay still and
white, a bloodstain spreading across the smudged white-
ness of her bodice.

The members of the posse slapped each other on the
back, congratulating themselves for a job well done. Some
even stepped up to the bar for a glass of whiskey.

"Rayne?" Kevin crossed the room and stood looking
down at the rancher. A movement in the street caught
his eyes and he pulled his gun and fired. Numbly Rayne
glanced up. He didn't see Thad Martin lying dead in the
street, and he was unaware Kevin had just saved his life.

At the sound of the shot, the men at the bar swung
around. They were shocked to see Rayne kneeling beside

the still form of the Texas Angel. Someone ran for the doctor, but the rest of the men stood shuffling their feet and averting their eyes, embarrassed to see a strong man like Rayne Elliott cry.

Epilogue

The excitement had finally died down. A new sheriff had been appointed, Tom Garner was run out of town. Rayne had declined the position. Thad's men were in jail and the district judge notified. The funerals had been held and the dead buried. The posse had dispersed and the men had returned to their ranches. The storm had passed them by and a dance had been scheduled for the following Saturday. It would be the last one of the season before winter set in. The town had turned its attention to other things and life went on.

The day dawned bright and sunny. A carriage headed down the street toward the doctor's office, its markings that of the Spencer ranch.

"Now, remember, you're to do absolutely nothing but rest in bed," the doctor said to his patient. She smiled, her dark eyes brightening. Her face was still too pale for his liking and he considered keeping her in town for a day or two more, but she'd been so miserable and unhappy he decided against it.

"I'll take it easy," Gaby said. "I just want to be home with my little boy."

"You were very lucky," the doctor reminded her, and Gaby smiled; then her face grew somber as she thought of Mrs. Schafer. They'd buried her a few days before, but Gaby had been too weak to attend. The ranch wouldn't seem the same without the stiff-lipped, kindly old housekeeper.

"I have been fortunate." Gaby sighed and thought of

433

all the people who had been pulling for her. They'd come to wish her good health. None of them had been allowed in to see her, but they'd brought cards and gifts. In fact, so diligently had the doctor guarded her the past few days, that she'd seen no one since that night she'd opened her eyes and found Rayne seated in a chair nearby. His face had been gray with fatigue and worry and he'd gripped her hand so tightly it had hurt, but she hadn't minded.

"Hello," he'd said softly, his eyes warming her with his message of love.

"Rayne," she'd whispered, and tried to ask about Kevin and Billy.

"Shhh, don't talk now," Rayne had said. "Everything's all right. Just rest and get better now." His large hand had smoothed her hair back from her forehead.

"Don't leave me," she'd whispered.

"I won't," he'd reassured her, and she'd slept again. Only later, when she'd awakened, he'd been gone and she hadn't seen him since.

"You have a visitor," the doctor said now. "It's Rayne Elliott. Do you want to see him?"

"Rayne?" Gaby exclaimed, her eyes shining. She began to smooth down her hair and check her collar. From the radiant look on her face, the doctor guessed Rayne Elliott was just the medicine she needed now. He went to let the man in.

Rayne looked wonderful standing in the doorway, his broad shoulders blocking it for anyone else. "How are you feeling?" he asked, his blue eyes studying her face.

"Better." There were still hollows under her cheeks and dark smudges of shadows beneath her eyes, but the spirited smile was there. " 'Course I won't be dancing for a while."

"No, I expect not." He smiled briefly. Silence fell between them.

"How's Billy doing?" she asked.

"He's back at the ranch and Jacinta's making a fuss over him."

"You got Jacinta back?" Gaby said in surprise.

"She came back while you were here. She said we Elliott men needed someone to take care of us."

"She's right."

"Gaby . . ." Rayne cleared his throat. "About Danny. I'm sorry for the threats I made. I won't be trying to take him from you."

"Rayne, let's get married and then we'll both have Danny, the way it should be."

"Nothing's changed, Gaby," he said.

"What do you mean?" A cold chill of apprehension swept over her.

"There's going to be a trial. Thad's father is fighting back with everything he can. His defense for his dead son is to cast suspicions elsewhere. The rumors are already starting up again. If we're together, people will believe they're true."

"Some won't. They'll know the Martins for what they are, liars and murderers. We can't live our lives being afraid of what they say and do."

"I came to tell you I'm leaving Texas."

"Rayne, you can't."

"If I leave, the talk will die down soon."

"I won't let you go."

"Don't make this harder, Gaby. It's for your own good and Danny's. When the boy gets old enough, tell him . ." He paused, slapping his hat against his thighs in a familiar gesture. "Tell him I love him."

"Tell him yourself, because I won't," Gaby cried.

"Good-bye, Gaby."

"Don't you dare leave," Gaby commanded. "After all we've been through together." He wasn't listening. He had already left the room, striding across the doctor's waiting room. "Rayne, come back," Gaby called, but the door closed behind him.

"Damn you and your pride, Rayne Elliott." She clenched her fists in blind rage. It would be the last time he walked away from her, she vowed, and suddenly was fearful that it was so. She beat angrily at her pillow, wishing it was Rayne Elliott's shoulder, then threw herself down to weep.

When Kevin came to take Gaby home, he was astonished at the ravished face. He'd expected to see her smiling and happy to be seeing Danny again. Carefully he bundled her into the buggy and started the ride home.

Gaby was strangely silent, and after a few attempts, Kevin finally gave up.

"Rayne's leaving Texas," she said when they were drawing near the ranch.

Kevin glanced at her. The pain in her voice ran through him like a knife. "He'll come back, Gaby," he said. "He loves this land. He can't stay away from it for long." She seemed to find little comfort in that, and Kevin took a deep breath. He couldn't change the way things were, as much as he wanted to. Gaby belonged to Rayne. "Rayne loves you, Gaby."

"I know," she replied softly.

"He was like a crazy man up in those mountains. He wouldn't rest until he'd found you again. The others had given up. Rayne wouldn't."

Gaby began to cry softly, not able to understand how a man could show so much love for someone and then walk away.

"It must be frightening to love someone as much as Rayne loves you, especially for a man like Rayne."

"What do you mean?" Gaby asked.

"He seems like a man who's not used to loving or being loved. He wouldn't know how to handle it. Maybe he'd be a little bit afraid of his feelings."

Gaby mulled over Kevin's words. He was right, she realized. Rayne had never had much love in his life. He wouldn't know how strong and constant it could be, especially in the face of adversity. He thought he was protecting Danny and her by going away. But there was something more. He was leaving because he was afraid that one day they'd stop loving him and blame him for not protecting them from the rumors or for not providing them with all the wealth he thought they wanted. Gaby couldn't see the ranch house for the tears that filled her eyes. Her brave, tough Rayne. He was like a small child in some ways. There was so much they needed to learn about each other.

Rayne was frightened of the legend of the Texas Angel. He'd forgotten that underneath she was still Gabrielle Reynaud, the girl he'd rescued on the wharves in New Orleans. She was still a woman who needed the man she loved. In that instant she knew what she would do.

The buggy drew to a stop before the ranch house and Abigail Spencer stepped out on the porch, a simpering smile on her lips. Gaby took a deep breath. Before she was free to go to Rayne, there were things here she must attend to. Purposefully she stood up and let Kevin help her from the buggy.

"Gaby, this is Mrs. Pierce," Abigail said. "I took the liberty of hiring someone to replace poor Mrs. Schafer."

"How do you do, Mrs. . . . . er . . . Spencer," the woman said, and bowed with exaggerated gentility. "I have tea for you in the drawing room."

Tightening her lips, Gaby moved toward the parlor, pausing for a moment in the doorway as she remembered how Mrs. Schafer had tried to save her from her kidnappers. Suddenly she felt weak and shaken. She drew in a breath to steady herself and turned back toward Kevin and Abigail.

"Won't you two join me? I have some things to discuss with you."

A light flickered in Abigail's eyes, but she smiled. "Of course we will, my dear," she said smoothly.

"That will be all, Mrs. Pierce. I'll pour," Gaby said. "You may go to your room now and pack."

"I beg your pardon?" The woman blinked uncertainly and looked at Abigail.

"I'll have one of the men drive you back to town. Your services are no longer required," Gaby continued in spite of Abigail's outraged gasp.

"Oh, my," the woman said, and cast another look at Abigail, who sat with her mouth open. When Gaby turned to face her, Abigail closed her mouth and sought to compose herself.

"That was most unwise, my dear," she said tartly. "It is hard to find good help out here. It won't be easy to replace Mrs. Schafer."

"It will be impossible," Gaby said, thinking of her old friend. Her face hardened as she looked at Abigail. This smiling woman was the reason for some of her grief, and would have cost Gaby so much more if she'd had her way. Gaby poured a cup of tea and handed it to Kevin.

"You've come to love this ranch very much, haven't you?"

"I can't imagine being anywhere else. I hope you'll let me stay on, Gaby."

"The ranch needs you," Gaby answered. She looked around the serene parlor. The fine old ranch house had been a haven for her in her times of trouble and unhappiness. She glanced at the window. Beyond it she could see the corrals and barns and the bunkhouse. The sturdy buildings were trim and neat with a fresh coat of whitewash over their wattle-and-brick exteriors. They'd been built to last for generations. Had Aaron hoped that someday his son would come to carry on for him?

"I'm giving you the ranch, Kevin," Gaby said, and felt a weight lift from her shoulders.

Kevin could only stare at her with startled, disbelieving eyes. Abigail gave a gasp of surprise. Neither could she believe they'd won.

"Oh, Kevin, isn't that wonderful?" she cried, jumping to her feet in her excitement.

"You're going back to Rayne," Kevin stated flatly.

"Yes," Gaby answered simply. "I love him. I'm sorry if this hurts you."

Kevin shook his head slowly. "I've known that's how it would be ever since you were kidnapped. You're giving up the ranch for him, aren't you?"

"None of it means anything to me without Rayne."

"What about Danny?"

"Danny is Rayne's son," Gaby said, and saw fresh surprise and hurt in Kevin's eyes. "Aaron knew I was carrying Rayne's child when we married. He claimed Danny as his own. I never stopped to think how unfair it all was to Rayne." She fell silent.

Kevin sat absorbing all she'd told him. "This is quite a shock," he said. "I'd gotten used to thinking of Danny as my brother."

"He still is your stepbrother." Gaby smiled, and finally Kevin returned her smile.

Abigail had remained strangely silent, although her eyes gleamed triumphantly. "Just think, Kevin," she said now. "We can sell the ranch and go back east where we belong."

"I'll never sell the ranch," he said.

"Of course you will," Abigail urged him. "You'll grow

tired of playing cowboy out here and you'll want to go back where people are genteel and mannerly." Kevin looked pained as his mother went on and on. He thought of what his life would be like in the months and years ahead with his mother constantly haranguing him to sell. At first she would be subtle and reasonable in her attempts to influence him, but as it became clear he had no intention of selling, she'd grow bitter and abusive. He sighed heavily. It was a small price to pay for staying on his father's ranch.

But Gaby had foreseen Abigail's intent. "The ranch can't be sold," she said now. "If Kevin decides he no longer wishes to stay on the ranch, it will revert to me or my descendants." She saw the look of gratitude on Kevin's face. "It will be so stipulated in the contract Jeremy Wallace prepares."

"You can't do that," Abigail cried.

"I can," Gaby said implacably.

"Mother," Kevin admonished his mother, "Gaby has been most generous."

"How generous is she?" Abigail huffed. "She gives you the ranch but retains control. Why, you're hardly more than a hired hand."

"Kevin will take all profits from the ranch and have complete say-so over it. I can never change my mind and take the ranch back. Only Kevin or his descendants can decide to give up the ranch."

"Thank you, Gaby." Kevin crossed the room to put his arm around her. Gaby clung to him for a moment, remembering Aaron and his gentle strength. Somehow she felt she was repaying him a little for the things he'd done for her.

"Be happy, Kevin," she said. "That's what your father would have wanted for you."

"I will be," he said. "I could be happier if you were here to share the ranch with me, but I know your heart is elsewhere." Gaby smiled, and for a moment he caught a glimpse of the gay young girl who had first come to Texas, her head full of dreams, her heart full of love for just one man. He felt regret that she couldn't look like that for him. Rayne Elliott was a luckier man than he could ever know.

"Well, this is all very nice," Abigail said, and her eyes were bitter and resigned. If she must stay out here in this dry prairie among dull, cloddish ranchers and their dowdy wives, then she must make the best of it. At least she would be the mistress of one of the biggest and most important ranches in the territory. She would take full advantage of that. She would take these ranch wives in hand. In no time they'd understand what real society and class were supposed to be.

She'd begin with Gaby. After this she would be little more than a poor hardscrabble rancher's wife, struggling to make ends meet. Regally Abigail crossed the room, her hand extended graciously like a queen conferring a special honor on one of her subjects.

"You must come to call often, my dear," she said with cool politeness.

Gaby only smiled, ignoring the proffered hand. "Kevin, I'd like to speak to your mother alone," she said, and with a final nod he left the room.

The polite smile on Abigail's face vanished. "Well, you've finally done the decent thing," she said flatly. "Don't expect me to thank you for giving back to Kevin what belonged to him in the first place. It's unfair of you to make such a stipulation that he can't sell it, but if we must live with it, we will. I can make the best of it, I suppose."

"You won't have to make that kind of sacrifice, Abigail," Gaby said mildly. "You'll be going back east. It will be safer for you there."

"I wouldn't dream of leaving Kevin here," Abigail began, then turned to look at Gaby suspiciously. "Why would I be safer there?" she asked.

"If you go back east, you won't be tried for complicity in murder."

"I don't know what you're talking about," Abigail sputtered.

"Don't you? I know about your agreement with Thad Martin that you'd sell the ranch to him if he killed Danny and me."

"I . . . I . . . had nothing to do with it."

"Didn't you? I'm sure Thad Martin's foreman will tell a

different tale. I overheard him talking to Slade Harner when they held me captive."

"He lied," Abigail cried, her eyes wild and frantic.

"I don't believe he did, and neither will the sheriff."

"It will be my word against his," Abigail cried.

"Do you want to take that chance?" Gaby asked quietly. She could see the panic in the woman's eyes, the mottled red of her face. "Tell Kevin you want to go east. He loves you, he'll provide the money you need to live on modestly. Not quite in the style you might fancy, but adequate. Go east, Abigail, while you have the chance, and stay there. Don't come back or I will tell the sheriff about your involvement in this whole affair."

"You bitch," Abigail raged. "How dare you dictate to me what I can do with my life? I've found out about you. You're little better than a whore. Texas Angel, indeed. They treat you like you're a saint, but you're just a woman like me, conniving to get what she wants."

"Yes, I am," Gaby said. "But I am not a murderess. You are getting far better than you deserve, and that's only because of my fondness for Kevin."

"I won't go."

"You tried to have my baby and me killed, Abigail. Folks don't take kindly to that kind of thing. They hang horse thieves. What would they do to the would-be murderer of an innocent child?"

"So you've won," Abigail hissed. "One thing will console me when I'm back east. You won't be sitting in the lap of luxury either. Take your bastard child back to his father, and all of you be damned."

"I intend to do just that," Gaby said blithely. It was all behind her now, all the worry, all the decisions. She was committed, and there was no turning back. Swiftly she left the room and the bitter, defeated woman who lingered there.

"Maria," she called, running up the stairs. "Pack Danny's things, we're going home."

It didn't take Maria and Gaby long to pack trunks and boxes with their clothes. Kevin and a cowhand carried them down to the buckboard.

"I'll send for the rest of my things," Gaby said, giving Kevin a final hug.

"It's not going to seem the same without you and Danny," he said, placing her trunks and cases on the back of the buckboard. "Mother is going back east at the end of the week. I'll be alone here."

"You won't be alone, Kevin. You have Ben and the other cowhands. You'll be so busy with the ranch you won't have time to be lonely."

"That's true." He placed the last trunk in the back and stood leaning against it, his gray eyes studying her. "Still, it won't ever be the same without you. If things don't work out at the Elliott ranch, Gaby, come back here. The ranch is still yours too."

Gaby looked around. She'd been secure here, but she'd never known real happiness. That would come at the Rocking E Ranch with Rayne. She smiled. "I won't be back, Kevin." Standing on tiptoe, she kissed him gently on the cheek and climbed up in the wagon.

"At least we'll be neighbors," he said wistfully.

"And friends, always," Gaby said, and slapped the reins across the backs of the horses. She didn't look back as the buckboard made its way down the dirt road and out across the prairie. Despite the chilly wind that had sprung up, Danny gurgled with happiness to be outside in the sunshine. His bright eyes took in everything, pondering the magnitude of the horizon and the immense prairie.

Gaby thought of the stormy night she'd fled across this prairie, running in her pride and stubbornness from the very man she loved and needed. How young and foolish she'd been then. If she'd only been willing to stay and try to understand Rayne's fears. Her impetuous flight had cost them so much. She slapped the reins against the horses' backs, urging them to a faster pace.

The wind had picked up by the time they reached the Elliott ranch. Gaby pulled the wagon to a stop in front of the low ranch house. The door opened and Rayne stepped out on the porch. Cole followed him out. There was a flare of hope in Rayne's eyes; then it died away, to be replaced by resignation. He carried his rifle and saddle-bags, bulging with food and ammunition. His horse was already saddled and waiting at the railing. A packhorse stood with its back loaded down with bedroll and other gear.

Her gaze went from the horse back to Rayne's face and she saw all the sadness, uncertainty, and fear there. He loved Danny and her. He was still trying to protect them, but he was trying to protect himself a little too.

"What are you doing here, Gaby?" he asked, making his voice cold and impersonal.

"I've brought your son home," Gaby answered, and her gaze was just as fierce and unyielding as Rayne's. Cole gasped as he heard her words. He peered at Maria and the baby.

"We have nowhere else to go," Gaby said. "I've given the ranch to Kevin." She didn't tell him she still owned Jessie's ranch.

"That was a damn fool thing to do," Rayne flared. "You just gave away a fortune."

"My fortune is with you."

"Gaby . . ." Rayne took a deep, ragged breath, thinking of the irrevocable step she'd taken. "You can stay here until Cole can take you to Galveston to the ferry back to New Orleans."

"To do what, Rayne? Go back to the Court of Angels? Do you want your son to grow up there?" She could see him struggle with the thought of Danny being raised in a brothel as she had been. Beside him, Cole peered at his grandson, his face trembling. He remembered another baby. A little boy with a widow's peak forming at his hairline and brilliant blue eyes like his mother's. In his preoccupation with his own grief, he'd ignored his son and missed the opportunities to show him love. Now Cole looked at his grandson and realized he could have another chance. Gaby was offering it to them all, if only they could give up their pride and take it.

He plunged down off the porch and held out his arms to his grandson. Uncertain, Maria looked at Gaby, and at her nod of approval, handed the baby down. Danny looked at the tall man and patted him on the cheek and gripped his nose, then laughed delightedly. Cole held the baby in his arms and felt some of the coldness that had gripped him all these years begin to melt away.

"What's his name?"

"Daniel Cole Elliott," Gaby said.

"It's a good name," he said, and his lips parted in a

stiff grin. It wasn't much, but it was a start. They would both learn about each other. They had a lot in common now.

"I guess I'd better clear my gear out of that spare room," Cole said, and still carrying Daniel, turned back to the house. Maria cast another quick glance at Gaby, then climbed down and started taking the baggage out of the wagon. Gaby watched her for a moment, remembering that tomorrow she'd have to tell Rayne about the other ranch and send Billy and Maria over to the house. There would have to be a wedding, and she and Jacinta would help Maria make a home, just as they had helped her. Gaby glanced at Rayne and stayed where she was on the wagon seat. She'd come so far for him. He had to give up his pride and meet her part of the way. He stayed where he was on the porch.

"Are you sure, Gaby?" he asked wistfully, unknowingly echoing the words he'd asked so long ago on a boat halfway between New Orleans and Texas.

"I belong with you, Rayne." Gaby repeated the words she'd answered then. Remembrance flashed behind his eyes. He thought of all she'd given up for him. He saw how courageous she'd been. She'd never faltered in her love for him. Why had he ever doubted her?

He ran down the steps and pulled her from the wagon and into his arms. His laughter rang out joyous and unrestrained. The light in his eyes blinded her with its message of love. He set her on her feet and stepped back. His expression was serious as he got to one knee in the dust of the ranch yard.

"Gaby, will you do me the honor of becoming my wife?" he asked humbly. His words took her breath away.

"The honor is mine," she said gravely.

He buried his face in her bodice, drinking in the fragrance of her. Gaby was home. He'd never let her leave him again. He'd never give her cause. His arms tightened around her thighs, pulling her closer.

Gaby leaned over him where he knelt, her arms cradling his dark head against her breasts in a gesture that was tender and protective; then he stood up and pulled her against his tall, lean body, and once again he was the protector.

"I love you, Gaby," he whispered, and held her tightly. She could feel his strong body tremble.

The chill Texas wind blew across the prairie, swirling the dust at their feet, then sent it dancing across the yard. It tugged at her skirts and hurried on to whistle around the corners of the sheds and barns. It was a lonely sound, but Gaby didn't notice. Together she and Rayne went up the steps and into the house where their son waited for them.

About the Author

Although Peggy Hanchar travels with her husband, Steve, they return often to their lake cottage in Delton, Michigan. She has four children, and in addition to writing romances, she quilts and sketches with pastels.